DA

"You know how bad I want you, Lilly?" Shadoe said.

"No," she whispered, her voice splintered with fear.

"You're afraid of me, Lilly, just like I'm afraid of you."

"I'm not afraid of you."

"Liar."

"I am not."

Shadoe pulled her tighter to him, his lips brushing her cheeks. "Not so, honey. We're both afraid of each other, and we have a right to be. You and I are a dangerous combination."

"Dangerous?"

"One kiss is a dangerous thing between a man like me and a woman like you," he said as his lips parted to claim hers.

Temptation

JANE HARRISON

LOVE SPELL **NEW YORK CITY**

A LOVE SPELL BOOK®

September 1993

Published by

Dorchester Publishing Co., Inc.
276 Fifth Avenue
New York, NY 10001

Printed in the United States of America.

For Virginia Brown Bianchi and Patricia Rorie.

Special acknowledgments to the late Freddy Sue Shaw, Adele Leone, Ralph Leone, Joanna Cagan, my parents—Charles and Pauline Harrington—and my sisters—Laverne Brigman and Liz Britt—for supporting this project with sincere enthusiasm.

Temptation

Prologue

Late October 1891
Harney County, Southeastern Oregon

It was endless, senseless, and dizzying. And there were moments when Shadoe Sinclair thought he might go crazy thinking about it—just one day, twenty-four hours, a dull Wednesday in the middle of the week, when his life had suddenly gone haywire.

It was the day his friend, Sam Miller, died. Shot in the back of the head, in the middle of a foolish argument that had turned frenzied and insane and left Shadoe arrested and branded a murderer in some eyes.

An untold day. With untold secrets, lies, and misery, and too many decisions mixed with conscience, regret, and aching doubts. But it had happened, forever changing all the days that would follow.

The past was over. The future fixed. Choices made and remade.

He rode deep into the Steens Mountains the same week he'd been released from jail—the day after Sam Miller was buried—following a secluded trail that soon disappeared between two shelves of solid rock.

He'd been easily acquitted of murder, the judgment being self-defense, but the guilt gnawed at him like some wild and hungry vermin, teeth sunk deep into his mind, painful, worse than any inner voice. The memories hurt, and they would keep on hurting.

When he reined his horse across the colorless canyon floor, the sight of it brought Shadoe little relief. The flat, morning light fell across the naked slopes and bald bedrock in an eerie and deathlike whiteness.

Shadoe felt a shiver, and hung his head for a moment. Sighs and whispers. A dying wind in his ears. Voices of yesterday . . . *This is the land of legends . . .*

This is your place, secret and inviolable . . . tierra de leyendas . . . *the place of lost treasures and strong spirits . . . of peace and contentment, solitude, and forgiveness. . . .*

He lifted his gaze and looked at it, knew in an instant that he would find no peace and forgiveness in this canyon. Located on the southernmost end of the Double S ranch, the rocky ravine and surrounding land had been a gift from his father in a rare moment of tenderness. The Spanish had said that the canyon held a secret treasure and that the Indians used it for a burial ground. Shadoe had never found a trace of either, but he had cherished it, kept it in his own private sanctuary, a place where he rode to escape the realities of his life.

Now, it was difficult to look at it with any real pleasure. And he knew why. Lilly . . . sweet, sweet Lilly. . . .

He had hoped to share the secret place with young Lilly McFall, a wedding present in the summer following her sixteenth birthday, not even a year away.

Stirrings in his body. *Oh, mercy. . . .*

They would have honeymooned there, he and Lilly, all wrapped together in a warm night full of stars and hushed whispers. Her body would have moved against his, struggled with his. Hair in her face. Love on her lips. Everything dark, wet, and warm.

Shadoe closed his eyes against the thought, felt a thick swallow pass down his throat. Everything had gone wrong, crazy. The canyon would always be just rock, sullen and eroded, cold and sterile. Never dark. Never wet. Never warm.

He shivered again, and the canyon's emptiness seemed to devour him. There was nothing left but his mind ringing with echoes . . . *You will never come here again. You will never marry Lilly McFall. And you will never forget . . . never forgive. . . .*

And it was true. That same day Shadoe was planning to tell Lilly that he was marrying another woman.

When she saw the rider, Lilly McFall frowned. The land between the Double S ranch and her own home was high, flat country, no edge to it but the sky, so she had seen him clearly for a while, making his way slowly toward the line shack, the Oasis, which sat almost dead center between the Sinclair ranch and McFall property. But he was riding too slow. Not the usual brisk gallop when he came riding to meet her at the Oasis.

Lilly closed her eyes, and for a moment, thought about the years she'd ridden up here to meet Shadoe. It had begun when she was a child, riding with her older brother and some of the ranch hands as they gathered and drove the cattle over the valley and highlands for summer grazing.

Even then, she had been quick to follow every movement that Shadoe Sinclair made: the way he sat in the saddle, the way his blue gaze flicked back and forth. He was knowledgeable and full of experience, and she had been drawn to that as much as she had been drawn to his silence and strength, to the way he always tilted his hat when he smiled at her. And he had always smiled at her. And she had smiled back.

There was nothing ordinary about him. Not the way he looked. Not the way he talked. Whereas the other men had been nothing more than dusty and tired cowboys, Shadoe had been an enigma. And as the years passed, Lilly had developed a great and unshakable love for him.

When he reined his horse next to hers, Lilly was still frowning. Something about the way Shadoe was looking at her protested any tenderness. Her hands pinched together over the saddlehorn, and she trembled as she stared back at him, watching his eyes and lips, ready to hear what he had come to say.

"Been here long?" he asked, his voice so low that it was almost lost in the October wind.

"A few hours," she replied quickly. "I said I was riding out to do some painting." She nodded toward the supplies which were strapped to the back of her saddle, some stretched canvas, oils, and brushes. "But, it was a dumb excuse." She looked up at the gray sky smudged with passing clouds. "Painting in this weather? All I could say was that I wanted to paint the storm that was approaching."

"You lied."

She glanced back at him. "Papa would never have consented to my seeing you, Shadoe."

At that, he sighed heavily, and his face, which had been expressionless, turned hostile as though her words had affronted him. "I'm not good enough to talk to the princess now that I've killed a man. I'm just a loathsome outlaw, a man who shamed his father and caused misery for others. An outcast among you."

Lilly flinched. "I didn't say that."

"But you thought it, didn't you?"

She hesitated, then nodded. At fifteen, she was still too unworldly, even a little naive. All she knew was that Shadoe had killed a man, and her father and everyone in the valley were raging over the motive. The rest was just a horrible blur in her mind, a senseless vision. Sam Miller was dead, and Shadoe had suddenly changed into a man she didn't know.

"It's impossible to think of anything else these days. Killing a man is a serious offense whatever the circumstances," she tried to explain. "And as close-knit as this community is, well, the effects are bound to be consequential."

"True."

"You can't blame everyone for being shocked . . . even a little outraged."

"No, I guess not, but that isn't what I wanted to talk to you about."

Her anxiety grew. "It's not?" Lilly was truly surprised. Somehow she had thought Shadoe had asked her out to the Oasis so that he could explain the facts concerning Sam Miller, so that she would know why he had suddenly became so indifferent to everyone. "Then what?" she asked.

He shifted in his saddle, looking more and more uneasy, and a long weighty moment passed. Lilly suddenly felt her heart beating wildly.

"You know, Lilly," he began, "between some people, well, things just happen. You don't know how or why. You don't question it."

Bravely, she asked, "Are you referring to you and me?"

He nodded. "Yes, you and me. More to the point, the feelings that we share."

Love . . . He was speaking of love, though neither of them had ever uttered the word or anything even remotely like it. But, nevertheless, it had been understood, taken for granted, not only by them, but by everyone who knew them. They had loved each other for years. And for the last few months, they had been *in love*, teetering on the edge of passion.

Lilly suddenly felt very afraid. There was something wrong about him, something wrong about the way he was looking at her. Seeing the cold, disturbing glint in his eyes, she desperately wanted to ride away, ride with the wind in her ears until she was deaf to everything. But she didn't.

The chain on the bridle rattled, and she steadied her horse. "I don't understand why you'd bring our relationship up now. Could you not have waited—"

"Waited for what? A more suitable time?"

"Maybe."

"No." His voice turned abrupt. "There will never be another time, Lilly."

She gazed at him. She heard her heavy breathing. "What are you implying?"

"I'm leaving the valley."

"Leaving? Why? When?"

He turned away from her and said with a long drawn-out sigh, "You know that I care about you, but sometimes things just don't go as we plan." A pause. Still staring away. "People change . . . For one reason or another, they go in different directions because they have to . . . because it's the right thing to do. The honorable thing. The sensible thing. It doesn't mean that they stop caring for one another, it just means that they need to move on with their life . . . face realities . . . understand their situations."

She was even more confused. "What are you talking about now?"

He still wouldn't look at her. No telling eyes. No soft mouth. Only an outline of dark hair and hat.

"You and me," he said. "I'm talking about you and me."

His voice had an ache to it, and Lilly felt the pain move into her body. She wanted to see his eyes, see the blue of them.

"Look at me, Shadoe."

"I can't."

"Please look at me."

He shook his head.

She grew impatient, angry. "Then finish it. Tell me what you are really talking about."

Slow and plain and easy, he told himself. "I have to marry Anne Woodward."

She gasped, instantly shocked and hurt. For a moment, she thought that maybe she hadn't heard him right, but then he said it again, the same words, the same horrible and hateful words.

But even then, Lilly resisted the thought. *Marrying Anne Woodward! Why, Anne is my brother's sweetheart!*

Her mind fumbled. Yes, it was true that Joseph and Anne had become distant and even argumentative since her brother had decided to leave Oregon for England, but this . . . this was some horrible mistake!

"You're lying!" she screamed. "It's not true!"

He turned and glared at her. "Yes, it is."

"But you don't love her! You don't love her! Say you don't love Anne! I know that you don't love Anne!"

Shadoe scowled at her. "She's pregnant, Lilly! I have to marry her!"

For a moment, Lilly thought she was dying, literally dying. Her heart rolled in her chest, and she couldn't breathe, couldn't swallow. She couldn't even see Shadoe clearly. Everything became a blur, suddenly rounded and dark. It was as though she were sinking somewhere, falling into a hole in the earth. She felt faint. She started crying.

Pregnant! She could barely think it. Shadoe and Anne together like that, making love, making a baby. Oh God! She knew he was a man, handsome and forceful and virile. She knew that he even cared about Anne, flirted with her, but. . . .

She stared at him through her tears, and cried, "Oh, Shadoe . . . no . . . no . . . no . . ."

Lilly didn't know when she stopped screaming, or even how she had gotten home. Only that she was there, safe in her bed, remembering, remembering Shadoe as he tried to ease her tears, and how she had fought and cursed him.

Shadoe and Anne marrying . . . a baby . . . It made no sense. It would never make any sense. . . .

In the spring of the following year, the senselessness turned to tragic drama. Anne Woodward died in a fall at the Woodward Ranch while visiting her ailing father. A few weeks later, Lilly's brother, Joseph, left for England. By April, Shadoe Sinclair was gone, too.

Nothing left—and nothing told.

Chapter 1

April 21, 1897

The rumor was true. For two weeks, the story had been the gossip of the town, spread from mouth to mouth, household to household, until each person knew the tale front and back. Every detail, every single word of the account had been repeated and second-guessed. No one was sure of the origin. It had blown through the town like a tumbleweed.

And yet, when the riders rode slowly into Montfort, people stood on the streets, gawking. The prodigal son had returned home after a five-year absence. The phantom of so many whispers in the night had reappeared, no longer the dreaded illusion, but reality. Shadoe Sinclair.

He nudged his horse to the center of the dusty road, edging a clear path around a slower buckboard directly ahead of him. From beneath the brim of his flat-crowned hat, he squinted, taking

18

a casual glance at the buildings.

The sleepy little town had grown since he had last been there. He liked the way it looked now, the red brick buildings and large gray stone structures that had replaced the former squats, the jerry-built stores. Yet he resisted the pleasure. It was still a small nowhere place in the middle of a nowhere county that refused to yield to civilization.

Montfort, Oregon, I hoped never to see you again, he told himself, and it was not the first time that he had thought those words.

He shifted his gaze toward the dusty street, whistling lowly at the large black dog that was straying to the side of the road.

"C'mon, Dragon," he said. The dog quickly heeded the order, moving back alongside the horse, and both rider and dog fell into a cadence.

They passed the post office, the barber, the bank, then the saloon. Knots of cowboys strutted along the wooden sidewalk, some joking noisily with a group of lusty prostitutes who were leaning over the railing of the second-floor balcony. Piano music played in the background.

But it was one particular building that caught the rider's eyes. Down the street, coming up on his right was the Episcopal Church. It had been painted white, its shutters a deep green. Shadoe stared at it for a long time before her name flooded his mind. *Not Anne's,* he thought. It should have been Anne's name, but it wasn't. Anne had been his wife, carried his name on her marker, right there on her grave beside the church. It was the other name, the one that had plagued his days, burdened him with both guilt and desire. Lilly McFall.

Lilly, I hope that I don't see you again, he told

himself, and it was not the first time that he had thought those words either.

Lilly McFall had just stepped out onto the boarded sidewalk in front of the dressmaker's shop when she heard some of the murmuring.

"It's really *him*," came a low anonymous voice, and everyone in the small crowd next to Lilly ogled, their curious glances directed toward the middle of the street.

The heavy sounds of the bay's hoofbeats thudded against the dirt. One rider followed the lead of the other, and the dog was now in between the slowly trotting horses.

"Shadoe Sinclair's come home . . ."

"Still got that crazy demon of a dog . . ."

"I'll be damned," one of the older men gasped. "It's Lewis Smith riding with Sinclair."

"There's gonna be trouble fo' sure," commented another.

With the last remark still clear in her mind, Lilly took a cautious step forward, taking a hard look at what everyone else was talking about.

One gloved hand lifted to her brow, shielding her searching gaze from the glare of bright sunlight. She blinked in irritation, focusing on the small cloud of dust that moved just in front of her, and a deep breath caught in her throat at the sight of one of the riders.

Lilly suddenly had difficulty swallowing. Although it had been years since she had seen him, Lilly could never forget, not even if she had wanted to. She moved closer, glancing over the ponies tethered to the hitching posts. Yes, she had heard the rumors, but then again, she'd heard them before, never believing for a moment that he would come back yet all the time hoping, but knowing and fearing that it was possible that he would not even come back to bury his dead father. There had been no real anticipation, nothing that had prepared her for the sight of him.

Her mind reeled with sudden apprehension, and as she stood watching, her heart twisted in her chest.

Five years! Five damn years! she cursed silently, and he still influenced her in a way that no other man could or ever would.

Tall, lean, muscular, he sat in the saddle with a particular ease as though he belonged there, controlled in presence, poised in strength. His hair, still very long and dark brown, was pushed back under the crown of his black plainsman, hanging in thick, wayward folds against his broad shoulders.

She could still remember her own hands pulling those same thick strands back into a ponytail, her fingers teasing playfully as she wiped the hair from his jaw, pushed an unruly lock from his sweaty brow.

Oh, Shadoe, you've really come back . . . come back. . . .

Lilly shivered and gazed in fascination. Around Shadoe's neck, weaving in the strands of thick hair, was the same deep blue bandanna, tied loosely, the printed scarf her brother, Joseph, had given him.

Her hand covered her opened mouth, and she leaned toward the street, straining, drawn by his nearness. Even beneath the low brim of his hat, she could see his blue eyes, voltaic and intense, framed by heavy brows and dark lashes. His jaw was square, forceful, shadowed by a fresh scrub of beard. He was as she remembered him—ruggedly handsome, dangerous, always controlled.

She felt dazed, slightly disoriented, and for a brief space of time—just a few seconds yet it could have been minutes—Lilly couldn't be sure of anything—Shadoe had turned to stare at her, his gaze slanted with bold appreciation across her face.

She felt herself go cold, then hot, a rush of color spreading over her cheeks, a stab of anxiety pushing through her heart.

"It's hard to believe," a familiar voice said, a voice filled with loathing.

Lilly jerked to see Tom Woodward standing beside her. His mahogany-colored eyes were filled with anger, his comely face lined with concern as he looked at her.

"Can you believe that he has the nerve to show his face in this town after what happened? I thought he was gone for good." He stroked his beard thoughtfully. "Heard he'd made some money in San Francisco . . . gold, shippin', or something."

She could say nothing, only shake her head.

He continued, "Funny, but it don't make no sense why he'd wanna come back to Montfort." He made a light mocking laugh. "And look who's ridin' with him . . . Lewis Smith. Next thing you know silly ole Luke will be ridin' down to help the two of them tear up the saloon. I swear, Lilly, if Luke Miller even looks at you, I'll . . ." His words faded into a blur of mumble jumble.

Lilly swallowed again with great difficulty. Her throat was tight and dry. She felt as though she couldn't breathe properly. She really hadn't heard a word Tom said, just the first sentence or two, after that, his words had all run together. Had he said something about Lewis Smith? Luke Miller? The Whitten brothers? The boys over at line shack number four? Poker?

She wasn't sure. She didn't care about Smith— the former Double *S* foreman—or Luke Miller, or even the members of Tom's little gang. Tom's buckaroos didn't interest her. All she remembered was "Can you believe?"

And she couldn't. He was here. Shadoe was really here.

"I can hardly believe it myself," she said truthfully before dragging her gaze back to Shadoe's moving form. "I never thought he would come back."

And it was true. The day Shadoe Sinclair had left Oregon, Lilly was certain that she would never see him again, never feel the touch of his fingers against her cheeks, never know the feel of his gaze on her face—that special gaze so often filled with masculine hunger, and then with restraint and denial. But she had hoped. . . .

Shadoe touched his horse with his spurs, nudging the bay into a canter toward the edge of town. Lewis Smith followed hurriedly, and the big black dog ran behind.

"It just don't make sense, him and Lewis comin' back here together, I mean . . . I didn't expect it . . ." Tom's constant stare spoke of his pain.

Lilly glanced at Tom and flinched. He was twisting nervously at the top button of his blue plaid shirt. Beneath the hate, she could see the smolderings of anguish.

She took a deep breath, struggling for some sense of control. Since Shadoe's and Joseph's departure from Montfort, Tom and his brother, Jesse, had been her devoted companions. Even when she was away at finishing school in Chicago for two of the five years, Tom had constantly written her letters. She quickly reminded herself that he'd been a good friend, supported her when she needed him. Now he needed her. This was bound to be a difficult moment for him.

"Maybe . . . he won't stay long."

"Any time is too long for me!" Tom spat, looking down at the splintered boards beneath his boots.

She lifted her brows and gave Tom a reproachful look. Even to her, it was obvious that Shadoe had come back to town to bury his father.

She touched his arm in a gentle gesture. "His father's dead, Tom. Don't forget that. It would have been shameless if he had not come home to give Mister Sinclair a proper Christian burial." Her voice grew faint as she added, "So just let it be for a while. He has a right to be here. It's the only decent thing that Shadoe could do."

Tom shifted his gaze to her, looking straight into her eyes. Lilly saw his dissatisfaction. "Decent? When was Shadoe Sinclair ever really decent?" He inhaled deeply. "And tell me why Shadoe would care to bury his father? They hated each other in the end. Nothin' between them but misery. I tell ya, there's something goin' on here. I don't trust 'em one bit, Lilly."

She wanted to argue, but Lilly knew that the point was moot, for in spite of any defense she might have found, Shadoe had already been declared guilty of every transgression that Tom might care to name. And Tom and Jesse both had named his sins over and over the last couple of years.

Each time, she had silently defended Shadoe. But she knew the Woodwards had their reasons, their anger, and their fears. Even she could not forget her own hurt.

The cool spring breeze tugged at her hair, and Lilly reached up and brushed a blond strand from her narrowing eyes.

"I won't quarrel with you, Tom, not here, not now, but I still say that Shadoe has the right to bury his father. According to your mother, Mister Sinclair had no other family left. Shadoe is probably in Montfort to take care of business."

Tom was clearly surprised at her words. "When did you talk to Maw about it?"

"Last week."

There was a look of interest in Tom's watchful stare. He crossed his arms, then stroked his beard again with his gun hand. "Old Simon Sinclair was broke, you know," he told her plainly. "Ruined with his gamblin'. If I know Shadoe, he's probably here to sell the place and run with what money he can git. A man like him would never want to stay on and take care of a ranch. There's too much bad blood in this valley for him to live here now. He's been too lucky in California to want to stay here. Yep, he'll sell the ranch and clear out with the money."

Lilly grew taut at Tom's apparent pleasure in his own words. As long as she had been alive, the Sinclairs had lived on the Double S Ranch.

"I don't believe it!"

Tom smiled at her excitement, a particular smile that doused Lilly as if she'd been showered with a pail of cold water. "That's the rumor."

Her mouth fell open once more.

"If so, the Double *S* is mine," Tom finished. "Jesse and I are goin' to buy it. Been waitin' for this moment for years."

Lilly lifted an eyebrow. "What?"

"I said I'm goin' to buy the Double *S* when Sinclair sells it."

Lilly choked back a gasp. It was unbelievable what Tom was saying, and her aching heart pounded out the reality of his words. If Shadoe was selling the ranch, then he was leaving Oregon forever.

Leaving me forever . . . forever . . . forever . . . And there would be no more hope, little as it was. It would all be gone, her fantasies and dreams . . . her memories. She grew defensive.

"Sell the Double *S?*" she questioned. "Why, Shadoe would never do a thing like that!" Lilly blurted, her voice soon an overflow of tumbling words and nervous sputters. "He couldn't . . . I won't believe . . . What about . . . You can't buy . . . And how could *you* buy it? Where would you get the money?"

Tom's face grew tight at her heated words, and he tossed Lilly a sour glance. His lips thinned, and he didn't answer her question.

"He's not a fit man, Lilly," Tom warned. He wiped the beads of perspiration that suddenly dotted his forehead in spite of the cool weather. "Sinclair has always been trouble. And he always hurts the ones he's close to. He ain't got no business here. And there's one thing more. I ain't gonna let him near the house. If he does come near our place, me and Jesse might have to teach him a lesson or two. Things have changed since he left. He cain't just come in here and take over like nothin' ever happened!"

A faint flush colored Lilly's skin, and she quickly thought of another reason that might have brought

Shadoe back to town, a reason far more important than selling the ranch. Looking at Tom, she could see that reason in his tortured gaze.

Shadoe had left behind his child with Anne's mother. If he had come back for that child, then there would be trouble, serious trouble.

She stiffened at the thought, but it was soon followed by a wave of tenderness that washed over her, tugged at her heartstrings. Shadoe as a father. It made her feel teased and tormented, the mere thought of Shadoe wanting his child after all these years. It made her want him more, swallowed up her hurt and frustration, swallowed up the distance of the five years apart. Shadoe was home. And if he was after the child, there was hope.

Her voice softened. "Shadoe was my friend . . . my—" she started.

Tom interrupted with a scowl, "Even his own father disowned him."

"Simon Sinclair is dead. The past is dead—"

"My sister is dead, too!" Tom said in a voice that vibrated with anger.

Lilly sighed heavily and stepped off the boardwalk.

All that was left of Shadoe was a trail of dust blowing in the wind. She stared off into the distance, hoping for a glimpse of anything that reminded her of the man whom she had once known so well. All she saw was a blur of color melting against the horizon of wind, sky, and desert lands.

She felt Tom move closer, and she half-turned.

"I think it's best if you stay away from the Double *S* until he leaves town, Lilly," he told her. "And don't go talkin' about this with Maw. I don't want her bothered with anything that has to do with Sinclair. There's no need openin' up old wounds. Let him do his business and be gone."

Lilly faintly heard Tom's words.

"The shorter his stay, the better it'll be for everyone."

She said nothing.

"Did you hear me, Lilly?"

"I heard you," she replied softly.

"Besides, you're my girl *now*." Tom's face relaxed as he reached for her. "And the future Mrs. Woodward don't need to be consortin' with the likes of Sinclair. People might git the wrong notion, think you still care for him. We don't need no more gossip."

She turned as he pulled her closer, snaking his arm through hers. "Tom, I wish that you would stop saying that."

"Sayin' what, Lilly?"

"Saying that I'm the future Mrs. Woodward. I've told you before that I'm not ready to marry anyone. I won't have you thinking otherwise."

"And you know that I've told you that I'm never goin' to give up askin'. It's been only you and me for so long, Lilly, all these months since you returned from Chicago. I reckon it's time we made plans." There was a slight smile on his face, and Lilly made a nervous gesture with her hands.

She had been stupid to deny Tom's prediction about the Double S, rash to speak of Shadoe with any hint of intimacy. Tom was very possessive, and now he was bringing up marriage again. She hated thinking about it, but she also knew that any debate was useless. Besides, she didn't relish the idea of quarreling with Tom while standing in front of the dressmaker's shop, especially when he was calling her "his girl" even when she knew she was not.

"I need to find Aunt Martha," she suddenly said, "and I'm tired of all this talk about Shadoe."

Tom's fingers tightened on her arm. His eyes were haunted when he told her, "I don't ever want you to think about that man again."

She gave him a slight smile as she patted his arm reassuringly.

"I wonder if Aunt Martha is over gossiping with Mrs. Burton. It's Monday, you know, and Mrs. Burton always serves chicken and dumplings on Mondays at her boarding house. Aunt Martha is absolutely silly about the dish! Maybe she intends to stay the afternoon," Lilly guessed as she ambled down the sidewalk, her skirts brushing against the splintered wood, her arm hooked with Tom's.

She glanced at him and could see that he was taking quite easily to her words. Lilly relaxed. "I told Papa that we would be home by one. But I'm famished, and it's already two o'clock."

A low laugh sounded in Tom's throat. "Maybe we should have some lunch, and then I could ride out to the house with Miz Martha and you." He gave her a playful tug on her arm.

Lilly nodded, fully aware of Tom's possessive gaze, of the way he held her arm too tightly. It frightened her.

If only she could make Tom understand that she loved him more like a brother. She felt the same way about him as she did Jesse. A shiver whittled through her as her thoughts returned to Shadoe's ride through town.

The present situation had a strange and fascinating resemblance to the past.

Chapter 2

The old Chinese man smiled when the riders dismounted. Shadoe and Lewis quickly tethered both the bay and Lewis's pinto in front of the barn.

"Mister Shadoe. Welcome . . . welcome home," he said, bending low, again and again, in respectful bows toward both Shadoe and Lewis. Two long pigtails swung from beneath his straw hat. "Mister Lewis. Welcome. Welcome home." The old man's wide grin was full of white pearly teeth, and his dark, slanted gaze sparkled with pure joy. Pulling his bags from behind his saddle, Lewis grinned back at Lo Ching.

Shadoe said nothing at first. He couldn't even smile. The effort just wasn't in him. He looked up from under the brim of his hat, quickly assessing his surroundings. It looked as if nothing had changed. The place was the same, except for a few broken boards, wind-worried, sundried, and unpainted. He pulled his Winchester from its leathered sleeve, untied the saddlebags, throwing them over his left shoulder. It was almost overwhelming to be home under the circumstances.

"Hello, Lo Ching," he finally managed with a weak smile, amused at Lo Ching's standard attire of a dark cotton padded jacket, loose black trousers, and wooden-soled sandals. He remembered sending Lo Ching boots and different hats over the years. But there the Chinaman stood in the same attire he'd always worn.

"Howdy, Lo Ching," Lewis added, walking over to the older man. He grinned down at Lo Ching who wasn't very tall, not much over five feet if you stretched an inch. "Ain't aged a day . . . No, ya ain't. I don't know what it is with your kinda folk, but you look as fit as a hound dog during hunting season. And just look at me." Lewis pointed to his bulging stomach. "City life nearly ruined me. Too many women. Too much rye."

Lo Ching laughed. "You a fine man, Mister Lewis. Just need some fresh air . . . good food." The Chinaman's gaze strayed cautiously toward Shadoe. "It's hard to believe these poor old eyes of mine, Mister Shadoe. I never thought you both come here again. No sir, Mister Shadoe. I thought you big, rich man now, you send fancy lawyer to take care of ranch. I sure glad I was wrong. It the right thing to do, Mister Shadoe. You a very wise man. A man needs to face his deeds."

"Still talk too much, Lo Ching."

The Chinaman grinned and made several more bows. "I still cook good grub, too, Mister Shadoe."

Lewis gave the small man an attentive smile. "I sure did miss your cookin', Lo Ching. Them fancy restaurants in San Francisco ain't got nothing to compare to the grub on your table. Ain't nobody, Chinaman or not, can cook the way you do. The things you do to a rabbit make a man marvel. Yes, they do."

"What he means, Lo Ching, is that he's been eating beans and jerky for two weeks now." Shadoe gave Lewis a mocking laugh. "What I need is a stiff drink to wash the sand out of my mouth. Let's go, you two."

Shadoe walked toward the large two-story frame house in which he had grown to be a man. Lewis, the big black dog, and the old Chinaman followed quickly.

Inside the front door, Shadoe frowned, an expression of uncertainty knotting his brows. Things were not the same after all. The house, once a monument to wealth and luxury, looked like a tattered quilt just pulled from a dusty trunk in the attic, worn around the edges, its brilliance faded away into mold and neglect.

"Where's Flora?" Shadoe asked when the silence stretched too long. His father's loyal housekeeper had kept things clean for years.

"Gone, Mister Shadoe." The Chinaman lifted his hands in a gesture of explanation. "She's been gone for nearly a year now. Your father never allow another woman in this house after that."

"Gone?" Shadoe slanted him an irritable glance. He had not known.

"Yessir, Mister Shadoe. She just up and quit one day. Went to stay with her sister in Denver. I had the preacher write her a letter about Honorable Mister Simon's death."

Shadoe took a few steps into the parlor. He ran his free hand across the top of the piano where an inch of dust had settled, then stared at the furniture draped with linen.

He was annoyed at the neglect. He was annoyed at himself for some reason, as if somehow he was responsible. But he quickly shook the thought off. This was not his decay. It was his father's.

"Looks like no one lives here, Lo Ching," he commented dryly.

"Just a little dusty, that's all," Lewis commented, trying to ease the growing tension. "Lo Ching must be gettin' lazy."

The old man's lips pinched into a white line. "Since Mister Simon's illness, there's been no people here, Mister Shadoe. With the money problems and . . . rustling, your father took no interest in the house. I try to keep clean, but only upstairs." He paused, a grief-touched glint in his dark eyes. "For last few months of his life, Mister Simon no come downstairs."

"See if you can get it cleaned, even if you have to hire some temporary help," Shadoe said almost bluntly. "Don't worry about the money."

"Yessir, Mister Shadoe," Lo Ching replied. He shifted from one foot to the other, the soft clicking of wood against wood humming in the background as he spoke. "I'll go to town tomorrow morning and see to it. Yessir, Mister Shadoe. I'll find good help."

"And buy some food, too, Lo Ching. I don't aim to starve while I'm here."

"Yessir."

"Whiskey, too," Shadoe continued as he strolled casually through the parlor, carefully examining his surroundings before wandering back to the foot of the stairway. "I want everything in this house washed. Everything. Think you can get it done?"

"Yessir, I'll see to it, and I'll stock house just as before, Mister Shadoe. Lots of food and plenty whiskey."

Shadoe drew a heavy breath, and weary distaste flickered in his eyes. "Buy plenty, Lo Ching. Buy some hard candy, too."

"Candy?" Lo Ching's expression was clearly startled.

"You heard me. Hard candy. Maybe a few toys. Some books and such things."

The Chinaman quickly nodded.

"And the men, Lo Ching? Are there enough to run the ranch for a while?" Shadoe asked.

The old man thought for a moment. "There are many who stayed on. But most gone now. No grub. No rifles. No wages."

"No wages?" Shadoe made a mocking gesture, and his words were quick and bitter. "There was plenty of money when I left. Where did the money go, Lo Ching?" It was a question that really didn't need an answer.

The old man lowered his head, saying nothing.

A troubled expression shaded Shadoe's eyes. There had been rumors of his father's financial troubles, reports that insinuated more than just bad investments. There was talk of some mysterious gambling, gambling that amounted to a severe loss of capital. Looking around, Shadoe now believed the talk. His home was almost in ruins. It wasn't that he felt personally responsible. It was just that Shadoe knew that his father had needed him, and he had not been there. But how could a son come home to a father who didn't want him?

There had been no letters. Nothing from Simon Sinclair because he had not forgiven his son for Sam Miller's death and all that followed—the elopement, Anne Woodward's tragedy, and the McFalls' anger and pain. It was as if the rest of Simon Sinclair's life had been to punish his son for those sins.

"He lost it all, didn't he?" came the quick, cold question, a question that didn't need an answer. Shadoe's calculating gaze pierced Lo Ching's guarded expression, and the old Chinaman shrugged helplessly.

"I won't say, Mister Shadoe. I don't know about such things. I just cook. All I know is your father was good man."

"So I've heard." Shadoe turned to give Lewis a curious exchange. Lewis slightly shook his head.

"I'll check the bunkhouse and see what can be done," he told Shadoe.

Shadoe nodded, then started for the steps that led up to the second floor. He had a funeral to plan.

"Give me a kiss," Jesse Woodward said to Molly Andrews on the back porch of her father's dry goods store in Montfort that same afternoon.

His brother, Tom, had already passed by with Lilly on his arm, but Jesse had hardly noticed, though twice he had slumped back on the porch railing to look down the alley at the main street.

He'd heard from some of the men that Shadoe Sinclair had camped ten miles south of Montfort the night before, and more than likely would be riding through town, and Jesse wanted to see it for himself. But he'd missed it, missed it for trying to get Molly to kiss him. And the minutes had soon passed into hours.

She was reckless today, he felt, reckless and willing with her mouth all full and rosy as she teased him with a pouting smile.

"Jesse Woodward, you so much as touch me, and I'll start screaming for my maw!" the young girl warned, though it was somewhat a weak warning. Her smiling eyes betrayed her.

"Aw, c'mon, Molly darlin', let me kiss you. One little kiss won't hurt nothin'." He pressed his face closer to hers. "You're as pretty as a peach today, sweetheart."

But Molly pushed away and shot him a scolding look. "We ain't even engaged yet, Jesse Woodward, and here you are, trying to kiss me right on the street. It's shameful! And you say you love me."

"We ain't on the street, darlin'. We're on your father's back porch. Ain't no one gonna see us. And I do luv ya," he finished with an easy smile.

"But it ain't proper."

He leaned, wrapping his arm around the porch post. Molly stared at him, her long dark lashes fluttering teasingly.

"Engaged or not, you know I luv ya," he said.

"Those kind of words are cheap. My maw told me a man don't go around kissing his intended before he asks her paw for her hand in marriage."

"Well, I told ya, Molly darlin', that soon, I'd be able to ask for your hand. Didn't I?"

"You did, but those words are just as cheap as the others. You never told me why I had to wait. I'm sixteen years old, Jesse, and most girls my age are having babies."

She blushed at her last words, and Jesse leaned

closer, and took her loosely into his arms. "Everyone knows that we're gettin' married, sweetie. I've told ya that. Tom and I are tryin' to settle things right now. It just takes time. But I promise you this, darlin'. Come Christmas, you'll be a bride."

Her eyes rounded. "A Christmas bride? Really?"

"Sure thing, sweetie. And we'll have a home of our own."

"Our own house?" Molly was clearly surprised.

He laughed and pulled her closer. Her soft, round body pressed lightly against his thin frame, and he let one hand trail bravely, but ever so gently up her rib cage. He was so eager to possess her in the way a man possesses a wife.

Molly giggled. "Maw would whip my hide if she caught me letting you touch me like that."

His hand slipped higher where his fingertips faintly grazed the soft curve of her breast. "Give me that kiss, Molly," he whispered.

She looked straight into his eyes, those dark round eyes that stared at her with such hunger. "I'll give you more if ya ask Paw right now for my hand, Jesse."

Molly pressed her body closer to his. All pretense vanished. "Come that picnic at the church next month, I'll cook you a chicken dinner, and you can buy it, and then I'll let you take me walking for a spell. We'll go off through the cemetery and then out toward the grove behind it."

Jesse bent his face to her neck, smelling the perfume in her hair, inhaling the scent of her womanliness. For a moment, he closed his eyes and tried to imagine how it would be making love to her. All that soft skin and silky hair. The warm breath. The physical pleasure he'd only felt in his dreams.

He shook with the thought. Sure, Molly had teased him before, but never with more promise than a kiss. He'd never had a woman, though Tom had offered him one of the whores at the saloon. He'd been waiting, waiting for his sweet little Molly to be willing enough to let him touch her. And now, she was going to let him love her.

Instinctively, he pulled her tighter against his body, and her eyes widened in understanding. She shifted her body against his, her frame rubbing against the front of his pants. Her breath was warm as it fanned against his twitching lips.

Jesse moaned with the slow grind. His groin pressed against her, hot and already full.

"Molly, darlin', can you really mean what you're sayin'?"

"Just ask Paw," she told him bluntly, but her voice was still soft, seductive.

That same afternoon after a few broiling kisses from Molly, Jesse wandered nervously into Andrews' merchant store and watched as the old man flicked a rag across the dusty shelves. The words came out haltingly, and stoic Pete Andrews never once looked at the boy. He just nodded when Jesse nervously asked the long-expected question.

After a quick conversation with his future father-in-law as to what he could provide for Molly, Jesse bounced up the stairs like a tight rubber ball, reporting with a smile the good news to both Molly and her mother.

Not too long after, he left to go home and give his mother the news.

When Jesse sauntered breathlessly through the front door, he found his mother sitting in a chair,

rocking, singing one of her sweet lullabies. A dull
fire glowed in the hearth.

"Where's Tom?" he whispered over her shoulder.

"Out. Said he'd be back in a day or two." It was
a low, hoarse reply.

Jesse frowned, forgetting his good news of Molly, ignoring the fact that his mother might have
been cheered up by the engagement. The news
that Tom would be gone two days made him angry,
even confused.

"Where'd he go?"

"Up to the lakes. Said he might drop in and
see Luke Miller. Since the river dropped last year,
there's been some nesters who settled east of line
camp two."

Jesse's confusion surfaced. "But that's property
Simon Sinclair gave to the farmers." Jesse paused.
"Besides, Tom ain't never liked Luke. Why would he
go up there? He ain't been up there since Shadoe
shot Sam Miller. Luke don't like Tom at all. Not
at all."

She shook her head. "Tom says the nesters are
on Double *S* property, and he wants Luke to let
him have the line camp to set up a post."

Jesse slid into a nearby chair. He pushed his hat
back and stared into the flames of the fire, then
over at his mother.

Something was wrong. Something had been
wrong for a long time, and it was driving him
crazy not knowing.

"Tom ain't owner of the Double *S* yet, Maw.
Besides, even if we buy the ranch, it would cause
a war if we started puttin' out the farmers."

"Tom wants the water rights back."

"So, how does that concern the farmers?"

She gave her son a hard look. "Under common law, the owner of the shore line is given ownership to the middle of the stream or lake. It's called riparian rights, son. If a nester lives on the shore line, then he can claim to the middle of the river."

"But there's at least five or six families livin' up and down the Blitzen, Maw. Tom cain't put them all out. Why, Alva Springer and her boys live on the river and the Daniels' homestead runs to the Blitzen and almost clear up to Malheur Lake!"

"I know, Jesse. I know, son, and I want you to remember that." She coughed, a low, deep gasp that vibrated through her entire body. Jesse flinched at the sound of it. Catching a breath, she gave him a warning look. "You have to remember that Tom's a lot like his paw. He wants this entire valley to be his. It killed your paw when Anne married Shadoe. Ruined his dreams of a Woodward marrying a McFall. I'm afraid that Tom is just as obsessed as your paw was. And it's dangerous to want something that bad."

"It's just some fancy wishin'. We'll do good to buy the Double S from Shadoe. Take every dime and more. No, Maw, this is just some fool notion of Tom's."

She turned to look down at the sleeping bundle on her lap. "I know. How well I know. And there's gonna be bad times ahead because of it," she murmured. "Bad times."

Chapter 3

Friday
April 23, 1897

He had been home two days, but his father's burial had been waiting for two weeks.

Shadoe cast a narrow hard-eyed look at the open grave, watching in stiff silence as the zinc-lined coffin was lowered into the raw hole. It was all that was left of the man who had ventured to Oregon some twenty-five years earlier to carve a home out of the uninhabitable desert range lands of the rugged southeastern territory.

In the early spring of 1872, Simon Sinclair had left the Willows country of California with his two-year-old son, 1,200 head of white and roan short-horn cattle, ten trusted *vaqueros*, and a Chinese cook named Lo Ching.

When he'd died two and a half weeks earlier, he'd left a ranch of some 42,000 acres, a little more than

half of the 80,000 he had once owned in the 1880s.
A poor businessman, the elder Sinclair had sold
off thousands of acres to settlers who drifted to
the Blitzen Valley of Oregon looking for land to
farm. The farmers had found what Simon Sinclair
had known for years: The flat desertlike land would
yield rich wheat grass.

He had practically given the land away, but then
the rancher had his own debts. Simon had managed to gamble most of his money away, for a
good game of poker was his main vice.

As Shadoe listened to the Scripture being read
over his father's grave, he bitterly realized that it
was too late for a reconciliation. His dark, listless gaze lingered on the dirt being shoveled. The
closed grave ended any future causes; the past was
unalterable and fixed, continuous with regret and
conscience. *If only we had talked. Just talked . . .* he
thought.

The black-robed preacher finished his sermon,
saying, "The spirit shall return unto God Who gave
it," and the crowd quickly dispersed. A few ranchers, many of the local farmers, and some of the men
who had worked for the Double S for most of their
lives moved away from the grave. Lo Ching went
to the kitchen to prepare a meal for the mourners.
Even Lewis stared at Shadoe with understanding,
finally wandering off to the bunkhouse, leaving the
son to reflect on the father.

Shadoe stood alone at the grave site under
a grove of Lombardy poplars that his father
had planted in 1873. He could visualize Simon
dismounting his horse that first time in 1872 to
look at the soft green knoll near the Blitzen River,
and deciding that this was where he would event-

ually build his saw-lumber house.

Surely Simon had never dreamed that only five years later he would be selling steers at the railhead in Winnemucca, Nevada, making more money than he could have imagined, or that he would be gambling the profits away at the saloon in the same town.

A knot formed at the back of Shadoe's dry throat, and he swallowed hard, forcing the memories from his mind. He would not let himself forget one of the main reasons that brought him back to Oregon. He was going to sell the Double S Ranch.

Thinking about the latter, he hastily placed his hat back on his head and began walking through the poplar grove and down a path that led toward the river road. The big black dog was at his heels.

There was no hurry to head back to the house where he would have to endure persistent questions from his father's well-meaning friends. One more platitude on the righteousness of caring for his father's land and Shadoe knew there would be an exchange of words. The last thing he needed right now was that kind of trouble. There was already enough gossip about his return. All Shadoe wanted to do was get his business over and leave town.

He had just crossed the road when he spotted the small buggy rolling down the shaded lane. One hand dropped lightly to graze the butt of his holstered gun, an old habit from his younger days on the ranch.

And then his hand relaxed.

The young woman saw him and the dog. She steered the rig over to the shoulder of the road, then pulled back and tied the reins. Grabbing her black straw hat from the seat, she leaped agilely to the ground, smiling when she cleared the rig without spoiling her gray silk dress.

Turning quickly toward Shadoe, she gave him a frankly examining glance. "Hello there," she called.

Shadoe's steady gaze took in every detail, recorded in a second's time her small oval face, her clear wide eyes the color of a graying dawn. Her hair was a wealth of rich blond strands laying across her shoulders, shining like burnished gold in the sunlight.

She would have been a pleasure to any man's eyes, but as she took a step or two nearer to him, the sight of her became painfully uncomfortable in its familiarity. His gaze clouded.

"Well, aren't you going to say something?" she asked in a wavering voice that betrayed her uneasiness.

"Yes. You're trespassing."

His tone was bland, and she gave a start, then steadied herself with a smile as she looked down at the dog.

"Am I? Hello, Dragon." She leaned over and patted the black beast on the head. "Good dog, you still remember me, don't you, Dragon?"

The animal acknowledged her presence with a generous lick, then a wag of his tail as she continued to run her gloved hand down his back.

"Now that's a good . . . good boy," she was saying to the dog.

"You're trespassing on my land," Shadoe repeated, "and I see that you're still trying to steal my dog."

Her gaze lifted, and she stared back at Shadoe.

Her voice was light and casual as she told him, "I guess you could have me arrested, but then again, you'd have to call the sheriff out to the ranch, and, of course, Sheriff Smith, being the scandalmonger that he is, would tell everyone in town and they'd all know that I was here. I'd be ruined, absolutely ruined. Papa's little English lady off without her chaperone, entertaining a scandalous rogue in the woods. As they say back in England, I wouldn't be fit for the marriage market. Papa would most likely have you killed, shot in the back when you least expected it just like Jesse James."

A hint of a smile tugged at the corner of his mouth. She had changed, and yet she was still the same. It made him feel easy for a moment.

"Maybe I should just put you over my knee and give you a good spanking like I used to do."

Lilly laughed softly as she drew closer to him, stopping directly at his feet, close enough to look straight into his eyes.

"Hello, Shadoe," she said, her voice honeyed and sweet.

"Lilly." The single word almost stuck in his throat. *Curse her!* he quickly thought.

"Why, you do remember me after all," she teased, smoothing back the wayward strands of her hair that had blown into her face. The wind was growing stronger, pushing thick clouds across a heather-colored sky.

"How could I forget?" he slowly replied, then added quickly in a cold tone, "what in the hell are you doing here?"

Her smile faded. "Don't you think you should welcome me first, Shadoe, instead of scolding me like I was a pestering child?"

Shadoe shifted slightly. He was uneasy with the way her teasing words sliced through his body without warning, at the way her hair shimmered in the light that danced through the trees. Just being with Lilly brought back so many memories.

Damn her, he thought. *She's here to make me suffer. She's here to get revenge . . . some sweet revenge. . . .*

Shadoe tensed, his face changing, closing out any tenderness that he might have felt. But he had to struggle to keep his body under control. Just the sight of her drove him to the edge.

"Right now, you are pestering me," he warned. "And maybe you need a good scolding, though I can't remember one ever doing you any good. What in the hell do you think you're proving by coming out to the Double S? This is no child's game. You could cause a whole lot of grief if anyone found out you were here with me."

"I'm not a child anymore, Shadoe. And I'm not playing games. I do just exactly what I want."

His gaze quickly took in the womanish curves of her body, the small round breasts, the narrow waist, and a cruel smile twisted at his lips, an expression layered with years of skepticism and suspicion. Lilly was no longer a blossoming fifteen-year-old schoolgirl, but a woman, a beautiful, strong-willed woman, and he still wanted her, knew it the minute she jumped from the buggy. Not even five years had killed his desire for her.

He stiffened. "You still remind me of that pesky *kid* who used to follow me around, worrying the hell out of me, causing me nothing but trouble, spending my money at the store in town whenever you could talk me out of a penny or two. Maybe you still like trouble? Is that it, Lilly?"

Shadoe's tone took on a serious note as he added, "Did you come here just so your papa could have a good excuse to kill me? Do you want revenge, too? I'm sure your papa still blames me for what Joseph did and would like to see me dead. Well, I don't want any trouble, especially *your* kind."

Lilly met his gaze which was now calm and detached. "What does that exactly mean . . . 'your kind?' Sounds sordid."

"The female kind," he told her bluntly. "And, yes, it can get plenty dirty!"

She drew back. "Any other lady would probably slap your face, but I won't! You're hopeless, just hopeless," she said with a sudden coldness. "And too big a fool to waste my time on!"

Hat in hand, Lilly turned away from him. She slipped on her straw bonnet in the thick silence, playing with the wide black ribbon, her fingers twisting the supple and satiny fabric into a perfect bow just to the left of her small chin.

"Maybe you would feel better if you slapped me?" he told her, thinking back to the day he had left her to marry another woman. She had wanted to hit him that day. "Some females get a perverse thrill slapping a man. Makes them feel kinda good inside."

She heard him, and twisted to meet his stare once again. A defiant smile curled her full mouth. "Yes. I might at that. You deserve a slap, you know, but once I start hitting you, I might not be able to stop and I know what kind of man you are."

"Afraid I might slap back?"

"You've been known to," she reminded him. "And I don't relish the thought of having my face marked." Her voice turned sweetly sarcastic. "There's a dance a week from Friday at the Railway Inn, and I want to look my best. I just had a pretty blue gown made special for the occasion. As for the perverse thrill, maybe you're speaking of yourself. You always had a violent streak."

She was mocking him, and Shadoe knew it, but he let it pass. He deserved it. So he stood in silence as she continued her sarcasm.

"Then again . . ." Lilly paused, a flush on her face. "There might be a time when I just might risk a slap on the cheek for the pleasure of smacking yours, Mister Sinclair. Perverse and all."

Shadoe smiled slightly with a hint of constraint. Her tone might have suggested playfulness, but he knew otherwise. Lilly was as tough as nails. He tried to relax, but he was having a difficult time.

Lilly, Shadoe thought, the sweet little "princess" of the English Weatherly castle, the princess who liked to play damsel to his knight. The little maid who picked tiny yellow and orange wildflowers that bloomed amid the lava rocks and stunted sage of southeastern Oregon and gave them to her warrior come home from battle when in actuality Shadoe had returned from a roundup on one of the southern draws, deep in the Steens Mountains. Or from his hiding place, the lost canyon.

The canyon . . . Lilly had pretended as a child that it was full of dragons and evil sorcery and that Shadoe went there like a young Arthur to meet his Merlin and learn the secret ways.

She had been his darling girl, the one who had wanted to run away with him when she was only fifteen years old, who at that very age had already reached an astonishing degree of maturity. She had a beguiling smile even back then, and now it was devastatingly provocative.

He looked deeply into her eyes. They were clear and lucid, He looked closer at her mouth which was deep pink, full and barely pouting. He wanted to kiss those lips, crush them, bruise them beneath his own mouth. Everything about her was so adorably seductive. And, yes, he loved her, just as much as he did the day he left her.

If only she had not been so young at the time, six years younger. If only she had not been a McFall. If only he'd not been Simon Sinclair's bastard son, the son of a whore in a San Francisco saloon, if only Sam Miller had lived. . . .

There had been too many ifs in their lives.

Even though he'd planned on marrying her, there were times he'd never quite felt good enough for Lilly. It just seemed as though there were too many walls between them, too much distance. He'd reached out to touch her many times, then pulled away. All those many times alone with her, he'd held back.

He had been too old for her. He had never even kissed her, but God, he wanted to kiss her now.

He swept off his hat and raked an agitated hand through his hair. "Why are you here, *Miss* McFall, if it's not to stir up a hornet's nest?"

Her dark lashes swept low, masking her expression which had clearly become downhearted. "I've come to pay my respects to your father."

There was a thick pause, and Shadoe looked away, and shrugged. "I see."

"You don't mind, do you?"

"No." His gaze once again shifted to her pretty face. "But you might have had a little foresight about the situation."

"I gave it a great deal of thought," she protested.

"Not enough apparently."

"Oh, more than enough. I know exactly what I'm doing."

He didn't doubt her. Lilly had a will of iron. What she wanted, she often got. She had never been the simpering English coquette that her father wanted. She was willful and reckless. In fact, she was plain dangerous at times.

Shadoe's predicament suddenly struck him. If she wasn't there for revenge, she was there for something worse—him.

Instinctively, he reached out and hooked his arm in hers, dragging her in the direction of the buggy, all the time scolding her. "Then if you thought this out, you must realize that coming here was a very bad idea, Lilly. It's best to leave things as they are."

Stumbling to keep up with his long-legged stride, Lilly said, "I hasten to disagree with you! I told you that I came here to pay respects to your father."

"Consider it done," he quipped as he tugged her along with his hasty steps.

"But that's not all. I wanted to talk to you."

"We have nothing to say to each other, remember?"

"Not so! We have a lot to say." He knew she meant it. "There are wounds to heal. I'm weary of all the feuding between your family and mine. Papa misses you. I know he does." She grabbed at her hat pushed back by a sudden gust of wind. "It's time that the feuding ended, Shadoe. I think there's been enough misery—"

"You still shouldn't have come here," Shadoe cut in, still dragging her toward the small rig.

"Why shouldn't I be here?"

Shadoe stopped abruptly and turned to glare at her. "Your father just for starters," he said with mounting anger. "He's an Englishman by blood, an aristocrat, and no Englishman wants his daughter out strolling with a man like me. Your old man told me so often enough." His words were true. "Don't you think I remember that you and Joseph are bluebloods while I just bleed red like the rest of the riffraff around here. No." Shadoe was shaking his head. "Your father wouldn't like you here."

Her chin tilted in stubborn defiance. "My father is not my conscience."

Shadoe shook his head again. "All right, then— *me* for the other reason!" As he continued half dragging her resisting form, he added, "I don't want you here."

"When did I ever listen to you?"

Never, he thought, and part of him loved her even more for it.

His fingers pressed more tightly around her small, gloved wrist. "Look, my father's dead, and he doesn't know one way or another who's here or not here, so it doesn't matter who pays their respects. Even if it's me. I just came home to sell the ranch."

Lilly came to a sudden stop just a few feet from the rig, bringing him up short. She gaped at him in angry disbelief, her light gray eyes fading into smoky darkness. "That's the coldest thing I've ever heard you say, Shadoe. And the meanest. You couldn't have meant it! You just can't sell the ranch!"

"I aim to."

"But you can't!" She looked at him, disgusted.

"The Double *S* was your father's life! Your life, too! You just can't sell the ranch! You can't just pick up and leave again! Why, I won't . . ." Her words faltered.

"Are you going to stop me, Lilly?" he mocked, suddenly amused at her protest.

"You're serious, aren't you?" She jerked her arm from his. "You plan to sell the ranch just like Tom said. Sell and run with the money."

"Tom?" The single word held a wealth of malice. "Tom Woodward?" Shadoe slanted a curious glance across Lilly's flushed face. "Is Tom your new beau, Lilly?"

She hesitated before blurting, "Well, if he is, it's none of your business!"

"It might be my business if you're out here spying for him, nosing around trying to see what's going on at the Double S. I've heard nothing but bad things about that *boy,* and if you're here on his behalf, I think I might give you that damned spanking."

She looked up at him and he saw the disbelief in her eyes.

He returned the expression as though it were a verbal reply.

Lilly's mouth tightened. "I don't like people telling me who I can have as my friends. And, yes, Tom Woodward *is* my friend," she defended. "He didn't go off and leave Montfort, running away from everyone. He had to pick up the pieces, and live with it. Oh, he's not perfect," Lilly commented, adding with a deep frown, "but neither are you!"

"So he is your beau," Shadoe muttered. "Well, don't that beat the hell out of everything!" He wanted to laugh, but couldn't. The thought of

Lilly and Tom together sickened him. He looked at her with renewed interest, realizing for the first time that she was really a woman ready for a man's touch. But he knew what it would be like for her with Tom, stiff and quick, under the sheets, in the darkness. She'd probably never imagined what a man and woman could be together, naked, twisting, sweating, aching for pleasure.

He swallowed hard, realized that he was lusting after her again, that his body was rigid with desire just thinking about her. He raked his hand through his hair again, struggling to forget. He had to forget.

Looking away, he said in a slow, checked tone, "The McFalls and the Woodwards. Just like before. So little Lilly has finally grown up and found her a real honest beau, one who's acceptable to her father, to that great design of his and Woodward's— the valley as one."

"I didn't say he was my beau!" Lilly returned, clearly irritated with his attitude.

He stared at her coolly. "You don't have to, honey. It all makes sense to me now. Woodward has his ranch. He intends to buy my ranch, and then he's going to have Weatherly through marriage." Shadoe gave a hoarse chuckle. "The boy's smart, I'll give him that!"

She gave him a rebellious look. "How could you?"

Shadoe smiled lazily at her anger. "How could I what, Lilly?"

"How could you insinuate that Tom was marrying me for Weatherly?"

His heavy brows lifted as Shadoe cast her a quizzical look. "Ah, so you are marrying Tom."

"I didn't say that at all!"

"But you did," he pointed out. "You're all red in the face because I said Tom was marrying you for Weatherly."

"I did not! And my face is not red!"

He smiled helplessly at her. She was so pretty, so very pretty. "Maybe not, but it's pink . . . pretty and pink."

She touched her face instinctively, then stopped, thrusting her hand to her side. "Okay, so I'm a little flushed. But that doesn't mean that I'm marrying Tom."

"Then what did you say?" he baited, wanting her to argue with him. Arguing with Lilly was always fun. It reminded him of the way they were so many years ago when she was just a young girl, and he was a man wanting her to grow up so that he could kiss her. God, he could kiss her now. Damn, why did she have to come near him?

She never answered his question and Shadoe could see that Lilly was clearly as flustered as he was.

"You look speechless, darlin'. Cat got your tongue at last?"

"Oh, I hate you!" Lilly blurted childishly before she could stop herself.

"I see that I spoke too soon—"

"I really do, Shadoe!" she cut in. "I hate you! You never were anything but coldhearted. Rude! Unappreciative! Scurrilous! Go right ahead and sell the ranch! Everyone will be glad to be rid of you! You can take the money and run back to wherever it is you've been hiding all these years!"

"Now this is the sweet little girl I remember so well, the small and pretty ragamuffin with a mouthful of nickel words." He laughed scornfully. "Talk to me some more, darlin'."

"You beast! I do hate you! I do!"

He relaxed in her frustration. In it, Shadoe found some control, and he teased her on with a taunting smile.

"Oh, sweetheart," he said.

"Damn you!"

"My sweet, sweet little princess!"

Lilly gritted her teeth. "You're hateful!" she swore as she lifted her shirts, stepping up into the buggy.

When Shadoe reached out to help her, Lilly swept his hand away, snapping, "You must have a faulty memory! When was I ever sweet?"

He stared intently. Her voice had altered. It was colder than he'd ever remembered it being.

"After all," she continued, "I had you as my role model, and you were a serpent in the grass, a coiled snake ready to strike at first sight!"

Lilly snatched up the reins and gave Shadoe a smile laced with ridicule. "You were an illiterate scoundrel, Shadoe Sinclair, running off with your best friend's girl, getting her with child. Leaving me when you knew that I loved you."

He stood back, stunned at the last of her words, so amazed that they—the I-love-you words—seemed to echo in his ears.

"Yes, I loved you! You hear me? Loved you more than my own pride! But now, looking at you, I'll never know what Anne Woodward saw in you and what was it about you that was worth her life."

His face whitened, and their gazes locked. It was a clash of wills, and somehow Shadoe felt that Lilly had just won the first battle in a war that would continue as long as he stayed in Oregon. Yes, he knew that she loved him, but she'd never said the words. No one had ever said the words. Not his father. Not his mother. Not even Anne.

He felt himself sinking into somewhere dark. But he wasn't about to show Lilly the weakness that he always felt in her presence. He gave her a scornful look, cold and ugly, laced with the feelings all knotted up with Joseph, Anne, his father, the Woodwards.

And then from out of nowhere, Shadoe laughed bitterly at her, a short laugh that quickly faded.

"You sure know how to welcome a man home," he told her.

"Yes . . . welcome home," she choked out, then slapped the reins against the horse's rump.

Shadoe moved back as the rig lurched forward. He stood in the middle of the dusty road, watching the rig grow smaller, while the name Anne Woodward reeled through his head. The two words were so relentless and unforgiving, that five minutes later he thought his skull was going to explode.

Chapter 4

Jesse Woodward met his brother, Tom, directly at the fork of the road that led to Montfort. Apparently, they were both going in different directions, none of which led home.

Stopping, the younger man leaned back in his saddle and gave his brother a curious stare.

First of all, Jesse was surprised that Tom wasn't going home, seeing that a storm was brewing, and Tom never liked to leave his mother alone on a stormy day.

Anne had left on a rainy day, when she ran off and married Shadoe Sinclair, and ever since, Sarah Woodward had hated storms, hated when even a sprinkle started to fall.

Even in his youth, Jesse had known what it was. It was as if fearing the storm was a lot easier to deal with than fearing for her daughter's future. And after Anne's death, Sarah's fears only grew. His mother hated the rain.

One look at Tom, and Jesse knew that he had been somewhere else, and it wasn't on the road. He knew that Tom had been gone for two days, and yet he was clean, even had a shave, and was wearing an ironed shirt. Jesse thought that Tom had the look of a man who had just enjoyed a welcomed bath and was about to go visiting.

"Where ya headed?" Tom asked first.

"I was goin' into town. And you?"

Tom pointed. "Weatherly."

"That explains some things. Goin' to see Lilly, I reckon." Jesse pushed back his hat and frowned. "Storm's gonna be on our heads soon. I asked one of the womenfolk to stay with Maw and Joey. She was feelin' poorly so she took one of Doc's powders. She was sleepin' when I left. Hope she sleeps through this one. It might git bad."

"What's the rush for town?" Tom asked, obviously avoiding the comment about their mother.

"Got myself officially engaged." Jesse grinned. "They're havin' a dinner tonight."

Tom sneered. "You really gonna marry Molly Andrews?"

"I reckon so."

Tom laughed as he shook his head. "You fool." Then he quickly added, "I'll go on home."

"No need. Maw's sleepin' real good. She won't wake for hours. Go on over and see Lilly."

"I don't know," Tom said, staring up at the sky.

"Don't worry. I plan on makin' it a quick evenin'. Molly's mother has been on me ever since I proposed. She wants one of those big church weddings. Talks of nothin' but lace and linen and flowers."

"I told you, Jesse. You should've listened to me.

Whores are better. You're too young to be tyin' yourself to a girl like Molly. She'll make you miserable."

Jesse frowned. "I don't want your whore!"

"I could give you a couple of dollars and she'd be so willin' to make my little brother happy. Forget Molly for a while. She'll make you poke her under the covers in the dark. Most likely have her nightgown on. You need a good seasoned woman, one who'll take all her clothes off, fall to her knees, and make you feel like you're dyin'." Tom laughed again.

"You just been with her!" Jesse accused between gritted teeth.

"What if I was?"

"And what about Lilly?"

Tom made a grimace. "Lilly is a lady. She ain't like Molly. And she sure ain't like the girls in the saloon! She don't know a damn thing about what goes on between a man and woman. Girls like her hardly kiss before the wedding night, and even then, they're scared out of their wits. They're refined. Virgins. Aristocrats. They breed bloodlines."

"But to touch a whore and then court her, I think it's sick."

"You think too much. You think like a boy. Let me worry about Lilly."

"And Shadoe?"

Tom jerked on his reins and gave Jesse a hard look. "What in the hell do ya mean by that?"

"He's here, and she ain't a girl no more. He ruined our sister. He might ruin Lilly if he takes alikin' to. Then what ya gonna do about your precious bloodlines!"

"Shut the hell up!"

"Well, I ain't gonna. You may be scared of him, but I'm ain't. I done told ya, Tom, I ain't taking nothin' off that man. He's too dangerous to leave alone."

Tom drew his horse closer to Jesse's. "I told you not to start any trouble, Jesse. Sinclair will pay for what he did, but leave it be. I'll handle it."

Jesse said nothing. He reined his horse, dug in his spurs, and rode hard toward Montfort.

Chapter 5

It was three miles from the grave site at the Double S to Montfort, and from there, it was another two miles to the large stone house of Weatherly, home of the English McFalls.

Lilly lifted her whip and popped it loudly. For the last mile of her journey, she had driven the horse unnecessarily fast, more out of frustration than out of need. Even though it had been drizzling rain since Montfort, there had been no hurry.

The small rig leaned on one wheel as it rounded the corner, driving hard up the often-used pathway which led to the house. The three-story castle stood high on a hill, overshadowing the land with its impressive size and overwhelming sense of power. Surrounding it was a rock wall built by James McFall against attacks by the Paiute and Bannock tribes. The Indians were gone now, trapped by the military from Idaho Territory in 1878 and moved to the reservation at Fort Simcoe.

A low rumble of thunder shook the damp air as Lilly tugged firmly on the reins, bringing the buggy to a sharp halt in front of the main doors.

She secured the horse with a ranch hand, scurried up the steps, and opened the door. The sound of voices greeted her from the hallway.

"Where have you been?" It was James McFall who asked the question, but Lilly could see that it was Tom Woodward who desperately wanted to hear the answer. She had heard as she passed through town that he had been looking for her all afternoon.

Raindrops clung to her eyelashes, glistening in the lamplight of the oppressively dim room. "Out," was her only reply, and she took a step to pass both Tom and her father.

Her father's voice stopped her. "I think you owe me an explanation, young lady. I told you that I do not like you riding off the ranch without Martha or one of the foremen. The least you could do is tell us where you are going," James McFall said in a tone that warned Lilly she would have to give him a satisfactory answer.

She turned to him. "I went out for a ride, that's all, Papa."

"Riding where?"

"I went into town."

James McFall's brows drew into a frown. "I went to town myself. You weren't there."

"I went for a ride. Honestly, you sound as though I might have done something wrong." Lilly ran a hand across her flushed cheeks and the damp windblown curls straying across her temples. Her deep gray eyes glowed with indignation beneath the brim of her hat. She knew that her father was aware that she was telling him only a half-truth.

"No explanations?"

"None," was her quick reply.

Looking over at Tom, the older man forced a smile. "You should have a daughter like mine one day," he said. "See these gray hairs? Everyone of them I attribute to my children. I thought Joseph was stubborn, but this girl makes him look like an angel. She's been more trouble than any boy. I've done my best to make a proper lady out of her," he finished with a shake of his head.

Tom laughed, and Lilly, too, smiled, though it was a lame effort on her part. She took a few steps closer to freedom.

"I need to change. The weather turned raw on me. Been sprinkling constantly since I left Montfort. I'm afraid that I'm soaked," she said as she ran her gloved hands down the front of her wet dress.

A clap of thunder exploded, vibrating throughout the foyer. The fine drizzle was turning into a splattering of heavy rainfall.

Tom glanced nervously at Lilly, and somehow she could see that he knew where she had been, knew who she had been with. A muscle twitched in his jaw and she knew he was struggling for control.

"I better be gettin' home myself." Tom's words were addressed to Lilly's father.

"I'll have no such thing, my boy. You'll have dinner with us before leaving this house. I've already told the servant to prepare another place at the table." The elder man patted the younger one on the back in a friendly gesture. "The cook has prepared a fine rib of roast for our pleasure. Rare roast beef, cooked to perfection with just the right touch of garlic. Nothing better to the palate. Don't you agree?"

"Sounds temptin', but I . . . don't know," Tom said with hesitation. "I'm gonna be late as it is with this storm. And Jesse's in town tonight eatin' dinner with the Andrews. I don't like leavin' Maw alone."

"Nonsense, Tom! You need a fine, hot meal in you if you're going to ride back to your ranch in this rotten weather. I insist. Besides, I'd like to finish that conversation we were having earlier. There's going to be no end to this mess of rustlers unless we find a way to stop them. Look at the trouble old Sinclair had this last year, and now my herd . . . There's a method to this stealing, method and cleverness I tell you. This is the work of someone who knows his business."

Her father's comment caught Lilly's attention. She had heard the talk about cattle missing from the ranch. But no one had ever used the word "rustler" before today, at least not to her.

"Rustlers? Are you sure?" she asked.

"That's the conclusion."

"Someone has been stealing our cattle? I thought everyone considered it an accounting error."

James gave his daughter a skeptical look, his thick gray brows lifting. "It's time you knew the truth. I've had the men counting the herds for months." Grimacing, he added, "Although we can't ride up every draw and we're bound to miss hundreds of them, the numbers are too low. Dan Hadley and a few of the men even rode out to the highlands where some of the cattle go looking for good grass. The book count looks bad. People are starting to put up fences near the open range. Tom came here to tell me that Luke Miller has fenced every line of his property and is threatening to shoot anyone who crosses it."

"I can't believe anyone would attempt to steal our cattle." Lilly tugged off her gray gloves, peeling them from her small hands. "Where would they take them?"

"I don't know. But they're gone. Just like Sinclair's, and I thought the old man had sold them to pay off his debts. I should have helped him." A sorrowful expression dimmed the angry glow in McFall's eyes.

"They buried him today," she commented quickly.

"I know."

"I wanted to be there."

"Let's not speak of it," James suggested.

Lilly twisted the gloves tightly in her hand. "That's the problem around here. No one wants to speak of *anything*." She looked at both the men, lines of discontent forming across her brow. "A man dies, a man who was your friend for over a quarter of a century, and you won't speak of it! The cattle are missing and *you won't speak of it!*"

There was a deep hiss of indrawn breath and Lilly asked, "Where do you think our cattle have gone?"

"I just don't know," her father said, his gaze dropping to the floor.

Lilly stared at Tom who immediately shrugged his shoulders. When she looked back at her father, she saw an uncommon element in his appearance. Over the years, she had trusted herself to know each of her father's many and varied expressions—how his deep gray eyes narrowed and darkened when he was angered; how his lips suddenly pinched into a tight grimace when he faced frustration and fatigue; or even the way his burly shoulders drooped when thwarted. Tonight, he was all of these, and it was obvious to her that he was more than a little troubled.

"What are you going to do?"

"Do?" the old slate-eyed man boomed, staring at his daughter with determination. "I am going to catch the thieves and hang them!"

Hang them! The words refused to come, stuck somewhere in her constricting throat.

"Couldn't you just catch them . . . and put them in jail . . . and let the law do justice?"

He pointed his finger at her. "There's an unwritten code out here in the West, young lady. A man protects his property. When a rancher is threatened with thievery, he makes his own rules, dispenses his own brand of justice."

Lilly could see the anger in her father's eyes, and part of her recoiled. She loved this man, but he had been more than stern over the years, too harsh with her, too severe with everyone since her brother, Joseph, had decided to return to northern England. He had hate in his eyes now. And she knew where part of that bitterness sprung.

Obviously Tom and he had been discussing more than rustling—Shadoe's return. It was time she made her exit.

"I'm not very hungry, Papa, and I feel a chill coming on. I think I'll have my meal in my room if you don't object."

"I most certainly do object! You'll have dinner with Tom and me. As the future lady of the manor, you must learn to be gracious when duty calls. I won't live forever, child. Weatherly will be yours one day, and you might as well get used to doing things even when you don't feel like it."

Lilly didn't make any rebuttal. It was not that her courage had failed her. She just didn't want to aggravate her father any more than he already was.

"I'll just be a moment to change into some dry clothes," she said with a forced smile.

She left the foyer, moving with brisk steps from the room, almost running as she made her way to the top of the stairs. Once inside her room, she collapsed across the bed, her heart pounding in her chest.

Somehow she felt more frightened than angry, and began to cry, the quick tears falling from beneath her rich lashes.

Lilly was not thinking of stolen cattle, not even of her father. She was thinking of Shadoe Sinclair.

He had been so indifferent to her, and so quick to treat her like a child. He may have left a childish young woman, but that was not what he had returned to. But he had not returned for her, but to bury his father and obviously to sell the ranch. To leave again. To leave her again.

Oh, Shadoe . . . How could she still feel so much love for him after all these years? Maybe it was habit, the memories deeply rooted in childhood and adolescence. Maybe because as long as she had lived, Shadoe had been so much a part of her existence, and she did not feel complete without him. But maybe she was a foolish young woman living on the edge of a dream, too.

She sniffled, fighting her despair. She hated being weak, hated tears.

"Well, you are finally back!" a loud voice bleated, and Lilly raised her head to look at her aunt.

Chapter 6

Martha McFall stood in the bedroom doorway, her hands on her broad hips. "I shan't ask you where you've been. God only knows what foolery you have been up to!"

"Well." Lilly narrowed a curious eye at her aunt, wondering the same thing herself. "*You* weren't at Weatherly when I left this morning, and you weren't in Montfort either. Should I ask where you've been?" Her tears were fading into irritation as she sniffled again.

"I went for a ride," Martha replied.

Lilly gave a hollow laugh and rolled over on the bed, propping her chin in the cup of her palms as she gazed at her aunt.

"What's so amusing?" Martha demanded, a slight frown creasing her forehead.

Lilly ignored the question, and asked her own. "When did you get home?" She smiled up at the gray-haired woman and wondered if her aunt had been riding in the same direction as she had herself.

"Before you did, young lady," was the quick retort, and the older woman drew herself up into a quivering knot of affronted regard.

Lilly sat up at her aunt's excited words. Her gaze came to rest on the older woman's hair. The thin wisps of silver curls around Martha's round face were clearly damp.

"Did you get caught in the rain, too, Auntie?" Lilly teased.

Martha raised her eyebrows and looked intently at her niece. "I guess there's no keeping the truth from the likes of you, young lady!" Turning, the older woman strode across the room and threw herself into a chair, a despairing expression shadowing her face. "I went to Simon's funeral," she admitted with a heavy sigh. "And don't make one single remark concerning it."

Martha wagged an accusing finger at Lilly. "And I know that you went there, also. I saw the buggy leaving the ranch."

"So?"

"Did you see Shadoe?" Martha asked.

"Yes, I did."

Martha's expression revealed her discomfort with the news and also a touch of curiosity. "And?"

"He looked well, but then you know that yourself. He hasn't changed much. Still the same man, single-minded, cold when he wants to be, even a bit cruel. He practically threw me off the Double S, and not one kind word for the Woodwards. As always, defensive, afraid to get too close to anyone."

Lilly paused, remembering, a troubled look on her face. Without thinking, she blurted, "It's strange how the passage of time can clear your head. God knows, I've been thinking. And I have to wonder if there's more to the Anne Woodward story than we all know, than we all cared to know at the time. I never thought it made any sense. I mean Shadoe and Anne marrying . . . her pregnant. Shadoe didn't love her, not the way he loved me. But there was something about it, some deeper meaning."

Her aunt looked rather shocked, but Lilly didn't hesitate in her speculations. She could not forget that last look on Shadoe's face. She had wounded him deeply with her words about Anne.

She bit her lip. Tugging at the ribbon of her bonnet, she remarked with a soft voice, "I know that Shadoe still loves me, Aunt Martha. I briefly saw it, love and want, in his eyes today when he gazed at me, that same look of childish hunger, that same spark, a connection. All these years, not one word, not a single letter. Nothing. And today, it was just like the last time so many years ago when we were happy and together, riding on the range. For a moment it was as if we had never parted unhappy with one another."

"It was your dreams you saw, child, that's all. He married Anne Woodward. Can you forget that?"

Her hands fell away from the ribbon of her hat. "Yes. God, yes! I can and I will. I looked into his eyes, those blue eyes of his, and saw only myself and what I wanted. Not Joseph. Not Anne. Anne doesn't matter. She's dead and buried. And I'm here, living and breathing, and needing him just like I did before. Just like before I want only him."

"I don't understand. Surely you can't forget how miserable you were at that time, how you suffered?" Martha wrung her hands together. "I don't want to see you hurt again. Shadoe never told you he loved you—not with words."

Lilly shook her head. "There are some things that need no words, no gestures. They just exist. A feeling. It's like Shadoe said that time long ago. Some things just are. You don't know why or how. You don't question it. And I won't question it now. We belong to each other in pain and in pleasure . . . two wild and unruly hearts." The tears flooded the corners of her eyes again. "I can't let him leave here again. I just can't face losing him again. I won't."

"You may have no choice in the matter," Martha said.

She gave her aunt a hard look, ignoring the comment. "Aunt Martha, do you think Joseph intended to go to England without Anne Woodward as his wife?"

"What?"

"Well, Papa seemed to believe that Joseph would have changed his mind about going to England if Anne had not married Shadoe, if Anne had told Joseph that she didn't want him to leave her. Papa said that Anne could have changed Joseph's feelings and they would have settled down here in the valley. But couldn't that have been his own distorted view of things?"

"I don't know. I wouldn't want to say that to you," Martha was murmuring.

Lilly added, "Papa has it in his mind that the reason Joseph finally went to England was because he couldn't bear to stay here after Anne's death."

Martha was silent for a moment, then said sharply, "The reason your brother went home to England is because he wanted to go. That's all. Your father inherited the northern estates of Montfort when his uncle died without an heir." Martha paused.

"You would have thought James would have been ecstatic, but he wasn't." Martha's face creased into a slight smile, as she continued, "He loves America, loves the wildness of it, the violence of the land. He came here, and made this place his Montfort in America. His own little British kingdom in the wilderness. When he inherited the title and estates in England, he had this notion that he would manage it through proxy, but Joseph startled him by jumping at the chance to go to England and play the rich aristocrat. About Anne Woodward? I really don't know. But I do know this. Your brother never cared for Weatherly in the same way that your father does. He never wanted the same things that your father did. He wasn't the man your father thought he was."

Lilly agreed. "Shadoe was more like Papa than Joseph. They were so close. He treated Shadoe more like a son than Simon Sinclair ever did." A new tear trickled down her flushed cheek, and she quickly wiped it away. "I can't believe how Papa turned against him."

Martha sighed. "Your father loves Shadoe very much. He was just so bitter when Joseph really decided to leave. He couldn't understand Joseph's desires and he couldn't accept them, Lilly." She looked kindly at her niece. "Remember how hurt and angry you were when Shadoe told you he was marrying Anne. You hated him that day, hated him as much as you ever loved him. That one morning and everything that followed swallowed up your love for a while. But, child, it was the anger and grief that helped you survive. The same for your father. James had to blame someone for Joseph's decision. But you know there was more to it, Lilly."

"You mean Papa's plans, his dreams for me?"

"Yes. When Shadoe married Anne, and you were so hurt, your father was almost destroyed. He was losing his son to England. He was losing you to all that pain and misery. He was losing Shadoe. James couldn't bear any of it, especially seeing you so unhappy."

Lilly finally pulled off her bonnet and hastily tossed it on the bed. "But there has to be more to it than just that. More than me! More than Papa's pride. I've always had this strange feeling about the situation whenever I was talking with Tom's mother."

"You shouldn't bother Sarah Woodward with it, Lilly. She has enough worries."

"I know." Lilly chastised herself, thinking briefly about how ill Tom and Jesse's mother was. "I know, but it's as though she wants to tell me something."

"Yes, maybe she does. I know Sarah aches for you when she sees you thinking about Shadoe." Martha quickly turned from the subject, and her voice lightened. "Anyhow, I think your father will soften when he sees Shadoe again."

"Do you really think so?" Lilly smiled lightly. "I was just wondering how I was going to tell Father about Shadoe, and that I don't ever intend on marrying Tom. But how can I if he won't listen? He was so angry when I got home today, so gruff. I was afraid that if he learned the truth, he would keep me housebound or worse, pack me off to England to keep me from seeing Shadoe."

Lilly shuddered at the thought, adding, "I hate for Papa to treat me like one of those simpering English debutantes who can't blow their own noses without instructions from their chaperones."

"When were you ever that?" Her aunt laughed. "I think your father long ago faced the idea that you are not going to be like your mother."

"But he still has English ways, Aunt Martha. He wants to arrange a marriage for me. He wants me to marry Tom. How he could accept Tom as my husband and not Shadoe is beyond me!"

A new flood of tears gathered in Lilly's eyes. She was so tired of struggling, hoping against hope that somehow her dreams would come true. She wanted to marry for love, and she did not love Tom. She hated it when he tried to kiss her, felt suffocated when he pulled her into his arms, and she always resisted.

For Lilly, there had never been any kisses. Not even from Shadoe, though she had dreamed of them, felt his lips in her thoughts.

"I just can't marry Tom," she spat at her aunt. "I do wish that Papa would stop trying to talk me into it every other day. Talk, talk, talk. Marriage. Grandchildren. His dynasty. You think when those three men first came to this valley, they must have sat down and planned the whole future out. A McFall married first to a Woodward and then to a Sinclair. The valley tied together by blood." Lilly laughed bitterly. "But then the dreams shattered. Only Papa still clings to hopes of a dynasty!"

"He feels guilty, I think, Lilly." Martha stood again, moving across the room toward the wardrobe. Her voice was kinder when she added, "He feels that Joseph should have married Anne, and somehow I think he feels that he owes the Woodwards for their loss. That's all. That's why he's pushed you at Tom."

Lilly sucked in an uneasy breath, and reached for the handkerchief tucked into the pocket of her waistcoat. Wiping her face, she swallowed some of her displeasure. "But Tom is becoming a problem. He's downstairs now, waiting for me to join him for dinner. He already thinks of us as being engaged. He calls me his girl all the time."

"Have you tried to talk to him?"

"Yes."

"And?"

"It's hopeless. He just keeps right on asking me to marry him."

Martha stood silently for a few moments as she rubbed her chin thoughtfully. "Maybe you should talk to Jesse. Those boys are so very close. Maybe Jesse could reason with him, make Tom see that you care for him in the same way that you care for his brother."

"Jesse has changed, Aunt Martha." Lilly frowned. "These last few months since Mrs. Woodward has been so ill, I've seen Jesse turn into someone I don't know any longer. He's too busy trying to be a man. I don't think Jesse would understand at all. He wants Tom and me to marry. Planning a double wedding with that shameless and stupid Molly Andrews!"

"But Jesse is only seventeen and he has always been such a sweet boy." The older woman was clearly surprised. "Molly Andrews? Why she's always becoming engaged until someone else better comes along! I can't imagine Jesse marrying her."

"Well, he talks of nothing else."

"Maybe Sarah's illness has something to do with Jesse's mood. The boys lost their sister, then their father the following year and now their mother is so ill. It's a hard thing to be on your own at such a tender age. He just wants some company."

Martha paused, gnawing on her lower lip. "It worries me . . . the situation over there. There's that sweet little child to think about."

"I know. I think about him all the time," Lilly retorted. "What am I going to do?"

"You'll do the right thing, I'm certain of it, Lilly. Don't fret over it so much. Time has a way of taking care of our problems. And maybe after all this time, Shadoe is going to do something about the boy." Martha turned and fumbled through the dresses. "Which gown do you want to wear for dinner, my dear?" she asked, changing the subject. "I'm sure that James and Tom are anxiously awaiting us."

Lilly trembled slightly as she glanced at the two dresses she had laid out that morning. She wasn't hungry, and at the moment, she didn't want to see Tom. "I think I'll wear the green-and-gray brocade silk to dinner," she decided. It brought out the color of her eyes, and was one of her father's favorites.

While her aunt moved to pick up the gown, Lilly stood and began fumbling with the buttons on the front of her gray-and-white dress, all the time her mind darting from one thought to another.

If Shadoe was back to get the boy, there would be lots of trouble. Tom wouldn't give up Anne's child without a struggle, especially to Shadoe. Anne's death had been mysterious, and everyone had been so quick to blame Shadoe for all the misery. The Woodwards. James McFall. Even herself. Everyone except Joseph.

Lilly frowned at the odd thought. Joseph had been faithful to the end. Even after Anne and Shadoe's betrayal, her brother had spoken only kindly of his friend, never once showing any anger.

But he has to be angry. I've been angry and bitter, waiting, living out the years in memories and pain, all the time wondering and fretting, wanting to know, wanting to see Shadoe as I struggled through the days, never forgetting, never not hoping. Not one day went by that I didn't think of him, hope he was thinking of me, hope that he was guilt-ridden and miserable, too. Joseph has to feel the same way and yet. . . .

At the time, Lilly hadn't cared to notice, but now, with Shadoe's return, she remembered the past with stark clarity. Joseph had been cold and indifferent. Joseph had been silent. Joseph had finally gone. Then Shadoe, too.

Only Shadoe had come home, and he still wanted her.

The glance from under her thickly curling lashes was slightly defiant, and a smile widened her full lips. She would dress and go down to dinner. She would even be the perfect hostess for her father, even smile at Tom.

But only one thought was in her mind as Lilly slipped off the wet dress and reached for the moss-colored gown. *Somehow I am going to find out the truth and that truth is going to lead me back to Shadoe. I'm going to marry Shadoe Sinclair if it's the last thing I ever do.*

Shadoe lay in his narrow bed. His dog was sleeping, curled around his feet, and he could hear Dragon's breath, slow and relaxed, and Shadoe wished that his own breath came so easily.

A flame lurched above the wick of the lamp, sending a flicker of light around the walls. He watched it. His eyes were hazy as he stared steadily into the light, as though he was a moth drawn into some heated disaster.

The continuous sound of rain splattered against the roof. It hummed in his ears, and finally he broke his gaze away from the light.

Shadoe sighed and glanced thoughtfully at Dragon, a huddled clump of black fur. A slight grin twisted at one corner of his mouth. A dog was always dependable, he thought, loyal, an easy companion who needed nothing more than a little affection, a few scraps of food, some water.

He rubbed Dragon's head with his socked foot, and the animal made a low growl of pleasure.

"Good dog, sleep."

Shadoe lifted the whiskey bottle that he'd been nursing for several hours, and slugged down the last drop.

Now women were different, he mused silently. He laid his hand against his chest, felt the slow thud of his heartbeat, and pondered some more. Women—they were trouble, that old fatal power of destruction. With them, a man could be as weak and as stupid as a puppy dog, running around, his tail curled between his legs, begging for one touch of affection. That was unless a man remained in total control.

Shadoe smiled lazily. He was a man of control. His life had been one lesson on how to forget pain, how to accept indifference. Yes, women were fine as long as a man stayed master.

He drew another long sigh, and stared out the window. Raindrops blurred the glass like some gray-vested misery, and he quickly scolded himself. His will was often more tenuous than strong where Lilly was concerned. A readied gun he could face, but he had a weakness for soft skin, gentle curves, silky strands of hair running through his searching fingers.

His mouth worked. "Damn her."

Dragon raised his head, looking at his master.

"They're all witches, playing games," he told the dog in a fierce mutter. "A man has to watch his back." He tapped the bottle against his chest in protest, then took a hard, empty swallow of air before he said the word that had been hanging in his throat all evening. "Lilly."

Her name burned inside of him, a fire far worse than all the secrets that he'd held for years. Not even the rain could quench the blaze consuming his soul.

His heartbeat quickened as he closed his eyes. In the blackness beneath his tired lids, he could imagine touching Lilly, one finger trailing slowly down the soft flush of her cheek, that fine white, porcelain skin, those gentle curves so perfectly shaped for his touch. His mind ached with the thought. His loins throbbed.

"God," he moaned as he rolled over, twisting in the sheets. The empty bottle fell from his hands, falling to the floor with a thud. Shadoe clutched a fistful of his pillow.

"Let me sleep, damn you," he slurred into the darkness. "Let me sleep."

But the moment was spinning wildly in his head. When he did sleep, it was not without dreams.

Chapter 7

The day after Simon Sinclair was laid to rest, Lilly was awakened with news that her father wanted her to come to the barn immediately. She was told to wear those riding pants that she often wore when working with the horses.

Breakfast was short and simple, a piece of bread, lightly buttered, then covered with some of Mrs. Burton's plum jam. Lilly was still licking the jam off her lips when she reached the round barn of Weatherly.

"What's this?" she asked, surprised at the sight before her. Dan Hadley was pacing back and forth, leading a pretty young mare.

"A gift," James told her.

"A gift?" She took an uneasy step, staring at her father, then at the beautiful young mare. It was one of Luke Miller's fine, spirited roans, a real beauty, a horse that her father would have given to no man, much less a woman, even if the woman was his own daughter.

Brushing the last trace of bread crumbs from her fingers, Lilly looked a bit disconcerted. "Why?"

"A peace offering if you like."

She saw a soft look in his eyes, noted the remorse. So he wanted forgiveness, she thought. A soft smile played at the corners of her mouth for she realized immediately that the moment was hers. This was her chance to settle some things with her father once and for all.

"What kind of peace are you offering?" she dared as she walked over to the mare. "A horse is not enough to make me forget last night."

"I should have known that you would exact blood from me." He drew an uneasy breath. The horse whinnied. James stared at his daughter as though he'd prefer whipping her to saying the words that soon poured from his mouth. "I was wrong to speak to you the way I did."

"And?"

He bit his lip, annoyed. His eyes grew narrow as he glared at her. "Blaze and bother! A man should not have to grovel to his daughter, especially when she was in the wrong, too—"

"Then don't grovel," she interrupted, "but you can send this pretty little thing right back to Luke Miller in the morning." She handed the reins back to Dan Hadley, the bit rattling in the quick exchange.

The foreman was clearly amused, and Dan smiled at her. "Don't ya want me to saddle her, Miss Lilly? She's the finest mare I've seen in years. A real beauty she is and got some legs on her. I bet she rides as quick as the wind."

"That depends on my father," Lilly commented

as she threw a look over her shoulder at him.

Dan grinned at the older man.

"You'd think she'd be a tad more kindly after all these years, wouldn't you, Dan? But, no, it doesn't matter how many times we've been through this scene. Each time she wants the very most of me. You'd think I'd learn by now. She's as hard as any man I know. Worse than most."

"I'll get that saddle," Hadley commented as he turned to stroll into the barn with the mare.

Lilly looked at her father, remembering how harsh he had been with her the previous night. She'd been miserable, hardly able to eat a bite of her food, and afterwards she could barely sleep for thinking of Tom living in Shadoe's house, sleeping in Shadoe's bed. She'd drunk too much wine, had a headache, dreamed the worst nightmares.

"Well?" she asked. "What were you saying?" She almost smiled at him, knowing that he was going to offer her any apology that she'd demand, but the gesture failed her.

He hesitated. "You're a wicked child, Lilly McFall."

"You were saying?"

"I was saying that I should have not forced dinner upon you, making you sit at the table with Tom and me, boring you with all that nonsense about brands and stock and breeding," he blurted.

Her lips pinched back in anticipation. She bridled and shot him an angry stare.

"All right! Damn you, child! You'd worry a man into his grave!" He rubbed his forehead. "I apologize for forcing you to listen to Tom discuss his plans for the Double *S*."

"How astute of you to realize that it was difficult for me."

"I was wrong."

"Yes, you were," she told him bluntly.

"It's a reality, Lilly. Shadoe intends to sell the ranch. Might as well face it."

"I will not."

There was a long stretch where father and daughter said nothing. Lilly kept her eyes on the ground, occasionally pressing the mud beneath her boots.

Her father finally broke the silence. "You can be very hard, Lilly," he said as Dan returned with the horse.

"I am your daughter, remember?" She gathered the reins from Dan.

"Too true. I only wish that you were a trace more like your mother."

She finally laughed. "What a hypocrite! You would not have ever subjected my gentle mother to a scene like last night. I'm just like you, and you adore it."

He nodded with a smile. "Yes, I do," he said, watching her rub the horse's neck. "I can see that you want more than an apology from me. What kind of agreement do you want? Something in blood?"

She eyed him intently, thinking, knowing exactly what she wanted to say, but hesitant.

"Go ahead, speak, girl. You'll never have another chance. I'm not likely to be this generous for a while."

Her face grew somber. "I'm not going to marry Tom."

Her words were blunt, and she could see that she

caught him off guard. For a minute, there was an expression of derision on his face, then it passed. He smiled, a lame effort.

"So you want to choose your own husband, young lady. Daughters in England do not have such pleasure."

"This is America. I want to marry for love." She rubbed the horse again, looking away from her father lest he should see her face. She was sure that she wore her feelings. She wanted to marry Shadoe.

"Love?"

"Yes, it's pretty simple when you think about it." She stroked the fine, shiny horsehair. "You marry the person you fall in love with, the person who you want to raise a family with, live all your days with."

"And what if you never fall in love?" He gave her a warning look as she turned to glance at him.

She didn't answer him, and she knew that he knew why.

"And if you fall in love, suppose it's a man who doesn't want you? Suppose it's a man who turned killer and crazy, who ran off and married your own brother's fiancée, not caring for all the hurt he would leave behind? What then, Lilly mine?"

Again, she didn't answer. Instead, she hastily mounted the mare, clutching the reins tightly in her hand.

"I'm riding out to the line shack on the southwest end," she told him before she spurred the horse.

"Ain't that on the Double *S?*" Hadley questioned as he watched Lilly ride away in a gallop.

James McFall nodded.

"Miss Lilly ain't got no gun, no provisions. Want me to follow?"

"No need." The older man's eyes narrowed in frustration. "Number nine is always stocked."

Line shack number nine. That's what everyone called it. But to Shadoe, it was called The Forsaken's Oasis. It was his place away from the rest of the world. He'd come there after arguments with his father or one of his friends, to be alone, to think, to clear his head after a long night of whiskey. The last time he'd been there was the day he told Lilly he was going to marry Anne Woodward.

It was cool for midday, he thought, almost cold for the last week of April. The air was still damp from last night's heavy rainfall. Sunlight spilled in through the window, and Shadoe stared curiously through the glass. Someone had taken extra good care of the place, stocking it with provisions, replacing boards, putting real glass over the wire that used to be in the windows.

And he had a thought to who that dedicated person was. It had been their place, his and Lilly's, and all these years, she'd still come there, to sit on the high porch in the rickety chair, looking at the softly rolling land.

The forsaken, he thought miserably. How fitting a name it was now, even more than before, when it had been named as a joke by all who wanted to get away for a night.

His eyes closed tightly at the thought. Somehow, someway, he'd never let himself think of Lilly as one of the abandoned. He'd never promised her anything with words. And she'd never done so with him—not until the other day when she had said that she loved him.

Everything was different now.

When he opened his eyes, he saw the rider.

Shadoe rested his arms on the windowsill, considering, but he knew, knew in an instant that it was her.

Damn her, he thought, *not now!* He wanted to run. Run. Run like the devil in paradise! But there was only one recourse. Shadoe walked out on the porch and waited.

Strangely, there were no words, no greetings.

He held the reins as she dismounted. He couldn't look at her, didn't want to. He had wished her away a thousand times in the last few seconds, even wished himself away.

"She's a real beauty," he said of the horse.

"Papa gave her to me this morning. One of Luke Miller's herd."

Her voice was nonchalant, and she was looking down at her hands. She'd forgotten her gloves. Tiny blisters had formed on her upper palms.

"Looks a bit saucy."

"She sure is." Lilly glanced up, gave the horse a weary look as she moved past Shadoe. "Fetch me a rope," she told him, catching the bridle in her hands. "She needs a rest. Not used to the taste of metal in her mouth. She jerked and gnawed on her bit for most of the ride. I'll let her hobble around for a spell before I start back."

Shadoe walked to his own horse which was tied securely to one of the porch posts. He took a lariat from the saddle, then returned, where he slipped it easily over the mare's neck. He began to unsaddle her.

"She needs a rest first, Lilly," he said, giving her the saddle. Shadoe ran his gloved hand down the sweaty spine of the horse. "Let's walk her awhile. Cool her down a bit before she starts eating."

Lilly agreed as she dumped the saddle over on its horn. "Where's Dragon?" she asked, staring around.

"Back at the house with Lewis. Dragon's getting too old to go with me all the time."

She looked at her palms again. "I can't imagine you without him. Without Lewis, either."

He ignored her remarks. "I can't imagine Mister McFall giving you a horse like this," Shadoe commented as they strolled, leading the horse a few yards from the shack. He stopped and grabbed the mare's mouth. "She looks a little too green for you to be pleasure riding. Look at her mouth. She don't like the bit at all."

"I know. She's a real mean one." Lilly laughed. "If I didn't know better, I would suspect that Papa deliberately gave me a bullheaded horse for spite. But I don't think Papa knew that she was so spirited. Luke's mares are usually so gentle."

Shadoe wasn't amused, and he looked at Lilly for the first time, meeting her eyes with a serious stare. Those eyes, he thought, those wonderful gray eyes, clear as sparkling spring water. A man could drown in them.

But he resisted, though the look chilled him for a moment, right down to the bone. "Wonder if she'd throw you?" he suddenly asked.

"She tried."

"Dammit, Lilly! You could have been seriously hurt, or worse, even killed. You should've gone back to the ranch."

"I was determined that she wasn't going to win," Lilly told him. "Look at her. By the time I get her home, she'll know who's master."

Lilly ran her fingers through the mare's long mane of reddish hair. Shadoe's eyes fell on her hands, those soft, nimble fingers, and he could remember them running through his own hair. He was sinking again. *God, stop, you fool!*

He turned away. "Better to let Dan or one of the boys teach her that lesson," he stated coldly.

"I don't want to break her spirit, Shadoe. I want her to like me. We'll be on equal terms."

The horse turned and stared, nostrils flaring. "See, she knows what I'm about."

Shadoe disagreed. "She looks mulish to me, and I have yet to see one like her ever take a master. A regular female, she is. One minute, she's blowing in your ear, all warm and cozy, the next, she's kicking you in the back." His jaw set, he cast Lilly a portentous look. "Can't trust a horse like this one."

Shadoe sighed. *Can't trust a woman like you,* he thought before adding, "You'll do good to get her home and send her back to Luke in the morning. Make him give you a sweeter mare. One that needs little attention."

"I will not! I like her."

"Mulish," he repeated.

Lilly took the lead rope from his hand. "Who are you talking about now?" she asked.

Shadoe didn't answer. He watched as Lilly led the horse back toward the shack. A muscle in his jaw twitched. He had come up to the line shack to think, to get away from everyone, and here she was, smiling, talking, fussing with him. Someone had once told him that the past had a sure way of stepping on the heels of the present. Could it be that his past was not far behind?

He cut the thought and followed her. *Control,* he reminded himself with every step. *Just take control of the situation.*

Chapter 8

The mare hobbled with a soft, braided rope tied loosely around her two front legs.

Lilly sat on the front porch, her legs dangling just above the ground. Shadoe stood, leaning against the open doorway.

Lilly was nervous, but not as much as before, when she'd first seen him on the porch, looking at her with those cold, dispassionate eyes. Blue fire, they were. Hot ice. One look at them and her knees went weak.

Control, she thought. *I just have to take control of the situation. Stay calm. Don't let him know that you're afraid of him.*

A pang of anxiety went through her. She was afraid, scared half to death. It wouldn't take much, and she'd fall at his feet, swearing love and devotion, making an absolute fool of herself. She could almost see herself begging him to stay with her. But she hadn't before. And she wouldn't now.

Years ago when he met her at the line shack and told her about Anne, she'd almost died inside. She had hated him that day, swore that she would hate him for the rest of her life, but then she hadn't. Shadoe, the person, had been ingrained in her for too long. It was the same for the love between them. Silent, deep-rooted and fixed, it had twisted itself through her existence like a tangled vine. To kill it completely, she would have had to lose herself totally and all those years of her life. Years and years with Shadoe.

Lilly looked out at the desertlike land, its fields now full of grasses wavering in the cool breeze. She could see for miles, and for a moment, all her fears faded. She loved this land, loved the boundless spaces, the feeling of endlessness.

"It's beautiful," she whispered, knowingly saying the words aloud.

"In a way," Shadoe replied.

She turned to him. "No, Shadoe, it's really beautiful. Not like the mountains or the seashores. Different."

He looked out over the vastness. "Just an irrigated desert. Without the river and creeks, nothing but sagebrush and scorpions could live here. Soon, the lakes will dry up. It's not pretty to look upon at all. A harsh land."

She shook her head.

"Then how so?"

She turned back to stare at the land, and Shadoe followed her gaze. "It's the waste of it, I think. The great width and emptiness of it that sucks up a person. The feeling of being solitary, the isolation. It makes a person feel as if the soul is like that . . . on and on, forever . . . wide and open and free."

"Dreamy words."

She tensed and turned to him. "You liked them once."

He crossed his arms, and a frown narrowed the corners of his mouth. "I was a man humoring a child. That's all."

"Then humor me now," she teased hopefully.

"You're not a child anymore."

She shifted and glanced at him uneasily, as if aware of his scrutiny. "So humor the woman."

He laughed slightly and sat down beside her. He waved a weary hand. "So you want me to look out at the land and tell you that I love it." He leaned toward her. "Well, I don't, and you know it."

"You did once."

She saw his lips draw back in a grimace. "I never did."

Lilly shook her head. "Why are you lying?"

He jumped up from the edge of the porch. "Let's change the subject. You're trespassing again, young lady."

She studied him for a moment. How handsome he was. And he loved her. Yes, he did. She strongly believed it because he had come back, and because nothing else was acceptable to her mind. He was going to be her husband.

Dreams. Oh, yes, dreams, and I won't let go of them yet.

Lilly suddenly smiled. "So, have me arrested," she said coyly.

"Seems like we have had that conversation before."

"And you know where it leads, don't you?" She didn't wait for him to answer. "Besides, this shack sits right on our borders on open range. I come any time I like. Remember?"

He made a mocking bow. "Yes. I guess I can't stop you. I don't like fences."

"I know."

"But I don't like you coming up here alone either, Lilly."

"I've been doing it for years."

"So I see." He nodded toward the door. "New door, new windows."

"I guess you've been wondering who's been helping me keep the place in shape?"

"Did cross my mind a time or two when I first got here. I know Dan Hadley didn't do this. Not his style."

"Lo Ching."

"That damn Chinaman! I'll have a word with him when I get home."

"Not about this, you won't. It's none of your business," she protested quickly.

"And how do you see that, darlin'?"

The word was a slip, and Lilly could see that he wished that he hadn't said it. She jumped off the edge of the porch. "Let's change the subject."

"I think we're running out of things to talk about."

She looked up. "The weather?"

"A bit cool."

"I like it," she told him. "Like the rain, too. Feels good and clean. Shall we move on to something else?"

"I never was good with idle talk."

"Then don't talk. Let's eat. I'm hungry."

He leaned over and pinched a blade of grass, twisting it between his fingers. Standing back up, he stared at her, amusement on his face. "Did the princess bring a picnic lunch full of those dainty sandwiches and little iced cakes?"

"No. Did you?"

He laughed, chewing on the bit of sweet grass. "I never was one for cucumber sandwiches and tea-cakes. This isn't Montfort, England, you know? A man likes a hearty meal, something . . . satisfying."

She took a step toward him and looked directly into his eyes. He was mocking her, teasing her. "Don't be rude, Shadoe. I'm hungry."

He turned aside, working his hands furiously through his pockets. "Nope. Nothing here. Not even a hard biscuit."

Lilly placed her hands on her slender hips and from under her thick lashes, she gave Shadoe an admonishing look. "Try and be of some help, will you? I left the house with only a bit of bread this morning."

"Oh, yes, and I forgot how much you can eat." He laughed. "Surely Lo Ching stocked this place with something. I thought I saw some cans in there, a sack of flour, some beans."

"I'm not in the mood for cooking."

"Oh, yes, lady of the manor." He met her eyes, winking at her. "The princess. Has a maid do all her cooking. How stupid of me to suggest that we might cook a meal ourselves. What do they teach you young ladies in those fancy schools, anyway?"

"Don't be mean."

His lips twitched with a grin. "Okay. I've got some cheese and bread, some whiskey. Good enough for the princess?"

She smiled at him, a big wide, appreciative smile. She was famished. "Sounds good to me. Let's eat."

In a few minutes, they were sitting on a blanket spread on the ground in front of the shack. Lilly took a helping of food, breaking the bread in her lap. She lifted her glass to Shadoe. "Pour me some of that rye," she demanded.

"Not for you," he muttered, his gaze on her face. Instead, he handed her his canteen. "Have some water."

"I'm old enough for spirits. Why, just last night I had four glasses of wine at dinner."

He eyed her thoughtfully. "I bet you have a head-ache today, too."

It was true, but she wasn't about to admit it. "Shadoe, I said to pour me some of that rye. You can water it down if you prefer. But I mean to have a drink."

He obliged her, filling her glass with rye, then water. Lilly sipped on it, finding that she liked the taste. It was the first whiskey that she had ever drunk.

"Why do I have the feeling there's more water than rye?" she commented after the second sip.

"Because maybe there is," he quipped. "I don't want you drunk, not riding that damn, stubborn mare home!"

She leaned back on her elbows, tossed her long hair, and gave him a rare look. "Maybe you'd like to see me drunk some other time, all silly and easy to handle."

She saw him stiffen, but there it was in his eyes, that starved, needy look. Something deep within her recognized it for what it was—masculine hunger. But it was more than just lust or anticipation. It was a sort of greed that was intensely singular and personal . . . and very physical.

She felt her cheeks color. All of a sudden, just looking at him made her yearn to touch him. But she admonished herself to stay in control, not to ruin the moment. It was too soon.

He sat cross-legged, staring at her, moody, as if waiting for her to do something, to say any-thing to change the way he was obviously feeling. He looked as though he was paralyzed. Lilly sat up, picked up another piece of bread. She grinned around the bite.

"What do you think I should name her?"

"The horse?"

His words spoke of relief, and Lilly smiled. "Yes, the horse."

"Haven't you already?"

"No. I told you that I just got her this morn-ing."

"She reminds me of a witch." He almost grinned, looked at Lilly with a sly expression. "Yes, that would be a good name. Witchy Woman. She's a vixen full of evil tricks if I ever saw one. A saucy, brazen shrew ready to do a person harm. Just look at the way she stands. Gentle and shapely. Danger-ous . . ."

Lilly laughed and reached for her glass. "No, don't like that one," she replied, sipping on her weak whiskey, eyeing Shadoe with care. He was playing with her, that familiar safe play of their youth. Well, she could play along, too.

"Try another," she told him with a smile.

"You try."

She mused. "Chastity."

He almost choked on his whiskey. "Hell! What kind of name is that for a mare like her? Does she look like a modest little lady? Hell no! Not her!

Give her a fitting name, woman! She's a damn scrub, a mean little vixen!"

"And what is fitting?"

"Gypsy," said Shadoe. "The kind that puts a spell on a man. Won't even let him sleep at night. She haunts his dreams until he curses her. He wants her out of his system, but he finds that he can't rid himself of her presence. It's as though she's part of his skin."

"Are we still naming the mare?" she teased.

"Who else?" he mocked, one brow cocked higher than the other.

She watched him pour himself a second, stiff drink, and down it in a couple of long swallows. His eyes were now smoky blue, dulled by the whiskey. She liked the way they looked, sleepy and warm. Shadoe rolled over onto his elbows.

Lilly took an uneasy breath, then wet her lips. Her eyes never left his face. "I was thinking more along the lines of Lady, something genteel."

"Ah, something for the English aristocrat." He let out a long sigh.

"Correct. After all, she's from some of the finest breed mares in this part of the country."

Shadoe looked lazily at the horse and then back at Lilly. "This one may look like a blue blood, a lady, but it's all on the surface. Inside, she's a hellion, full of fire and red-blooded. Hot-tempered."

"Mmm . . ." Lilly took another sip of whiskey, letting her gaze fall over Shadoe's long lean frame. She was attracted to his body, to the way it rested against the earth. She swallowed another sip, and it rolled slowly down her throat. She could remember him, working on the ranch in the summer, his arms and chest bare, the tight muscles, sweaty as a horse. Her eyes drifted downward.

She suddenly imagined his belt buckle dragging across her abdomen, his thighs rubbing into the fabric of her dress.

His watchful gaze followed hers, and Shadoe frowned, a sharp distinct look of pain.

Lilly caught the expression, realized that he could read her thoughts, that he was turning cold on her again. *Not yet*, she told herself. She turned and looked toward the mare.

"So what do you think we should name her?"

"We?" He laughed, and it was a callous laugh. "She's yours. Not mine. Name her whatever you want. I've said enough. Chastity . . . whatever! Call her Miss Prude if you like!"

He moved quickly to his feet, gathering up his things.

Lilly started, watching the way he jerked at the canteen, the bottle of whiskey. He was clearly angry.

"What are you doing?"

"I'm heading home," said Shadoe. "Got too much to do to be lying around with you, making small talk that don't amount to a hill of beans."

"What?"

"You heard me. I said that I've got better things to do than this. And hear me now, Lilly. I don't want you to come here again."

"But—"

"Don't come out here anymore, Lilly! This is my place, and I don't want you hanging around. You might get hurt or something."

Part of her immediately told her to shut up, to oblige him with whatever words would suit him, but she couldn't. She still had her pride.

"I'll come out here any time I want, Mister Sinclair! After all, you're selling the place. Remember? If Tom buys it, he'll let me have this line shack."

Shadoe glared at her, then turned to move back to the shack where he picked up her saddle and returned to the mare. Lilly followed behind him, matching his steps with her own angry ones.

"I don't need your help."

"Don't think I'm being kind, Miss Blue Blood. I'm just trying to get you out of here so I don't have to fool with you anymore. You're starting to get on my nerves."

"You bastard!"

"That's true. My old man never married my mother. I'm a true bastard, legal and all."

Lilly's mouth fell open. "I didn't mean that!"

"I don't give a damn what you meant," he told her, a tight, unpleasant expression on his face. He finished saddling the mare, bridled her, then reached down and easily slipped the rope off the mare's two front legs. Grasping his lariat in his hands, he suddenly grabbed Lilly.

"That hurts," she protested, but he held on to her arm.

"I'll burn it, Lilly. I'll burn the Oasis to the ground. Every last board if I have to. No Woodward will ever have it."

She jerked away. "Don't touch me that way, you—you—" She stopped and glared at him. "You're a bloody coward as Papa says. Just a bloody coward. You can't face your feelings. Go ahead and burn it. I'll raise it up a thousand times if I have to. And what will you do then, Shadoe? Burn it each time I rebuild? You can't stop me from living

just because you have! I'm a hellion . . . a witch . . .
a gypsy . . . red-blooded, remember? And I'm going
to live with or without you. I'm going to lie beneath
the stars right here at this shack and make love to
a man for God and all to see!"

His face drained.

She mounted and took the reins in her hand.
"Why? Why do you do this to us?"

Shadoe looked up at her, ignoring her question. "I just thought of a good name for this
mulish female. Suits her fine and real aristocratic.
P—r—i—n—c—"

Lilly slapped the reins against the roan's neck
and dug the heels of her boots against the mare's
flanks. The rest of Shadoe's words vanished in the
sound of hooves and wind. She rode hard, angry
at him, disappointed with herself.

She shouldn't have let Shadoe get the best of her.
It was all a defense, a game of warring words to
keep from being tender with her. She'd seen that
look in his eyes. She knew how he felt. She had
only to prove it to herself and to him.

When she got back to the barn, she could see the
relief on Dan Hadley's face. She knew her father
was somewhere, worried, too. They were all worried, she imagined. Fools! Shadoe wouldn't touch
her! He'd probably cut her throat first.

"Thought I'd have to come out to number nine
and fetch ya," Dan called when he knew she was
in hearing distance.

"I'm fine," Lilly said, quickly dismounting. "Just
hungry." She handed him the reins. "I gave her a
real hard ride. She's really worked up a lather.
Mind taking care of Princess?"

Dan grinned from ear to ear. "So you named

her." He patted the horse. "That's a good name. She looks like a princess. A real beauty. A fine little lady any man would be proud of. Underneath all that feistiness is a real delicate lady, someone that wants a little love and care, a gentle touch."

"Yes, that's what I thought," Lilly remarked, walking off.

Chapter 9

Jesse spat at the ground, then he cursed. He'd sat in the distance, watching Lilly and Shadoe, unable to hear their words, yet imagining what they might have been saying. He'd heard them talk before, years ago when all of the gang used to ride up to the Oasis. Number nine. Those had been happier times for everyone.

Jesse spat again, then leaned back in his saddle. The leather creaked beneath him as he stretched. He'd spent most of the morning watching them, and Jesse was convinced that he was right. Shadoe Sinclair was back, and he was after Lilly. Not for Weatherly. Not for breeding a bloodline. It was pride and lust.

And it didn't take much thinking. He knew that Shadoe had been bitter about losing Anne, angry over being cast aside by James McFall when Joseph left for England. Shadoe wanted Lilly, wanted her more than he did anything else. Having her would be the ultimate act of revenge on everyone. And he knew that Shadoe could be a man possessed.

He didn't need any more proof other than what he had seen that morning. Shadoe had been so busy trying to seduce Lilly that he hadn't even noticed that the two of them were being watched.

Jesse cursed again, said his sister's name, then rode slowly home.

Stooping, Tom was busy inspecting the wound on one of their horse's legs when Jesse came into the barn. Dressed in blue britches and a faded brown shirt, the older brother seemed small next to the large chestnut gelding.

The brothers looked at each other.

"You and Molly been fightin'?" Tom mocked before turning his attention back to the horse's leg. The gelding was tied where it couldn't move, but at Jesse's approach, the horse nickered, attempting to belly-blow his attendant. Tom was quick, moving, then pushed back at the animal before he added, "That face of yours reminds me of this old toad frog that I used to play with at the pond. Ugly and miserable."

The scent of hay and manure was strong, and Jesse frowned as he took a breath. After a heavy rain, the air in the barn always seemed to choke him. "I just left number nine," he muttered between coughs.

Tom glanced up nervously, then back at the wound. "So?"

Jesse coughed again, then retreated toward the open door. "He was there just like he used to be . . . and Lilly was there, too."

Tom said nothing for a few minutes, and Jesse stood silently, watching his brother dig viciously into the horse's wound with a knife. "Mind your

business," he finally said. "I swear, Jesse. Mind
your own damn business."

The gelding snorted, shifted uneasily, then
dropped its forefoot. Tom pulled the knife back.

Jesse moved inside, closer to his brother. "And
I told ya before, Tom, I ain't scared of him. He's
gotta pay."

Tom released the leg, jerked around, and pointed
the knife at his brother.

"And I told *you*, Jesse, leave it be! And I don't
want to have this conversation again. Ya hear me?
Nothin'. Not a word about Lilly. I'll take care of
her, too."

Jesse frowned. He leaned against a stall door.
His thoughts changed. He rubbed his forehead,
letting his mind wander. There were so many problems. Molly and her mother. Tom's strange behavior. And now his mother was wanting to go into
town.

"Maw wants to take the boy into town," he suddenly announced.

"What the hell for?" Tom asked before turning
his attentions back to the horse. He began apply-
ing the liniment. "I told you as long as Sinclair's in
town, I don't want the boy to leave the house."

"I know what ya said, but Maw has her mind
settled. She wants to go to the cemetery."

A frown knotted between Tom's brows. He
reached over and gathered up the strips of lin-
en, wrapping them slowly around the horse's leg.
"The answer is still no."

Jesse kicked at the sawdust and hay on the floor.
"Then you tell her. I ain't got the strength to look
in that tired face of hers and refuse her anythin'."

Tom stood and cast his brother a stony look.
"Okay. I will."

Chapter 10

It was the following Friday night when Shadoe tied his bay outside the saloon and walked inside, moving through the batwing doors and into the smoky room with deliberate caution. This was his first time in town since he had ridden through that first day on his way to the ranch. Most of the men looked up at his entrance, but when they met Shadoe's rigid gaze, they quickly shifted their curious glances elsewhere.

He took a step, then stopped. One particular rumble of voices caught his attention. Shadoe glanced through the haze of smoke, seeing some familiar faces. Tully and Martin Whitten, David "Dice" Jennings grumbling beneath the sound of rattling poker chips.

Tom's buckaroos. Only Pepper Maddox was missing, and Shadoe wondered if he had been killed by now. Probably. Pepper was a man who lived by the gun. He had been Woodward's gun years ago.

Shadoe cut the thought and realized that Tom was down at the Railway Inn, dancing with Lilly. He remembered her words about living, about loving a man under the stars.

Women, he moaned. *Sharp-tongued and moody. They could wound a man as quick as a bullet.*

He went straight to the bar and ordered a bottle of rye whiskey. He poured a shot into his glass and quickly gulped it, the warm liquid sliding smoothly down his parched throat.

I shouldn't have come back here. I shouldn't have looked at Lilly again, knowing that I want her, just like I wanted her all those years ago.

And she wants me. She still loves me. She even said it.

Another swallow.

Lilly's forgiven me when I haven't even forgiven myself.

And it was true. But he'd hoped that she had forgotten him, moved on with her life, fell in love with another man.

Lies . . . all lies. . . .

Licking his lips, he reached inside his pocket for one of the cigarettes he had rolled earlier that morning. After lighting it, he grabbed the bottle and poured himself another glass just as a young beauty moved up beside him.

"Hello, stranger," she murmured in a low sultry voice as smooth as silk, and Shadoe slanted her a careful look through the curling smoke of his cigarette.

Another woman. More trouble.

Shadoe said nothing at first, just watched the woman's face as he lifted his glass to his lips. She said hello again. She was pretty, a bit too thin, but with nice large eyes and a head of thick dark hair, curly hair that tumbled over her shoulders in a shimmering cascade of blackness.

Shadoe knew what she wanted. Women like her all wanted the same thing, a few drinks, some money, and a paying customer for the night. Inhaling on the cigarette, he blew out a stream of smoke.

"I sure could use a drink," she drawled.

Raising his glass, he stared over the rim at her, still silent, wishing her away. The last thing he needed was more gossip. No matter what, he didn't want anyone running to Lilly and telling her that he'd been in town, fraternizing with one of the saloon girls. But he wasn't the kind of man to be openly and coldly rude.

"Bartender." Shadoe motioned for another glass, and the young woman watched with silent pleasure as he poured a generous amount of whiskey.

Lifting the shot to her red-painted lips, she smiled around the rim of the glass. "You're new in town," she commented.

Shadoe laughed slightly. "Sorta, sweetheart."

"What's that mean?"

"I used to live here. Just got back. But not staying. Only passing through for a few days."

She gave him a thoughtful glance. "Where did ya come from?"

"California." He drew deeply on the cigarette, then exhaled. She looked confused. "You have heard of it, haven't you?"

She lifted her chin, watching as the smoke drifted out of his open mouth, a thin lazy curl of white smoke rising in front of his strongly set features.

"Yeah, I know the place. Ain't stupid." She stared

with a thoughtful gaze. "Gotta a name, honey?" she purred.

He didn't want to tell her anything. "What would you like to call me?"

But she only laughed, apparently amused. "Well, I might could think of a few good names, but a proper name is always the best kind to begin with, honey. So what's it gonna be?"

No more play. He was weary of women and their games, games that could cause trouble, amusements that could break a man's heart.

"Sinclair. Shadoe Sinclair."

Her eyes widened with recognition, meeting his cool, challenging gaze. "You don't look like the devil to me," she said with a surprised sigh, and Shadoe saw her glance quickly roam over his body. "But then again you might be ole Lucifer himself."

He chuckled hoarsely, and downed another shot, then drank straight from the bottle. "The devil? Is that what they're calling me these days? I think my reputation has improved." He rubbed his chin thoughtfully, pushed the bottle toward her.

She laughed, her voice bubbling with pleasure. "Well, Mister Sinclair," she said as she poured herself another drink. "I kinda like my men a little sinful, if ya know what I mean."

There was an invitation in her tone, and Shadoe twisted slightly, easing away from her just as she edged closer to him. Her hand slipped around his waist. He looked down at the gesture.

"Well, I'm sure that you would appreciate a little wickedness now and then," he said, glancing back at her face. He moved her hand away from his body. "And God knows, you probably need a little mischief around this dismal place, but if you're looking for it tonight with me, you're looking in the wrong place. What did you say your name was?"

"I didn't, but it's Naomi," she snapped. "And you're just as ill-tempered as they said. Mean as a snake. I thought you knew how to treat a woman, Sinclair. Heard that you were a real ladies' man."

"Like I said, I'm just in town for a few days, passing through. And you shouldn't believe everything you hear."

He dropped his cigarette, crushing it on the floor with the toe of his boot. "Good-bye, Naomi." He flipped out a silver dollar and casually slipped it in the silk of her scarlet bodice and then smiled. "Better luck, next time."

"Why you sonuvabitch—"

Shadoe laughed. "Don't take it so badly. It's nothing personal. I've just got too much on my mind."

"Then let me take you upstairs, Sinclair. A woman like me knows how to make a man forget his problems."

She leaned over and lightly rubbed her body against his chest. Shadoe could feel her taut nipples beneath the silk of her dress.

For a moment, he felt like succumbing to her charms, but he shoved her away. A woman like Naomi could make a man forget many things, but a quick drop in the hay with a saloon girl would never make him forget one moment that he had shared with Lilly.

"Forget it," he told her.

He paid for the bottle of rye and moved across the room. Naomi quickly followed, the bottle of whiskey in her hand.

"You're a man in trouble, Sinclair. You need a friend. Let me earn the money."

Shadoe shook his head and walked on.

Chapter 11

The double doors of the saloon swung open, and Jesse strolled in, moving quickly toward the bar. He needed a stiff drink if he could talk the barkeeper out of one.

Everything had been going wrong lately, everything meaning Tom and the ranch, and, of course, Molly Andrews.

Jesse couldn't exactly figure out what was wrong with Tom and the ranch, but he knew precisely what it was with Molly. She was teasing him without mercy, and tonight despite his objections, she'd danced with Luke, that damn womanizing Luke Miller who only had to look at a female and they'd start giggling with delight.

Lilly had danced with Luke, too, and that thought caused Jesse to think about the really important problem—Tom. He worried Jesse in the worse way. For weeks, Jesse had been full of suspicion where his brother was concerned. Tom was doing something, planning something, and somehow, it all had to do with Lilly McFall.

He'd seen how Tom looked at Lilly tonight, how she had become the most important person in his life, as if Lilly represented Tom's whole future.

She was the belle of the ball, Jesse thought as he swept off his hat and ran his nervous hands through his shaggy head of hair, the belle of the grand and English Weatherly, too.

God, everything seemed such an awful mess. He put the black hat back onto the crown of his head, and darted between the tables.

That damn dance at the Railway Inn. He'd left it himself because he was having such a bad time, watching helplessly when Molly felt like dancing with some of the other young men. Why were young women so fickle? Even engaged ones? They still liked to banter with all the young men, even the old ones!

And Lilly, too, thought Jesse. She was as fickle as any of them. And she was pushing Tom to the breaking point with her whimsical ways.

Jesse was really scared. He knew that Tom didn't like to see Lilly with other men, smiling at them with her bright clear eyes, holding their hands, making polite conversation. Tom didn't get mad in the same way that he did. Damn! Why couldn't Tom just let off steam the way most men did by getting drunk or getting in a fight?

No, Tom would let his anger smolder awhile. And it would go deep, the fires of discontent, for Jesse knew that the sight of Lilly in another man's arms only reaffirmed Tom's suspicions that she didn't really love him, that she would never marry him.

Jesse swallowed hard.

But she'll marry Shadoe Sinclair . . . that dog . . . that no good riffraff that ruined my sister's life, he fumed silently.

"Damn all women," Jesse grunted as he moved faster toward the bar, his anger mounting until he glanced up and saw Shadoe Sinclair. Astounded, he muttered, "What the hell?"

He paused to draw in a steadying breath. Before him stood the man who had destroyed his sister and who was standing between Tom and Lilly. His guts twisted with weeks of anxiety, and a rush of recklessness swept over his trembling frame. But his mother was dying, and there was Anne's child to think about.

Jesse shot Shadoe a vehement look. The man had to be stopped before everything was soured. Before Maw . . . before Tom . . . before Lilly . . . before. . . .

Jesse moved quickly.

Shadoe jerked in surprise when the young man ran into him. The bottle in Naomi's hand fell to the floor with a loud, splattering crash. Naomi immediately screamed, and when Shadoe whirled around, he was staring straight into Jesse Woodward's tormented face.

Suddenly everyone in the room was listening, attracted by the fall of the glass, by the sudden stillness that had filled the crowded saloon, by the growing tension building between the two men.

"Well, if it isn't the squanderin' cur come home at last," Jesse hissed.

Shadoe tensed and pushed Naomi aside. "Hello, kid," he said, his voice restrained.

"Kid?" Jesse made a mocking laugh. "Who ya callin' kid?" Jesse stared around. "I don't see a kid here anywhere. My name is Mister Woodward to *you* trash."

A muscle in Shadoe's jaw twitched, and his lips thinned in anger. He didn't intend on killing a boy, but he didn't plan on taking any more verbal abuse either.

"You seem a little nervous, *Mister* Woodward. Maybe I should buy you a drink."

"Buy me a drink?" Jesse snorted, and his thin face flushed with revulsion. "I wouldn't drink with a Sinclair."

"Whiskey is whiskey. Tastes the same no matter who does the buying, and you certainly do look like you could use a drink."

"It'd sour in my stomach comin' from the likes of you, Sinclair."

A slight grin twisted at Shadoe's lips. "Go home to your mama, boy."

Jesse wasn't wearing a gun, but his hand dropped to his side instinctively, and Shadoe's eyes followed the move with interest. He knew that look. The boy would kill him if he had the chance.

"You don't have a gun, Woodward, but even if you did, it'd be stupid to go for it. I'd kill you in a second, before you even had a chance to get your gun clear of the holster. Why don't you go on over to the bar and have a drink, and I'll forget that this ever happened."

"Forget it!"

Shadoe grimaced, and he nodded toward the back corner of the saloon. "Tom's pack of wolves are playing cards. Why don't you go over with them?" He took a few steps. "Just leave me be, boy. I don't want to hurt you for nothing."

"You're a bastard, Sinclair. And ya talk big with a gun on ya."

Shadoe stopped. "Listen, kid. I don't aim to kill you, but if you don't go on about your own business, I might be forced to beat some sense into you. My words plain enough?" He leveled a stern gaze at the younger man. "I'm tired, boy, and I'm going home."

"Your whore has bad taste in customers, Sinclair."

"Okay, Woodward," he growled. "I know you're mad, but I don't need trouble. Not with you. Not now. But I don't like your talk either." Shadoe pointed to Naomi. "She's not with me, you got that. But I don't call any woman a whore. You apologize, or I'm going to give you a good beating right into the ground with the other dirt."

"I'd sooner die than apologize to that whore!"

Naomi's face turned red. She sank back against the stair railing with a look of defeat lined across her frowning face. She gave her companion a pleading look. "It's all right, Sinclair. His words don't bother me none."

"Well, they bother me," was the gruff comment, and Shadoe stared at Jesse. "Are you going to apologize to Naomi, Woodward, or am I going to have to beat the damn words out of you?"

"I know you're a fightin' man, Sinclair, but I ain't afraid of ya." Jesse scowled. "I'm callin' ya out now. Just take off that gun, and we'll fight man to man."

"Man to man?"

Jesse bristled. "You got a problem with that?"

"No. I was just wondering about how much of

a man you are, *Jesse*. Five years might have put some experience on you, but you still look like a kid to me."

"Just take that gun off," Jesse repeated, shifting on his feet, his fists knotted into tight balls of anger.

A slow smile crept across Shadoe's mouth as he reached down and began to unbuckle the leg strap to his holster.

Jesse's gaze followed. He danced closer, tense and waiting.

Before the leather strap was out of place, Shadoe moved, whipping up a quick, short punch to slug Jesse dead straight in his chin, knocking the young man back against a table that crashed to the floor under his weight.

The card players had already pushed back their chairs, familiar with such a scene. None of them seemed interested enough to protest.

"Don't get up," Shadoe warned, but Jesse wouldn't listen. Though dazed, he jumped to his feet and ran at Shadoe, smashing away at the older man with both fists.

"I'll kill ya, bastard," he panted, and Shadoe pushed at him as they both tumbled to the floor.

They rolled on the dirty floor, hats falling, exchanging blows. The crowd was on its feet, most of them now yelling for one or the other. Jesse clawed at Shadoe's face, and when a trickle of blood oozed from a cut over Shadoe's heavy brow, the older man knew that he had had enough. With one quick kick, he knocked Jesse back, just far enough to deliver an underhand right to the younger man's exposed belly.

Jesse reeled with the blow, clutching at his stomach, the pain blasting him. He curled up into an anguished knot and moaned. The fight was over.

After finding his hat, Shadoe dragged his shirt sleeve across his brow, wiping at the blood, then he brushed away the dirt on his clothes. He turned his gaze slightly and with a dispassionate eye glanced at the boy.

Jesse made a move as if to rise.

"You'd be a fool to get up now, kid," Shadoe warned.

"He won't," a crusty voice interrupted, and Shadoe looked up at the man walking across the room. "What's goin' on here?"

It was Jackson Williams, one of Shadoe's old drinking friends. A silver star was pinned to Jackson's vest.

"Hello, Jack," Sinclair said without emotion.

The deputy sheriff's quick glance immediately appraised the situation. He frowned. "I knew there'd be trouble, but I was hopin' not so soon." He stared down at the floor, shaking his head at Jesse. "Boy, you ain't been nothin' but trouble for the last few months. I hate doin' this to your ma, but I'm gonna have to lock you up for the night. Let you see what trouble can bring ya if you ain't cautious."

"Why don't you just take him home?"

Jack looked at Shadoe firmly. "This ain't about you, Sinclair. I've been foolin' with this kid for weeks now, warnin' him about comin' in here. It's not the first time."

Jack motioned to his deputy. "Take the kid over to the jail and lock him up. Have Doc Brewster come over and give him a look just to make sure that Sinclair didn't burst his gut or somethin', then go on down to the Railway Inn and let Tom know that his brother's goin' to spend the night in town. I don't want Sarah Woodward troubled by this. Poor woman can't take much more without it putting her in a grave."

A flicker of disquiet darkened Shadoe's gaze as he stared at Jack, suddenly thinking about Sarah Woodward and all the letters she'd written him over the last year. She was ill, maybe even dying, and Shadoe was worried. He'd been in town for over a week, and he'd heard nothing from her, though they had planned to meet. "Sarah Woodward okay? I mean, she's still up and about?"

Squirming on the floor, Jesse overheard Shadoe's question. "Don't you even say my maw's name," he moaned as the deputy leaned down, pulling the young man to his feet.

Jesse staggered for a moment, then shot Shadoe a vehement look. "You'll pay for this. You'll pay for everythin'."

Jackson exhaled heavily and jerked his thumb toward the door. "Get him out of here. Now!"

"The kid sure has changed. Reminds me of Tom," Shadoe said as he watched the young man disappear through the batwing doors of the saloon. "I never thought to see it. He was a good kid."

"Been lots of changes around here the last five years, Sinclair."

"So I see." His full gaze settled on the bright shiny badge pinned on Williams's striped vest. "Looks like you finally made something of yourself, Jack."

A hint of a smile tugged at the corners of Jackson's mouth. "I like this side of the star, Sinclair, though I ain't sure that bein' on this side makes life a helluva lot easier."

Shadoe's thoughts returned to Jesse. "What's going to happen to him?"

"He'll spend the night in jail to cool off, and I'll give him a few wise words in the mornin', but I suspect they ain't goin' to do him much good."

Coming up behind him, Naomi slid her arm around Shadoe. "Let's go on upstairs, honey," she commented with a strange look in her eyes.

Shadoe ignored her. "Never thought Jesse would remind me so much of Tom," he told Jackson.

Williams laughed bitterly. "He's worse, 'cause he ain't as smart as his brother. You better be careful, Sinclair. That one is crazy. If you're plannin' on doin' what I think you are, you might end up with a bullet in your back."

Shadoe's smile was cynical as he saw the wary look in Williams's gaze. "I've got eyes in the back of my head, remember?"

"Yeah, I remember, but what I think you're plannin' is gonna cause a helluva ruckus around here, especially if you're plannin' on stayin' in Oregon."

"Just what do you think I'm planning, Jack?"

"Well, there's Miss Lilly McFall for one thing." Williams smiled, but Shadoe quickly frowned so the lawman asked the question that he had been wanting to ask for days. "The boy?"

"I do have my rights, don't I, Jack?"

"What are you two talking about, honey?" Naomi asked.

"You didn't answer my question, Jack. Do I have rights?"

"You got rights, but them Woodward boys ain't goin' to like it one bit."

"Then maybe I ought to get your help," Shadoe said.

Williams shook his head and ran one hand across his unshaven face. "This land was made for the strong," he told Shadoe, "made for the ruthless, and you're capable of being both, but you might look at the boy in another way. You might consider a trade, Sinclair."

"Trade?" Shadoe shoved one hand in his pocket and reached for a rolled cigarette. He struck a match, then lit his cigarette. Blowing out the flame, he held it, the smell of sulfur sharp and acrid as he drew in deeply.

He gave his old friend a strange look. "Why should I trade for the boy? Seems a peculiar thing even to consider in this situation."

"I've been hearin' talk . . . about the ranch. Heard you're plannin' to sell it. Heard that Tom Woodward wants to buy it. Maybe you could throw in a little barterin' along the way? The boy and a fair price for the ranch?" There was a twinkle in Jack's eyes, a blue gleam of awareness as he squinted through the smoke of Shadoe's cigarette. "The ranch goes cheaper if you get your *goods*. Know what I mean? And you'd be happy, the Woodwards would be eased, and I'd avoid a whole passel of trouble. Woodward might not grieve so over the child if he gets what he really wants . . . your ranch."

"No."

Jackson Williams shook his head. "What are you goin' to do? Kill those two boys if you have to? I can't let you do that, Sinclair."

"Just like you said, the law is on my side, Jack.

Woodward knows why I'm in town. He knows I plan to sell the ranch."

"And the boy? What about that? Does Tom know?"

Naomi's gaze narrowed as she watched Shadoe shrug away the question. When he spoke, his voice was soft and deliberate. "I'm not sure what anybody knows about the boy, and frankly I don't give a damn, Jack. I'm here. And the boy is here. And Sarah Woodward is seriously ill . . . dying. It only makes sense that I get my son from her before she's gone."

Chapter 12

Just one look, Shadoe told himself. A single look and then he'd turn to leave, go back to the saloon, buy another bottle, and drink it on the way home. Get drunk, fall into bed beside his dog, and dream . . . always dream.

But he had to have a look at Lilly, just one simple look. It was safe, he judged. No touching, no eye contact, no words—tender or not—just watching her dance from a safe distance. He had that much control. At least he hoped he did. The devil take him if he made a mess of things now, especially after all these years of denial, of trying to get past what he'd given up for others. Oh, Lord, would he ever get past what he'd given up?

The room at the Railway Inn was full of people, and as impossible as it may have seemed, when Shadoe walked through the doorway, the first person he saw was Miss Lilly McFall.

He stopped, shivering in a sudden chill. The

sweat on his body cooled beneath his clothes. His face strained. He clamped one hand inside the other against the urge to reach out to her.

Run! Run, you stupid fool! Get the hell out of here! Move! Do it now! an inner voice cried. But Shadoe was mesmerized, struck almost dumb by the sight of her. She was more than he'd anticipated, and a thousand repressed feelings flooded his veins, pumped through his heart, fed his lungs and brain.

Again that damned voice. *Get the hell out of here or else. . . .*

He took a step, tried to turn, but his emotional and physical needs far outweighed any amount of sensibility. She was there, and he wanted to look at her.

The sight of her—so pretty in her blue silk dress, its small, tight waist, the icy-blue folds of soft fabric swaying with every turn as she swirled around the room—made Shadoe yearn for her in a way that was hard to ignore.

I should leave, he thought, but knew that he would not. Could not. His common sense was leaving him. His body was taking control, and Shadoe held his breath as he watched Lilly dancing in the arms of a young man.

At least it wasn't Tom, Shadoe thought. But it wasn't himself either. It was Luke Miller, a comely looking fellow who had always been popular with the girls. Miller was tall, had dark hair and very fine black eyes with a moon-eyed expression that made some women catch their breath.

Of course, what impressed Shadoe was Luke's strength. Despite his brother's untimely death and a great deal of other obstacles, Luke had turned his

ranch into one of the finest in Harney County, even
in the state of Oregon. While in California, Shadoe
had heard about Luke's fine breed of horses.

He quickly recalled the young and mulish mare
and then the morning he had spent with Lilly at the
Oasis. He'd never forgotten the way she had looked
at him, her eyes roaming over his body, and now,
he couldn't help wondering if she'd ever looked at
another man that way.

Maybe Luke? Sooner or later it would be someone. Lilly would look at someone. . . .

His mind reeled as he moved toward the wall,
lounging against it. His lips pinched as he stared
at Luke holding Lilly in his arms. Luke was only a
few years younger than him and had never taken a
wife. Shadoe knew that the younger man would be
a sensitive husband for Lilly, a good man to take
over Weatherly, to run the whole Blitzen Valley.

But there were still secrets and Luke shared
them.

Shadoe dropped the thought and stared. Luke
and Lilly—they were smiling at one another, laughing, talking, dancing. They were touching!

Mercy, they are touching! He grimaced, shifted a
little against the wall. Why couldn't he be happy
about it? And why in hell had he left Naomi at the
saloon without so much as a promise to return? He
needed a woman in the worst way. He was almost
shaking, and the blood roared in his ears.

But he knew the reason, and nothing else mattered. Not Weatherly, not the Double *S*, not Tom,
James, or even Luke. Nothing but the feel of Lilly
in his arms—just once. *Just once*, he told himself.

Fool! the other voice cried.

* * *

"May I?"

Lilly jerked at the sound of Shadoe's unexpected voice.

"Howdy, Shadoe." Luke grinned, pulling both Lilly and himself to a slow halt in the middle of the dance floor. "Heard you were back." He paused awkwardly for a moment, then suddenly said, "Sorry about your father."

"Thanks," said Shadoe, but he wasn't looking at Luke; instead, Shadoe's gaze fixed on Lilly's face.

Luke glanced at Lilly who was looking intently at Shadoe. He smiled again, looking back at Shadoe. "Want to dance with Miss Lilly?"

"You mind, Miller?"

The younger man laughed and shook his head. "That'd be kinda dangerous, wouldn't it?" There was something strange in the tone of the comment, but it went ignored as he quickly offered Lilly's hand to Shadoe. "No, you take her. I'm ready for a cool drink. This dancing's hard on a man. Besides, I'm going to have to call it an early night. Leaving at first light for the ranch."

Lilly started to protest, but one look at Shadoe and she changed her mind. He had that greedy look on his face again, and his eyes were smoky. Her stomach tied in knots. Tonight might be her chance, her only chance to persuade him to stay in Oregon. She lifted one hand to his shoulder in consent.

"You were right," Shadoe said, pulling her into his arms.

"Right about what?" she asked faintly, her voice almost gone. She was looking up into his eyes, her gaze dark and narrowed. Part of her wanted to tremble, but she didn't dare let her body betray the shock and excitement that she was feeling.

He pulled her closer, and their glances held and burned.

"Right about your dress. It's very nice, Princess," he murmured close to her ear. "Remember? You were telling me about it just the other day."

His clear gaze dropped to her low bodice, slanting appreciatively across the soft swell of breasts. He smiled instinctively. "It would have been a shame if anything had spoiled your pretty . . . face . . . for tonight. You are by far the loveliest little lady on the dance floor."

"Thank you," she said softly, knowing that it was not her face of which he was speaking.

"You're really all grown up, darlin'," he commented in a playful tone.

"Girls usually do," she told him, regaining her composure. Her nerves steadied. "I hope you like what you see."

"A beautiful woman?"

"A woman, yes," she reiterated.

The grin on Shadoe's face widened. "I sometimes forget that five years has passed between us. And, yes, I like what I see very much," he said. "You're one of the few things in this town that has improved with age."

Lilly heard herself laugh despite the tension. "Glad that you found favor with something." She grew bolder in her determined confidence, in knowing that he lusted after her the same way that most of the young men in town did. "But why do your compliments always have a ring of concupiscence to them?" she asked in a tease.

He was clearly surprised at her playfulness.

"Concupiscence? Is that one of those big English words?" He grew thoughtful. "Ah, you mean, pure lust . . ." He leaned almost against her. "Maybe because they do, darlin.' "

"And that is supposed to be comforting to me?" She pulled back slightly, putting some distance between them, and then her gaze was somber. "It's hard for a lady to accept flattery from a man who is looking at her bodice as though it was the first course of a seven-course dinner. Could you not be a bit more subtle?"

Shadoe chuckled, whirled her in a circle around the dance floor. "I'm not the delicate type. Remember?"

"Yes."

"And do you remember how we liked to dance together in the barn, just you and me?"

The smile on her face vanished. How could he be so cruel to think that she could ever forget? She looked away from him for a moment, thinking how quickly he could become vicious when he wanted to. He'd always been that way, as cruel as he could be kind, moody and distant, and yet at the same time, very passionate. What Shadoe felt, he felt to the core of his being.

But he had left her. He could leave her again, and that was reality.

Shadoe is a dangerous man, she warned herself. *He doesn't always play by the rules.*

Her intense gaze met his again. She'd try a more direct approach rather than just sense-less bantering. "What are you doing here?" she asked. She eyed his clothes. He wasn't dressed for a dance.

Shadoe evaded the question. "I'm just here," he

told her, adding with a wink, "pretty little ladies like you shouldn't know too much. Ruins a man's advantage."

The music died, and Shadoe slowed to a stop, but he did not let go of Lilly's gloved hand as they stood waiting for the next song. The touch of his hand felt warm to her, too warm. She looked into his eyes. Catching a glimmer of the ambivalence that was so often there, the same indecision that she knew he had felt on first seeing her again, she felt certain that he was hiding something. But what? Would she ever know? She'd play the game and hope. Keep on hoping. . . .

"It's the woman who needs the advantage, especially where you're concerned, Mister Sinclair," she said. "Always silent and full of secrets. You must have had a good reason for coming to the dance tonight."

"Maybe I had a few reasons."

Lilly didn't doubt him. She turned away, her eyes wandering around the room. Everyone was looking at her, whispering. And Lilly knew what they were saying. Shadoe Sinclair was one step above being an outlaw.

Then Lilly looked at Luke. He was watching them, smiling, sort of happy, and she suddenly wondered why Luke had never hated Shadoe for killing his brother, or why he'd never really courted her, asked her to marry him as so many of the young men had.

Something is not right here and Luke knows what it is.

Lilly tensed, cut away from Luke's appreciative gaze. Instinctively, she pulled her hand away from Shadoe's, and began clapping with the other guests.

"Scared of what they're thinking?" he asked her.
"No."

Shadoe's face tightened. "I think you're lying to me. You always cared too much for others' opinions."

"I did not!"

He grabbed both her hands tightly, but his voice was soft as his face moved very close to hers. "Then dance with me again, Princess. I don't give a damn what any one of them thinks."

Lilly snatched her hands away. "I don't think this kind of social is your idea of a good time, Shadoe. So tell me the truth. Why did you come here? It certainly wasn't to dance in a room full of people!"

"I wanted to see you," he suddenly announced.

"Me?" she questioned, startled at his reply. "You wanted to see me? What about the other day?" Her voice turned sarcastic. "If I remember correctly, you were very definite about not seeing me again."

"I never said those words. Besides, that was another day. This is now. Dance with me," he replied sardonically.

"No," she told him firmly, adding, "we didn't exactly leave each other on the best of terms."

His mouth loosened into a gentle smile. "I thought we left each other on the very best of terms," he teased. "It's good to know where one stands. Dishonesty has a way of choking the very breath out of us. And then, darlin', there's no strength to say anything. True words, even sharp ones, are better than a bunch of soft pretentious lies."

"That's a strange thing to say, especially coming

from you. But then you can speak from experience, can't you? When I think about the times you lied, especially to me."

"I've never been dishonest with you."

This time Lilly gave an unexpected chuckle. "You're probably right." Glancing at him from under her eyelashes, she gave him a questioning stare. "You may not lie to me, but you certainly have a way of avoiding the truth when it suits you. There's more to what you don't say than to what you do say. Men like you always have a way of twisting words to suit their fancy. You sweet talk your way into a woman's heart, then you break it."

Shadoe's eyes narrowed as he studied her. "You are a shrewd one, Lilly. And here I thought you were a sweet little *innocent*, knowing nothing about men."

"I know a lot about men," she informed him, her cheeks hot. He was staring at her with such a direct gaze.

"Do you?" he teased again. "From the look on your face, Lilly, I think you're about as innocent as any virgin could be. Tom may have already claimed you as his intended bride, but I'm certain that he hasn't claimed your heart or anything else for that matter."

The music began again, and though everyone fell into the rhythm of the melody, Lilly protested heatedly when Shadoe pulled her into his arms. "I think I need to go home," she said, pushing away from him.

"Did I say something wrong?" he asked. "Or do you just want to go home?"

"Both," she said, moving to walk across the room.

He followed her into the lobby of the hotel.

"Who's going to take you home? I don't see your father or Tom Woodward. Someone's got to escort you home to the castle. Maybe Luke's next in line for the position."

She stopped abruptly at the door and turned to face him. There was a strange look of appreciation in his eyes, and she knew that he was taunting her. But she could play that game, too. "Don't you think that I can get myself home if I wanted to?"

"Certainly you could. But there are all kinds of bad things out there in the dark, Princess, and I don't aim to let you go wandering at this hour of the night."

She tensed slightly at his suggestive remark. There was a passionate look in his eyes, and Lilly was both excited and anxious at the way he was staring at her.

"You don't have much to say about it, Shadoe. I've been doing just fine without your help these last few years, and I don't think I need it now. Besides, you're probably the most dangerous thing prowling around in the dark. Wolves, both you and Dragon."

Touché, he said with a chuckle, adding, "but I aim to take you home tonight, Princess."

"Dan Hadley is taking me home, thank you." Lilly added quickly, "And I wish that you would quit calling me Princess."

Shadoe glanced over his shoulder into the next room, a nasty grin on his face. "That's a cruel demand," he told her, finishing in a drawl, "asking poor Dan to take you home when he's dancing his heart out with Widow Daniels. Seems that Hadley is still trying to marry that woman. You wouldn't want to spoil his chances, would you? Where would Dan find another woman with four sons, a spot of land, and some cows?" Shadoe turned to lean in close to Lilly. "And I've always called you Princess."

A frown knitted Lilly's brows as their eyes locked for a moment, then she quickly looked away, staring with uncertainty into the room where Weatherly's foreman was with Polly Daniels. Dan had been courting the widow for the last six years, hoping for marriage. Only lately had Polly given him any real hope.

Lilly turned to give Shadoe a nervous stare. He was collecting his hat and holster. He intended to take her home, but she was in no mood for playing the game any further. If her father knew that Shadoe had escorted her home, Dan would suffer the older man's foul temper.

"If I walk out of here with you, the whole town will be talking, and what will Papa say?" she protested weakly when he returned and reached for her arm.

"So I'll get Dan's permission if that will make you feel better. We'll make it legal and proper so to speak."

"What good will that do?"

"Listen, Lilly. You've already shared a dance with me. The gossip's already flying." Shadoe motioned with his hat. "Look at them. They're already wondering what's going on. So what difference does it make if I take you home, or if Dan does? I don't understand what all the fuss is about. Besides, I want to speak to your father."

"You want to speak to Papa?" she asked, surprised. The two hadn't said a word to each other since the day Shadoe had told the sheriff that he had killed Sam Miller.

"Yeah."

She was stunned by the remark, dazed and happy, but she could barely accept the thought. Shadoe was going to speak to her father. It was more than she had dared to hope. A miracle! A tiny little miracle that moved her closer to her dreams.

"All right. But you better tell Dan that we're leaving. This is probably going to start a whole lot of trouble, and I don't want to involve Dan in anything that would cause a conflict between him and Papa."

Shadoe narrowed his eyes at Lilly's apparent hesitation. "If you want me to, Lilly, I'll just walk out that door and forget that I was ever here. Do you want me to do that?" he asked, his tone clearly filled with irritation.

She didn't, and she wasn't about to pretend. "No."

"Good. I'll just be a minute."

Lilly watched as Shadoe moved into the crowded room. She looked on nervously as he told the older man of their plans. Suddenly all her resolve failed, and she shook at the thought of being alone with him for the two miles to Weatherly.

They were both silent the first mile, sitting in Dan Hadley's buggy. Shadoe's bay was tied to the back, following.

Fool! Fool! Fool! Here he was in the buggy with her, when he should have been on the road home, taking care of his business, or better yet, getting drunk and forgetting.

But, no, he was here. And it was crazy. This was

the craziest thing that he'd ever done. But there was no lying to himself at this point. He was here because he wanted to be.

And why? The answer was easy enough. He needed her, and he couldn't stand the thought of another man needing her the way he did.

Love? God, yes, he loved her, but tonight it was different. This was more than just the years of emotional love that tied them together. Tonight, his body wanted to be close to hers. Heat. He could feel her heat. And he burned miserably in his own. Tonight, they were not Shadoe and Lilly, but a man wanting a woman.

The way she looked, smiled, talked. Her smell. He could smell crushed lavender on her skin. How could she get lavender to smell so sweet? It never seemed that honeyed before. He even wondered what she would taste like. He'd never kissed her, and he needed to kiss her, but at the same time, he hated himself for feeling so weak.

Oh, jump out and ride home before you ruin it all. But Shadoe didn't. Instead, he listened to questions buzzing in his head, the questions with no answers. What would happen if he touched her? What about his plans? What about the lies he had been living with?

He stiffened. She could never know the truth. He loved her too much. If he touched her, there would be no stopping the landslide of emotions, no stopping the consequences, no stopping. . . .

Mercy! His whole body tied in knots at the thought of it. He glanced at her, watched in thick silence the soft profile of her face. She was so sweet, so really innocent.

Dammit! I can't let myself do this. I can't let myself

make another mistake . . . take another risk.

His life had been full of mistakes. No more!
Shadoe gritted his teeth. Somehow, he would find
a way to get her home without incident.

They rode, listening to the sounds of the night,
but the second mile stretched longer and longer,
and soon the silence was deafening. It rang in their
ears, all the words that were left silent and needed
to be said.

And finally it was time. . . .

Chapter 13

"Are you still mad at me for what I said to you the other day? You know, those things I said about you coming out to the Oasis?" Shadoe asked, trying to break the strain between them. He was watching the road in front of him, and every few seconds he would lightly shake the reins as though playing with them.

"No . . . not really. It's hard for me to stay mad at you about anything. Remember? I guess I'm a greedy person in need of punishment. I just can't let the past go."

He nodded, a half-smile on his lips.

Lilly continued, "I was thinking earlier that you had a right to be angry with me. I sometimes say too much. You know how I get when I'm mad. And I've been known to be too pushy. But I'm sorry that I said those things, especially about Anne that first day on the road. It was unfair of me. I should have apologized at the Oasis, but I just didn't get to it.

I never seem to get to what's important—"

"No," Shadoe interrupted. "No apology from you. Not ever. You weren't unfair. I shouldn't have been so rough with you. And at the shack, I shouldn't have said those things. I mean about burning it down. I would never do it." His voice turned thick. "I was trying to be indifferent, hoping that somehow I could keep my past at arm's length while I was back in town."

There was a pause. Lilly tilted her head back and looked up at the sky. "Dear God! How did you ever think you could do that?"

He grinned. "Just stick to business, I told myself."

"And?"

"Have I stuck to business?" he asked, peering at her in the darkness. He pushed his hat back on his head, then shifted on the seat. There was something about Lilly that struck him with an impulsive hunger even when he was determined to stay cold. And just talking to her had warmed him again.

"Have you?"

He could see that she was waiting for his answer, the clear look of anticipation in her eyes. But all he could see was that young, sweet girl whom he had known and loved so many years ago. No, that was not true. All Shadoe could see was a woman, a very beautiful woman whom he loved now. God, she was so pretty, ivory-skinned, her body made for a man's hands.

His yearning for her surfaced again, and he shifted uneasily on the seat. The whole scene had the feeling of a schoolboy about to face the teacher on examination day.

"Yes and no," he answered finally. "It seems that my business in Montfort is changing, getting more complicated by the minute. But I know that it's better if I keep things simple. And if that means being rotten a time or two, then I am. I can't let things get in the way of what I really need to do here."

"I understand." She half smiled at him, then turned to gaze down the road. She folded her hands stiffly on her lap. "You've always been mean, Shadoe. I didn't expect you to change," she told him stiffly. "But I did expect some courtesy from you. After all, we were friends, more than friends actually, so close, and now I feel, even sitting here in this buggy, I feel that we are so far away from each other . . . as if you are determined to put a hundred years between us. We used to laugh together, trust one another. Now all I see is you tearing us apart for no reason at all. I told you that I was sorry about Anne. Sorry about everything. I'd forgiven you long ago. I never stopped caring."

Shadoe said nothing. And the moment passed where he could have told her how wrong she was, about how much he cared, too. Instead, he was silent, watching her as she sat stiff and hushed. He knew the hurt in her heart. He saw the restless look on her face, even a touch of fear. And he turned away. This was not what he wanted, not what he had intended.

After several minutes, he crooked his head slightly, looking back at her, suddenly feeling agitated as he watched her. She was staring straight ahead, and he could tell that she was growing more and more overwrought, and he knew it was his fault.

Tonight, he had wanted her to feel at ease with him. After all, this was probably the only time they would have together. It was a stolen moment, and he knew it. He'd stolen it for himself, and now he realized that he had stolen it for her, too. They had to make some kind of peace.

Shadoe said, "I wish you would say something, anything. I'd rather have you mad at me than—"

"Than what?" she broke in, her voice strained.

"You act as though you're *afraid* of me." His words were blunt, and they had the effect that Shadoe had hoped for.

"Afraid? Me? Of you?" The words rattled from her lips with defiance. "I've never been afraid of anyone. You know that, Shadoe."

"Then why so quiet?"

"I was thinking," she told him.

"Do I have to give you a whole nickel for those thoughts?" he asked, laughing.

"I never was cheap," she remarked with resolution. "Remember when I was younger, you always had to give me five pennies when we went into town."

"I spent more money on you than any other female in those days, that's for sure."

"I was worth it," she told him, a soft smile on her face.

He sensed that she was beginning to relax with the conversation.

"Yeah, you were . . . still are." He reached into his pocket and pulled out a silver dollar, handing it to her. "This will buy you a whole sackful of candy and then some, Lilly."

She took the coin, rolled it over in the palm of her gloved hand. "You'll have to do better than this, Shadoe Sinclair! I'm all grown up, remember? My tastes are more expensive."

"So you want frills and things, now. Maybe a pretty new bonnet, a new dress? Or a kiss?"

He'd said it, though for the last mile, Shadoe had repeatedly promised himself that even if he thought about kissing her, he would never say the word.

Lilly flushed, pink spreading over her warm cheeks. "I suppose you think I would enjoy kissing a man like you!" she exclaimed with a defensive laugh.

Shadoe lifted a brow at her unexpected words. "You might," he returned cautiously.

"You're wrong," she retorted. "I wouldn't."

A faint smile, almost like a sneer, curled at his lips. She was playing games with him again. His first instinct was to kiss her, prove to Lilly that she would enjoy kissing him, but he held back. He couldn't touch her. He had already touched her too much. But God, how he wanted her.

"No. I don't suppose a young woman like you would enjoy a kiss from a man *like me*," he finally said in a flat tone, hoping that his statement would end the dangerous discussion. "A woman like you wants a more refined man. A man who would come courting you, wooing you with pretty words and gifts. Women like you like to think about love, being in love, but when it comes to the real thing . . . Well, women like you live in dreams."

Her brows drew together. "Lives in dreams? Just what are you talking about?"

He didn't want to explain.

The carriage rolled noisily. The chains on the harness clanked, and Shadoe looked down the road, wondering why he'd ever started the conversation.

Lilly began again. "Either you want to kiss me, or you don't! Either you think I'm a woman, or you don't!

"Are you through?" he inquired when she paused for a deep breath. "Because if you are, I'd like to change the topic of conversation."

"Didn't we do that the other day? Shall I say stupid things about the weather?" She made a mocking gesture. "Stars out tonight. Looks like we'll have a clear week ahead." She stopped, smirking at him. "Shall we name another horse?"

"Maybe. Those are things you know about. Easy things. The other?" He shook his head.

"You are ill-bred," Lilly accused him. "Just what kind of *woman* enjoys a kiss from a man like you, Shadoe? And what kind of woman do you think I am? Stupid? Silly? Ignorant of the ways of love?"

Shadoe frowned. "I don't think we need to talk about such things, Lilly. You don't know anything about what goes on between a man and a woman. And I don't think I'm the one to tell you." He drew in a quick breath, suddenly feeling pinched for air. "Besides, things like that are not easy to tell . . . a person . . . Well, you just come by them naturally."

Her stare was perplexed. "*Now* what are we talking about? I thought we were discussing a simple kiss?"

Shadoe was silent. She couldn't understand. If he ever kissed her, there'd be more. He cursed himself. Why was Lilly so different from other women? If she had been anyone else, he would have pulled her into his arms and kissed her so ruthlessly she would have surrendered all, and he wanted to desperately. He looked closely at her.

"You're a beautiful woman, Lilly. That's why I find it difficult to talk about such things . . . intimate things. Talking about kissing with you is not so simple to do."

"Kissing ought to be simple enough."

"No kiss is simple, not for me."

It was a warning, but Shadoe knew that Lilly didn't understand.

"I suppose you know a great deal about women, don't you?" she asked, leaning closer to him. Not waiting for his answer, she added, "Especially the kind of women who live above the saloon in town."

Shadoe stiffened. "How so?"

"Well, I'm not stupid, Shadoe. I've heard some of the men talking when they didn't know I was listening. There are two kinds of women, two kinds of kissing."

"What?"

"You know what I'm talking about. Men act one way with a certain kind of woman, say with one of the saloon girls, and with a woman, well, like Polly Daniels, men act another way—"

"That's stupid," Shadoe cut in.

She frowned, and Shadoe pulled back on the reins, bringing the buggy to a halt, staring at her.

By God, she was beautiful, he thought, beautiful and innocent. His gut tightened with the next thought, and then suddenly Shadoe knew. Lust. Desire. It was there, raising its command in more ways than he'd wished to acknowledge. But it was there. He had tried to deny it, fought it, and now it had bested him, swamped his well thought-out plans with feelings that he could no longer ignore.

Mercy, you can't leave her like this, not thinking the way she does.

He sighed. Could she be so silly as to believe what she said? Two kinds of love? Two kinds of women? He looked at her, wondered for a moment if she was still playing games with him. He would never know.

I am going to kiss you, he told himself.

Chapter 14

"What are we stopping for?" Lilly asked when the buggy suddenly halted.

"Cause I want to take a good look at the mess of trouble I'm getting myself into, that's why." His voice was lazy and seductive and Lilly suddenly went cold.

"What trouble?"

"You, Princess. I have a feeling that you're nothing but trouble, and as hard as I've tried, I can't seem to avoid it. I'll just have to pay my dues later and hope that the devil is kind."

Shadoe caught her in his arms, his hard body pressed tightly against hers, his blue gaze sweeping over her face with more than just simple admiration. "You know how bad I want you, Lilly?"

"No," she whispered, her voice splintered with fear. Surprised at his sudden and unexpected confession, all she could do was tremble under his powerful stare.

Shadoe's strong hands plundered her hair as his eyes wandered heavily over her face again. Lilly's heart pounded in her chest.

"Shadoe . . ."

He stilled her moving lips with his fingers.

"That day on the road when you asked if I remembered you . . . Well, the answer was yes and no. I knew a girl, but I could hardly have imagined the woman that she would become." Shadoe lifted a thick strand of her hair and pressed it between his fingers. "You know the first thing I thought about when I saw you. I thought—no hope is a better word for it. I hoped that you still felt the same way about me as you did all those years ago."

Lilly could hardly breathe.

"Do you?" Shadoe murmured.

She couldn't answer.

"Aren't you going to talk to me, Princess?"

"I can't," she said, her voice caught in her throat.

He leaned over and pressed his face into her hair, smelling the sweet scent. "I knew you were at that dance, and I wanted to see you there, dressed like an angel, smiling, being the darlin' of the party. I've gotta be crazy."

Lilly felt her throat tighten.

"You're afraid of me, Lilly. I know that, just like I'm afraid of you."

"I'm not afraid of you," she lied.

"Liar."

"I am not."

He pulled her tighter to him, his lips brushing her cheeks, his warm breath fanning her skin with desire. "Not so, honey. We're both afraid of each other, and we have a right to be. You and I are a dangerous combination."

She felt the breath catch at the back of her throat, and a strange mixture of terror and delight began to run through her body. "Dangerous?" she queried in a broken voice.

"One kiss, Lilly. One kiss is a dangerous thing between a man like me and a woman like you," he murmured into her hair. "You see, Princess, there aren't two kinds of kissing for the likes of us. There's only one kind of passion that we can share."

She began to tremble in his arms, truly apprehensive. It was the first time that a man had ever held her so, the first time that she had ever felt such fire. But she needed him, wanted him with every fiber of her existence.

"I'm . . . frightened." It was a hesitant admission.

He looked at her again. "I know."

"I've never been kissed," she whispered.

"I know. God, how I know," Shadoe murmured as he began brushing her hair with his fingers. His thumbs pressed softly against her temples, then his fingers slid down around her ears, his palms over her cheeks as he held her face to his own. "Lilly," he said as his lips parted to claim hers.

His mouth covered hers, plundering gently, savoring the honeyed sweetness of her lips. His tongue slipped easily between her teeth, and Lilly melted against him, her body yearning to touch his. Shadoe quickly dragged his mouth across her cheek, murmuring in a harsh breath. "This is madness, you know. You smell so good. I can't keep my hands off you."

Lilly clung to him, desperate in her new feelings, seduced by the touch of his hands on her body. "I'm dreaming," she told him.

"No dreams, Lilly, darlin', it's real enough. Maybe too real."

"Kiss me again, Shadoe."

He obliged her easily, smothering her mouth with a fervent kiss that demanded more than Lilly knew she had to give. She pulled away slightly, baffled by this new direction, but he held her on course, coaxing her as he lifted her into his lap, leaning them both slowly against the back of the seat.

"I need you," he whispered in a hungry growl when their mouths parted, sending a wash of shivers up and down Lilly's spine.

She held to him like a withering vine, her body weak, her resolve completely vanquished. She was entirely mastered by his touch, the feel of his hands as they roamed up and down the curves of her body. He was kissing her again, but not her mouth, just tiny little kisses, like droplets of fire, falling down the curve of her neck, across the soft swell of her breasts that peeked modestly over the bodice of her gown.

Lilly moaned with delight, and Shadoe reached up a hand, gently persuading another invitation as he touched her. "Mercy me, you have the softest skin. You are so beautiful." His hand ran under her bodice. "You like?"

"Mmm," was all she replied. She was in a mindless wonder, not knowing how her gown had fallen from her shoulders, only knowing the feel of Shadoe's mouth on her breasts, realizing that his hands were more urgent than ever as they ran up and down the silky folds of her skirt.

She moaned with pleasure. "I love you," she told

him in a husky voice. "I've always loved you, needed you like this." She reached, grabbed a handful of his hair, brought his face close to hers. She kissed him.

He tore his mouth away. "For God's sake, you make a madman out of me, woman. I need more . . ." His hands plundered viciously at her skirts.

"Then teach me," she told him in a low voice that wavered with anticipation.

For a moment, his hands were crazy on her body, and then Shadoe looked up into her face.

A pause. A ragged breath. He paled, and Lilly saw the strain, the look of self-condemnation. He was pulling away, scared of what he had started, afraid to finish.

"No . . . no." He shook his head and muttered a string of curses.

"What's wrong?" she gasped with a pleading look.

"We can't do this. I can't be with you. Not now. Not ever. Not for any reason." He pushed her slightly away.

Lilly reached out for him, but he grabbed her fingers, crushing them. "No."

A warm blush quickly spread over her face and she looked away. "I—I don't . . . understand. I thought . . . I don't know—"

"What's going on?" he snapped. "Look at me, Lilly," he demanded, and she forced herself to meet his gaze.

"You and I don't belong together, not like this. It was crazy. It just got away from us, that's all. But nothing happened."

"But—"

"But nothing happened. We didn't go too far." He grunted slightly, then cursed again. "It was nothing! You hear me?"

"Is making love nothing?" she asked.

"You and I shouldn't be making love," he said, his voice growing cold.

"We shouldn't?" she questioned, her eyes wide with the anger that she was starting to feel.

"You understand that I just have needs and a man like me finds it hard to resist a sweet little thing like you. But that's all. I'm hungry for a woman—"

Her mouth fell open.

"Any woman," Shadoe continued. "It's no more than that. Making love and being in love are two different things. You understand?"

She flushed again. Yes, she knew. Sex. Physical pleasure. Desire. But she had not thought. It all seemed so different, and Shadoe had called her so many sweet names.

"Yes. I understand completely. You're trying to tell me that you don't care about me, that you just wanted to satisfy your physical needs. Like the men who go to the saloon. Is that right?"

She didn't wait for him to answer. Lifting her gown back over her shoulders, Lilly added in an acid tone, "Well, it seems a complete contradiction of what you said earlier. You told me, if I recall correctly, that I was stupid to think that there were two kinds of women, that there was only one kind of kissing for the likes of you and me, and now you're trying to tell me that you kissed me just because you couldn't control yourself. Damn you, Shadoe! Now you're telling me that you only wanted me in the same way that a man wants a whore!"

"I didn't say that!"

"You did, too!" She pointed an accusing finger at him. "You come to the dance, run my partner off, then insist on taking me home. On the way, you try to seduce me, saying those sweet words, and then all of a sudden you stop, telling me that what's happening between us is *nothing!* You're just like Tom said. A man who knows how to break a woman's heart!"

His face went blank, and he reached for the reins. "I need to be getting you home. I've already got a great deal of explaining to do as far as your father's concerned."

"And no explanation for me?"

"We've already said enough, Lilly."

"Papa would kill you if he knew what you really did to me tonight." She wasn't teasing.

"Then maybe you ought to tell your father and let him put me out of my misery."

She shook her head. "Tell him? No. I wouldn't dare let him know that I was such a fool." Her anger subsided and she drew a tired breath. How could she love this man? Was there no way to reach him?

Frowning, Shadoe looked at her. "I have plans, Lilly. You know why I'm back. I want to sell the ranch and get the hell out of Montfort!"

"Just you and Joey and good ole Lewis?"

He stiffened. "Yes."

Lilly straightened her dress across her shoulders, and Shadoe dropped the reins and instinctively reached over to help her loop the buttons at the back of her neck.

She let him, knowing that she was too angry and nervous to perform the task properly. She didn't want anyone at Weatherly suspecting what had passed between her and Shadoe.

"You don't want to stay here?" she asked him while his skillful fingers did their work. There was a quiver in her tone, one that revealed how breathless she still felt by his touch.

"No. I've never liked ramshackle towns on the edge of nowhere." His voice was cold again, and Lilly looked up at his face to see the anger glistening in his eyes.

Her remark about Tom had caused the appropriate damage, and she was glad. Let him think about her and Tom. It would punish him the way he was punishing her.

"Well, I never want to leave," she told him, feeling a bit stronger. "This is my home. It's where I belong, and you belong here, too."

"I hate this place." He finished the buttons, pushed back away from her, sitting up straight on his side of the buggy.

"You hated what happened, but not this place, never this land."

"Let it be. The past is dead, Lilly, and I want to keep it there. You can't understand how it was for me . . . why I left."

"I understand. It's the same reason you can treat me so warm then so cold the next minute. I might be young and foolish in your arms, but I know you, Shadoe Sinclair."

Lilly gave a chilling laugh. "I'll survive tonight," she defended, adding in a mocking tone, "but I'm not so sure that you will. You love me, Shadoe, and I know it." She smiled. "Burying the past will mean burying me. And you don't have enough guts to do that, to see me giving up on life just because you have."

Shadoe was silent, but he slapped hard at the reins, and the buggy lurched forward in the dark.

Chapter 15

When James McFall saw Shadoe Sinclair stroll into his library with Lilly at his side, the old man almost choked on his brandy.

One look at his daughter and James suspected the worst. They were still in love. The two of them were together as they had been all those years ago, inseparable, attached.

He stiffened at the thought and at all the memories that it suddenly brought back to him. In the old days, James had hoped that when Lilly had matured into a young woman, she and Shadoe would have married. Naturally, his son, Joseph, was to have married Anne Woodward. It was all a very tidy plan. The three largest ranches in southeastern Oregon tied together through marriage, and McFall's dreams of a dynasty in America finally fulfilled.

But it never happened. Without warning or

explanation, James had seen Shadoe grow into an uncommunicative and difficult young man. He had killed a man for no reason, and then he had seduced Anne Woodward, gotten her with child, and married her.

But most of all, Shadoe had betrayed Joseph. James had always felt that if Shadoe had not deceived his son, Joseph would have forgotten about the offer from England and stayed in America. The thought of Shadoe in his house sickened him.

"What the hell?" he questioned, rising from his leathered chair. "What are you doing in my house, Shadoe?"

Lilly started to protest. "He brought me—"

"Go to your room, Lilly!" her father interrupted. "Now!"

She jerked at his brutality, but Shadoe only grinned, casually taking off his hat. "You haven't changed much, Mister McFall. Still giving orders to everyone in that same aristocratic tone. Well, remember what I told you before. This *ain't* England, and I'm not some weak-minded and scared servant ready to jump at your every command."

"How dare you!" James clenched a fist. "Get out of my house!"

Lilly's face paled, and she glanced up at Shadoe.

"You can have me thrown out, if you have a liking to, but I'm not leaving. I came for a reason and I aim to stay. I need to talk to you," Shadoe bluntly told him. "Now."

"We have nothing to say to each other, young man."

Shadoe shook his head. "We have a great deal to talk about."

"I can't imagine that we have anything to talk about, Shadoe. You said it all years ago when you put a bullet in Sam Miller's head." James drew an uneasy breath and he shot Shadoe a disgusted look. "I heard you were here. Knew that you would bring trouble. Just like before."

He glanced from Shadoe to Lilly, then back to Shadoe. "You shouldn't have come back to Montfort."

Shadoe moved further into the room. "I couldn't agree with you more, but I assure you that I don't want any trouble. I just need to talk to you about the Double S. The rustling."

James gave the young man a blank stare. "How does that concern me?"

"I aim to sell the ranch, but not before talking with you about it, Mister McFall. There's words that need to be said."

James grew tense as he looked at Lilly. She was staring up at Shadoe with a peculiar glint in her eyes.

"Where's Tom?" he asked her. "I thought he was bringing you home."

"He received an urgent message and had to leave," Lilly answered.

Shadoe scowled, moving toward the older man. "Tom had to go to the jail. Jesse was fighting in the saloon. Tried to kill a man. Stupid kid."

"I don't believe it!" Lilly responded in surprise, and her father shook his head in dismay.

"Well, it's true. The man he tried to kill was *me*," Shadoe explained.

Lilly's mouth fell wide. "You were at the saloon?"

"Yeah, I was."

"Why would Jesse want to kill you?" James interjected.

"Kid acted kinda crazy. Got that funny look in his eye. I tried to reason with him, but he just wouldn't let it go. He was mad as hell about something. Just itching to tangle with me. I think he knows that I'm here to get Joey." Shadoe raised his arm, making a friendly gesture. "That's one of the things I wanted to talk to you about."

"You're going to get your son after all this time? I don't understand," James said, truly baffled. He had understood that Shadoe had completely abandoned the child after Anne's death.

"Like I said, there are words that need to be said." Shadoe glanced back at Lilly. "Mind leaving us alone?"

A wounded look clouded her eyes. "If that's what you want?"

"Yeah, I do."

She looked hurt, and her voice faltered. "Then I'll say good night."

"Good night."

She looked at her father nervously, almost afraid to meet his gaze. "Good night, Papa."

"I'll talk to you in the morning." It was a warning, and Lilly turned immediately.

Saying nothing, Lilly walked from the room, and Shadoe watched her go. When the door shut, he turned to stare at her father. "She's quite a lady, the princess all grown up. Just as spunky as ever."

"Yes, but I don't want to discuss my daughter with you."

Shadoe stood steady, holding his hat, the crown in the palm of his hand. He brushed his other hand through his hair, looking at the older man with an expression that told of his weariness. "You've never forgiven me?"

"Why should I?"

"I don't know. I was just thinking out loud, I guess," the younger man grumbled as he moved across the room.

"Are you going to sell the Double S to Tom Woodward?" James asked, shifting to pour himself another brandy.

"I don't know. I was wondering if you wanted to buy it, instead." Shadoe swung around and gave James a firm stare.

"Tom has made it clear that he would like to buy the place," James said, sipping on the brandy. He didn't offer Shadoe one.

"I know that, sir. But I don't want to sell it to him. I would rather sell it to you."

James grimaced. "It seems that you are determined to sell it to someone. Why? Why would you want to give up the Double S? I don't understand."

"I want out. I'm taking the boy and going back to San Francisco. I have a business there. A home for the boy. I even found my mother." He grinned a little. "Got a ten-year-old sister in a convent. The boy will have a good life."

"Your mother is . . ."

"A soiled dove?" Shadoe finished with a strained look.

"I wouldn't have said that," James blurted.

"Why not? It's what she is, always was, and will always be. She's a soiled dove. Works on the Barbary Coast. Owns her own place." Shadoe paused, then looked at the older man. "She explained my father to me. How he could never forget that she was a whore. That he could never love me because of it. That's why he was so indifferent to me all those years. That's why he drank and gambled. So I felt that I was never good enough for him."

"And Lilly?" James eyed Shadoe carefully. "Are you good enough for her?"

A dark expression flew across Shadoe's face. "Lilly has nothing to do with any of this, you know that."

James shook his head. "I don't think that's true. Somehow, I think she has everything to do with this."

Shadoe said nothing.

Noting the younger man's reluctance to answer, James persisted, telling Shadoe, "You know how she feels about you."

"Yes."

"And you don't have any plans for her?" There was a trace of disbelief in James's voice, one that demanded an explanation, but Shadoe didn't give him one.

"None intended," he said lowly.

"What's that mean? Yes or no?"

"It's hard to answer that."

James stared back. "Well, you're going to have to answer. Lilly means everything to me. Everything. I don't intend to see her hurt again, Shadoe. I couldn't face that pain. She means everything . . . everything to me."

"She's always meant a lot to me, too," Shadoe said. "Very special. I want the best for her. I have never wanted her to be anything but happy. I'd never hurt her again."

James grimaced. "Then try to keep those feelings in mind, Shadoe. I know how the girl feels about you. She worships you just like she did her older brother. And look at how Joseph hurt her. You can't know the pain his leaving caused her. You can't know the pain your leaving caused her—"

"I know—"

"Then you must realize that she is very vulnerable now that you're back in town?"

"I do." Shadoe moved closer to James and looked straight into the older man's face. The younger man cleared his throat as he lifted his hand and pointed at James. "But I also know that I don't want her to marry Tom Woodward!"

James grew angry. "You have no right to any objections!" he roared at Shadoe. "None! Do I have to remind you that I wanted Lilly for you? Wanted you as her husband one day, but, no, you wanted to prove something. I don't know what. I'll never understand it . . . all that running around with Lewis and the others, Luke and Sam Miller, Jackson Williams, pranking like young bucks until you killed Sam and caused all that misery."

Shadoe stiffened, remained silent.

"Shadoe, were you so uncertain of yourself that you had to prove your strength in the most miserable of ways?"

"I'm not going to apologize for being a man or for making mistakes. And Sam Miller's death was an accident. I told you before that there's things you can't understand."

"What's to understand? You shot him through the head."

"He had a knife. It was an accident."

"Accident? I imagine that Anne Woodward's death was an accident, also?"

Shadoe's jaw set. "I don't want to talk about any of that."

"I don't imagine you do," James retorted in a sarcastic tone. "So here we are back to the start of our conversation. Back to your offer of selling the Double S to me. Is that it, Shadoe, just so that a Woodward won't have it? Well, I won't get involved. I don't need the land."

"Maybe, but then again, sir, there's more to think of than the land."

James narrowed his gaze. "What are you talking about?"

"Control of the Blitzen Valley."

James McFall gave Shadoe an inquiring stare. In the middle of the Blitzen Valley was the water, and the Sinclairs had always been free with it. A nervous feeling flooded through the older man as he watched the strange look in Shadoe's eyes.

"Whoever owns the Double S would control the rights to the water," the younger man voiced.

"So?"

"Are you so sure that Tom and Jesse Woodward are the best choices as controllers of the Blitzen Valley?"

"Tom will marry Lilly. She'll have part ownership."

"Can you be certain? Things happen. People die."

James's brows lifted at the last remark. "Whatever are you talking about?"

"Just talk, Mister McFall. But let me remind you that you had plans before, and look what happened. Life has a way of taking its own course sometimes. We plan and then one day we wake up and everything's changed. I know that firsthand.

You know that firsthand. If I was you, I'd make sure that those water rights are secure instead of depending on Lilly's ownership through some foolish marriage that will never happen. There are things going on around here. Bad things."

James grew gruff. "I don't think I like what you are implying!"

"You don't have to like it." Shadoe paused, and took a deep breath. "In truth, I don't give a damn what happens to this valley. It could burn to the socket! But Lilly does. And I care about her. I wouldn't be here, wasting my time if I didn't think that Tom Woodward was rotten and you know *that* if you don't know another damn thing about me." Shadoe hastily placed his hat back on his head, then headed for the door.

James watched him walk away and hurriedly followed. "Come back."

Shadoe stopped, halting near the door.

James almost smiled. A small part of him was glad to see that Shadoe had not changed much. "You were always hotheaded, impulsive. Doing without thinking. Never letting others know what you knew. Full of secrets."

"I'm thinking. If anything, I'm thinking too damn much!" Shadoe blurted. "I can't quit thinking. I want to leave this valley as much as you want me to leave this valley." He shook his head. "But I won't leave until I am sure that things are settled, that the valley is secure, that Lilly is safe and happy."

James was still silent.

"You want the truth. That's the truth. Can't you believe me?" Shadoe asked. "After all these years, can't you look at me and know that I wouldn't have come back here unless I had good reason?" Shadoe paused, frowned deeply. "I could have sent for the boy, or better yet, Lewis could have fetched him for me. I didn't need to come back just for that. But the ranch is different. A lot of people depend on the water rights being fair. Can't you believe me for once?"

"I believe you. And I believe that I need another drink." James poured the liquid and then raised his hand toward Shadoe. "Care for a brandy?"

Chapter 16

Weatherly Castle. The stone structure rested on the largest ranch in the state of Oregon, its fearful gray-and-red brick towering over the flatlands like a sacred icon.

James Farley McFall owned over a hundred thousand acres of mostly irrigated meadows, but the summer grazing lands he used in the Catlow Valley and on the highlands of the Steens Mountains totaled to perhaps another million. He was by far the richest man in Oregon.

The second son of an English earl, James had always been a soldier of fortune, a man who reached out for new dreams instead of relying on his family's connections. Nevertheless, he was nobility, a man who knew what blood flowed through his veins. When he'd first arrived in Oregon, he had built his wife the elaborate castle, a smaller version of one that she'd admired during their honeymoon while traveling on the

Danube River. It was a pretentious, gaudy house, a reminder that he was still lord of the manor, even in the wilderness of southeastern Oregon.

Every year, on the second Saturday of May, McFall held a barbecue, invited every man, woman, and child in Harney County. Next to his Christmas parties, it was the biggest event of the year, even taking precedence over the Fourth of July celebration. This year, Lilly thought, was the biggest celebration ever.

She had snaked her way through the wedged vehicles parked in the open field between the house and the round barn. Dust motes constantly filled the air as did the sound of guitars and fiddles. Excitement and socializing everywhere.

A large, wooden platform had been built especially for the dancers. On a lawn nearby, a few of the townfolk pattered, playing croquet, sipping on cooled lemonade, reveling in the English dignity that Weatherly represented.

Lilly had danced several times, four dances with Luke Miller alone, and Tom Woodward was jealous, seething when she refused him the waltz for the sake of sharing it with the handsome horse breeder.

She had felt guilty and yet, she'd been relieved when Tom finally complied with her wishes and left the dance area to talk with some of the men. It was during the waltz that she'd taken the first step in her new scheme to get Shadoe to stay in Oregon; she persuaded Luke Miller to meet her at the tables next to Weatherly's pseudo-English garden. Everything was going smoothly, everything but Jesse.

Jesse Woodward had been another matter. Lilly had watched the way he had looked at her and

Luke, saw that he disapproved of her behavior. She knew in her heart that Jesse had been sincerely hurt by it all, and a little ashamed, Lilly had totally avoided him, only offering a lame smile when she met Jesse and Molly on the dance floor.

But even dealing with Tom and Jesse wasn't her biggest complaint of the day. Nothing vexed Lilly more than being ignored, especially by the men, particularly when they were discussing the future of the ranch. From the moment that Weatherly's annual barbecue had begun, most of the big ranchers had been huddled under a large shade tree, away from the music and dancing, to discuss the latest news on the area's plague of rustling and murder. Two nights before, one of the local homesteaders had been killed, shot in the back. He had been putting up fence. It was a senseless, cold-blooded murder.

Lilly had passed by the men several times, eavesdropping, hoping to hear what her father was saying, but the excursions had been in vain.

"What do you think they're planning?" she asked her aunt as she paced nervously.

Martha was sitting, eating her lunch at one of the many tables placed on Weatherly's wide lawn. Lilly had purposely chosen one close to the formal garden which provided some shade and a good view of her father and the others.

"I don't know," Martha replied, watching her niece.

Her answer only flustered Lilly, and she continued to pace. "Damn! I can't make a thing out of what they're saying, but it must be something important. Just look at the way they're chomping on their cigars."

"Good Lord! Sit down, child, you're making me jittery with all that pacing." Martha gestured with her hand. "Back and forth and, for heaven's sake, please watch your language!" She grimaced, took a sip of her water. "What if someone had heard you?"

Lilly drew a long sigh and obliged her aunt. Sitting down in her chair, she stared at her father for a moment before commenting, "It's the stealing. Papa can't believe that anyone would have the grit to steal Weatherly cattle. The thieves must be dangerous men." She leaned against her chair, resting her back, and proceeded to peel off her gloves. It was hot, and her hands were sweating. "What do you think they're going to do?"

"They're going to do exactly what your father said last week," Martha replied between bites. "They're going to catch the rustlers and hang them."

"Without an official trial, you think?" Lilly questioned before reaching to take a sip of her lemonade. In all her years, she'd never heard of a lynching on Weatherly land.

Her aunt nodded silently.

It wasn't a civilized notion, and the thought of a murdering mob revolted her.

She opened her mouth to protest, but before she could utter a word, another voice concluded, "If they capture them red-handed, the rustlers will be strung up on the spot, as they say."

She twisted to see Luke Miller. He was staring pointedly at her. "No trial, Miss Lilly, not even a word of explanation. I've seen it happen before when some men stole a horse," he told her in a quiet, but firm voice. "If a man steals, he pays with his life. It's the law of the land. They don't even give rustlers a decent burial."

"So I've heard." Lilly frowned, thinking of the stories she'd heard of lynchings and burnings. "Seems so violent an act in this civilized world. Barbaric."

"And not a pleasant thought," Martha remarked.

Luke agreed. "But both you ladies need not concern yourself with it. It's a man's duty, his worry." A little smile, mocking or teasing Lilly, yet gentle, came into his eyes for a moment. "Better for you ladies to think about that charity social coming up in a few weeks."

Without asking, Luke pulled out a chair, turned it around, and straddled it. "Every young lady in the county is talking about it."

Martha smiled at him. "And every young lady in the county admires you, Mister Miller. So are you going?"

"I don't rightly know, ma'am." His brow furrowed. "With all this trouble, I got plenty of work to keep me up north. Hate to leave my horses for too long. Already spent enough time in Montfort socializing and such." A reluctant look crossed his face as he glanced at Lilly. "But I have to admit, I sure will miss dancing the waltz and looking at all the little ladies holding their lunch baskets."

"I'm not going either," Lilly admitted for the first time. Three days had passed and not a word from Shadoe. She was miserable. Had not the barbecue been on Weatherly soil, had she not wanted to see Luke, she would have happily spent the day in her room, reading and brooding, and of course, plotting. It seemed that where Shadoe was concerned, she was always plotting.

"Not going?" Luke questioned.

"Not going?" Martha echoed.

Lilly stared at her aunt, then at Luke. "No." The next words just fell from her mouth uncontrollably. "They're planning to auction off those box lunches, and if I take one, I'll end up spending the whole afternoon with Tom Woodward and right now, I just couldn't bear it. Not a minute of Tom's talk."

Her blunt words caught Martha off guard, and the older woman balked at the comment before falling into a cough. Martha had been suffering from a cold.

"You are most certainly going, young lady! We've been planning it for months. Those proceeds from the lunch-box sales go to my favorite charity." She paused to cough, then looked at her niece with a chastising expression. "Why, Lilly McFall, you know that your box will bring the most money of all."

"I know. I know." Lilly admonished herself miserably. "That was mean of me." She glanced at Luke, then set her glass of lemonade on the table. He had that knowing look on his face, not a smile, not displeasure, but a straightforward look.

"And I know what you're thinking, Luke Miller. You're thinking that I'm a horrible spoiled child. Papa's precious and pampered English lady."

"Not so, Miss Lilly."

"I think Mister Miller is being kind." Martha snorted. "You are horrible to speak of Tom in that way, especially in the company of others."

"Not so." Luke grinned at Lilly. "Begging your pardon, Miss McFall, but I don't think Miss Lilly is horrible at all."

"How could you not?" Lilly asked him sincerely. "It was an unbecoming comment on my part. After all, Tom is my friend."

"Because your words were the truth. And the truth is better than a bunch of double-dealing." His tone implied more, and Lilly met his gaze boldly. She'd never imagined him to be so blunt with words, to say exactly what he was thinking. After all, for years he'd said little if anything. Martha gave him an uneasy smile, but Lilly was clearly appreciative. Luke apparently knew a great deal more about what went on in the Blitzen Valley than anyone imagined.

More than I ever realized before, Lilly thought as she leaned over and softly touched his arm. *Luke, you know something and I need to find it out.*

She smiled at him. "Luke. I just thought of a way to solve the problem." She tapped her finger on his shirt sleeve.

"What problem?" he questioned.

"Tom."

"And is that why you wanted to talk to me in the first place?"

"No."

He smiled shyly. "I didn't think so. I was hoping that it'd be something simple, that you'd be wanting to teach me that game you're so popular at." Luke pointed toward the croquet players, and Lilly laughed.

"Do you really want to learn? I would think that knocking little balls around on the grass would be silly, maybe too nonsensical for a rugged cowboy like you?" She arched an eyebrow. "You never showed the least interest in it before."

"Well, that's true, but the little ladies seem to like it." There was a playful look in his eyes as he grinned devilishly at Lilly. "I was thinking today that it might be a good form of . . . Well, how do you put it?" He stroked his chin thoughtfully. "A good form of contact."

"Why, Luke, you are a shrewd man!"

Martha laughed. "Now I see how you managed that ranch all these years. Diplomacy and guile!"

"Caution," Luke teased. "Just caution, Miss McFall. And a game like croquet is cautious, slow and easy. It lets a man be careful in his thinking, in his speaking. A good game to play with a woman."

"Well, I'll teach you today," Lilly told him quickly between laughs.

Martha smiled. "You'll probably be sorry, Mister Miller. Come next year, half the women in the county will have you cornered on the croquet field."

"Exactly my thoughts, ma'am." He looked at the field, watched as one very pretty female tapped a wooden ball through a metal wicket. After a moment of thought, he returned his attentions to Lilly. "So, what will you want in return, Miss Lilly?"

She didn't waste any time asking. "I was hoping that you'd ride over to Weatherly a day early so you could escort me to the charity picnic."

"What about Tom?"

Lilly glared at him. "Yes, our little problem—"

"*Our* problem? I ain't got a problem, do I?" he suddenly asked.

"Tom is the problem, Luke," she answered. "Yours, mine, and Aunt Martha's." Lilly could only smile at the sudden confusion on her companions' faces. "Let me explain. I want to go to the social with you," she told Luke. "Tom wants me to go with him. So that makes him your problem. If I have to go with him, I won't go at all. And that would make Tom Aunt Martha's problem because she'll have to do without the funds from my lunch box. Now do you understand?"

Martha shook her head. "I don't understand at all."

"Neither do I," Luke said. "But I can see that logic has nothing to do with this. It's plain that all this is leading to something else besides just an escort. What is it you're thinking, Miss Lilly?"

"Come that Sunday social, Luke, you are going to bid on my lunch box."

"What?" Martha interjected.

"And, Luke, I mean to have you buy it." Lilly squeezed his arm reassuringly. "No matter what. Do you understand? I don't care if it cost a hundred dollars!"

"A hundred dollars?" Luke's mouth fell open. "But what for?"

"Don't you think my lunch would be worth a hundred dollars?" she teased him.

Martha was struck silent by the bold remark.

He faltered on a few breaths, started to say something, then stopped himself.

Luke was clearly amazed at her suggestion, caught in her web like a wounded insect, and Lilly knew it. All he could do was just stare at her, amusement on his face.

"Well?" Lilly asked.

He stood abruptly, shoving the chair out from under him. "Pardon me for my boldness, but I have to say that women are the most curious creatures. A man can trust his dog, his horse, but a woman? I feel like I've been snarled in a roll of barbwire, and I don't even know how I got here." He knitted his brows in a perplexed stare. "Miss Lilly, a hundred dollars is a mighty expensive price to pay for cold chicken and a game of croquet."

"I promise that you'll have a good time," Lilly tempted.

"You better promise to give me that game of croquet before it gets too late in the afternoon," he warned.

"I'll see you in an hour at the field."

"Good." Luke scowled and gestured toward her with a pointing finger. "But let me warn you, I'll not spend one dime over a hundred. Promise or not, there's a place where a man has to call halt to his own foolishness!"

"What was that all about?" Martha asked heatedly when Luke was far enough away not to hear her.

"Exactly what it sounded like. I've got Luke to bid for my box."

Martha grimaced. "You're not fooling me for a minute, child! There's more to this than you're telling." She glanced at the men who were disbanding. Tom was walking straight toward Luke.

"You're going to get that young man in trouble," Martha scolded her. "Tom isn't going to like it for one minute. You're playing a mighty dangerous game with this performance."

Lilly only smiled. It wasn't Tom whom she considered. It was Shadoe Sinclair. And she had just set the scene. Now, she had to make sure the players were all arranged.

Chapter 17

When Shadoe dismounted, he was unaware that Lilly was playing croquet with Luke Miller. Walking through the crowds, he cast a searching eye for her. Either she'd decided not to come, holed up in the stone castle, or she was somewhere on the grounds, eating and talking, maybe dancing.

His heart sank in her absence, sank deep. He needed to talk to her, to try to explain about the other evening. He had left her to assume the worst, and he hated himself for it, realized that he couldn't leave Oregon with her on his conscience. Not this time. Not the way he left her before.

For a reason he didn't quite fathom, Shadoe desperately wanted Lilly to know that she did mean something to him, that he really cared, that somehow she would always be the most important person to him. But she also had to know that as much as that mattered, it was impossible for him to stay in Oregon. It was impossible for him to marry her.

Marry her . . . marry her! The two words rolled over in his head like two heavy stones. Silently, Shadoe groaned. For the last few nights, he had lain in bed, thinking only of her, how she felt in his arms, soft and warm, how her sweet breath fanned lightly against his skin. And he knew that he loved her, loved her even more than he had all those years ago.

It was strange how their relationship developed over the years. He had been tied to her through his relationship with Joseph. But Shadoe now knew that it was Lilly all along whom he really loved and wanted. She was his princess, the fair beauty of the castle, and she offered him a love and a life that he'd only dreamed about. With her, loving her, he was no longer the bastard son, but her prince and lord of the manor.

But it would never happen now. Sam Miller's death had changed all that. Sam and then what had happened to poor, poor Anne. Those two things, tied together, would never allow Shadoe to give Lilly the total commitment that she needed. He could never live with her as a husband and not share his soul. And God, he couldn't share his soul—his dark and shattered soul.

But he loved her! And it was suddenly important to him that Lilly not only forgive him for leaving her all those years ago, but for leaving her again now. Maybe if she did, if she told him that she could go on with her life, he could forgive himself for all the secrets, the lies that had torn him away from her in the first place? He had to try. What else was there to do?

Shadoe weaved in and out of the parked wagons and buggies, following the sound of the music. When he turned the corner of a buckboard, he started straight on the path that both Tom and Jesse Woodward had taken.

Shadoe didn't hesitate, though he could tell that they were apparently upset at the sight of him. Neither said anything as they passed him. Shadoe mimicked their actions, and it appeared for the moment that discretion would be the by-word between the three of them.

Tom was no fool, Shadoe thought. He would never risk exposing himself for the bastard that he was. *One sorry jackass, one silly fool*, Shadoe swore silently before moving in another direction. *And the jackass wants to marry the princess. No . . . no . . . no!*

She was hungry after the two games of croquet, thirsty, too. But Lilly glanced with boredom over the platters of desserts: rich pies, fresh-baked breads, and cakes. All she could really focus on was how to keep Shadoe in town for several more weeks. As long as he was there, she had hope.

She set down a half-finished glass of lemonade and proceeded to help herself to a piece of Mrs. Burton's famous chocolate pie.

"Looks good," came a familiar voice, and Lilly glanced up to see Tom standing over her.

"It is," she answered quickly. "I thought I'd have some pie. Want some?"

Tom shook his head, then reached over to take Lilly's unfinished glass of lemonade in his hand. "No, thanks, but I'll watch you eat yours if you don't mind."

There was a wide smile on his face, and Lilly mused that he looked particularly handsome in his own way. She smiled back at him, and thought that it was easy to like Tom when he wasn't trying to seduce her, or talking ill about the Sinclairs, or planning the future.

Poor Tom. If only he didn't care so much, if only he didn't want so much. And then she quickly caught herself, regretting all those past ill thoughts toward him, particularly her conversation with Luke. She felt suddenly guilty. Tom had never been anything but good to her. And it struck her that he might need a friend, particularly now when his mother was so ill.

"Let's see if we can find some shade," she told him in a gesture which stemmed directly from her desperation to make amends. Seeing that Aunt Martha was engrossed in a conversation with Widow Daniels, Lilly turned to walk toward the garden that ran adjacent to the side of the house. In the wide open pastures of Weatherly's large cattle ranch, the small grove of trees offered the only respite of privacy.

"We'll sit there," she commented, pointing her finger, and wordlessly Tom followed her away from the crowds.

"You should try the pie, Tom. It's delicious," she said, finding a seat on one of the ornate benches. They had been imported from Europe.

"I couldn't eat. Not now."

"Why?"

"Shadoe's here."

Lilly was both happy and dismayed at the news. Why hadn't she seen him? Where was he? She quickly cut a sharp glance toward the path that led to the open field.

Tom followed her gaze. "I'm surprised at your father. Very surprised. Thank God I didn't bring Maw out today. She'd had a fit if she saw Shadoe here."

Lilly took a bite of her pie and listened, trying to stay calm, but a silent rage was building in her soul.

"Maw's been feelin' so poorly these last few weeks, well, I hate to think—"

After she cleared her throat, Lilly cut him off. "Do we have to talk about him? I just hate it when you start this mess. What happened between your family and the Sinclairs is in the past." She paused and reached for the glass of lemonade which he had been holding in his hands. Lilly took a sip, attempted to swallow the knot forming at the back of her throat.

"Don't you think that you could just leave well enough alone?" she asked, setting the glass down beside her. "Here I was wanting to talk to you, to comfort you because I felt you needed a friend and now all you can talk about is Shadoe. Shadoe this. Shadoe that. Why, it just drives me mad hearing his name all the time. I do swear, Tom, I think you're obsessed! Just stop thinking about him."

"How can I?" Tom's gaze narrowed with thought. "You should have seen what he did to Jesse the other night. Whipped him right there in the saloon, right down onto the floor in front of everyone. I wish I'd been there."

"It doesn't matter. I would rather talk about something more pleasant."

"Damn, Lilly, I don't want to talk about anythin' else!"

Lilly tensed at his tantrum and shot him a look of ire. "You have no excuse to be rude to me, Tom. None whatsoever! Why is it that you insist on making me miserable with all this talk of Shadoe? You know that it is just as hard for me to have him around as it is for you!"

He leaned over and grasped her arms. The plate fell from her hand. "Do you realize what you've just said?"

She did, but only after the fact. Tom would be foolish not to realize that the reason it was difficult for her to bear Shadoe's presence was because she was still in love with him. Lilly turned her head so she wouldn't have to look at his accusing stare.

Suddenly, Tom leaned closer and kissed her, a small stab which sucked against her lips before she could deny him.

"Don't, Tom," she complained, moving her head, but he insisted. He took his hands, forcing her face to meet his, and his mouth fell over hers in a punishing kiss.

Lilly tried to push away, but Tom pressed even harder against her mouth. She felt one of his hands grab her hair, then the other grab the back of her neck. She struggled, then finally slammed her hand across the side of his head, knocking his mouth from hers.

"Stop!" Lilly gasped.

"I'll stop all right!"

Lilly struggled against the tears filling her eyes. "I can't believe that you'd do this, that you'd act this way. Why, Tom?" A silky brow arched in disbelief. "Why are you being so cruel to me?"

She stood. The plate of pie lay splattered on the

ground, and she stepped around it as she walked toward the crowd, muttering as she went, "I don't understand."

"Because I want you to hurt," he said hotly, coming after her. "I want you to know the pain of lovin' someone who will never love you. Cause that's exactly what you have to look forward to, Lilly!" He grabbed her arm. "I heard about Shadoe comin' to the dance, takin' you home. Do you know why Jesse and Shadoe were fightin' at the saloon?"

She shook her head. "He didn't mention it to me." The tears were falling now. And she didn't really care. All Lilly could think of at that moment was rage. "I don't care why he was in the saloon," she cried.

"I bet you don't."

There was mockery in Tom's voice, sarcasm so thick and heavy that Lilly gave him a watchful stare. She could see a glimmer of triumph in his gaze as though he had somehow won a small battle in a very large war, a fixed, set expression in his eyes—cold and hard. It frightened her.

"Why are you looking at me that way, and why would you say something like that in that tone?"

He laughed for a moment. "Don't you know?" he finally asked in a sneering little voice.

"Know what?"

"So you really don't know? I'm not surprised. What did he do, Lilly? Drive you home, talkin' sweet, tryin' to seduce you, playin' those games of his, pretendin' that he cares when really all he wants is a quick tumble in the hay?"

Her mouth flew open. "How dare you!"

Tom grinned sweetly at her. "Oh, Lilly, dear. I told you that he would use you. He was at the saloon with a woman—a whore!"

"A woman!" She couldn't say the other word, but Tom repeated it for her.

"*Whore.* He was walkin' with Naomi when Jesse ran into him."

"I don't believe you!" she roared.

"Why would I lie? Anyone there will tell you the same story."

Lilly couldn't speak. Her face paled suddenly with the thought of Shadoe making love to another woman. Wiping at her damp cheeks, she glanced at Tom and could see that he was telling her the truth. Shadoe had been at the saloon. He had admitted as much to her father. But a woman? How could he have been with a woman and then kissed her the way he did?

No . . . no . . . no. It was a lie, another one of Tom's jealous tantrums! Her gray eyes clouded, dark with rage. She shook all over. But the thought remained, stuck in the corner of her mind like a sticky web: Shadoe in the saloon talking and teasing with another woman. She felt crushed.

Maybe Shadoe had been truthful when he said that the kisses had meant nothing. Maybe a woman was just a woman, and she was the same as any of them. She struggled with her thoughts.

Tom frowned, coming closer to her. "It's plain to see that this news troubles you." He reached out and gently stroked her hair. "Forgive me, Lilly, for hurtin' you like I did. For being the one to tell you these things." He shook his head in dismay. "I hate being full of so much anger. But I know what Shadoe did to my sister. He killed her. Drove her to her death. I don't want to see you hurt. I couldn't bear for that man to hurt you like he did Anne."

Lilly looked at Tom a moment, struck by the

intensity of his remark. She could see that he meant it, and that he really said all those things because he wanted to protect her from a man he didn't trust.

But his motives gave her little comfort. "Go away . . . Tom. Leave me alone for a while," she said to him in a voice choked with new tears.

She moved away, wiped at her eyes. The sun's rays flashed through the tree limbs. They were bright and hot, and threw a shadow in front of her as she began to walk blindly toward the crowd. And she walked slowly, step for step in a new kind of misery.

The afternoon passed. Night came, and the moon burned coldly through the raveled and yellowed edge of a cloud. Lilly gazed up at it and felt a shiver. How like the moon she was, dying in her isolation, cold and chaste. Cold and chaste, shriveling inside.

She had felt that way since the day Shadoe and Joseph had left Oregon. And tonight it was worse. The ghostly smear in the night sky seem to haunt her, laugh at her—a symbol of unrequited love.

She turned and gazed at the dancers, the soft firelight of the lanterns skittering across their happy faces. It was good that Tom and Luke had found some business to keep them from her, that Aunt Martha had to retire because of her cold, that her father was too busy with his friends to notice that she stood, in the garden, alone, with tears in her eyes.

But then, from nowhere, came the word, "Hello."

The word was too easy, and in her numbed mind,

Lilly was unsure that she had even heard it. She stepped back, standing in a pool of moonlight.

Then it came again, a little firmer, closer to her ears, Shadoe's voice, her name on the night breeze.

"Hello, Lilly."

She clutched her skirts in one hand, ready to run from the figure she could not see. And then he was there, standing beside her, too close for her to escape if he protested, so she dropped her skirts.

She looked directly into his eyes. "I thought we were not going to see each other again," she said in a voice that wavered.

"We were."

"So why did you come here?"

"I want to say good-bye just in case I don't see you again before I leave for San Francisco."

She was startled at his words, and forgot her fear and anger. Even her thoughts of the saloon, of Tom's remark vanished in her new anxiety—his departure.

"Are you really leaving?" she asked.

"Maybe faster than I'd hoped. Your father has agreed to buy the ranch. A gift for you, I think."

"Buy the Double *S*?" She couldn't have been more surprised. "For me? A gift? I don't understand?"

"You know I came back to sell the ranch. I've spent the last few days talking your father into buying it. It is fitting that you own the Double *S* and I'll be comforted knowing that I left something for you."

Left something for you. Lilly pushed the thought away in resignation, in a feeling of finality. She looked up at the sky, the stars peeking through the black foliage of the trees.

"So it's done," she murmured.

There would be no time for her schemes, no time for hopes of love. No time to unravel the secrets. As before, Shadoe would ride out of her life, never looking back.

"Not exactly," he replied. "I have to get Joey."

She looked back at him. "Joey? Oh, yes. When will you get Joey? How?"

His gaze flickered across her face, cautious, restrained. "I have my plans and you're better off not knowing them, just in case."

"Just in case I tell Tom, is that it? I could have already told him that you were here to get Joey. But I didn't," she fussed. Lilly waved her arm in a gesture of disgust. "So you don't trust me."

He moved closer to her, and Lilly flinched as he lifted his hand to touch her cheek with his finger. "I may never see you again," he told her in a strange voice, completely ignoring the way she had scolded him. "And I wanted you to know that I'll miss you. I really will miss you."

There was an element of sorrow in his expression, and Lilly momentarily succumbed to the unexpected tenderness in which he looked at her. Her heartbeat quickened and she asked, "When are you leaving?"

"In four or five days if everything goes as planned." His hand brushed her cheek, then drifted to her hair. "As hard as I try, Lilly, I find it impossible to leave you alone. Do you know that? Do you know what you do to me?"

She felt weak with his words, but the conversation with Tom suddenly flooded her mind. He had been at the saloon, possibly with one of those painted women!

She knocked his hand away, and Shadoe

flinched. "Is this something you say to all the women you leave behind, Mister Sinclair? Or did you intend this tenderness for my ears alone?"

He didn't answer her question, just watched for a moment, and a spark touched his eyes. Whether he was angry or amused, Lilly did not know, but she suddenly felt resolved. So he was going back to San Francisco, breaking her heart just like he did all those years ago. Well, this time, she was going to give him a dose of his own medicine.

One crazy scheme developed. An act of revenge.

Lilly stiffened. "I'm glad that you came to say good-bye. Truly I am. There is something that I want to tell you." She paused, preparing herself for the lie, summoning all the strength she could muster. "You see, I wanted you to hear it from me, instead of someone else. So that I could explain."

He appeared confused. "What are you talking about?"

Lilly's heart began to pound with panic. She had to say the words! She had to hurt him if she could!

"I'm marrying Tom," she announced, her face expressionless.

A fierce light, such as Lilly has never seen before, came into Shadoe's eyes. He glared at her, a sterile, frigid look that fell across her face like a netting of paper-thin ice. She reached up as if to wipe it away, but it clung to her skin. She was shaken and cold, ready to scream.

"Well, aren't you going to say something?" she asked, hoping that he'd explode before she did.

"I guess I should congratulate you," he told her softly and the unanticipated reply incensed Lilly. But before she could make a rebuttal, Shadoe stooped swiftly, pulling her into his arms.

He looked at her, the devil's own taunt in his eyes, a wide, crooked grin on his face. No longer was there coldness. His mouth fell on hers, molding against her lips in a wet and fierce kiss. Lilly struggled at first, her eyes open, her hands beating him, then the world went black. She could see nothing, hear nothing, only feel the pleasing warmth that settled through her. Her arms circled his neck, and she kissed him back hungrily.

When their mouths parted, Shadoe started to laugh, his breath warm against her face, and Lilly gazed at him, perplexed, not understanding what was so amusing, wanting him to kiss her again.

"What's so funny?"

"That you would marry a simpering fool like Woodward. What a waste!"

She struggled against his embrace, but Shadoe held her tight. "Now don't be angry at me, Lilly. I couldn't help myself. I had to kiss you, teach you a lesson."

"A lesson? What are you talking about?"

There was an odd glint in his eyes. "You're a bad liar, Princess. I know you better than anyone, remember? How could you even consider marrying that boy? Why, he wouldn't even know how to kiss you properly, and believe me, Princess, you're made for kissing. I just proved that."

She blushed furiously and wiggled in his arms. "Oh, I do hate you! I do!" she cried, and her chin raised defiantly. "I'll marry him! I swear to you that I'll marry him!"

Shadoe became somber and his mouth tightened into a thin line. "You'll never marry that boy. Do you understand me?"

"And what do you care? You know that I love

you." Her voice came softer, and tears wet her cheeks. "But you never cared enough to stay with me."

"I care."

"Then why did you leave me? Why are you leaving me now?"

He pushed her away gently. "I have to go. You know that. I can't stay here."

"Then I'll go with you," she pleaded, leaning against him.

"No."

"Please, I love you."

"I don't want you to go with me, Lilly."

Lilly stepped back. The familiar coldness was there again, fixed in his stare. "You can't love anyone, Shadoe Sinclair! You never could. Papa always said you reminded him of some animal in the wilderness. Like the land he said, wild and free and uncaring. Well, don't tell me who I can marry and who I can't. All these years, I've been hoping, praying, looking everywhere to find what I felt with you. But it just isn't there. So don't tell me not to marry Tom. I'll not be an old maid! Tom loves me, wants desperately to make me happy. And God knows, I want to be happy!"

"Tom could never make you happy!"

She gave him a wicked look. "Maybe I'll marry Luke Miller instead."

"Luke?" He turned a little and gave her a sideways glance.

"Yes, there aren't many women in this part of Oregon and Luke needs a bride. Maybe I'll marry him."

Shadoe was truly stunned. "Luke would never marry you. He couldn't."

She was surprised at the quickness of his words, at the tone of confidence. But there was something in his stare that told her that he was speaking with knowledge.

"Is that so?"

He turned, looked away from her sudden curiosity, and Lilly knew that he had said more than he had wanted.

"Don't you think Luke might want to marry me, Shadoe?"

"Well, he might want to marry you." He faced her again. "Any man would want to marry you. But Luke is a man with lots of loyalty, pride." He paused. "I've thought about it myself, but I know better. There's things you don't understand about Luke. As much as he likes you, he'd never marry you."

Lilly frowned at his expression, knew that his words held a great deal of truth. Next to Shadoe and her brother, Luke Miller was the most eligible bachelor in Harney County. Yet, he'd never taken a wife, had never come down from the lakes to court her or anyone else. Just horses, just the ranch since his brother, Sam, was killed.

"Well, don't underestimate my abilities," Lilly told Shadoe. "I just taught him croquet this afternoon and come that charity event next month, he's riding up a day early just to escort me." She paused, took a needed breath. Her chest was tight with anxiety. "Remember, Luke is *just* a man, and if I want him, I'll get him. I always had what I wanted."

And a thought flickered through her mind, *except you . . . except you. . . .*

Shadoe wasn't amused. "You scheming little

witch. You're planning it, aren't you?"

Lilly laughed. "Of course I am! You stupid brute! Did you think I would just pine away forever? I have needs, lots of needs, just like you do!"

"Still got a sharp tongue, don't you?" Shadoe snapped. "Well, that's fine. You marry whomever you please!"

"I have to have some happiness!"

"You'll be miserable!"

"You sound jealous." She shook her head at him, a defiant smile on her face. "I won't be miserable. I'll be having another man's babies!"

He half-turned. "Don't expect me to stay just because you threaten me with this marriage. I have my reasons for leaving and you're just as much a part of them as anything else. But I won't have you throwing your life away on a man you don't love."

"But you'd have me throw it away for the man I do love," she retorted. "Have me live in loneliness with only my memories of you. Well, life's a queer thing. We don't always get what we want, do we, Shadoe?"

"No, we don't, Princess."

He turned and walked away, and she watched him leave.

Her heart raced, but not any faster than her thoughts. What were Shadoe's reasons for leaving? And why was she just as much a part of them as anything else?

Chapter 18

The woman looked tired. She entered the cemetery gate, threading her way through the gray, weathered headstones, moving toward Shadoe, who watched intently the little companion who trailed behind her.

She stopped at one particular stone, a thin block of white marble, and leaned over, placing some flowers on the soft mound of green grass. Her smaller escort did the same, crouching beside the tombstone as if to play.

For Shadoe, the scene had the look of familiarity, and he was correct in his opinion. The youngster soon sat down, withdrew a small spoon from his shirt pocket, and began to plant his handful of flowers with the expertise of a seasoned gardener.

The woman looked down, smiled, then tapped the boy on the shoulder. "Stay here," she told him before she turned to look back at Shadoe.

Shadoe brooded over what to say. It had been

so many years, and now as he stared at her empty expression, he could only feel regret that he had waited so long to see her. The years had not been as kind to her as they had been to him.

"You're too ill to be here," he cautioned her immediately.

She walked slowly, almost struggling, and Shadoe did not like the way she looked. There was something in the way she moved that gave him warning. It ate momentarily at his resolve.

The woman half smiled. "It has to be done," she said. "Besides, it's such a pretty day. A good day. Don't you think?"

He nodded and watched her reach into the sleeve of her dress to pull out a handkerchief. She wiped the moist skin beneath her brown eyes, then turned to give the toddler a careful look.

Shadoe followed her gaze. He stared at his son, sitting in the grass, digging. *His son.* The words sounded unnatural, and yet, legally, they were true. Though he had never been a real parent to his child, the boy carried his name.

Shadoe watched him play, planting the yellow flowers. How like Anne the boy looked, the same dark hair, the same brown eyes, the little nose, perfect except for the tiny crease at the end. He swallowed hard. The comparison pained him, caused Shadoe to hold his breath, blink his eyes a time or two. And it suddenly occurred to him that this was the wrong place, that he didn't want to be there, standing over Anne's grave, taking care of business like she didn't matter, like nothing mattered at all.

"We should have met somewhere else. I should have come out to the ranch," he said in a stumble of hasty words.

She shook her head and leaned over against a tall stone made in the shape of an obelisk. "It's the only way," she replied, out of breath. She closed her eyes for a moment as she rested her head on the marker. When she opened them, her dark and misty gaze was intent.

He could see her determination, felt swallowed by it. As weak as her body was, her mind was still as strong as that day so many years ago when she had persuaded him to leave the boy behind. Shadoe wanted to leave the cemetery right then, but he couldn't, didn't. He just stared at her, silent, waiting for her to say something, anything.

"Jesse drove us into town," she started slowly, and he listened anxiously. She turned her head, her gaze moving from man to sky. Shadoe did the same. There was not a cloud to be seen. The sky was blue and wide, and a flock of birds flew overhead, flapping their wings in short, quick movements.

"It will be good to die," she commented. "I'm tired. Everything here is so heavy and wasted. Sky looks so wide. Light as a feather. Like an angel, I imagine. I don't think I'll mind feeling like that one bit."

He swallowed hard again, listening to her words, struggling for some of his own, finally able to summon his voice.

"I know you're in pain. Let me take you back to the buggy," Shadoe suggested.

"No time. Jesse will be back soon. He's at the barber shop now, seeing about cutting his hair for that Sunday dinner at the Andrews's. I think he finally has decided to marry that girl. Poor Jesse. I wish—" She stopped, fighting for a fresh breath.

"I'll see that Jackson looks after him." It was a strange thing for Shadoe to say, sudden, without thought or planning, but it just came out naturally, as if he really meant it and was not just humoring a dying woman.

"Would you?" she asked in a ragged whisper.

"You know that I will." Shadoe moved to her. "Let me take you back to the buggy. You can't stay here."

She made a gesture to refuse. "No. This is it. I'll never have another chance. Jesse wouldn't have brought me at all had I not insisted on coming to the cemetery. He never had a thought about it." She gestured with her hands, pointing toward the boy, then back to Shadoe. "He never had a clue that you would be here to fetch Joey." A heavy sigh. "But all the same, I still had to force him to bring me. There'll never be another moment for us."

"Does anyone know?" asked Shadoe.

"That I came to meet you?" She shook her head. "It's better this way. I couldn't trust anyone. Tom's so bitter. I hate for him to think that his mother betrayed him."

"I understand."

She smiled at him, a weak but bright smile that animated her features. Her dark eyes sparkled in the sunlight. "You were good to me, Shadoe, letting me have the boy all these years. With him, I saw my young Anne again, an innocent and playful child. I want to pay you back for your kindness. I want to put things to rest." She grew stiff, standing straight. "I hate dying with these lies. Lies are heavy things, you know, and I want to be as light as a feather. You should tell the truth."

"No," Shadoe told her. "There's no point to it

now. What good would come of it? It's better just
to let it rest. If we were going to tell the truth, we
should have done it years ago."

"But you and the McFalls? Do you want to go to
your grave keeping all these secrets?"

"For Anne I would. For Lilly. For the old man."

"And the rest?"

"They're of no account in my mind." It was a
quick, cold reply and a selfish one, too. Shadoe
shifted his gaze, thinking that he had never thought
of the others—meaning Tom and Jesse. How would
it be now if everyone had known the truth? He
pushed the thoughts away, shuddered at facing
them.

A frown was on her face when he turned to look
at her. "You're as hard a man as you are kind,
Shadoe Sinclair." She stopped to cough, and it
stuck in her throat, gagging her on the fluid that
had been slowly consuming her lungs for months.
Shadoe took the ailing form in his arms.

The young boy, alarmed, ran to grab his grandmother around her knees. His thin, small hands
clutched tightly at the folds of her skirt.

"Mawmaw . . ."

Sarah Woodward finally caught her breath.
"Take the boy," she gasped.

"I need to be getting you to the doctor," Shadoe
complained.

She shook her head. "Nothing the doctors can
do. Take Joey and go."

Sarah looked down at the small face which
was covered with a spray of freckles. Smiling,
she moved from Shadoe's arms, leaning over to
give her grandson a kiss on the tip of his small
upturned nose.

"You be a good boy, Joey, and go with this man. He's your paw, you know. Mister Sinclair. Got your name. Remember the stories I've been telling you about him. Well, he's come to take you to his house."

The boy scowled, tears forming in his eyes, and Shadoe thought how scared the youngster looked. After all he was only five years old. But hesitation wouldn't help the child now. There had already been too much time between him and his son.

He reached down and scooped the youngster up in his arms. "It's all right. I'm going to take care of you," he said in a slow, gentle voice.

"Mawmaw?"

Sarah smiled, patting the boy on the hand. "He's gonna be a good paw to you, Joey. Mawmaw's too sick to take care of you anymore. Now you promised Mawmaw to be a good and brave boy. You be good."

She shifted her attention to Shadoe, a glimmer of pain in her eyes. "Here, take this. You might need it," she said, handing him a piece of paper she had dragged from her pocket. "Go," she finally requested. "Go now and don't look back."

"I hate to leave you here," Shadoe protested. "At least let me see you back to the buggy."

She resisted his arm. "Please, go away. Take the boy and go away. I want to be alone."

Shadoe said nothing as he watched her tears. Yet, somehow, it was fitting. Somehow in its twisted justice, it was right. He'd done his duty. It was finally over. All of a sudden her face looked cold, remote to Shadoe, as though she were a stranger standing before him, some woman whom he'd never known or cared about in any small way.

Clutching the boy in his arms, he left the cemetery, his quick and incautious steps moving across the flowers and small spoon scattered on the grassy mound beneath Anne Woodward's tombstone.

It was Widow Daniels, coming to pay respects to her husband's memory before she agreed to be Dan Hadley's bride, who discovered Sarah Woodward in the cemetery, slumped on the ground. Her screams caught the attention of another Montfort citizen who immediately summoned Doctor Brown, then the sheriff.

Sarah Woodward had collapsed. Her lungs, no longer able to provide her body with proper oxygen, had put a strain on her heart. Though she was only fifty years old, she was dying apparently of congestive heart failure.

When Jesse strolled toward their family's buggy, he spotted the crowd gathering in the cemetery. Instinct and fear told him what had happened, and his heart was in his throat when he reached his mother. She lay in Doctor Brown's arms, looking like death, though she breathed, short, violent rattles that shook his masculine resolve.

By the time they had carried her to one of Doctor Brown's rooms, Jesse was crying, and Sarah Woodward was unconscious. Tom was summoned, and at a quarter past ten on that bright and sunny Monday morning, Sarah Woodward drew her last breath in the presence of her two sons.

It was the tenth day of May.

Her grandson, young Joseph Simon Sinclair, was conspicuously absent.

Chapter 19

Lo Ching stared at the boy, who with his fork was piercing the tiny pieces of beef on his plate. After each bite, Joey Sinclair would look up at the cook as if he needed some kind of approval, and the Chinaman would oblige him with a nod and a smile.

When Lo Ching wasn't looking, the boy would drop a piece of meat on the floor, and Dragon would graciously lick it up.

"He do well, Mister Shadoe. Young Master Joseph is a good little man. Smart. He going to be just fine here with us."

"Yes, he is," Shadoe remarked, and thought how true it was. He knew that coming home to fetch the child had been the best thing he'd done. For this, there were no regrets.

Lo Ching pointed to the dog laying directly at the boy's feet. "Just look at the way Dragon take to him. Dog finally like someone besides you, Mister Shadoe."

"So he does." Shadoe sat back in his chair. It creaked heavily. He was cleaning his gun. Every now and then he would take his thumb and roll the cylinder, staring at the spotless metal as though it was his mistress.

His gun had been his strength for years. When he thought about it, he realized that today was the first time he had ever worried about not beating a man to the draw. Maybe, it was because he was older, less focused, a parent. Shadoe didn't quite know.

When he was young, he was remarkably capable, with speed of hand, with a steadiness that made his aim direct, always on course. He never deliberately directed a shot; he just pulled his gun and fired. Yet, he thought, that no matter how good a man was with a gun there was always someone who was better.

Tom Woodward wasn't. But he could hire a gun, and Lewis had found out that Pepper still worked for the Woodwards.

Only a fool would be too confident. Shadoe loaded his .45 peacemaker and slipped it in the holster. He was no fool.

Lo Ching watched as Shadoe was thinking. "You worried about somebody coming here to make trouble, Mister Shadoe?"

"Yeah. Anything's possible after today."

The cook shook his head, and his slanted gaze strayed to the boy. "You think we should talk about what's been going on today? I mean . . . the boy needs to know something."

The "what's been going on" was that Sarah

Woodward had been laid to rest in the small cemetery behind the Woodward house.

"I'll do it when the time is right. I have other things on my mind," Shadoe commented. He prodded his vest pocket, retrieving a match, then lit the cigarette that he had been holding in his mouth for several minutes. "I might be sending you and the boy ahead, Lo Ching. Lewis will take the two of you. Maybe as soon as this Sunday."

"But I thought you say that we need to stay longer?"

Shadoe needed to stay longer, not them.

"But for us to go on alone . . . the boy?" Lo Ching protested. "He already scared enough."

The child raised his eyes to Shadoe. The expression unnerved Shadoe for he suddenly realized that he'd made a mistake. Another pitiful mistake. Now everyone would pay dues for his weakness.

And it was true. Shadoe knew that it was a careless mistake, leaving Joey behind with the Woodwards. Though he had thought only of Anne and her mother at the time, he should have seen further down the road toward the misery it would finally bring. And with Sarah Woodward dying, it was a mistake more destructive than he had ever imagined.

He scowled, took a deep drag on his cigarette, and looked out the kitchen and adjoining dining-room window which faced the front of the house. He exhaled slowly, staring, then his eyes narrowed.

"Expecting anyone, Lo Ching?"

"No, Mister Shadoe," the Chinaman muttered nervously as he rushed to the window. "Trouble come?"

"Maybe." Shadoe stood and strapped on his gun. "Take the boy upstairs."

There was no hesitation. The cook picked up the boy, and hurried through the parlor that separated the kitchen and eating area from the main foyer. Before Shadoe had collected his rifle and moved to the front door, Lo Ching and Joey were safely up the stairs.

There were four riders approaching the house. One rider he knew to be Jackson Williams. The other threes' identity he only suspected until he walked out on the porch.

"Sheriff Smith . . . Jackson." Shadoe said nothing to Tom and the other man. He dropped his cigarette and crushed it with the toe of his boot. The black dog stood beside his master like a waiting sentry.

"I guess you know why we're here," Smith began, but Shadoe cut him short.

"The boy's mine and he stays with me."

"Like hell, he does!" Tom blurted.

"Stay calm," the rider next to Tom said. "Let the law prevail upon this man."

"The law is on my side," Shadoe replied coldly. "Joseph Simon Sinclair is my son. And Mrs. Woodward surrendered him to me the day before yesterday." Shadoe looked at the sheriff. "I've got papers and *this* if necessary." He raised his rifle and gave both Smith and Jackson a hard look. "I don't want any trouble, but I'm not giving him up. I gave him to Sarah, and she gave him back. That's all there is to it."

Smith frowned. "But the Woodwards do have a claim, Shadoe. You abandoned the boy."

"Not true."

Tom smirked at Shadoe's quick remark. "Then what the hell do ya call it?"

Shadoe looked at Tom, but his words were directed at everyone. "The boy's grandmother begged me to leave him with her. I agreed."

"That's a damn lie!"

Smith and Jackson both looked at Tom who shifted nervously in his saddle, then the two of them glanced at the other man.

"Mister Seegrove is an attorney," Sheriff Smith began.

"Good for him," Shadoe interrupted. "Then he knows that a man has his rights. The boy is my son legally. I've got papers that say so."

Smith dismounted, quickly moving to Shadoe. "I know your abilities firsthand. You're good and quick with a gun, but I'm a peaceable man. I'd rather talk than fight. You wouldn't happen to have them papers on you?"

"I thought you might be dropping by sooner or later." Shadoe reached in his shirt pocket. "Here." Shadoe lifted his hand to the sheriff. "His birth records from the courthouse at Winnemucca and this. It's a letter from Sarah, explaining."

At the sound of Shadoe's words, Tom hastily swung off his horse. Jackson quickly dismounted, moving to stand between Shadoe and Tom.

"Don't get too antsy, Tom," Jackson challenged. "Let the sheriff handle this."

"I ain't gonna do nothin' of the kind." Tom took a step past Jackson. "If my mother wrote something, it's my right to see it."

"Let him look," Shadoe told the sheriff. "He does have a right. Just like I've got mine."

Tom grabbed the piece of paper, his hardened gaze scanning the words scribbled in a trembling hand. He was shaking his head as he spoke, "This cain't be. She never said nothin' about askin' Sinclair to leave the kid until she died . . ." Tom's voice trailed off, and he looked up at Shadoe. "You left her in the cemetery, you bastard, left her there to die."

Shadoe swallowed hard. "She wanted it that way."

"It ain't right, you comin' here and gettin' the kid."

"Your mother wrote to me in San Francisco, Tom. She told me to come."

The words were meant to hit hard, and Tom tightened his fists. "You lie like a dog! My mother ain't never wrote you."

Shadoe straightened his rifle. "I don't want any trouble," he said when the sheriff took the letter from Tom's hands. Smith walked to Seegrove and handed the lawyer the piece of paper.

"Take a look at this."

The man read, then looked at Tom. "Mister Sinclair is right. Apparently, he didn't abandon the child. I'm afraid—"

Tom jerked around. Revolt was in his eyes. "He cain't have the kid. How can you let a murderer have a kid?"

"I didn't kill Anne, Tom. You know that."

"Same damn thing," Tom spat at Shadoe. "You tried to force her to go away with you again, just when she had come home. You as good as pushed her down those steps!"

"You know that's not the truth—"

"All right, you two." Smith looked at Shadoe and Tom. "The both of you are through discussing this, you hear me?" Smith directed his gaze at Shadoe. "Shadoe, I'm gonna have to take your papers as well as Mrs. Woodward's letter into town for the judge to see."

The older man turned to Tom. "And, Tom, I don't want you coming back out here until I can make some sense of all of this. You hear me, boy?"

Tom said nothing, just looked at Shadoe.

"Tom, don't come back out here," Jackson reiterated.

"I hear ya."

Nothing else was said, and the three men mounted their horses.

Shadoe walked into the yard, following, watching the riders leave. He stood until they faded into the distance.

When Shadoe turned, Lo Ching was moving through the front door.

"Trouble gone, Mister Shadoe?" he questioned with an imploring frown across his face.

Shadoe drew a heavy sigh. "Trouble gone. At least for a while."

Chapter 20

When Lilly heard the news from her father, she didn't know whether to cry for joy or just get angry. So Shadoe hadn't abandoned his own child, after all, but gave Joey to Sarah Woodward out of a moment of tenderness.

The judge had forbidden young Joseph Sinclair to leave Harney County until a hearing was held concerning the facts related to the custody case. Judge Hardwick heard the case on the nineteenth day of May, exactly nine days from the day of Sarah Woodward's funeral.

The outcome was quick and final. Sinclair was the father and he had every right to claim his child. The judge finally told the Woodwards to stay away from the boy. Though Jesse was furious, Lilly, on the few occasions that she'd seen Tom, was surprised that the elder Woodward was so easily assenting to the surrender of Anne's child. She had expected to see Tom angry, ready to kill

202

the judge, ready to fight, do anything to keep Joey from staying with Shadoe Sinclair. But from the day Judge Hardwick had issued his decree, Tom had never mentioned the young boy again.

It was eerie. Tom's silence. His inactivity concerning the matter. Lilly had thought that Tom was too calm . . . too calm.

For several days, no one in Montfort talked of anything else, until the night Dan Hadley showed up at the mansion to tell James McFall that some fences had been cut on Polly Daniels' homestead. Polly and her four sons lived near Malheur Lake which was thirty miles directly north of Weatherly. Their place was across the river from Luke Miller's horse ranch.

Hadley also had some tragic news. One of the new homesteaders on the west side of the Blitzen River had been shot and killed just a few yards from where Double S's most southern lines ran. It seemed that the rustling was taking on a new dimension, spreading over the whole Blitzen Valley, some thirty-six miles that ran from the Steens Mountains to Harney and Malheur Lakes.

The news greatly disturbed James McFall, and Lilly was shocked at his sense of confusion. It was plain to her that he had not expected such boldness from the rustlers and was demoralized by the scope of his responsibility since Shadoe and he were signing the final papers on the sale of the Double S Ranch the following morning in Montfort.

That news disturbed Lilly the most. The thought of Shadoe leaving her again exploded in her brain. Shadoe gone? Forever? Nothing left. No hope. No dreams.

She thought often of her schemes, her plans to discover Shadoe's secrets, but if he didn't stay in Montfort, if he sold that ranch, the secrets would always remain hidden, and all her life she would hunger for their untold meaning. She couldn't live like that.

It didn't matter how much Shadoe had hurt her, she still loved him, still wanted him, and there was only one way to keep him in Oregon. She had to stop him from signing those papers! And she would.

Lilly's father had repeatedly warned her not to ride at night, never into Montfort. Times were dangerous and she might be mistaken for someone else on the road. Or she might meet with a stranger who was no stranger, or worse, meet with one of the rustlers.

But Lilly had disobeyed her father and even her own conscience as well as her logic. But logic had little to do with desperation, and she was desperate.

As she reined the horse down the dim path toward the Double S, she stopped frequently to listen. It was a cloudy night, no moon, no stars, just the blackness and void of the land.

So far, she was not being followed, and there was no evidence of someone else on the road. When she came upon the knoll on which the house set, Lilly saw the light in one of the bedroom windows. It was just after midnight.

She knew Shadoe was cautious. It would be difficult, if not impossible, for a rider to come near the house without being seen. He would know that she was there. Maybe he already suspected a rider approaching. Her only hope was that he wouldn't send her straight back to Weatherly that very night.

She was amazed that he let her ride all the way in without so much as a sign that he knew she was there. No greetings on the front porch. No hasty rebuttals. Nothing. Even when she slowly dismounted and tied her horse to the railing, there seemed to be a thick quiet wrapped around the house.

When the front door opened too easily, Lilly knew. Shadoe was waiting for her, sitting in a chair in the parlor.

"What do you think you're doing?" he asked her quietly. There was no anger in his tone, just a kind of benign acceptance.

She turned sharply to the right. "Coming to see you."

It was dark in the house, and she could barely make out his form slumped back in the chair, but she could hear his breathing. It was heavy, anxious.

"It was a fool thing to do," Shadoe chastised.

"I had to see you. I had to come."

"Don't you know what's going on around here? You might have been hurt, even killed." His voice hardened as it grew louder. "It was reckless. I'm glad that I knew it was you. But what do you think you're doing coming here now?"

"I came to ask you something. There's something I must know before you leave for California."

He rose from the chair and walked over, stopping just a step or two in front of her. She could still barely make out the lines of his features. But her heart wrenched in her chest. She wanted to touch him, but her fingers recoiled from such an intimate act. She locked her fingers into a fist and repeated her previous statement, but this time in a firm voice that demanded a reaction.

"You rode five damn miles to ask me some stupid question?" Shadoe barked.

"Yes."

He was clearly angry now. In the dimness, she could see his disapproval. "Well, for goodness sake! Speak! What could be so important?"

She hesitated for a moment. Thought about how to word it. The answer was important. But asking Shadoe about Sam Miller had never been easy. She remembered years ago, when Sam had died, how Shadoe had refused to talk about it. He might refuse now. But she had to ask. She was running out of time.

"I want to know why you killed Sam Miller?"

Something about Shadoe's appearance suddenly altered, too subtle for Lilly to grasp. But whatever it was, it went as quickly as it had come. He was soon looking at her, as though she were a fool.

"What in the hell does that have to do with anything?" He stepped closer to her. She could feel his warm breath, see his expression. A deep frown settled across the lines of his face. "I can't believe that you'd ride out here to ask me this," he commented before he paused to take in a deep, shuddering breath. "Dammit, Lilly, I should put you over my knee for this one!"

"Scared to answer?"

He said nothing, just turned away from her, walking back into the parlor. In a few moments, he had lit a lamp. The soft, pearly light filled the room with a warm glow. "Sam Miller was my friend, but he was hot-tempered and too easy with a knife," he told her as he sat back down in the chair. He pulled a cigarette and match from his pocket. "He just let both get away from him one time too many, that's all."

Lilly leaned against the doorframe, looking at him. "So you just killed him?"

"Yes."

"Was Joseph with you when you killed Sam?" she asked, watching him smoke.

He clamped his lips together and stared beyond her. The smoke rose in front of his face which was now expressionless. In a few moments, he shifted his gaze back to her.

"I don't see why you're asking all these questions. Sam Miller's dead and buried. What difference can it make to you now? What difference can it make to anyone, except maybe Luke?"

"You aren't answering the question."

"And I'm not going to." He took a deep drag of smoke, then blew it out. "I've got some of my own to ask. Like what in the hell am I going to do with you?"

She smiled lazily at him, prepared for this question. She had been rehearsing the answer since she left Weatherly. "You're putting me to bed. I'm staying the night."

"You're what?" The cigarette dropped to the floor, and Shadoe nervously stamped it out.

She took a short step into the room. "I said that I'm staying. It's five miles back to the house, and I don't relish the thought of making the trip again so soon."

Lilly stretched in a teasing fashion, watching with delight as Shadoe's gaze flickered with interest over her body. "Why, every muscle in my body aches. I'll go back in the morning."

Shadoe practically jumped out of the chair. "Like hell you will! You'll go back tonight!" He looked at her, his eyes wide, almost startled as if she had suggested something sinful, and she had.

Lilly looked at him and broke out laughing, amused at his apparent discomfort. "I'm staying the night so you might as well accept it. I'll sleep in your father's room."

"The boy's in there."

The house had only three bedrooms. That left two, Shadoe's and Lo Ching's. Lilly knew that he would not trouble himself to give her his own bed, at least not without a struggle and maybe not alone. "Then I'll sleep on the sofa."

Shadoe shook his head. "And what would your father say about that?" he finally asked. "Are you rattled? He's gonna raise hell! That's what. And not just at me, Lilly. When he finds you're gone, he's gonna ride out here." He moved, quickly grabbing her by the arm. "I'm taking you back tonight."

Lilly jerked her arm away. "You'll have to tie me to the horse, Mister Sinclair. I'm staying and there's nothing you can do about it. I'm not a little girl anymore, Shadoe. I'm twenty years old, a woman who can take care of herself. I'll handle my father." She drew a much needed breath. "Besides, he won't know that I'm gone. He's planning to meet you in Montfort first thing in the morning. I told him that I was sleeping in, that I'd see him when he returned."

He appeared defeated. "Lilly, you can't stay here. You just can't."

"Why?"

"Because . . . you just can't. It's not right."

"What's not right about it?"

He looked away for a moment. "You know why. We've talked about this before."

"I remember." Her soft words drew his attention.

"Then you know why you can't spend the night here," he told her. "I can't be responsible for . . ." He stopped and bristled with his next words. "You can't stay!"

She stared into his eyes. He was looking at her curiously, uneasily, almost with fear. "Because you're afraid of me? Is that it, Shadoe? You're afraid of what might happen if I spend the night here with you?"

He was silent, and she knew that he would never answer her questions, at least not now.

Lilly smiled. "Oh, I see. It's not me that frightens you, it's yourself. Why would you be frightened of yourself?"

He was silent again, and Lilly could see that he was choking with the idea of being alone with her. She almost laughed at his weakness, at her sudden moment of triumph, but at second thought, the amusement faded. She knew what it meant to stay the night in his house. If he could, he would take whatever he could from her. But would he ever give? Would he ever stay? Would he love her forever? She didn't know the answers.

Lilly shuddered briefly, then summoned all her courage as she teasingly asked, "What did you call it that night?" She paused, feigning an expression of deep thought as she rested her finger on her chin. "Oh, yes. A man like you just has needs, physical needs and well, it's hard to resist . . . What did you call me . . . 'a sweet little thing.' "

He stared at her steadily, an urgent appeal in his full, pale blue gaze, a gaze now fixed strangely on her face, as though he was admiring her with affectionate malice.

"Do you remember saying that, Shadoe?"

"I do. But I think that I can control myself," Shadoe told her in a sardonic voice. "I'm strong enough to resist. I did before. Do you remember that?"

Her own eyes were now wicked. "Yes, but then again, you didn't have to put up with me all night."

"So that's it, you silly witch. You've come here to seduce me! Think that you can keep me here in this damnable place with the pleasures of your body." Shadoe laughed. "Well, I'm not stupid enough to fall for such an adolescent trick!"

"Well, I'm glad to hear that because you know how weak I am when it comes to you, Shadoe." She blinked her eyes at him. "So willing that night. Easy as the girls in the saloon, the ones with rouge on their cheeks, rye whiskey on their breaths. I'm glad that you have so much resolve. Otherwise, I could lose my virtue tonight."

With her words, Shadoe grunted, then muttered a string of oaths before moving past her toward the stairs.

Lilly bit back her growing laughter.

"You're shameless!" he cried. "You're reckless! A tease!"

"I'm yours!"

"Mine? Then you're mad! That's what you are! Mad enough to do anything!"

"Mad for you!"

"Mercy! Lord! You silly witch!" He grabbed the stair railing and shot her a wild look that bordered on despair. "If I had any sense, I would tie you to that damn horse right now!" he bellowed. But a deteriorating look in his eyes warned her that he had no intentions of letting her go. He was going to prove to her that he was strong.

"Put me to bed, Shadoe," she whispered.

She saw him swallow hard. His gaze appeared to mist over with a kind of desperate longing. "I'll put you to bed," he told her with a hint of anguish in his tone.

She smiled gratefully, watching him mount the stairs. "Thank you."

"You better save your thanks," he roared over his shoulder. "Thank me when the morning comes if you please, but God, don't thank me now!"

She slumped against the wall, relieved, almost exhausted. She had won the first battle of the night. But it was going to be a long night, and there were several battles yet to be fought.

A shudder eddied through her. What if she weakened in his arms, weakened under the weight of his desire until she lost the strength even to care about trying to keep him? What if tonight was all she had?

Lilly looked cautiously at his moving form. She had to stay strong. He could not lure her away from her goals. She was the seducer. There were questions that had to be answered. She could give him her body, but he had to give her something in return. Answers.

"Shadoe," she called after him.

Her summon halted his steps mid-flight. He turned sharply and looked down at her. "Had a change of mind, Princess?"

She shook her head and pointed to her clothes which were worn and dusty from the long journey. "No. It's not that. I was just wondering if I could get a bath? I'm so dirty—"

He cut her off and hollered up the steps, "Lo Ching!"

Chapter 21

How a simple minute could have appeared as an hour, Shadoe could not understand. How he ever got himself into this predicament was even a greater mystery. Whatever, the darkness dragged and dragged, and then it seemed as though it had come to a stop, languishing with some sort of mocking pride. It laughed at him, and in its stillness made him realize just how weak he was as a man.

Mercy! Where was the first sign of morning light? Lilly would leave then. Just a quick bath, a clean shirt, some sleep, and then she'd promised to go away.

Shadoe listened, heard her sounds, then put his hands to his ears. Still the sounds came, splashing water, her low giggles, a moan, then a long drawn-out sigh that seemed like music, rising out of her throat, pure liquid, almost a complete melody. He thought he would die.

She was there, Lilly, bathing in a tub of warmed

water. No, not Lilly, just soft skin, wet and warm, just light and fire in her smoke-colored eyes, and heat. Yes, heat.

Even though a door was between them, he could feel her heat, and he burned, curled like an ash in a blue flame.

He was dizzy. He was desperate. Where did Lo Ching go? he thought. Wasn't that little man always around? He needed him. Oh, yes. That brave little Chinaman could save him, watch him with those slanted accusing eyes so that he wouldn't turn the knob and open the door. Only Lo Ching was not there to stand guard, but finally asleep in his room.

The water splashed again, and Shadoe sucked another anguished breath. He could wake the man again. Play cards. Do anything. Do something.

Shadoe shook his head. He should have stayed downstairs on the sofa with his cigarettes and whiskey, but her sounds had led him up the stairs, her wicked, womanly sounds.

He knew that she was waiting for him, and the hard heat of his body made him stiffen. Where had been his resolve? Gone, scattered to the winds? Where had been that great battle of the wills, his against hers? Vanished, lost in their mutual desire?

He loved her, and the darkness beneath his closed eyes suddenly filled with the color of her, bright, hot, and blinding. Burning. Burning. Burning. Shadoe groaned. Her sounds pulled and sizzled within him. And he could stand it no longer. He was on fire, and he would have her and pay his dues to the devil! He would love her, worship her body with his hands, and whatever the consequences, he would accept in defeat. After all, where Lilly was concerned, he was already a man destroyed.

Lilly . . . sweet . . . sweet Lilly . . . Shadoe smiled, then reached out with his hands and twisted the knob of his bedroom door.

When Lilly heard the door creak, she was wrapping a linen sheet around her wet body. At the sound, a shiver ran through her, strong, relentless, bringing with it a strange kind of excitement, flashing like electric currents, running strand for strand in the thin layers of water on her skin.

She felt on fire! And a thousand thoughts suddenly flooded her mind. What to do? What to say?

Yes, Shadoe was there. Shadoe was coming to her.

She blinked, and the door opened. Her heart fluttered like beating wings. And then she saw him.

Words were out of her reach. The capability to think was lost. Everything around her was suddenly very much in the present and very physical. Her body had irrevocably become her master.

There was a long stretch of silence as she watched him close the door, and then he stared at her as though she was unreal, as though she was just a terrifying dream floating like a white-draped ghost in front of his eyes.

For one heady moment, Lilly thought she saw love, but then his gaze narrowed, and Shadoe smiled at her, a slow, burning smile that somehow felt rough against her eyes. This was a man she didn't know.

She swallowed, and her saliva ran thick down her throat. Instinctively, she stepped back from him.

"Come here," he told her.

Her feet were rooted to the floor.

Shadoe called her again, same two words, too blunt and too compelling. And suddenly Lilly felt an overwhelming sense that this was wrong, that this was not the way she wanted it to be, not nearly the way she had planned.

Her mind screamed, *I have no control! I have no control!* And then another dizzying thought, *Shadoe will swallow me up until I am nothing.* And still, another voice cried, *Let him have you.*

"Come here," he repeated a third time as he lifted his hand toward her. He took one step, then another. "I need you." And his words fell on her like chains, dragging her toward him.

She took a step, stopped, struggling against them. *Words . . . words . . . words . . .* She could fight them.

Another step.

Too many questions. Where was that vixen? That witch? That intent seducer who had schemed and schemed for this moment? Where was that woman so anxious to get this man in the bedroom? *Gone,* thought Lilly. Someone else stood in her place, a lone shapely mess of flesh and bone, engulfed in feelings that were new and strange and exciting.

His eyes burned her, and though he had yet to touch her, Lilly ached between her thighs, a deep, gnawing feeling.

"This is what you wanted," Shadoe told her. "There's no going back now."

And Lilly knew it was true. But she'd not thought, not imagined that it would begin like this. What was this? No seduction. No tender words. Just raw and open sex. It certainly was not like that night in the buggy!

They matched each other's steps, finally face to face. His hand touched her face, and Lilly closed her eyes. The ache between her thighs was now almost painful. It called to her, called again and again as his thumb ran over her cheek, called her in a language that only her body knew.

"You have the softest skin," he whispered.

Lilly opened her eyes and looked at him. His shirt was opened. She touched him, heard Shadoe moan slightly as her fingers ran up and down his chest. His breathing was ragged, but she liked the way it sounded, shallow and fast, the way her heart was beating. Then Lilly circled her arms around his neck. The linen dropped to the floor, crumpled at their feet, forgotten.

Shadoe leaned over and took her in his arms, kissing her, his teeth nipping at her lower lip, letting go, playing with her mouth. And Lilly kissed him back with a sense of urgency and unfamiliarity.

When he pulled away, she licked his lips with the tip of her tongue. "I need you."

He said nothing, and Lilly thought it was right that he didn't, that for the moment everything had been said.

She followed him toward the bed.

Shadoe fell against it, his back against the headboard. He pulled her down onto him, and at first Lilly thought he was going to roll her over, but he didn't.

His hands grabbed the back of her thighs, drawing them apart, drawing her on top of him.

"I love you," he told her suddenly, and Lilly thought she'd faint at the sound of his voice. It was altered, strangely hoarse, those love words

filled with the tenderness that she had been waiting years and years to hear.

She leaned over him, kissed him, let her hair fall
in his face.

Shadoe moaned again, reached out and pressed
his hands against her body, his fingers, then
thumbs stealing over her breasts, her nipples in
slow circles.

She pressed her weight against him, trying to
satisfy the ache that was now pounding. Shadoe
grabbed her buttocks, pushing her against his
pants.

"Feel that?"

She moaned, "I'm dying."

"Not yet, but you soon will."

"Then kill me," Lilly told him as her body arched
again and again against his jeans.

The material was rough and hard against her
skin, but she liked the way it felt between her legs,
the way it seemed to ease the gnawing.

She cried with pleasure, and her voice made
Shadoe move. In one quick, mercurial moment,
he slid his body halfway out of his pants, then
pulled Lilly down firmly onto his lap. There was
no warning as he rushed into her, hot, hard and
relentless, and then he stopped.

Lilly gasped, and her head fell back. She gripped
his shoulders. The relentless ache was vanquished,
dissolved around the hardness of his body. Impaled, she was suddenly afraid to move.

"More?" Shadoe whispered.

She shifted her gaze to his face. Her eyes closed
and opened, and closed and opened as she stared
at him. He was sweating. He looked almost as
drunk as she felt, and she smiled at him, a weak

smile as she started to move against the sweet ache that was rolling up inside of her. Somehow, that first discomfort had faded.

"Shadoe, I need to move."

Her words appeared to be all he wanted. His hands gripped her body, pressing as he pushed. The two of them merged completely. The ache grew and grew, and Lilly wanted to scream, but the breath caught in her throat.

She closed her eyes again, the black against her lids suddenly red, then white, then nothing. She could feel him growing more urgent, feel the rough denim sliding against her legs, faster, faster, and she was suddenly lost.

"Oh, Lilly," he muttered.

She could barely hear him, but she felt him, deep, deeper, hard, harder, one thrust after the other, each more urgent than before. Between her thighs was a fire. Pulsating, desperate, it was Shadoe consuming her, swallowing her, and she let herself go.

His hands twisted at her flesh, clawed at her, pressed her body onto his with the crudeness of an animal, wild and frenzied.

Lilly cried, a small, tight scream that was soon smothered by his wet mouth. He still moved, once, twice, and then the final thrust that pushed a breath from his lungs, sharp and ragged, a guttural sound that rushed to the back of Lilly's throat.

She gasped, and fell against him, a slumped and spent form. Shadoe kissed her again and again, and between kisses he murmured her name over and over. She heard him tell her that he loved her.

Lilly lifted herself so that she could see his

face. His eyes never seemed bluer, his face never handsomer. Yet, she found that she could say nothing as he smiled at her.

"Speechless for once," he said in an amused tone, and Lilly knew that he was pleased at her response.

She nodded.

"I understand." He stared intently at her. "Nothing will ever be the same," he remarked as he reached up to run his fingers through her damp hair. "We're different and everything will be different to us in some way."

She found her voice. "Even this?"

Shadoe laughed. "Especially this!" He gave her a quick kiss on the tip of her nose. "The more we do it, the better. There are things you've never dreamed of, Princess. Things I want to show you. Mercy, if only you knew what a man and woman can be with each other."

Her expression altered. She'd not thought of a second time, only the first, but now it seemed imperative that she knew he would make love to her again. "Then we will do—"

"Oh, Lilly! Yes!" He rolled her over, lying atop her. "Yes and yes and yes. As much as you want to."

She squirmed at the sensations she was beginning to feel. "Now?" Lilly questioned with an imploring smile.

"Mercy, woman, give me a moment! I've just barely got my breath again."

"But, Shadoe, I have that strange feeling again."

His gaze narrowed. "Where?" he asked with a smile, his hand sliding easily down to her thighs. "Here?"

She couldn't help but moan at the way his fingers sank so effortlessly into her body. Already, he knew so much about her, knew ways of touching her, of bringing her pleasure, and Lilly wanted his knowledge. There was no embarrassment. No shame. Only need and love.

She stirred against his hand, and the blood rushed to her cheeks. "Don't tease me! Not now. Not like this."

"Who said I was teasing?" His mouth fell on hers again, and this time it was a hard kiss. When their lips parted, Lilly gasped as she pushed at him in protest.

"What's wrong?"

Her brows furrowed as she declared with a hint of desperation, "For God's sake, Shadoe! This time, do take off your pants."

Chapter 22

At first light, Shadoe and Lilly quickly rode out toward the Oasis. Halfway between his house and Weatherly, the line shack was a good place for them to stop and rest—and talk.

Shadoe knew there were more words to be said, questions, answers, decisions, too many words. And God, he had already said so much to her, told her that he loved her, whispered words in her ears, tender things that he'd never said to another woman. But he was afraid to say more. And he didn't want any more questions. From the shack, Shadoe had planned for them to go their separate ways, he to Montfort, Lilly to Weatherly.

"What are you going to say to Papa?" she asked him when they arrived at the line shack.

The question was quick, said in a firm tone, and though he was reluctant to say anything at all to her, Shadoe knew that he would have to give Lilly a substantial answer. But it did not come out right.

The first words that poured from his mouth were, "I haven't decided."

She frowned miserably at his reply, and Shadoe knew instantly that his uncertainty troubled her.

"What do you want me to say?" he asked her.

They were sitting on their horses. Lilly leaned back in her saddle, and looked at him for a long moment. With no hat and brim to hide her face, her eyes caught the sunlight. They sparkled bright and clear in a kind of achy gaze.

"Do you have to ask?"

He turned away from her question, afraid to look at her pain-filled gray eyes, afraid that they might suddenly fill with shimmering tears, and he couldn't face her tears, not now, not after their lovemaking. He heard her long sigh.

"You know what I want, Shadoe," Lilly said, and he listened, though he didn't look at her. "I don't want you to sell the ranch. I don't want you to leave me again. I want you to tell Papa that you've changed your mind, that you love me. I want you here. I want and want and want." A deep breath followed, and her voice strengthened. "But what do you want? That's the real issue."

He shifted his gaze back to her, saw that her lips were pale and trembling, and he heard himself say so easily, "To stay with you."

But Lilly looked anything but happy at his words. "Then why don't you?" she asked in a desperate tone. "Isn't it enough that we love each other? That we have always loved each other? Isn't it enough that we are here now, together?"

"No."

It was a small word, but a grand and forceful one. Shadoe saw Lilly stiffen at the sound of it.

"I knew it. Dammit! I knew it!" she exclaimed. "It doesn't matter. Nothing I do matters. You left me before. You're capable of doing it again." Lilly twisted her reins. The small mare threw her head back nervously. "Nothing matters at all!"

"Not true," Shadoe contradicted as he reached out and grabbed the reins from her hands. He calmed the mare, then attempted to calm Lilly. "Everything you do matters to me. It always has. It's just . . . just that—"

"Just what?" she asked, her voice edgy. "What could be so important that it could keep us from happiness? Tell me! Give me some reason why you can't stay with me. I need to understand."

Shadoe shook his head. How could she understand what he barely understood himself? Tell the truth? He stiffened at the thought, resisted and resisted as the past rolled through his head like a muddy, murky stream of garbage. The lies had become his way of life. The lies had been his choice. His decision. Could he ever tell the whole truth?

Yes, Lilly had forgiven him for leaving her, for marrying Anne without even an explanation. But there was more to it than Lilly could imagine. Secrets. Dark secrets that lay at the edge of Lilly's heart, and hearts could be such fragile things.

No. He was afraid to take the risk. He couldn't stay. There was misery here. Misery and maybe even more death.

He flinched at the last thought, watching her face, her shining gray eyes so full of pleading, and a part of him longed to tell her, to cleanse himself of the past, but he'd promised himself, promised others.

And he had his pride. A man needed his pride, Shadoe told himself with justification. If he told her, what would have been the value of hiding the facts for so long? Of living the way he had lived? And wouldn't he appear weak for choosing to do so now just because he had touched her, made love with her? Wasn't his pride stronger than that?

Tell her the truth? Satisfy her? Shadoe swallowed hard. Would truth ever lead to satisfaction?

Inside him, a voice warned, *The past is dead.*

"I can't tell you," he suddenly said.

"Why?"

No answer.

She scowled at him. "Then just tell me one thing, one simple answer to a question that I've already asked you?"

He was puzzled. "What are you talking about?"

Lilly shook her head. "No, Shadoe. I won't explain. Just promise me now that you will tell me the answer. It's not about why you left. It's not about Anne. It's not even about why you are determined to leave me now." She leaned closer to him. "If you won't tell me the truth, then at least let me have the chance to find the truth for myself! Don't I deserve that much from you?"

You couldn't, he thought, *you could never discover the truth. Not with a single answer. Not from me.*

He hesitated, shifted restlessly in his seat, and a thousand ambivalent thoughts rattled his brain, until he thought he would go crazy.

Shadoe stared at her, really stared at her. God, how he wanted to marry this woman! From the beginning, she had been everything to him: as a child—happiness; as an adolescent—hope; then as a young woman—love and finally desire. *Oh, Lord, help me. . . .*

"Please, Shadoe, for today, for the love we shared today," he heard her saying, and the sound of it touched him.

"Ask," he finally replied.

"Then promise me the truth."

"I promise."

She stared pointedly at him, and Shadoe suddenly wished that he had not committed himself. His throat tightened as he watched her face. There was an odd glint in her eyes, one that warned him that she had intended this moment from the beginning of last night's events, that this was as much a part of the seductive scheme as coming to his house and taking a bath.

"Oh, Lilly, spill it. What do you want to know?" he growled.

"Was Joseph with you the day you shot Sam Miller? I know that you said he wasn't. That he said he wasn't. But I've always felt uncomfortable with that story. I don't know why, but that one day changed you. It's as though Sam's death was the beginning of everything that went wrong. For you. For Joseph. For my father and me. I need you to tell me if Joseph was there when Sam died."

For a moment, he was too stunned to reply. *The wily little bitch!* He almost laughed, but couldn't. It was too damn wicked to laugh about. So, she was more clever than he'd imagined. That one question, the one that she had popped in the door with last night, was now demanding an honest answer. It was obvious from the keen look on her face, from the curiosity in her voice that Lilly thought Sam's death was the thread that would untie the knotted mystery. But would she really want to unravel it?

"Well?" she asked.

Shadoe took a breath. "What difference would it make if he was? It still won't change the past. It won't bring Sam back. It certainly won't decide what I say to your father." He tried to discourage her. "Besides, some answers are a little hazy around the edges. Once you find them, you don't know what to do with them. And I'd hate to know that you're wasting your days—"

"Maybe I would. Maybe not. All I know is that it would be a beginning. And God knows, Shadoe, you may not need the truth, but I do."

He looked away for a moment, then quickly glanced back at her. There was a strangeness about her, a strength that he didn't know she had, and it scared as well as enticed him. She wanted the truth so bad. Maybe too bad, and Shadoe suddenly thought of Joseph. "Lilly, are you thinking about asking Joseph about this?"

"I've already asked."

He held back his surprise, his fears. His eyes narrowed. "And?"

Her voice turned light, and she smiled at him. "He gave your story down to the last word. Sort of silly it was when he told it . . . wrote it in a letter to me after I had come back from finishing school in Chicago. That's what got me to wondering. I never really thought about it until I read the way Joseph described it—you and Sam in some fight over a game of cards. Sam drunk, pulling out a knife and your shooting him in self-defense. Right down to the last detail, just as you told the sheriff, almost word for word."

"So that should have ended it for you."

"Maybe he lied to me."

Startled, Shadoe suddenly chuckled. "What?"

"I said maybe Joseph was lying to me."

Shadoe repressed the urge to laugh again. He pursed his lips and viewed the flat land, thinking of how absurd it was to have Lilly ask this question after all these years. If only she had asked that day at the line shack, that morning when he was leaving her for Anne. If only he had told her the whole story? If only. . . . He frowned. It was too late, and the question was almost painful.

"Did Joseph lie to me?" she asked.

Shadoe glanced at her again, and asked very calmly, "What if he did? Is it really all that important, especially now?"

She nodded.

But he only shook his head. Lilly had always adored her brother, too much, idolized Joseph. Shadoe suddenly frowned, for he had idolized Joseph, too, loved him too much, loved him like the brother he had never had. He sighed, thinking. Looking back, the reasons were simple. The McFalls had been his true family, the family that the bastard child needed in order to feel whole, to feel accepted and loved. The McFalls had been everything to him, and he had loved them all too much, loved them until he was blind.

He stared achingly at Lilly. She was as blind as he had been, but somehow there was happiness in being ignorant, of not knowing and understanding reality, of seeing the world only as you wanted to see it. There was peace in unawareness. *Oh, Lilly, you're better off not knowing.*

He resisted telling her anything. "I know you, Lilly, and I can't see you believing anything false of that golden-haired brother of yours. You worship him just like your father worships him. The laughing, brilliant boy with the world at his feet. The heir and aristocrat. A lie passing from his lips? Not in a million years."

"Maybe there's a reason he lied. A good reason?"

He turned darkly amused at her hopeful speculation, knowing well that though she was asking the right questions, she was still far away from the truth. But he couldn't get serious about this, not now, or he would tell her everything, spill his guts in a moment of anger. And now was definitely not the time to be telling tales.

So he fought for some distance, teasing her, smiling, joking as he asked, "Protecting me? You think Joseph was?"

"Someone is protecting someone. That's obvious. But why and who and what for, I don't know."

"And you're gonna find all that out by yourself?"

She smiled that determined and brave smile. "Well, you certainly aren't going to tell me anything."

He shot her an admiring look. "Well, I'll tell you that one answer. Might as well." Silently, *After all, you have guessed the truth on this count and, besides, I want to end this conversation here, now.* He also wanted to ride away. "All right. Yes, Princess. You get the truth. But no more questions." He nudged his horse and moved past her, saying as he went, "Joseph was there, right there when Sam Miller died."

When Shadoe rode off to Montfort, Lilly was watching, still smiling, thinking of her lover, relishing the look of defeat in his tired blue eyes, the way he had reluctantly answered her question. Oh God, that simple, obvious question that should have been asked so many years ago.

Why didn't I ask it? The answer to the question told so much, and yet . . . Why had Joseph lied? She quickly lost her smile, frowned heavily as she thought about Joseph, about the relationship between him and Shadoe. Recalling her girlish poetry notebooks, she remembered those days when as a young adolescent girl, she had secretly cloaked her life and love in desperate metaphors and bad similes. Joseph had been the sun, and Shadoe the moon, both light and shade, twin spheres ruling the earth, not as equals, but as one mixed influence. And Shadoe had been darkness, the icy moon, the sun's vassal.

Lilly winced at the symbols in her mind. Misused, but true! How true! Whatever Shadoe did in those days, somehow Joseph was involved.

As a young girl who loved and idolized her handsome, older brother, it was difficult for her to see Joseph and Shadoe's relationship as anything but good. But now?

She was a woman, a woman in love with a man who was obviously torturing himself. She was also the sister of a man she'd not seen in years, a brother who had lied to her about Sam's death.

But why? Why didn't Joseph want anyone to know that he was there? What was the point? More important who was lying to protect whom? Had Shadoe lied for Joseph instead of the other way around? And if so, how many times had Shadoe lied for Joseph all those years together?

Dear God! Whose failings are whose? she asked herself.

And then she was thinking only of Shadoe again, of his lips and hands, the way they had felt on her body.

She looked up at the sky. Morning. A time for new beginnings. A chance. A chance for love . . . for Shadoe in her life.

Hope had finally come home again, and she felt so very happy. Shadoe loved her, and even if he wouldn't tell her the truth, she knew she could find it.

Luke Miller knew some of the answers.

Her plans. She had so many schemes, and they were all unfolding, one by one.

Lilly gently nudged the mare. "Let's go home, Princess. We've got work to do."

Chapter 23

Before Lilly had ridden very far, she spotted the riders in the distance. She quickly lifted her hand to her brow, shading the sun's glare. She was riding east, and the light was shining hot in her eyes.

Was she in any danger? The fact that Shadoe was riding to Montfort to see her father, that he might be signing away the Double S suddenly evaporated from her mind.

She pulled her rifle from its sleeve and counted. There were six riders, and they were coming directly toward her. She watched them carefully, saw the direction of their path, and knew immediately that they were not from Weatherly for they were too far south on the open range, deep into land that belonged neither to the Double S nor to her father. Maybe they were riding from Montfort.

As they drew closer, she finally relaxed. They were from the Woodward ranch, presumably cut-

ting across to the road that led north upside the
Blitzen River.

They all passed, but one. Lilly recognized every
face. Casey Whitmore. Tully and Martin Whitten.
Dice Jennings. Next to last in line, the gunman,
Pepper Maddox.

She eyed him carefully. He never looked at her,
and Lilly shivered at the sight of him. Pepper was
a real gunfighter. For years he had followed the
boom towns of the West, hiring out for jobs that
no man would speak about in public. Fifteen years
ago, he had come to the Blitzen Valley, working for
the Woodwards exclusively.

Lilly didn't like him. Who could? Flat-faced, a
deep scar over his left brow, those strange, black
and menacing eyes, he was ugly and every bit the
gunman who was the epitome of lawlessness. He
had actually killed a man one time for simply
ordering beer instead of rye. The fact that this
man was riding with Tom made Lilly strain with
thoughts, thoughts that had never really occurred
to her before.

Pepper hated Shadoe, and Lilly unexpectedly
realized that if Shadoe stayed in Oregon, sooner
or later, the two would face a shootout.

Shootout! The lone word struck her painfully.
How could she have been so self-centered not to
realize that if Shadoe stayed in Oregon, he would
have many enemies to face again?

The realization collided with her recent happiness, quickly reminding her that she had been acting almost childishly in her pursuit of Shadoe.
She also began to understand Shadoe's motives
for leaving, for staying away. Staying in Oregon,
facing the facts would be easier said than done.

When Tom reached Lilly, he yanked back on his reins and stared, his dark eyes wide and curious at her presence. She could see his bewilderment, plain and hard in his expression.

"What in the devil are you doing out here this early?"

"Trying to tame this new mare of mine," she told him with a half-smile. "Thought a good hard ride would do her some good."

"She's a pretty mare."

"Thanks. One of Luke's breed."

His gaze narrowed at her reply, and for a moment, Lilly thought she caught a glimpse of anger, but then he smiled at her. "I ain't seen much of you lately."

"That's not my fault," Lilly was quick to say. "I've ridden over several times only to find Jesse alone at the house." She paused, then bluntly remarked, "He's brooding too much, Tom. There's something worrying him. And it's not Joey."

"Jesse thinks too much, that's all. Thinkin' and a moonin' over Molly Andrews."

"I don't think it's Molly who's bothering him."

Tom pushed his hat on the back of his head and squinted against the morning light. Sweat dripped from his chin, and he reached up to wipe it on the sleeve of his shirt. "It is. That young girl he's plannin' to marry is drivin' him silly."

"Maybe he needs you around a little more, some emotional support."

"What the boy needs is to stay busy!" Tom snapped. "He just sits around the house."

"You seem busy enough," Lilly commented dryly. She shifted her gaze to the riders who had stopped about thirty yards to the north. So Tom was riding with these men. It was not a new thought. But for the first time, it appeared a threatening one. "Where are you riding so hard for?" she asked.

Tom pointed north. "Up to the lakes for a day or two. Got some business."

"And you need Dice and Pepper for *business?*" she questioned cryptically. "What's going on, Tom?"

His expression was shuttered as he looked at her, and Lilly suddenly felt queer inside. Why would Tom and Pepper be heading up to the lakes? And why would he be so sullen about her interest?

Her expression became frantic as she spoke, "Has something happened? At the Daniels' place? Luke's?"

"Luke?" Tom voice held a hint of malice. "Why would you be so worried over him?" A slight frown marred his forehead. "Are you seeing Luke Miller?"

She hesitated. "Why do you ask?"

"Because I hadn't realized that Luke interested you at all. Now here you are ridin' one of his mares, worrin' over him. It makes me wonder if he's not sweet on you."

"Well, now that you mention it, I'm planning to go to the church social with Luke."

Tom's mouth fell open. "I thought you were goin' with me?" He raised his hands over his head in a sort of mute resignation.

"I never said so, Tom." She paused and watched him carefully. He was genuinely shocked at her news, and she could see that he was furious with her decision, so she told him rather plainly, "You've been so busy, Tom. And so distant since your mother's death that I thought it best if we didn't go together. It just doesn't feel right anymore, us being together, that is. I think it's the proper thing to end the relationship now." She feigned a smile. "Of course, we can always stay friends, but it's time that I made new friends. I've depended on you and Jesse for too long now."

"You're takin' a lot for granted, ain't you, Lilly?" Tom gave her a serene smile, and in a composed voice, he said, "What makes you think you can go and change everyone's way of thinkin' with just a few pretty words? Huh? Saying it don't make it so."

She grew tense at his hasty words which seemed so out of character coming from Tom. Too calm, she thought, too full of underlying meaning. She'd expected him to balk, but never did she expect steely words layered with a threat. That's just how the words sounded, foreboding, as if she was stupid to think that she could really ever have anyone else but him, stupid to think that he would accept her explanations.

She tried to smile at him, but the tension in her face restricted her attempt. All Lilly could do was stare at him, abruptly fearful that somehow she had unintentionally created some sort of vengeful monster.

Yes, Tom looked different, every bit the man who could ride with his wild buckaroos, and Lilly thought that the moment reeked of irony. *Why now? Why should I feel this fear the morning after I've made love with Shadoe? Why should I start doubting on the morning that offers me so many chances?*

Lilly grimaced. She had clung to Tom in Shadoe's absence, never realizing in her obsessiveness for Shadoe that Tom was not whom she thought him to be at all, and suddenly, she was sincerely regretful, knew that it was not really Tom's fault for feeling the way he did about everything.

"I'm sorry, Tom. I have wronged you."

"Wronged me?"

She nodded. "Yes. Wronged you. All this time, I was selfish with your feelings, using them like some foolish young girl. But I'm not a girl anymore. I'm a woman, and I realize now that I've made a terrible mistake."

The morning breeze tugged at the strands of hair around her face, and Tom's gaze followed them as they floated in front of her eyes. "A woman are you? Since when?"

"Tom, please—"

"A woman since Luke started courtin' you?" He snickered. "Maybe Shadoe?"

Her eyes widened at the suggestive questioning, but she steadied herself, giving him a rebellious look. "I don't think I have to answer questions like that."

A whistle sliced the air, and Tom looked to see Pepper waving him on. He signaled at the gunman, then turned to cast Lilly a tired look.

"You know, Lilly. It's not your lack of love that really bothers me," he suddenly announced in a voice filled with sarcasm. "I knew that I was never really good enough for you from the beginning. But I'd hoped, even planned on it. Nope. It ain't none of that, not really. It's that damn Sinclair. He's been back barely a month and look at all of us. Maw's dead. Joey's gone. He's even talked your father into buying his ranch just so I cain't have it. I hate that bastard! And now Luke Miller and you goin' to church together." Tom chuckled hoarsely. "I guess if Shadoe had to pick a man for you, Luke would be him. Yeah, Shadoe likes ole Luke. Always did."

"You can't blame all that on Shadoe!"

"I can and I will! In fact, I already have!"

"But it's ridiculous!"

Tom turned his mount, gathering his reins tighter in his hands. "Say what you want. It don't matter. You really ain't never planned on marryin' me," Tom muttered. "So be it. But I promise you this, Lilly. Sinclair will be sorry. He'll pay for the misery he's caused my family, and I cain't let my love for you git in the way of it. Remember that."

He kicked his horse.

Lilly anxiously shifted forward in the saddle, as he joined the others. She watched for a long time, seeing them disappear into the bright horizon.

And suddenly, everything went awry in her mind. She'd seen Tom's face, heard his words. They rang through her head like wild bells in a storm, tolling some impending disaster.

"Oh, God!" she cried, covering her mouth with her hand. Could it be possible? Could Shadoe be in danger?

"Oh, no," she moaned. If Shadoe stayed in Oregon, Tom would kill him.

James McFall sat in the law office, worrying. For the last hour, while he waited for his solicitor, he had been looking at his jittery companion. Shadoe had barely said a word to him, and from the moment the young man had arrived, he had been pacing constantly. Back and forth across the room, Shadoe had walked, smoking one cigarette after another.

The air was thick, and James found himself growing more and more uncomfortable.

"I wish you'd be still for a while," James said. The older man gestured with his hand. "All this moving from here to there is making me dizzy. Do sit down, Shadoe!"

Glancing at him, Shadoe stopped, and James could see that something was terribly wrong. The clear eyes were dull and listless. The face was awash with anxiety. He watched anxiously as Shadoe sank into a chair. "What is bloody wrong with you?"

Shadoe looked at him, and James noticed that he was having difficulty getting the words out.

"Well, speak. Say what's on your mind!"

"I'm having trouble with this, sir."

"Trouble with what?"

Shadoe turned away before he spoke. "I don't think I can sell the ranch. Not now. I thought . . . But now I just can't . . ."

James was still looking at the back of Shadoe's head, and he heard the younger man draw a heavy breath. "What are you talking about? You can't sell the ranch? It's all I've heard about for weeks from you!"

"I can't leave here," Shadoe said as he pounded his fists against the arm of the chair. He turned back to give James a cold, hard stare. "I can't leave now. Not even if I wanted to. Damn her! Damn her! Damn her!"

James's brows knitted together, and a deep scowl settled across his face. *Her*. The word screamed through his head. He poised himself. "What are you saying?"

Shadoe grimaced. "I can't leave Lilly."

"Why?"

"Because I love her."

"You what?"

"You heard me."

"Yes, I did, but I'm hoping that somehow my ears deceive me!" James stood, moving to Shadoe's chair.

Shadoe looked up into his face. "I love her, McFall, and I don't intend on betraying her again. I can't. I just can't. I won't betray myself either." He rose from his seat, and James flinched at his closeness. He stepped back from the younger man.

"So you mean to stay and marry her!" James spat.

Shadoe shook his head. "Marry her? I don't know that at all. Marry? Lilly may not want to marry me when all is said and done." Shadoe drew a long breath. "But she means everything to me, and I know what the Double S means to her. Not just the land. But Sinclair blood on the Double S. I never realized the depth of her feelings until . . ." Shadoe paused. "I can't sell the ranch. I can't leave here without giving Lilly a chance for what she really wants. No matter what it costs me or anyone else. In the end, she may find that she really doesn't want me. But dammit! I mean to give her that chance!"

"What in damnation does all that mean?"

"You'd never understand," Shadoe said. "How could you? You never thought I was good enough for Lilly from the very beginning. And you made me feel that way, even though you cared for me. Even though you talked of us marrying, you never really thought I was fit for her. But I loved Lilly. I needed her. Somehow, she made everything I was better. And what I did, I justified by saying that I did it for her and you, but now I see what it's all brought. Just misery. I thought I could put it all to rest, but I see now that even if I could, Lilly never would. It wouldn't matter at all whether I stayed or went. Lilly would still be caught up in the past, searching for her answers, longing to know why I abandoned her. She's the kind of woman who would carry that need inside of her for all her days. It's not the legacy I intended."

"What in the hell are you talking about? Speak plain!"

"Joseph . . . that's what. I lied for him. Time and time again, I lied! And one lie led to another until I lost sight of what was really the truth."

James bristled at the shocking words. "How dare you speak of Joseph that way!" He raised shaking fists to Shadoe. "How dare you speak of love! You broke my daughter's heart, left her for Anne Woodward. And as for Joseph. He was a brother to you. Gave you everything, and what did you do? You broke my son's heart, too!"

"That's the biggest lie of them all!" Shadoe blurted as he moved hurriedly to the door. He reached for the knob, jerking. The door snapped open, and Shadoe turned to stare at James. "Joseph McFall never had a heart, you foolish old man! Never had a heart at all! And as for what he gave me. Shall I tell you what he really gave me?" Shadoe's expression loosened. "A son. That's what he gave me, old man, a son. Anne Woodward's child."

James paled at the words. His face pinched as the door slammed shut in his face. He was shaking, unmovable, so angry that he could have struck Shadoe. But he stood fixed.

A son! A son? Anne Woodward's son . . . "Oh, God!" Then he muttered, "No . . . no . . . no . . ."

Chapter 24

The next day Lilly didn't leave the castle nor did she have any contact with her father. She passed the time in her room, trying to read, thinking a dozen foolish thoughts about Joseph and Anne. About Luke. About Tom. And always about Shadoe.

Sometimes she rehearsed in a low voice exactly what she would say to Shadoe the next time she saw him. But what could she say? That Tom was crazy, even capable of violence? Could she tell Shadoe, even though he had decided not to sell the ranch, that she wanted him to go back to San Francisco before there was serious trouble?

Not hardly. It would be almost impossible, especially after their lovemaking, to tell Shadoe that she had changed her mind about the ranch, about him, about everything. Shadoe was no fool. If she backed away from him now, she knew that he would be suspicious. Besides, it was a lie.

She loved Shadoe, worshipped him with every particle of her existence. And Lilly knew that if Shadoe left her again, she would wither in her bitterness. Her very survival was at stake.

So that left only Tom. But what could she do? Who could she talk to? Her father? Jesse? Shadoe?

One word said about Tom's threats, and Lilly knew what Shadoe would do. He'd force the younger man to a shootout. Lilly was well aware that Shadoe was the better man, but the thought of Shadoe gunning Tom down in a Montfort street seemed barbaric, terrifying, almost catastrophic.

Blood. Tom's. Shadoe's. She could already feel it on her hands.

When she went to sleep that night, Lilly dreamed she was struggling, suffocating in a thickness of danger and fear. Then she was running, fleeing in a stormy world where a strange red wind rushed straight at her, whipping her hair over her head, speeding wildly up the folds of her clothes. It filled her eyes, sealed her nose, her mouth. It smelled and tasted of blood.

And Joseph, Luke and Sam Miller were there. Anne. Even Tom was chasing her, and not far behind was Shadoe, a gun in his hand.

Her face buried in her pillow, Lilly awoke the next morning with a muffled scream.

"You're not to see him again, Lilly!"

Startled at James McFall's abruptness, Lilly side-stepped him and slanted her father a weary glance. It was obvious that he was speaking of Shadoe. The fact that Shadoe had decided not to sell the ranch and to stay in Oregon had everyone in a fluster. But Lilly hadn't expected her father to be so vehement about it, and she had just barely walked into the elegant dining room. No greeting. No smile. Nothing. Only angry words.

"Well, good morning to you, too," she managed to say. She walked to the sideboard, grabbed a Wedgwood plate, and went through the motions of filling it.

"Child, do you hear me? I don't want you to see him again. *Do you hear me!*"

The morning sunlight was harsh, and Lilly's eyes narrowed as she peeked sleepily at her father. He looked a bit wan as if he were cold all over, and his eyes were cloudy. His shoulders rounded conspicuously as he sat slumped at the head of the table, but Lilly knew that voice. It was a tone that brooked no argument from anyone.

"Does it matter?" she said in a cryptic tone, adding to herself, *I don't know if I can stand to hear all of this. Not now. Not with everything else.*

James shook his head, finishing a quick bite of muffin. "Yes, it matters a great deal," he said, watching her closely as she moved to the breakfast table.

"Then, no, I don't understand at all," she complained. Sitting across from him, Lilly carefully unfolded her linen napkin and placed it on her lap. She stared blankly at the plateful of food, the sight of which only sickened her. She glanced back at her father who was still gazing at her with a ruthless stare. "Do you want to explain why?" she asked him bluntly.

He started to say something, but stopped, his mouth already rounded for the word. And then a long moment stretched between them, ending with a heavy sigh from her father.

James finally answered her. "Well, no. I don't want to explain. In fact, there's to be no discussion at all. You don't have to understand my reasons. All I want you to understand is that I mean business." He leaned over and smeared some creamy butter on another muffin. "Just do what I ask."

Lilly toyed at her food with her fork, trying to stay calm, but wanting to scream, scream and shriek till her heart burst! Didn't her father realize that there was something more important than a man's pride? So he had lost the option to buy the Double *S*? But what did that really matter? Couldn't he see the misery in her face, the pain that was ripping her insides apart? Didn't he know that she was in trouble? How desperately she needed him, to tell him about her feelings about Tom, about Shadoe, about everything?

She bit her lip, gained a moment of control, then met his eyes straight on. He was frowning as he ate the muffin. "Why are you so angry, Papa? It's not like you wanted to buy the Double *S* in the first place."

James watched his daughter lift her fork to eat her eggs. He swallowed the sweetened bread, then reached over and poured himself some fresh water. After a swallow, he said, "Just promise me that you will stay away from him, please, Lilly. I have to sort all this out in my mind, and I can't do that if I am worried about you and Shadoe, worried over what's going to happen next. It's . . . just too much. I don't know what you two might end up doing!"

Lilly's temples began to throb. Her head ached, and her indignation was rising. Might do? They had already done too much! Done the deed! Made love! It was too late for her father to worry! In fact, he was too late for many things, and hassling her this morning just because Shadoe hadn't sold him the ranch was simply too much.

Her gaze swung to him with what could only be described as budding impatience. "For God's sake, Papa, you're acting as if I'm a child, as if you really had some control over Shadoe and me, over what we feel toward one another. Don't you think this is something that Shadoe and I need to work out all by ourselves?"

"I don't! That's exactly why I'm talking to you about him. I don't want you to be alone with him—for any reason!"

Lilly dropped her fork with a clatter. "Would you please quit screaming at me? I can hear you well enough. Damn! The whole house can hear you!"

James scowled. "You're not to use profanity at this table, young lady."

Lilly shifted a little in her chair. "I'm sorry." And she was remorseful, though her regrets included more than just blasphemous words.

"I'm sorry, too," James replied, drawing a tired breath. He looked exhausted. "I shouldn't have raised my voice to you, especially when I can't explain my reasons, when I know that you don't understand—"

"You're right. I don't! How in the world all of this business could bother you so much only baffles me. You'd think that Shadoe's not selling you the ranch was some major disaster."

He looked rigid. "It's not the ranch, Lilly." His words wavered. "It's . . . something . . . else."

Her heart fluttered at his low-spoken words. Not the ranch! Lilly really wanted to scream.

She stared at him, looked deeply into her father's eyes, and finally saw it. Oh God! That rare and dreadful emotion. Not misery. Not pain. But fear. Dread and terrible fear. The kind she had been feeling all night. James McFall was actually afraid of something. But what?

Her voice wavered. "If it's not the ranch, then what, Papa?"

He remained silent.

Lilly gathered her strength in a shiver of misgiving and confusion. A small voice inside her head told her what it was, but she could hardly ask the question, though she had been angling toward it for weeks. Never in her wildest thoughts did she expect the question to be aimed at her father.

"This is about Shadoe and Joseph, isn't it? Shadoe told you something the other day. Didn't he? Something about Joseph? Tell me, Papa."

"I can't."

"You mean you won't!"

James clenched his napkin between his hands. A vein pulsated noticeably at his temple. "Please, Lilly. You've got to trust me. I don't want you to see Shadoe. Promise me. Please, daughter. Promise me this." His voice broke, and Lilly thought for a moment that he was going to cry.

She fell back against her chair. Dear God! What had Joseph done? Her brother, the man she had worshipped as a young girl, the older sibling who had been her image of the perfect man had done something? What had he done to Shadoe? Lilly shook her head at the thought. What was the lie that Shadoe had been hiding all these years? And why had Shadoe told her father and not her?

Her father's eyes misted as he waited, waited for her to answer, but Lilly couldn't answer. Her back stiffened as a rush of ambivalence ran up her spine, and her fingers were now kneading the tablecloth in front of her.

She had wanted Shadoe home in Oregon. She had wanted this moment, the moment of truth, but now, she was squirming in her chair like a coward. It all seemed too much, this truth, opening old wounds. The memories of the past played in her head, round and round, reminding Lilly of the pain she and her father had suffered so many years ago.

Sinclair will be sorry, she suddenly heard Tom say. *He'll pay for the misery he's caused my family, and I cain't let my love for you stand in the way of it. . . .*

She shivered, pushed Tom and his threats from her mind.

"Promise me," her father was whispering, and Lilly dropped her eyes to the table, unable to look at her father's face.

What had she done? Was she responsible? If only she had plotted to go to San Francisco with Shadoe, instead of scheming to keep him in Oregon. She had never dreamed she'd hurt so many people in the process.

And yet as long as she and Shadoe breathed, they would be a temptation to each other. Their fascination for each other had begun so many years ago. He for the civilized princess. She for the untamed cowboy. They would always be tempted.

She sighed and knew the future. The secrets, the lies, they had to die before anyone else did.

She lifted her gaze, and squinted against the glaring light. But how torn she felt as to a solution. What she needed was time, time away from Shadoe, time away from Tom, time to figure out what was happening and why. In an awkward way, her father was offering her this.

She hesitated, but when the words came out, they came easy. "I promise."

James's expression turned wide with shock at so quick a resignation. "Then you agree?"

Lilly pushed away from the table and walked around to the other end. Leaning over her father, she wrapped her arms around him. "This is one promise I will keep, Papa."

The front door opened, and voices rose from the entrance hall. There were words, two male voices, then three. But Lilly ignored them as she hugged her father reassuringly, telling him that she loved him, that somehow everything would work out for the best.

James whimpered a thank you and squeezed her arm. "Oh, Lilly, say the words, say you won't see him so that I can truly believe you, that I can hear and rest."

"I promise, Papa. I won't see Shadoe again—"

"You'll have to break that promise," came the jarring interruption, and both Lilly and her father jerked to see Shadoe standing in the doorway.

Chapter 25

Both displeasure and impatience were in Shadoe's eyes, his stance, stoical and proud. He was looking directly at her.

Obviously, Shadoe had overheard her promise, and Lilly found herself trembling at the thought of it, at the sight of him. What a fool she was to think that she could look this man in the face and tell him to leave her alone! Shadoe was a temptation that would never die.

Beside him stood Dan Hadley and Lewis Smith.

"What in damnation is going on here?" James rose quickly from his chair, motioning violently to the men with his hands. "Couldn't this wait until after breakfast?"

For Lilly, Shadoe's immediate response faded in the rush of blood and excitement that pounded stubbornly inside her head. Lilly could see his mouth work, but not a word of what he was saying was audible to her.

All she could do was return Shadoe's stare, drawn to it like a white moth to a blue-burning flame. She felt hot, dizzy, slightly dazed. She tried to look away, but couldn't. She couldn't even utter a word of greeting.

It was strange, but the sight of Shadoe fascinated and alarmed her, made Lilly feel things that she thought impossible. It was as if her body remembered his hands, recalled, inch by inch, the hot force of his being thrust so deeply into hers.

But then reality came crashing in as Lilly heard her father almost screaming. "I'll ask all of you to leave and let me breakfast with my daughter!" James ordered. "I'll meet with you in the library later. But for bloody sake, leave my daughter out of this!"

"No, sir. It can't wait." Dan shifted nervously on his feet, looking at his employer with narrowed and troubled eyes. "There's a crisis, sir. And Miss Lilly needs to hear about it."

"Crisis?" James asked.

Lilly pulled away from Shadoe's hard gaze. "What kind of crisis?"

"More stealing . . . more murder." Dan faltered as he spoke the words as if he was embarrassed, as if he felt responsible, and Shadoe quickly stepped forward to explain.

"I lost a man last night out near the Oasis. He was camped with a buckboard of supplies. They didn't take a damn thing from him, just shot him through the head and left him there."

Lilly covered her mouth with her hands.

"What a bloody muck!" James shouted.

"Yes," Shadoe said. "It looks to be that the man was just in the wrong place at the wrong time. The cutthroats were coming through with some horses, and he saw them, that's all."

"The same culprits who have been rustling?"

Shadoe nodded. "It has to be," he said, motioning to Lewis. "Lewis tracked them. Same horses. Same tracks as when that homesteader was shot near the end of April."

"They're the same ole bunch," Lewis agreed. "There were six of them, riding, and maybe two dozen horses. I tracked them up the eastern slope of the Blitzen. They crossed on the northern border of the Double S, then turned, heading back south, but I lost their trail when they went into the mountains." He sighed and looked at Dan. "I was hoping Dan would give me some of your men to look further into the Steens. Maybe try and pick up the trail while it's still warm. Too much wind, and we'll lose it in the dust."

Lilly had been listening carefully, but Lewis's explanation confused her. "Doesn't make sense that they would go north across the river then turn south. What would be the point? They could have made better time going straight south from Weatherly."

"Too close to Montfort? Too close to the Woodward place, maybe? I guess they thought they would be safer riding down the other side of the river," Lewis commented.

James frowned and moved closer to Shadoe. "It still isn't reasonable. Number nine line shack is to the east of their way. Why would they be riding toward number nine if they were stealing your horses?"

"Not mine, but yours," said Shadoe.

Lilly gasped. "Weatherly horses?"

"What?" James stared at his foreman. "Dan, are you saying that someone stole horses off this ranch last night?"

Dan grimaced. "Not only were some of the greens stolen off the range, a few horses were stolen right out of the barn."

"Out of the barn?" asked Lilly in a weak voice.

Shadoe stared at her again, and she met his gaze.

"Yes, Lilly," Shadoe said. "Dan told me that they took your mare right out of her stall."

Later that afternoon, following a heated discussion, Shadoe, Dan, Lewis, and even her father, left, riding south to the Steens Mountains, hoping to pick up the trail.

They'd probably be gone for days, Lilly thought, just time enough to give her a respite so that she could calculate her next move.

Sitting in the library, listening to Martha chat about the post, Lilly closed her eyes as she laid down the pen. She was tired, so tired. It had taken all her strength to write just a few miserable lines on a sheet of paper. But then again, it was a letter to Shadoe.

Oh, Shadoe, love, will you understand or will you feel that I've betrayed you? Lilly didn't know.

The letter said: "Dear Shadoe, I have promised my father that I won't see you again. You must understand that I do this to give us time apart. It is time we need so that we can think clearly about what we are doing and why. Always, Lilly."

Ironically, the family had just received a package and letter from her brother, Joseph, that morning. *An accidental fate,* Lilly told herself. The letter was a perfect example of a paradoxical twist.

Her brother usually communicated with them four times a year, excluding their birthdays. This was Joseph's spring package.

The Earl of Montfort had sent his father a five-volume set of Shelley's poems. It was an edition edited by H. Buxton Forman, a particularly nice gift since James McFall had been acquainted with the late English poet's son, Sir Percy. Two small miniatures of Joseph and his wife were included, both painted by Sir Percy Shelley. Lilly's gift had been an expensive evening gown from Worth. It was an elegant ball gown of blue damask, covered with white tulle and garlands of pearls.

And Joseph's letter? It was always the same generous dialogue, asking about the ranch, wanting Lilly to come to England. Only this time, a hasty postscript was scribbled on the last page. Joseph had asked expressly for news of Shadoe. What irony. . . .

Chapter 26

Molly grinned, an elfish smile, the kind of expression that made others call her a devil's child. Sunlight and shadow spilled alternately across her face. The young man standing beside her put his hands on her waist and pulled her to him.

"Oh, Jesse, honey! I just have to have a summer wedding now that I have that beautiful new gown! I just have to! It's the most gorgeous dress I've ever laid my eyes on," she said, circling her arms around his neck. "Every girl in Montfort is going to be green. Green, I tell you. Green with envy."

That damn fancy dress from England, thought Jesse. *Why did Lilly and Miz Martha have to go and give it to Molly for a wedding dress?* It was all Molly had talked about for two weeks!

He brushed her rosy-colored cheek with his lips. For months, Jesse had waited to get Molly alone.

Alone. The word almost killed him with anticipation. She'd made promises about the church picnic back in April, and all through May, she had teased him unmercifully, even made him watch while she flirted with others.

But it was now June the twelfth, the day of the church picnic. *I can't wait no longer,* thought Jesse.

"I need ya, Molly," he whispered in her ear. "I need ya somethin' awful."

She giggled and pushed slightly at him. "Not here, you silly fool." Twisting in his arms, she shook her head at him, and Jesse saw that she was serious in her protest. "Why, Jesse, I can see your brother, Tom, from where we're standing. I can't lie down with you *here*. We might be interrupted, and even engaged, it'd be the scandal of the town."

"Where?" Jesse asked, suddenly cold with her news.

"Where what?"

"Where's my brother?"

She pointed. "Why, right through there. In the graveyard."

Jesse looked up and frowned, marring the warm expression that had been on his face. It was an unexpected sight. Through the trees, he could see Tom standing over Anne's grave. Fresh flowers lay clumped at the foot of her tombstone. And Tom wasn't alone. Pepper Maddox was with him. They seemed to be arguing.

Jesse frowned deeper and his body grew stiff with the thoughts that were flying though his mind. Tom. Pepper. The long trips north, then south. Something not right with all of it. Something wrong, something bad as his mother had said.

Molly leaned against Jesse. "What's wrong, Jesse?"

"Nothin'."

"Are you sure, honey? You look pale as a ghost. If I didn't know better, I'd think you were staring at Anne instead of Tom over there among those stones. Anne's ghost ahaunting you."

Jesse flinched. "Anne . . ." He turned and looked into Molly's face. A feeling of desperation layered the hunger in his voice. "I luv ya, Molly, girl."

She smiled nervously, and as if she knew the desperation in his soul, she said, "I know a place where we can lie awhile."

"Let's go," he said, pulling Molly by the arm. He leaned over and grabbed the large picnic basket that had cost him twenty dollars.

Though his hands often fumbled, Jesse made love to Molly like a grown man crazed with passion. He lifted her skirts, tore at her underclothes, then ran his eager fingers inside of her body.

And Molly liked it. Before Jesse had moved to unzip his jeans, she slid her hand inside the front of his pants and wrapped her cool fingers over his erection. Her fingertips lightly grazed over the silkiness of the tender flesh.

Jesse almost lost it, spilling his seed in his own pants. "Damn!" he cried.

After that, came the proof of weeks of promise.

"Fifty dollars," Shadoe called out, and everyone crowded in front of the Episcopal Church gasped at the new bid. Even Doctor Brown, who had graciously volunteered to play auctioneer, spouted a convulsion of drivel.

Lilly stood on the platform with her basket of food, staring pointedly at her lover. Hadn't he read her letter? Didn't he understand that she meant every word of it? What was he thinking?

For the last few days, she had been divided in two—crazy for wanting Shadoe, fighting to stay away. And now, here he was, clean and freshly shaven, smiling at her, looking so sure of himself— almost happy—as he bid outrageously for her tiny, English-cut sandwiches.

She frowned at him. He had been back a full week from the trail, after posting guards at all the line shacks, and setting up a makeshift bunkhouse at the Oasis. Seven days, and she had not seen him for a single moment, and now, today of all days, he had decided that he was going to end all that. Just bid on her lunch. Just smile and talk and see how easily she would break her promise to her father.

She knew what he was thinking; he was going to prove that her words meant nothing once he had her in his arms again. She frowned deeper. The bastard didn't seem to have a care in the world, but she needed more time.

"Seventy-five dollars!"

Lilly smiled with appreciation at Luke. The young horse breeder was sure keeping his part of the bargain, and Lilly was more than pleased.

Earlier that morning, as Luke had driven her into town, they had discussed his brother's death. Luke had finally admitted to Joseph's being involved and that Joseph and Sam had argued over Anne Woodward.

But Lilly didn't understand that, and she hadn't had enough time to make a connection between Joseph and Sam. Why would they be arguing over Anne? What about Shadoe?

When she had questioned him about Shadoe's part in the affair, Luke had shilly-shallied until she had told him her suspicions, that Shadoe had accidentally killed Sam while protecting her brother. To her surprise, Luke got defensive when she suggested that Joseph needed protection from Sam.

It appeared to Lilly that Luke had something to hide, and he wasn't going to give up the truth easily. If anything, her scheming little trip into town had proved little.

"Eighty," Shadoe said, giving Luke a fiendish grin, and Lilly gripped the handle of her basket tighter. She should not have come to this affair. With everything that she knew and felt, she should have stayed home, hid in the castle until she knew what to do.

Oh, God, what if Shadoe won the bid? How would she eat with him? What would she say? How would she act? And her father? Her knees grew weak.

"Ninety," countered Luke.

"Ninety-five."

Luke stared at Lilly, and she knew what he was thinking. "One hundred dollars," he said in an exhausted breath.

The crowd grew silent. No one had ever offered so much money for a lunch in the history of the church charity social. A minute floated on the warm spring air, and Lilly, along with a dozen other people, glared at Shadoe, waiting.

"Two hundred dollars."

She gasped and gave Luke a pleading stare. *Do it! Damn you, Luke Miller! Bid whatever it takes!*

But Luke was silent.

The auctioneer called, "Going once! Going twice!"

"Three hundred dollars!"

Lilly thought she was going to faint at the sound of the words. The crowd roared, and Luke Miller stepped forward, waiting to see if Shadoe was going to bid higher. But instead, Shadoe only tipped his hat at the *new* bidder.

"Sold!" the auctioneer cried. "For three hundred dollars, one lunch with Miss Lilly McFall purchased by Mister Tom Woodward."

"Why, Tom? Why?" she was still asking him when they had found a place in the grove of trees to picnic.

Lilly didn't know what to think. Not only was she wondering why Tom had spent so much money, she was also wondering what in the world Shadoe was contemplating when he let Tom have her basket.

She stood, watching as Tom spread out the blanket and sat down. A shock of lanky hair fell into his face, and he reached up to push it back under his hat. Lilly thought him handsome with his tie and clean suit, but she knew him too well to appreciate his appearance.

"Why did you bid, Tom?" she asked him again, this time her voice cold and demanding.

He looked up at her with his dark eyes, sincerely amused. "I did it because a man has to have some pride, Lilly. And because I wanted ya here with me, and I wanted to show Luke and Sinclair that I still can have ya if I want."

Lilly contained her anger. "There it is again."

"What again?" he asked.

"Pride. Men and their pride. Well, I don't give a flip for it. In fact, it sickens me!"

Tom laughed at her reproach. "Well, pride ain't everything. I'm hungry, too," he said with a trace of mockery. Leaning over, he reached in the basket and snatched one of her sandwiches. "Chicken . . . mmm . . . good."

"I don't want to eat with you," she told him bluntly. "I don't have to."

"But you'd eat with Shadoe."

"I wasn't planning on eating with Shadoe either."

Tom swallowed another bite, then reached for another sandwich. "Oh, yeah, I do believe from the looks of things that you were plannin' on doin' your eatin' with Luke Miller. Well, ain't it a shame. He drove you into town all for nothin'. Yep, poor Luke, left his ranch yesterday, rode all the way to Weatherly and spent the night in the bunkhouse just so he could drive you to the picnic. All that trouble and now he eats alone, and you got to suffer through a meal with me."

Lilly stood, shocked that he knew so much of her business. She started to ask him how, but then changed her mind. It was better to leave things as they were. But about eating with him, she had more than a few words to say.

"No, Tom. I don't. You paid for the meal, then eat it, but I don't have to sit here and take your abuse. I realize now just how full of hate you are."

"Do you now?"

There was a wide, nasty grin on his face, and Lilly shivered at the sight of it, an odd and cruel expression that suddenly made him look raffish and worldly, not the countrified boy she'd thought him.

"Yes, I do. You live in the past, Tom. No present. No future. Everything an extension of something rooted in the years gone by. Maybe I have lived there, too. But if Shadoe's coming back taught me anything, it's that you have to live in the present. It's all you really have."

"And forget the past? Forget the memories?"

"If need be."

"Could you forget that you love Shadoe?"

Lilly hesitated. This was her moment. It would be so easy to say the words, to lie and tell him that she could, but somehow the breath caught in her throat. She stared at Tom, white-faced and rigid, and she found that her hands were trembling.

"Don't answer that."

At first Lilly thought that Tom had said it.

The same voice again. "You don't ever have to answer that to nobody not ever, Miss Lilly."

Lilly looked around and found that Luke Miller was slipping through a knot of bushes. She couldn't help but relax, and a gentle smile flew across her face.

"Luke?" she called uncertainly, softly, as if the sight of him was too good to be true.

Tom hurried to his feet. "What the hell?"

"Don't get so bothered, Woodward," Luke said in a voice that was hard and quick. It seemed to rush at Tom like a zinging bullet, and Lilly thought that she had never seen Luke so commanding or angry.

"What's wrong?" she asked immediately, and Luke's gaze softened as he turned to her.

"There's been another killing at my place."

Tom shifted from one foot to the other. "Who?"

"One of the new boys I hired from Montfort last week to watch the greens grazing near old line camp two. The scum nailed him dead center."

"How awful," Lilly said in a strained breath.

"And that ain't all. The thieves headed south and on the way they got one of your men, Woodward."

Tom's eyes rounded. "What?"

"Yeah, winged him good. Tully Whitten. He dragged himself into the rocks, and hid. Apparently, they couldn't find him because they left him alive."

"Where is he?"

"In the back of one of my buckboards. Dead though."

Lilly gasped, but Tom looked as cold and hard as stone. "Did he talk? Say anything?" he asked quickly.

Luke stared at Tom again, his gaze filled with a smoldering anger. "Yeah, he said a little, Woodward. But not much that makes sense. None of us could understand what he was doing out there in the first place. Tully mighta looked stupid to the eye, but he was a crafty fellow. Didn't seem like the kinda mess he would have let himself get caught up in at all. I mean he had to know they were out there." Luke shook his head, and drew a long sigh. "Some of my boys tried to get him to say more, but there wasn't much life left in 'em. Maybe you can make some sense of it."

"What did he say?" Lilly was very curious.

Luke looked at her, then turned back to Tom. "Something about *tierra de leyandas.*"

"Why that's Spanish!" Lilly cried, astonished. "Was Tully part Spanish?"

"No! I didn't even know the bastard knew Spanish!" Tom shouted at her. Then without a word and in unexpected haste, he stomped away.

Lilly watched him leave, aghast at his speech, curious at his reaction. When he disappeared through the trees and bushes, she turned to Luke with a questioning stare. "Why would Tully say such a thing?"

"Do you know what it means, Lilly?"

She nodded. "It means land of legends in English." Lilly paused and looked at Luke, puzzled. "Where have I heard that expression before?"

"You think you know?"

"It's strange. But I have the most peculiar feeling that I do. Part of a childhood secret, a place in my dreams, an imaginary place that only . . ." She stopped and pinched her lips, saying nothing more to Luke.

But a serious thought entered her head. *Shadoe's lost canyon. The imaginary place that Shadoe teased me with, the land of dragons and fairies. Why would Tully mention that?*

Shadoe watched Tom leave. Then Luke. Both alone, without Lilly, he thought with pleasure, and she was still in the trees, probably nibbling one of her dainty chicken sandwiches, relieved that she had finally escaped from everyone.

"Lewis. Take the boy home for me."

The foreman didn't look surprised. "What about the men? You want me to send someone out to help Luke?"

"No need. Luke Miller always does things his own way. Besides, I have my own plans to catch these damn night riders. Luke's made it plain that he's going home to take care of his herd, then riding out to watch the area south of Widow Daniels' homestead." There was a heavy pause and Shadoe turned to stare at his companion. "You stay at the house with the boy and Lo Ching. I don't want them left alone for any reason. Hear me?"

"Yep."

"Send a few of the boys to push the herd grazing near the Oasis up farther north. Tell the men to camp. But everyone is to stay together. No loners and that's an order!"

Shadoe lifted Joey up in his arms. The boy threw his arms around his neck, and Shadoe smiled at the tenderness. In the little time they had spent together, he and Joey had already become very attached to one another.

"You tell Lo Ching to make you a chocolate cake, Joey," Shadoe said before he bent close and whispered something in his son's ear.

The child smiled, and Shadoe ran his palm over the small curve of the child's apple-colored cheek.

"Yes, Paw, I will," the boy said.

"Take care of him," Shadoe told Lewis as he deposited Joey back on his feet. "I'll be home later. Got some unfinished business."

Lewis took the boy by the hand. "I will, boss."

In a few minutes, Shadoe was standing alone, staring eagerly at the wooded area where Lilly remained hidden.

His throat ran dry as he thought of her. Mercy! She did things to his feelings that no one ever had. Even now, he felt edgy, pushed to doubts, queasy with brainwork.

The letter? She wanted time, and he could understand that. But he was desperate in his need for her. One minute was too much with the way he was feeling. Already, the situation between them had stretched much too long. He had to see her

now, understand if she meant to keep her promise to her father, and just how far that promise
would go.

But most of all, Shadoe wanted to know exactly
what James had told Lilly about Joey!

Chapter 27

When he was sure that they would not be disturbed, Shadoe sought Lilly out, finding her among the thick grove of trees that were located directly behind the little church cemetery. For a moment, he watched her, uninterrupted, looming over her like an adumbration, full of longings, cast-down desires that were hardly the kind expected at a church social.

Everything else aside, at the moment, he was only a man in need of a woman. A particular woman. Already his body was hard, his erection pushed painfully against his pants. In spite of his doubts—and he had many since his talk with James—Shadoe could only think of strong-arming Lilly to the nearest bed, and doing what needed to be done.

His gut tightened, ached at the thought of her clothes peeling away, layer upon gentle layer, at how her ripe body would feel under his possessing hands, even at the way her soft toes might

curl against the heels of his feet when she was
fever-pitched.

Shadoe shifted uncomfortably as he watched
Lilly with hungry eyes. She sat, dressed in corn-
flower blue, a creamy lace scarf at her neck. Her
hat was in her hands, and her wheat-colored hair
had blown free.

He imagined that she must have sensed his presence, felt the vague outlines of his need, for Lilly
glanced up at him, meeting his stare with a singular look.

*Oh, Lilly, darlin', I love you. Even in all this mis-
ery. I want you and need you. But you're going to
have to come to me. Just like before, you're going
to have to want me more than ever if we are going
to survive this, if we are going to fight the past,* he
thought quickly before he asked, "Are you hiding
from me, Princess?"

It was a valid question, and one that he felt
needed answering. His voice was purposely soft,
coaxing, and Shadoe could almost see Lilly smile,
but she held it back, held back the light that usually poured from her eyes. And he guessed silently
at the reason. James had told her the truth about
Joseph's being Joey's father.

*Papa's little girl is mad at me. Papa's little princess
is going to keep her promise if she can. Papa's little
girl hates me for lying to her all these years about
Joseph and Anne,* he mused silently.

He asked the question again, this time in a fine-
grained voice, but she ignored it.

"You shouldn't be here," she told him instead,
and her words were quick and blunt, nervous words
that sounded rehearsed to Shadoe.

He cocked an eyebrow at her, saw her anxiously twist the satin hat ribbon between her milky fingers. *God! Those wonderful fingers, so soft and white and. . . .*

Shadoe felt his lust surging, and his voice softened again. "Shouldn't I?" he questioned her. "I belong with you, Lilly, wherever that might be. If I recall rightly, and I *do* remember, you and I have already decided that we belong only to each other." He moved closer, taking a short step on the checkered blanket on which Lilly was sitting with her picnic basket, the small, carefully interwoven container that had earned the Episcopal Church of Montfort three hundred dollars, an offhand sum that gave Shadoe a disagreeable feeling.

His nearness apparently bothered her for she shifted back away from him.

"Please go away, Shadoe," Lilly scolded in a frosty tone.

"Go away?" Shadoe leaned over and playfully tugged at a strand of her silky hair, smiling as he told her, "You don't really mean that. Go away?" His voice turned almost whimsical. "Why, Lilly darlin', I think we need to talk. It's been days and nights since I've seen you, more since I've touched you." His hand lightly grazed her flushed cheek. "And, sweetheart, don't you feel that there's much to be said, so much to be done between us?"

Her response was to shoo away his hand. "Not now." She appeared half aggrieved, half angry. "I can't."

The words were terse, but her tone was firm, and Shadoe didn't like the sound of it. He stood straight, thumbed back his black plainsman, and gave her a slight frown. The sound of a bee buzzing in the afternoon breeze filled his head. So Lilly was going to be difficult, more hard-won than he had imagined. The thought worsened his mood, and he felt his temper rising.

"You mean you *won't* talk to me."

"No. That's not it at all. I *can't*," she repeated adamantly.

His gaze raked over her thoughtfully. For a heady moment, her sweet, soft scent was on him, and Shadoe liked it, liked the way her smell teased at him, connected them with some sort of intimacy, but he took a long, hard swallow, crushing the notion to take her immediately into his arms. If Lilly wanted to play games, he was willing, at least for a while longer.

"So you really intend like that stupid letter said— if you could call that damn thing a decent letter, a few cat-scratched lines, a bunch of silliness on a piece of thin paper . . ." He was losing track of his thought. "Dammit, Lilly! I'm worth more than four stupid lines of words!" He shook his head, recovering himself. "You really intend on turning round about, going on as if nothing happened between us? You intend on keeping that promise to the old man?"

"I most certainly do. I have to," Lilly said bluntly. She let out a harsh breath.

Shadoe caught the sound of it, and his gaze fell pointedly on her face. Her gray eyes had dulled, and her face seemed colored by the revulsion of his own expression.

"How can you walk away from me like this, Lilly? After everything, it just doesn't make much sense."

"If love was all that mattered, I would be with you."

He scowled painfully at her. "You mean you don't love me enough to forget the past?"

An odd expression filled her eyes, and for a moment Shadoe thought she might relent, might reach up and take his hand, press it to her face, and say that she could forgive him anything. But she didn't.

Instead, Lilly turned her gaze away. And he knew his answer. She couldn't forgive him for lying about Joseph, or even for telling her father the truth. She didn't like that her lover was the one to reveal Joseph for the heel he really was. She would hold on to her cherished misconceptions because they were easier, safer, and it meant she wouldn't have to face the pain of disappointment concerning her brother.

It was strange, but Shadoe understood. For years, he had thought his own father hadn't loved him—only to know too late the indifference and silence had been a replacement for Simon Sinclair's own difficulty with loving the child of a woman who had disappointed him by staying in a saloon instead of coming to Oregon and making a family.

It was strange, but Shadoe understood that people could invent their own realities. Reinvent them over and over. He had. Done so five years ago when he had chosen to protect Joseph because it was the noble thing to do, the supreme sacrifice, the gesture that would make him worthy of his father's love, of James McFall's respect, make him worthy of marrying the princess.

What an illusion, a cherished misconception, a faulty reality. God, he was so angry now that he wanted to scream the whole truth, but couldn't. He remained silent for a long time, speechless with his despair, growing taut like a cat ready to spring. Then he said in a ragged tone, "I feared this all along."

He saw her clutch the folds of her dress.

"Don't, Shadoe," she pleaded, still looking down at the ground. "Don't say anything more. I can't bear to talk to you. I told you that I need time, and I still need the time." A long and anguished sigh from her. "Oh, Shadoe, I can't talk to you. I don't want to talk to you!"

"I see," he said stiffly, feeling angrier and more hurt. "Talking doesn't suit the high-and-mighty princess right now!" He looked at her sharply, suddenly and overwhelmingly struck with the idea that he could really lose her this time, that she would stop loving him.

His head suddenly buzzed with stupid jealousies. "Yeah, I can imagine why you don't want to talk. That long ride into town with Luke this morning. You smiling, asking those sly questions while poor Miller tried to steer away from anything that might make him look bad. And Luke can be just as bad as I am, you know." His grin was surly as he continued, "The princess is already talked out, and then, of course, we can't forget dear ole Tom. He just had to go and buy your basket." Shadoe laughed in a sneering tone. "One can only marvel at why your little sandwiches and teacakes would be worth so much money. And who woulda thought that little Tommy would have such a sum to spend? Amazing!"

Lilly turned and stared at him. "Damn! Would you stop!"

Shadoe laughed at her, scorned her with a bright, taunting smile, though he could see that his mockery had drawn her to the edge of despair. Her gaze was mixed with tears, alarm, displeasure. A tight curve rounded her beautiful mouth.

"Let me love you, Lilly. Let me take away all the memories, all the pain, all the suffering. I can. I'll take you in my arms and crawl inside of you until you forget everything but me."

"For God's sake, Shadoe, would you please shut up! You're killing me! Driving me insane!"

"Talk to me, Princess. Say some more. You know I love it when you're mad. Your cheeks get all rosy. Your eyes sparkle irresistibly!"

Dropping her hat, Lilly rose quickly to her feet. She stared fiercely at him. He grinned appreciatively at her. "Shadoe, please. Let's not do this."

"Do what, darlin'?"

"Get in an argument. Say silly things. Hurt each other. Just go away so that I can think clearly. I don't want to quarrel with you, not today."

He stepped closer to Lilly, and jerked her roughly into his arms. "Hurt? Who's hurting who?" He inhaled quickly. His face turned sober, troubled.

"I hurt," she muttered, her warm breath fanning his face.

"Then let's see how painful a kiss can be."

Lilly looked at him, stricken. "No."

"No?" Shadoe demanded, and her appeal went unheeded with another indecent smile.

His mouth claimed her lips, not sweetly or kindly, but unmercifully, forcing her lips open with his tongue. At first, Lilly resisted, but Shadoe held her tightly against him, absorbing her hesitation, initiating compliance as he slid his tongue into her mouth.

She was shaking, but all Shadoe could feel was the blood roaring, pulsating through his ears. His hand slid to one breast, and his fingers squeezed gently. Lilly writhed in his arms, but Shadoe didn't care. Her mouth was wet, and his tongue danced against hers, lashing in a duel of desperation. Then, Lilly's arms wrapped around his neck.

Damn . . . damn . . . The curse rolled in his mind as he kissed her, as he felt her giving way to passion. He wanted her, needed her badly but not this way. This had meant to be painful, to hurt, to cause her anguish.

He reluctantly dragged his mouth away and looked down into her face. Her eyes were dusky, and her lips were dark and swollen from his kiss. For one brief second, he thought about making love to her, right on the blue-and-white quilt.

He took his hand, shaping his fingers against the soft curve of her jaw line. "The last time we were together, you were wanting to do more than kiss. I think the same is true now." He lightly brushed her mouth with his lips. "Shall we forget all the angry words? Shall I make love to you again, Lilly darlin'?"

"No," she said in a whisper that melted into his warm breath. "No. No. No."

"Then talk to me. Explain why you can't bear to talk to me. Let's get it all out in the open and go on. I need you, Lilly. I need you more than I can ever say with words." He pulled her tighter to him, and his voice turned husky. "I need to show you how much I need you."

She squirmed in his arms. "Please, Shadoe. I promised my father that I wouldn't do this."

He cursed savagely as he dropped his arms, letting her free. Shadoe took a quick step back, and glanced at her from head to toe. He saw her blush uncomfortably at his leering appraisal and he felt pleased. "You don't want to explain? You just want to forget, forget how good we can make each other feel?"

"Yes. For God's sake! Yes! Can't you tell? I want to forget! I need to forget!"

He gave the ground a hard kick with the toe of his boot. The dirt splattered, and Shadoe was clearly astounded, indignant that he could have been such a fool. For a week, he had walked around, anticipating her anger, prepared for her forgiveness and for the love she'd offered him before. But not this, not this coldness so thick and blinding that it actually made him fearful, made him feel the rage he knew she must be feeling. The pain ate at him. His blood went hot.

"Then you go to hell, lady!" he shouted. "'Cause I'm not the kind of man who begs. I left you before. I can again." She paled, and her response only fueled his cause. "Believe me, if you can forget this easily, then I'm willing to do the same. I don't need you. I don't need your *forgiveness* anymore!"

"Forgiveness?" Lilly asked as he turned to walk away. "What forgiveness?" She moved to follow him, a curious expression spread thickly across her features. "Shadoe, what are you talking about? What forgiveness?"

He turned sharply at her questions, a deep scowl on his face as he shook his head. She had offered him no explanations, nothing. He would do the same for her.

"Forgiveness?" His blue eyes became a little smaller, his mouth a little crueler. "Did I say something about forgiveness? Why, Miss McFall, I think you heard something you wanted to hear. I ain't worried about forgiveness, just forgetting. And like I said, I intend to do just that!"

"But—"

He cut her off. "I'm leaving Oregon, Lilly, and I'm never coming back. It's over. I can't take any more pain. I can't feel as though everything I do is never good enough to meet the standards of the high-and-mighty McFalls. I mean it this time. I'm leaving for good, and I won't ever look back, ever think about you again. I mean to survive. I have to, if not for me, then for the boy." Shadoe suddenly turned and walked away.

It was a real threat, and Lilly thought she would swoon at the sound of it, not his other angry words, not her own, not her old fears, not her new anxieties. Just the threat of his leaving and forgetting.

Her knees grew weak, her legs wobbled. Could he really leave her? Yes, he could do that, but forget? Could he really forget her? Forever? Shadoe gone forever? Their lives separate?

Lilly wanted to yell, and fought it, until it escaped from her quivering throat with a will of its own. She muffled the harsh sound with her hands, trembling, shaking fingers that felt her stinging tears.

Shadoe. Shadoe. Shadoe. I love you. I could forgive you anything but what?

Forgiveness. For the moment, it faded under the threat.

No! He couldn't forget! Oh, God! She hadn't meant for him to forget. She hadn't meant for him to leave Oregon.

Lilly shrieked and crumbled to the ground. Her spirit, shattered like a thin-shelled egg, cracked into a thousand tortured pieces, and she had no one to blame but her foolish self.

Chapter 28

Shadoe was hurting when he wandered into the Montfort saloon that Saturday afternoon. The batwing doors slapped open and shut, and Shadoe strode through the layers of cigarette smoke, making his way straight to the bar.

He ached so badly that he knew there was only one quick cure. A bottle of good rye whiskey. He'd get drunk, so slaphappy drunk that he wouldn't care about Lilly and her pitiful letter. He wouldn't care that no matter what he did, he would never be as respected as Joseph McFall had been.

What a joke! He was and would always be the son of a soiled dove who gave him away. The son of a man who knew as much about love as he did the value of a dollar.

And how ridiculous an ambition! Joseph may have been respected, but he was a scoundrel and a cheat.

Well, no more!

"Your best rye," Shadoe called.

The bartender put a bottle and glass before him. Shadoe licked his dry lips with his tongue, and flopped down a coin on the counter.

"Where's the music?" Shadoe asked of the empty piano stool.

"Gone. Doubles as the undertaker."

Shadoe chuckled, then poured himself a glass and swigged down the contents. It was strong and hot, and it ran down into his gut, easing the twisting knot that had formed there.

A chair creaked as someone shifted his heavy weight, and Shadoe glanced cautiously from the corner of his eye. At a nearby table, two men sat, playing a sleepy game of poker with a dog-eared deck of cards.

One of the men was Pepper Maddox, but the other, a big man with a square jaw, Shadoe didn't recognize. He had a greasy, red look about him, and Shadoe thought that he seemed to be out of place, sitting across from the thin, swarthy Pepper.

"Who's that with Maddox?" he asked with a nod of his head.

The bartender turned to give the two men a look, then shrugged his shoulders as he swatted a rag across the dusty bar. "Another gun, most likely. Pepper no doubt called him in cause of all this rustling goin' on. But I ain't sure. But then again, I don't ask many questions in my profession. I just listen."

Shadoe turned his brooding gaze on the bartender and lifted his glass. "You'd think that Pepper would be out at the Woodward place with the rest of the hands since Tully Whitten was killed last night?"

"Pepper ain't the kind to grieve for the dead," came the sneering reply. "Ain't none of those boys lamenting for Tully, not even Martin Whitten. I heard him and Dice talk about headin' north to Luke Miller's place."

"Luke's?" Shadoe downed the rye in a quick gulp.

"Yep. I heard they put ole Tully in a box, paid the undertaker, and then left ridin' north."

"So much for brotherly love." Shadoe poured himself another drink. He could understand Martin's callous attitude toward his murdered brother. Martin and Tully had seen lots of dying over the years, their parents, one brother, then a sister to smallpox. The harsh land of southeastern Oregon had claimed many lives, and it was enough to make a person harden to the pain that death often brought, but Shadoe couldn't see Martin riding off to Luke's without burying Tully first.

Shadoe drank his rye, this time more slowly, as if he was savoring each drop that slid down his throbbing throat. He frowned over the rim of the shot glass, sick to death of all the guessing, all the planning, all the wondering. He was tired of thinking. Anger, frustration, impatience had all channeled themselves into rivers of fatigue.

Lilly, he thought with a low curse that was meant to crowd out any last regrets. Somehow, it seemed as though they had been playing a game with each other. Somehow she had won and he had lost, cast away the control that he'd struggled so hard with all those years away from her.

Even now, the rye burned his throat, and so did her memory. The bottle was half empty, and still he hungered for her, needed her desperately.

The sound of laughter caught his attention, and Shadoe turned, leaning his long muscular frame leisurely against the bar. His dark and somber gaze lifted toward the stairs, finally resting on the engaging form of a woman inclined against the stair railing.

A slow, incredulous grin widened the corners of his mouth, and the woman broke into a smile. Shadoe stared fixedly. Her mouth looked red and forbidding. Her eyes sparkled. She was waiting, he told himself. Naomi.

His gut tightened. His mind tumbled. "No . . . only Lilly," he muttered as he pushed away the glass, grabbed the bottle, and headed for the door.

Lilly, I mean to have you one way or another, I mean to have you. . . .

"Who's there?" Her voice was a hoarse whisper as she tiptoed across her bedroom.

It was dark, and Lilly could scarcely see a hand in front of her face, for the lamps were out, and though there was almost a full moon, the spring sky was smudged with heavy clouds.

She lifted the skirt of her light muslin gown, and moved with care past the curtains out onto the small balcony of her room.

"Who's there?" she called again, this time in a firm tone.

But no answer came, just the same continuous noises—a low, dull rattle, the rustle of leaves against the brick of the house, the sound of the wind entangled among the twigs.

Lilly shivered in the night air, and looking down at the garden beneath her window, glimpsed a moving shape in the gloom. It reached out and pulled on the lowest branch of the tree that grew nearest the house, jerked and twitched the limb as if testing it, and then the farm covered the branch, cloaking it in total blackness.

Gone. The branch was gone. Lilly gasped, frozen with disbelief.

Then the shape moved again, as if it had no care at all, silently and quickly up the tree, limb for limb, toward her.

Lilly jerked, stepped back carefully, suddenly filled with fear, realizing that her circumstance was marked with danger.

But she had hardly moved before the apparition had landed directly in front of her.

She gave a scream, half-throttled, then fell back against the shutters of the door. "Shadoe!"

He moved, not too close, but close enough for her to know that it was really he. She could smell the whiskey on his breath.

"I came to rescue the damsel in distress," he said in a slur. "I've scaled the castle walls."

"For God's sake, I thought I was seeing a phantom!"

"Maybe a demon?"

Though she couldn't see it, Lilly sensed that Shadoe was actually grinning at her. "Close enough. You smell like the hound from hell!"

Shadoe took a generous step, almost meeting her face to face, nose to nose, and Lilly let her head fall back against the wooden shutter.

"That smell, my Lilly love, is the best rye that money can buy in Montfort, Oregon. I drank nearly the whole bottle on my way out here. Courage. A man has to have courage, even if he finds it in a bottle. And with a witch like you, I need all the whiskey magic I can find."

She narrowed her eyes at him. "You're drunk, too drunk to be climbing trees like a foolish schoolboy."

Laughter, howling laughter, and a cloud passed, the moonlight striking Shadoe's figure. The light danced in his blue eyes, showed the white of his teeth. He was grinning pointedly like a lone wolf lost in a herd of sheep.

"I thought you liked the schoolboy in me. If I remember correctly, you used to wait patiently for me to climb that tree," Shadoe said. "You wanted me then, and you *really* want me now."

"Do I?"

"Yeah, you do, Princess. In spite of everything you said at the picnic, I know you love me."

"Do I?"

He laughed, threw back his head, then looked sharply at her. "Lilly, I want to hurt you. Do you know that?"

"Yes, I know it."

"Do you really? Can you understand that I'm so full of pain that I'm ready to burst? All the way from town, I drank and cursed, cursed you with all my being. I wanted to climb up that tree and teach you a bitter lesson."

"Well, you seem to have drunk enough courage!" she snapped. "So get on with it—if you think you can."

He moved carefully for her.

Before Lilly realized his intentions, Shadoe let his fingers play across the top of her gown, fumbling at the knotted tie at her bodice. His hand was through the breach in one vigorous, but gentle stroke, under the gown, over her breast. Then Shadoe buried his face in the curve of her neck, and moaned like a wild and hurting animal.

Lilly made a small cry, and he kissed her ear, whispered in it, "So you thought I was a demon, a ghost." His breath was shimmering hot against her skin. "How silly of my little princess." His voice turned coy as his fingers kneaded the soft mound of flesh. "I'm real enough, darlin', and I aim to prove it." The loosened nightgown fell from one shoulder, exposing Lilly's breasts, and Shadoe ran his hands across them. "Mmm, honey, don't that feel sooo good?"

Heart, soul, nerves, everything about Lilly seemed to split open at Shadoe's touch. How could she let him do this to her? She had been so resolved to keep him away, to save both herself and him from the danger that their love could bring. But his hands, his voice, his smell intoxicated her. There would be no more time.

"Shadoe, please, you don't understand. Don't . . ." she protested in a soft whisper, wanting to explain.

He chuckled a hasty no, the sound muffled as his lips fell against her skin. And then he was strong on his feet, pulling Lilly, positioning her, his hot, wet mouth sinking against the nipple of one breast, licking it, sucking the beads of sweat from her skin, and Lilly thought the air had turned to sweet poison.

She couldn't breathe. She couldn't talk. No protest. Nothing. There weren't any words for the exhilaration of his hands and mouth ravishing her body.

She threw her arms in the air, her trembling fingers soon clutching at his broad shoulders. She heard him moan, felt the dance of his tongue and teeth lightly playing against both her breasts now.

Bite-light and richly, Shadoe consumed her, feasting on her resolve. A nibble there, a touch of teeth, he sucked her like a sweet morsel of delicious candy.

"Shadoe," she heard herself say, though it could have been another woman, not her, surely not her. It was a pleasure-filled voice that carried a desperate and urgent plea. "I love you. I need you. Don't stop. Don't ever stop . . ."

He said nothing, only moved his mouth slowly up, up along the ridge of her throat, then to her mouth. It was a fervent kiss, one full of need and savagery.

Lilly suddenly ached all over, a dull throbbing that spread from her breasts to her lips, then downward in a swirling path that settled like a scorching fire between her legs. She squirmed at the sensation, pressing against Shadoe, feeling the hardness of his manhood rubbing urgently against her.

She wanted Shadoe, wanted to feel him, demanding and hard inside of her. Nothing mattered but the fact that she loved him and he loved her.

Lilly felt her gown being handled, shoved at, manipulated. She faintly heard the sound of his suspenders scratching as they were pushed off his shoulders.

"You're so fine, darlin'. And I love you . . . want you . . . need every little piece of you."

Her hands were on his face, in his hair. "Oh, I love you, Shadoe. I do . . . I do . . . I do."

"Let me touch you . . . show you . . ."

She did, and beyond the rest of the world, they stood in pools of shadow and light, moonstruck and mad, making love to each other.

His hand slid up her belly and then abruptly down again, settling warmly between her opened legs. Her knees went weak. Such strong hands. Such spry fingers, playing with her, easing into her body, teasing her into bliss.

"I want this," Shadoe muttered.

His voice was soft against her face. Lilly stared at him. He was a little god, that demon of lightlessness that had crept into her heart, tempted her with his words, his lips, his hands. She worshipped him, loved him with a love that could conquer anything and anyone. He was everything. Even now, before he had taken her, she felt that he was within her everywhere.

"I can't fight you . . . can't fight myself," she whispered into his face. "Take me . . . take what you want."

"Why fight it, darlin'? We're meant to be together. There can never be anyone else for us. Even apart, we belong to one another. Nothing that anyone says or does means anything to us. Not now. Not after being together like this."

A feeble smile came to her lips, resignation in a final gesture as she leaned back, limp and ready, waiting for him, for his body to conquer hers.

But tears formed in her eyes as she closed them. "Oh, Shadoe, if only . . ." Her thoughts broke for a moment as she became lost in physical pleasure, drowning under his touch. Her eyes opened. "If only . . ."

He saw her anxiety, paused slightly in his pursuit. Not entirely, for he kissed her lightly on the neck, against her ear as he whispered, "What is it, darlin'? What is bothering you?"

It was hard to talk. It was hard to do anything but

respond to his lovemaking, and how she wanted to make love with him again, excited and complete.

He was touching and moaning, then whispering, "What is it, Lilly love? I'm listening."

She wanted to say *if only there wasn't Tom and all his threats,* but all she could manage was one word. "Papa," she uttered between breaths.

"He doesn't matter now. Nothing matters now, except that I love you, that you love me. Feel me, darlin'." His hand moved and Lilly moaned with pleasure.

Tell him, you silly fool. Tell Shadoe that you're afraid Tom will try to kill him, and that Tom will die doing it. Tell him that you're afraid of Pepper and the others, that you're bloody scared, scared he might die because he loves you. . . .

Instead, she said, "Papa does matter. His feelings matter."

His hands eased on her body as he moaned into her ear, "I don't care about your papa. I don't care about anything." His teeth nibbled at her ear lobe, and then he said so very softly, "Not even the forgiveness. It doesn't matter to me that you can't forgive me for Anne, for the lies I told about Joseph and her. About Joey. None of that matters now . . . just this and this and this . . . your lips and breasts and belly and . . ."

Lilly was suddenly cooled by his seriousness, by the words. Especially one word.

That word again. *Forgiveness.*

His asking for forgiveness. What was he really talking about? Hadn't she already forgiven him for leaving her for Anne?

She shifted a little, moved so that she could see his face. Something strange about him. Something about the way he was looking into her eyes. This wasn't about Anne, at least not the way she understood it. "I could forgive you anything. Don't you know that? What lies are you talking about?"

His hand fell away from her, and Lilly gasped at his release. She didn't know whether to be grateful or disconcerted. Her body was still trembling with hunger, with the need for him to make love to her.

"I don't understand you, Lilly. I thought—" In the wavering moonlight she could see that his mouth had thinned. "Don't you know about Joseph and Anne?"

Her eyes widened at the question, at the confusion lined across his face. Her brows lifted. "What about Joseph and Anne?" She pulled her gown back over her shoulders.

There was a weighty moment, and Shadoe stepped back with a stumble. He laughed bitterly, then cursed, "Damn the old man! He didn't tell you after all!"

She shivered at his words, quickly realizing that Shadoe had assumed that she had written him the letter because of what had happened between him and her father. But she hadn't. Her father had said nothing, and Lilly realized just how important it was to Shadoe that he did. He looked hurt, really hurt. That little scene at the picnic was because he thought she had abandoned him for her father's pride.

"Papa wouldn't tell me anything, Shadoe. That's not why I wrote the letter."

"I can see that now," he said.

"I'm sorry that I wrote it. It's useless trying to stay away from you. It doesn't matter what you did in the past, I'll always want you. You'll always end up wanting me."

"I can see that, too."

There was a long pause, and then Lilly heard the clink of metal as Shadoe fixed his suspenders. "Would you get dressed now, please?" he asked as he turned to move across the darkened bedroom.

"Shadoe! You can't go down that way. Papa would know! You can't really mean to tell Papa about this?"

She heard him stop, the sound of his boot heels thudding against the carpet. Even in the dimness of the room, she could see that he was looking sharply at her. There was a seriousness to his features, a look that wasted away any protests.

"You told me that you wouldn't fight me. Well, don't argue the point now. We're way past it, Lilly darlin'. If you really love me, if you want to be with me, trust me. Just put on some proper clothes and meet me downstairs with a packed bag."

"Bag?"

"You heard me. Packed and ready to go. Something small and simple. We're leaving tonight, *together.*"

She gasped. "But, Shadoe, it's not going to be that simple." She walked slowly, her hands rumbling across her gown. "Yes, it's true that I melt in your arms, that I love you and want you. But there are so many things between us. Not just Papa and the past. There's Tom—"

"I'm not worried about Tom as much as I am the past."

Lilly moved, reaching for the bedpost. His words exhausted her with both anxiety and excitement. "But, Shadoe, the reason I wrote the letter was about Tom—" she started, wanting to tell him her suspicions, but he cut her off.

"No buts. No talk about Tom. Get dressed, Lilly, and quit worrying. Everything is going to be all right. I promise you that." He pointed a finger at her and smiled. "But no more of this wrangling between you and me. The situation has dragged on for far too long. I love you more than anything, more than my own life, and I need you. I need you in my bed tonight and every night."

Then he was gone.

The door opened, and she could hear his hasty steps fading down the long hallway.

Collapsing on the bed, her body went cold then hot. Her smile faded into a frown, then reappeared again even wider. "I'm really going to marry Shadoe Sinclair," she muttered into the night air.

Lilly stretched out against the cool sheets, staring into the darkness. She was dizzy with thought, with anticipation and longing. Everything was going to be all right. Shadoe promised. She believed him. She loved him. And all her fears faded away in this love and trust in Shadoe.

Suddenly, like a schoolgirl, she began to giggle.

Chapter 29

The door opened in an earsplitting whack, the wooden edge slapping against the adjoining wall with a force so great that one of the heavy portraits hanging nearby crashed to the floor of the study.

Jerking his gaze from the pile of folded papers in front of him on his desk, James saw Shadoe Sinclair standing in the open doorway. The older man quickly jumped to his feet.

"W—what—"

"You bastard!" Shadoe interrupted as he stomped his way into the room, quickly crossing the short distance that separated the two men. "You didn't have enough guts to tell Lilly, and then like some coward you made her promise to stay away from me. Why?"

James ignored the query. His gray brows lifted, and he stared rigidly at the young, disgruntled man. How could he answer such a scorching question? For days and days, it had been hanging over him with no suitable answer. He was tongue-tied with grief, wordless in his efforts to deal with Shadoe's news about Joseph.

Why couldn't he tell Lilly? Why had he made her promise to stay away from Shadoe? Why? Why? No answers.

James met Shadoe's gaze with some reluctance. He stiffened, suddenly afraid and defensive. This man was here in his house, and his son was gone. Shadoe Sinclair had come home. Not his son. The truth be told, his son would probably never come home.

James shivered with the thought, forced away the dogging questions. Resentment smothered his fear and doubts. "How in the hell did you get into the house?" he asked coldly, his voice full of anger.

"Acid on your tongue? So that's the way it's to be." Shadoe's next words were calm. "I climbed a tree into your house."

"You what?"

Shadoe's sneer was almost cheerful. "I said I climbed a tree." He took a few steps, drawing closer to James. "You know, the tree nearest the house. The one I used to climb when I was younger." He took another step. "Only then I wasn't brave enough to climb in but tonight I dared the jump, and you know, your lordship, it was definitely worth the risk. As you say in England, I've mustered the courage to measure swords with you and the prize of victory is our Lilly."

James colored, knew exactly what tree Shadoe was speaking of, knew exactly what Shadoe was implying.

"Lilly?" The word escaped from his lips in a panic.

Shadoe smiled wide at the sound of it, a lazy grin mixed with delight and malignity. "Oh, Lilly's fine," he cannily informed James. "Just fine." The younger man paused to plunder his pocket for a cigarette. "And she's coming downstairs just so you can tell her the truth."

"How dare you!"

Shadoe grimaced and lit a match. "How dare I what?" He inhaled deeply on the cigarette, then blew out a thick stream of smoke which drifted close to his face. His eyes were smiling at James, mockingly, unkindly, but were warm and a scintillating blue. He pointed a finger at the older man. "How dare I go against your wishes? How dare I love your daughter? How dare I tell the truth about Joseph? How dare I tell you that you have a grandson? Just which one are you talking about, your lordship?"

James clenched his hand and banged on the desk. Books and papers scattered to the floor. "Joseph would have told me. He would have told me that I had blood."

"He didn't."

"He must not have known," James quickly countered.

Shadoe laughed, a sharp, stinging sound that bit at James's skin, mottled it with old fears and doubts. "Now that's really funny. Must not have known?" Shadoe brushed the hair back from his face, and stared at James, a look now stiff and ruthless. "The bastard knew from the very beginning." Shadoe shook his head. "But Joseph wanted England more than Anne, old man. And he knew that she wouldn't fit in with those grandiose ways. Poor Anne. She was the most beautiful thing I ever laid eyes on, but she was rather simple in her ways. The thought of Joseph going to England terrified her. She just couldn't face it. It was too much for her. And there she was all . . . all alone and pregnant."

"No . . . no . . . no . . . You're lying!"

"Lying? I've lied, all right! I've lied about Joseph time and time again."

"You're wrong. He loved Anne. He wouldn't have left her pregnant. He only left because of you and Anne. That's the truth of it! You betrayed him."

"What in the hell is wrong with you?" Shadoe moved quickly, crushing his cigarette out in the saucer of James's tea cup. He twisted and looked at James, astonished and confused. "I'm telling you that you got a grandchild, your own blood, and all you can say is that the boy isn't a McFall. All you can do is think to protect Joseph. Goddammit, James! Joseph left you as much as he left Anne, left that child. And you still want to make out like he was a saint. Well, you can forget it. Joseph was guilty of more crimes than I care to think about. But none of them matter now, except that you know that the boy is your blood, that I didn't abandon Lilly for another woman. I was just trying to help Anne . . . help everyone."

"I can't believe this. Not a word of it rings true."

"What a hypocrite! You *can* believe it. You know it's true. But it's just that you can't face it, can't face the idea that all these years Joseph hid the truth from you. You can't really face the idea that he was not the son you wanted, that he betrayed you as much as he did everyone else."

James clasped his hands to his ears, screaming, "I don't want to hear it! I don't want to hear it!"

"But you have to, Papa!"

It was Lilly's voice that called from the open door. She rushed into the room, grabbing her father by the arms. Her eyes were filled with tears, and her voice carried her pain. "Don't you see, Papa, you have to face it. It's the truth." She clutched a fist to her chest. "I've known it in my heart." Her voice wavered as she began to sob.

James dropped his hands and stared at his daughter. For a moment, he thought he was going to faint, but he steadied his wavering form. It was true, he thought with disenchantment. Everything Lilly said was true. But the pain ripped at his heart. It was like losing Joseph a second and final time. But admitting the truth killed years and years of dreams, hopes, ambitions.

"Oh, Lilly, I don't want to believe it," he told her with a pleading look. "I can't . . ."

"I know," she started. "I know." Lilly's hand touched her face, wiping at the tears.

Shadoe watched for the moment, saying nothing, his face expressionless, listening as Lilly continued, "But there comes a time, Papa, when we have to face the truth, live with the consequences, no matter what. It seems that all the years between Joseph's leaving and now have been years of just going through the motions of living for the two of us. But we have to go on. Look to the future."

She turned and looked at Shadoe, smiling slightly. "I wish that you would have told me yourself."

He was quick to answer. "I felt that it needed to come from him. Besides, I wanted you to have the time to think about us, and I was troubled, Lilly, scared that you couldn't find it in your heart to forgive me for lying to you, for leaving you to protect Anne. That I didn't have enough guts to face you then . . . just like now . . ." His voice died.

She moved to touch Shadoe gently on his arm, and it seemed that she was oblivious to her surroundings. "I could forgive you anything, you know that."

He covered her hand with his. "I want to believe it. I need to believe it. I really do."

James glanced at them, saw the way they looked into each other's eyes. For a moment, the old man felt a touch of the peace and acceptance they shared, then his misted gaze caught sight of the bag that Lilly was clutching in her hand.

All thoughts of Joseph faded with a new anxiety. His rage mounted again as he asked, "What's that bag for? What are you doing, Lilly?"

She turned to stare at him, and he could see it in her eyes, the anxiety, the look of pity. "I'm leaving with Shadoe," she told him bluntly.

He choked, found it difficult to swallow. Lilly was leaving him, and all he could feel was the pain of losing Joseph so many years ago. Shadoe Sinclair was taking his young and innocent daughter away.

"You can't! I forbid it!"

Lilly gave him a pleading stare. "I love him, Papa. I'm going with him tonight."

"But . . . if anything, it's indecent."

Shadoe laughed scornfully. "Don't talk to us of indecency." He pulled Lilly tenderly into his arms. "I plan on marrying her, McFall."

James looked at his daughter. "Don't do this, child. Not now. There's still too many unanswered questions. Anne's death, for one!" In a rage he turned and snarled at Shadoe, "What really happened at the top of those stairs, Shadoe?"

The younger man turned cold. "Anne's death has nothing to do with this."

Lilly agreed with Shadoe. "I trust him, Papa. I know that whatever happened to Anne, Shadoe had no hand in it."

Shadoe turned to move toward the door, and Lilly followed him.

"If you leave here like this, in the middle of the night, eloping like some low-bred riffraff, you will be forbidden a place in this house! Do you hear me, child?"

"Please, Papa!" Lilly stopped as Shadoe continued walking out into the hallway toward the front foyer of the house. "Don't do this. Don't say things you really don't mean—"

"I do mean it, Lilly. You're a McFall! First and always. A McFall. You don't run off with a man in the middle of the night . . ."

Lilly gave her father a defiant glance from under her lashes. "I'm leaving," she said, her voice almost a whisper, and then Lilly turned and ran after Shadoe.

James watched them leave the house, looked on in silence as Shadoe found his hat, mounted his horse that was brazenly tied at the front doorsteps.

The old man said nothing as he saw Shadoe reach down and pull Lilly to a position behind him. Instead, he slumped against the wall and closed his eyes. Why had this happened? Why couldn't he face the truth? Oh, Lilly. . . .

When he opened his eyes, Martha was standing at the bottom of the stairs.

"You silly old man," she called to him. "Don't you realize that Shadoe Sinclair lied as much for you as he did for Lilly?" Martha strolled across the room, touched his arm. "That young man loves you, James. He's the son you wanted. The son you never really had in Joseph."

The words were thick and hard against his ears. James sighed, settling on a bench in the front foyer. "Oh, Martha, what am I going to do? I've ruined it all with my pride."

"Pride?" Martha laughed softly. "I think Lilly will understand about men and their pride. It's all I've heard her talk about for weeks upon weeks, dear brother." She narrowed a cautious gaze at him, and James saw the earnestness in her eyes. "But you're going to have to let go of the dream of Joseph coming home one day, of all the resentment, of all the guilt." Martha paused. "I once told Lilly that you felt responsible for poor Anne, for the tragedy that has been the Woodwards, that you felt that you owed them a debt. And I think deep down inside, you always knew why. Joseph destroyed your dream for the valley, not Shadoe." She sat down beside him. "Lilly is not the debt that you owe the Woodwards. But the truth is. Those poor boys, living all these years, twisted with their father's vengeance. It's time to put an end to it all. It's time to tell Shadoe the truth, too."

James looked at his sister, awed.

"Don't give me that look. You understand me as well as I understand you. James McFall, you're going to have to tell Shadoe Sinclair that you love him, love him as much as you loved your own son."

*   *   *

When Jesse saw the tracks, he knew but couldn't believe it. He ran his gloved fingers over them again and again until the doubts faded, until the tracks themselves melted into the dry desertlike dirt.

For a moment, he felt giddy, even a little afraid, but the excitement of making the catch quickly strangled any anxiety. He mounted his horse and followed the hoofprints in the darkness, slowly walking his gelding so that he would not miss the trail in the wavering moonlight.

The tracks led over a sand hill, down past a rolling hitch of boulders, off to the left into a dry, sage-filled runoff that held the rain in winter months.

Jesse immediately recognized the place, though he had not been there in years. It was the remains of line camp number eight. He hastily calculated that his location put him directly north of Weatherly and almost dead center between the castle and the Daniels' homestead.

He sighed heavily, and his mind turned back to an easier time when he and Tom had rode the grasslands and desert, when both his parents had been alive, and Anne, young and beautiful, had been the belle of Harney County.

Jesse swallowed hard. It was gone, the dreams, the hopes, the plans, all of it, wasted in the hot night air, consumed by the sounds that played off the rocky soil just ahead of him.

He took off his gloves, wiped his sweated hands against the fabric of his broadcloth trousers.

Those sounds. He knew them too well. He had been following them since he left Montfort after dusk. Horses' hooves and low talking. The sounds of Martin Whitten and Dice Jennings.

Jesse stared fixedly, then pulled his rifle from its sleeve.

It all made sense now. The tracks. The tracks had been the telltale sign. They belonged to Tom's horse.

Chapter 30

"I want to kiss you."

Shadoe leaned back, cocked his head to the side, and slanted a curious look at his passenger.

"Now?" he questioned, tugging on the reins. It was the last request that he had expected from her.

Lilly squeezed his waist enthusiastically with her circling arms. "Yes. Right now. Right in the middle of nowhere. I want to kiss you . . . and kiss you . . . and kiss you."

Shadoe made a slight laugh. "Don't you think that we need to wait until we get to the house?"

"No," Lilly said.

She yanked off his hat, and ran her fingers through his long hair, winding it around one hand. "I love your hair. I've always loved the length of it, the way it hits your back. I want to braid it like a woman's, put a black ribbon at the end. I want to feel it in my face—"

"Wait a minute, Princess. Hold on." He stopped the horse, and slapped playfully at the tangled fingers in his hair. "I might give you my heart. I might even marry you, but I'm not going to let you plait my hair."

Lilly curled up against him, her breath hot on his neck as she murmured, "But, Shadoe, don't you just love the way my fingers feel?" She let her empty hand drop to his waist, then down to his groin. "Just think of how g . . . oo . . . d they—"

"Enough!"

Shadoe slung his leg over the horn of the saddle and jumped off the horse. He paused for a moment, staring up at her, thinking how wonderful she really was, how just the sight of her made him yearn to make love to her.

He held out his arms. "Get down here, woman."

"That sounds like an order to me," she teased with a half-smile.

"It is."

Lilly leaped into his arms. "I love you," she said, her breath warm and sweet in his face, and Shadoe moaned as he pulled her tightly to him, hugging her, lightly kissing her hair.

Lilly pasted his black plainsman on the top of her head, then snaked both arms tightly around his neck.

Shadoe glanced down, amused at the sight of his hat perched on the crown of her blond curls. "You have to be the boldest woman I've ever known. No scruples at all. Right mean when I think about it. Whatever you want, you get, Princess."

She pushed slightly at him, holding her head where Shadoe could see her face. "And I wanted you from the beginning. Remember?"

Lilly was looking at him with her silver eyes, shiny as newborn stars. Shadoe knew that look, that fatal, delusive warmth seen only in the eyes of a woman on the edge of giving herself to a man.

He stiffened, felt himself grow hot and hard with need. "I remember," he told her in a husky tone. "I remember everything about you, about us."

"Then make love to me, Shadoe. Right here. Right now. On this land of ours."

He hesitated. There were other plans, schemes to take her home, to woo her with sweet words and soft gestures, to feel a feathery bed and pillow against their skin as he made love to her, touched and kissed every silky inch of her naked body.

The mesa. The sky. The wind. It suddenly made sense to him. Nature as a background. That raw sex he'd dreamed of, the wordless, silent labor of their bodies, the need to be one, to be lost in something else, to feel for the first time the beginning of something new and greater than just the two of them. Shadoe shivered with the thought of it. He and Lilly, making love so pure and natural, unmistakably savage.

He got terribly serious, and his words almost wavered as he told her, "All my years away from you, Lilly darlin', have been years of confession. I feel for the first time that I have really come home. Home to you, home to love, home to forgiveness."

"Don't talk. Just kiss me, Shadoe."

His mouth took hers in a hard kiss, and Lilly moved, catching his face in her soft hands. Instinctively, without any thought or plan, Shadoe dropped to the ground, pulling Lilly on top of him.

His hands plundered her skirt, ran up the silky skin of her thighs. He soon discovered that she was still wearing her muslin nightgown, that she had no other clothes on beneath the simple garment.

He couldn't help but laugh. "You amaze me, Lilly."

"Take your shirt off," she said with a smile. "I want to touch you."

He inclined his head, tugged at his clothes, all the time feeling Lilly's nimble fingers playing at his pants. Shadoe obliged her, lifted his hips, letting her shove his jeans toward his knees. Somehow he lost a boot, kicked out of one leg, then reached to drag Lilly across the arch of his muscled hips.

She sat on him, her soft, wet flesh wrapped over his erection. She was smiling down into his face like a conquering queen sitting on a throne. His hat was her crown.

Shadoe smiled. Lilly moved. Shadoe moaned.

Then he gasped as he felt her hand reach out and grab his shaft. He closed his eyes, the world suddenly gone. Black, flat, and dull, his mind drifted with nothing but the thought of her body sliding over his in one deep drive.

He heard her cry, impaled, trembling, rocking back and forth against him, shaking with excitement, and he thought he would die. The breath caught in his lungs, burning. He inhaled violently as his hands reached for her buttocks. He needed her to move faster, faster. The moment was rough, almost tormenting, quick.

"Lilly . . ." Her name was nothing when the moment came. He held her down as he thrust up into her, hard, relentless movements that shook her, made her scream. Her fingernails sank into his flesh.

Shadoe opened his eyes and looked dizzingly at Lilly. The hat was gone. She was leaning closer, collapsing. Her long blond hair spilled like syrup, slow and thick across her shoulders, down her back, on his face, sugary-sweet against his lips.

He cried out, his voice lost in her breath as their mouths met. And he kissed her and kissed her and kissed her.

The wind and land whispered, and the moon, once golden, paled, waning toward the dawn.

Shadoe and Lilly had almost reached the Oasis when they heard the shots, not one or two, but a spray of rattling explosions that seemed like a thousand bullets echoing through the dry stirring air.

"What in the hell is that?"

"It sounds like firecrackers on the Fourth of July," commented Lilly.

He jerked back on his reins and gave her a warning look. "You stay here," he told her immediately. Shadoe pulled his rifle from its sleeve, and Lilly watched him check to see if it was loaded.

"You can't leave me here alone, standing in the middle of nowhere with no horse, no protection," she protested while Shadoe hurriedly pushed shells into the chambers. "I won't be safe if they're rustlers—"

"Don't argue with me, Lilly. You aren't going."

"Oh, yes, I am." She grabbed him securely around the waist. "We're safer together."

He drew a heavy breath and Lilly caught the sound of it. Resignation. His eyes narrowed while he studied the distance. "You may be right. I hated to think I left you here for someone to take hostage if need be."

Another salvo of shots fired, and Shadoe uttered a low curse. "Hang on and mercy, woman, keep your head low!"

The rope burned, and Jesse realized that his efforts were in vain. He was going to die, dangling at the end of a rope like a twisted sack of grain. He'd seen a thief hang once, black and blue in the face, gasping for that last breath of air, pissing in his pants.

The rope tightened, and Jesse tried to scream. *Stop, you fools! You've got the wrong man! You've got the wrong man! You've got the . . .*

Shadoe and Lilly rushed through the low bush and burst into the clearing near the bunkhouse. A mob of faces met them, and Lilly quickly recognized several of the men. Luke Miller and his boys were gathered with several Double S ranch hands. They were in the middle of stringing up three men.

For a moment, everything became an unbelievable blur of images: the men shouting and screaming; shots being fired; laughter; cursing; and then the sight of three men hanging from the rafters of the gable. Shadoe's new bunkhouse had been turned into a makeshift executioner's gallows.

Lilly screamed, felt her lungs explode. Her heart pounded in her chest as she stared up at the convulsive faces. "Jesse!"

Shadoe stared at Luke. "What in the hell are you doing? This is my property!"

"Stringing 'em up!" His dark eyes were filled with hate, and the sight of Lilly McFall leaping off the back of Shadoe's horse and running the short distance toward the bunkhouse didn't seem to matter.

"Get her out of here!" Luke hollered at Shadoe.

Lilly was desperate. The seconds seemed like minutes while she ran to Jesse's feet and held up her hands, reaching to give him support. His body was swaying from the lowest point, and she could see that he was still breathing.

"Shadoe, please. Oh, my God, help me! Someone please help me!"

He heard her pleading voice, looked with apparent suspicion at Luke Miller. "Cut him down," he said. "Now!"

Luke grimaced. "He'll hang with the other two horse thieves. I caught Martin and Dice red-handed with some of my breed. They killed one of my men. Butchers! All three of them." He pitched a chilling stare at Shadoe. "And Tom Woodward will swing just like his thieving brother!"

Lilly screamed as she heard Jesse gag. "Shadoe, stop them. Stop them!"

The seconds were passing, and Jesse Woodward was dying.

Shadoe pointed the rifle at Luke. At the same time, he slid out a knife. In one quick, fluid motion, he rode over and sliced Jesse's dangling body from the rafter.

Jesse fell across the crest of horse mane, and Shadoe dropped the knife to grab the folded, gasping figure with his free hand.

Lilly screamed, but the crowd hushed, a thick combative silence that quickly divided Luke's men from Shadoe's. They scattered.

"Damn you, Sinclair! You ain't got no right to do this."

"Cut them down, Luke, or I'm going to shoot you."

Luke glanced wearily up at the two remaining bodies. He thumbed back his hat and grinned at Shadoe. "Those two are dead, Sinclair."

"Cut them down anyway, or I'm going to put a bullet in your brain."

Luke carefully wiped the sweat from his face, and Lilly, watching, saw the anxious look in his eyes, realized that Luke was thinking of firing on Shadoe.

She moved back, felt her pulses jump.

"Don't do it. Don't draw against me on this one." Shadoe lifted the rifle in aim. "If we shoot it out, I'll kill you, Miller. Why get yourself killed over this one? If he's really guilty, he'll hang."

Luke's features stiffened, and his gaze turned vengeful.

"You'll take him straight to the sheriff. See that justice is done?"

"Of course he will!" Lilly cried, moving to Shadoe's horse. "But only after he's seen the doctor. He's hurt badly, you fool!"

Luke's gaze softened as he stared at Lilly's desperate efforts. She was struggling with Jesse's limbs, attempting to pull the wounded man off Shadoe's horse without causing him any more harm. One of the Double *S* men ran over and helped her, but Shadoe kept his aim dead center on Luke's head.

"What's it going to be, Luke?"

The young man sighed heavily. "Cut them down," he ordered one of his men. "Pack 'em up and take 'em in town for the law to have."

Luke turned, swung to his saddle. "I'm sorry you had to see this, Lilly." He tipped his hat to Shadoe in a mocking gesture. "Jesse may have been at the wrong place at the wrong time, but those other two deserved to die. If I was you, Sinclair, I'd watch my back. Pepper Maddox is out there somewhere, and he's guilty as hell. Dice and Martin admitted it."

"And Tom?" Shadoe lowered his rifle. "Did they mention Tom?"

"No. Nothing about Woodward."

With those words, Luke swung his horse around and rode quickly away, the remainder of his men following. They cut a direct path north across the grasslands, which looked grizzled and barren under the milky moonlight.

The rifle fell into its sleeve, and Shadoe dismounted. "Bring the buckboard!" he shouted.

Lilly sat on the ground, Jesse's head in her lap.

"How's he doing?" asked Shadoe as he bent over and touched her gently on the arm.

"Breathing . . . breathing." She looked up into Shadoe's eyes. Dust stirred in the air and in the steaming mist of light in front of his face. "Thank you. You saved him."

"I hope it wasn't in vain."

"What do you mean?"

"If Pepper's in on this rustling, then most likely Tom is the ringleader. Jesse may have known."

Lilly shook her head. Her fingers gently stroked the young man's face. Jesse had fainted in her arms.

"No," she said bluntly. "Jesse would never have been involved. Not with stealing, with murder. I won't ever believe that. Not ever, Shadoe."

The buckboard arrived, and Shadoe and the other men slowly loaded Jesse into the back of it. Lilly crawled in, and once again pillowed Jesse's head in her lap. She bent over him, listening for his breath, which was now unexpectedly low and quiet. And she smiled when she realized that his breathing was somehow coming easier to him.

Shadoe tied his horse to the back, then climbed onto the seat of the new buckboard. One of his men jumped aside, riding with a rifle between his knees.

The buckboard lurched forward.

Looking at the bruises on Jesse's body, the rope burn around his neck, Lilly suddenly trembled with fear. "Jesse Woodward, you are *not* going to die on me. You hear me, Jesse? Poor Molly just got that pretty new dress and she's planning on wearing it this summer when you marry her. Do you hear me, Jesse? Do you hear me?"

It was dawn when they reached Montfort, the sunlight bright red in the morning sky. A rush of wind swept through the streets, sending swirls of thick dust motes into the crisp air. It seemed to catch the buckboard in a funnel of choking wind, red and stiff, red and rough against the skin.

A red wind, thought Lilly, *a strange, red wind.*

Jackson Williams closed the door behind him. "Well?"

Williams looked painfully at Lilly and shook his head, a trace of indecision on his face. "Doc Brown says that he was beaten pretty bad. Neck's fine, but he's black and blue, every inch of 'em. From what the sheriff got out of Luke's men, they found him that way. But who knows? Maybe they did the beatin'."

Shadoe blew out a thick stream of cigarette smoke. "Not Luke's style. Dice and Martin beat him."

Jackson turned his gaze to Shadoe. "Where's Luke now?"

Shadoe dropped his smoke, crushing the fire with the toe of his boot. He reached over and grabbed Lilly's shaking hands. "When he left the Oasis, he was heading north. Probably to his place," he told the deputy as he stared into her gray eyes. "You all right?"

She nodded, but the tears quickly filled her eyes as she pulled away from him. Lilly turned her gaze to the hotel wall, slumped against it in a gesture of despair. "Jesse can't die. It's just too awful. Poor . . . Jesse . . . Molly."

"There's things in this world that we have no control over, Lilly," Shadoe told her. "We did what we could. The rest is up to Jesse."

Lilly sobbed uncontrollably, and Jackson walked down the hall toward the stairs.

When he was out of sight, Shadoe spoke her name. Lilly looked at him.

"Time we went," he told her.

"Where do we go, Shadoe?" she asked him with a hint of confusion, a trace of doubt. Nothing seemed to make sense for her after seeing Jesse hanging in the bunkhouse. She had this incredible feeling of disorientation. "Where do we belong?"

Strangely, Shadoe didn't answer her.

Chapter 31

The morning turned long and sticky hot.

Lilly slept fitfully in Shadoe's narrow bed and often—too many times to count—Shadoe would walk into the room and look down at her, watch her sleep and dream, and wonder if her mind was drifting with much the same thoughts as his.

Last night had certainly changed everything. But it was not Lilly's leaving her father that had altered his thoughts, not even the wild lovemaking on the road, but Jesse's hanging at the Oasis. That one horrible deed had complicated the past, the present, the future. Like a ghost, it rose from the dust of a grave, screaming out the sins of a lifetime. If Jesse Woodward died, it was sure to haunt everyone forever.

Close to noon, Shadoe roamed upstairs to see if Lilly was awake, if she was hungry enough to try some of Lo Ching's chicken pie, but he found her still resting. And part of him was happy for it.

Lilly lay on her side, her legs drawn up. Nothing but her bare toes stuck out from the muslin nightgown. And Shadoe couldn't help but smile at them, those soft pink toes.

He dragged his sleeve across his face, wiping the sweat from his brow. The hot, gummy morning had soaked through his underarms, drawing dark stains on his clean, white shirt.

But Lilly's skin looked powdery cool. Her bare feet, her porcelain face.

Shadoe desperately wanted to touch her. The smoky sunlight showed up the soft curve of her cheek, and her long, thick lashes. She was so beautiful, the kind of woman that made a man think and do crazy things. *Like now,* Shadoe thought, bewildered.

With all the trouble, the problems, the responsibilities, all he could think about was making love with her, being caught up in the flow of her movements, drowning thick in orgasm.

Damn! Lilly is driving me crazy. Everything is driving me crazy!

A cold wave ran through his body, and Shadoe shook as he stood before the bed. He couldn't think about making love with her again. Not now. There were things to be done, important things.

Oh, yes, Lilly was living with him at the Double *S*, but for how long, and how long happy? He closed his eyes, shut back the thoughts, but the images of Jesse hanging from the rafters flooded his head once again. Since the hanging, Shadoe realized that he had to tell Lilly, tell Jesse, even tell Tom, the whole and final truth about Anne, and the thought, contaminated with guilt and regret, even fear, soured in his stomach.

It seemed that the great lessons of his life had all been learned through error and self-condemnation.

Sure, Lilly had accepted Joseph's being the father of Anne's child, but what would Lilly do when she knew the rest?

His skin prickled with anxiety, doubts, all the longings that he had carried over the years. He started pacing in front of the bed, rubbing his hands as though they ached. His whole body ached with the present situation. If the past didn't destroy Lilly's happiness as well as his own ambitions, what about the mess that was going on now? The persistent rustling and murders had reached a furious pitch.

Yes, Lilly was at the Double *S*, but she wasn't safe. No one was safe with Pepper Maddox on the loose, thought Shadoe as he turned and walked quickly out the room. Something had to be done, and he was going to do it.

Lo Ching met him at the front door of the house. "You leave now?"

Shadoe nodded. "Soon. I need to talk to Lewis first." Shadoe glanced out at the yard. His eyes were fretful. "You seen him?"

"He's in the kitchen," Lo Ching answered. "Came in while you upstairs." The Chinaman narrowed his dark eyes at the stairway. "Miss Lilly still sleep?"

"Yes."

"You wake her before you go?"

"No."

Lo Ching frowned. "She be mighty angry when she wakes up and finds you gone, Mister Shadoe."

Shadoe opened his mouth to explain, but stopped

when his young son came bounding out of the parlor. "Papa! Papa!"

The words stretched at Shadoe. He felt his gut wrench, and a bitter taste filled his mouth. It was not the boy's words that goaded him, but his own stupidity.

"I should have told the truth years ago," he muttered, grabbing Joey, pulling the young boy up into his arms. With Lo Ching following, Shadoe walked hurriedly through the parlor and into the kitchen.

He sat down, across from Lewis, a frown plastered on his face. Shadoe ran his hand over Joey's hair, and the boy smiled in response.

"I keep thinking that this is all my fault," Shadoe said aloud.

Lewis was stirring a piece of bread in the thick chicken juice. "What's your fault?" he asked without looking up from his plate.

Shadoe gave the boy a little shake. "Get down, Joey."

The boy made no protest. Obediently, he sprang off Shadoe's lap, turning quickly, facing his father with a questioning expression spread wide on his face. "We go to the Oasis? You said we could go lookin' at the new house today."

Shadoe looked at the boy, realized how much he had missed in this child's life. It was painful to think of it, painful to think that he would ever break another promise to this precious and loving child. He took a thick swallow before saying, "Not today. Too hot for a ride. But very soon." Shadoe took the child's hand and smiled. "Remember what I told you. A man doesn't ride in the middle of the day, not in the heat unless he has to. You ride at night, when it's cool."

Shadoe lifted his gaze to Lo Ching. "It's so hot and he's bored. Maybe you should fetch him some cool water and let him bathe? Cool him off a bit. Let him play for a while."

"Oh, Papa. I'm already clean enough." The boy gave his other hand to Shadoe. "See, both hands, clean as can be," Joey pleaded with a wide smile.

Shadoe grinned. "But you can play in the tub."

"I'd rather play in the river," Joey said. "You said you'd take me down to the river . . . teach me how ta swim."

"Not today, Joey. Papa needs to talk to Lewis, and then I'm going to go into town. I need to take care of some business."

Lewis looked up from his food.

"Can I go? Can I go?" Joey yelled.

"No, maybe tomorrow. I told you it was too hot for a long ride." Shadoe paused, seeing the disappointment on the child's face. Very gently, he touched Joey on the cheek. "Miss Lilly is here, upstairs asleep. She'll be getting up soon, and I want you to stay here and keep her company. Can you do that for me?"

Joey beamed, his blue eyes wide. "Can we ride the new pony?"

Shadoe grinned. "Of course you can. Lewis will saddle her up for you later this afternoon, when it cools down a bit. Won't you, Lewis?"

"I sure will, and we'll saddle that little mare up for Miss Lilly and ride over to the river and find a good swimming spot for them lessons."

Joey clapped his hands.

"Keep a wide eye on your back, Lewis," Shadoe warned in a low voice.

"It'll be all right."

"Come on, little man, let's go upstairs and find some clean clothes," Lo Ching said as he reached to take the youngster's hand again. "Your papa got some talking to do, and I got some cleaning to do. We get this bath over in a hurry." He gave Shadoe a worried look, then guided Joey from the room.

When Shadoe was sure that he heard their footfalls on the stairs, he glanced sharply over at Lewis. "Maybe you should stay closer to the house."

Lewis swallowed a bit of chicken. "Maddox won't come here. You know that. Not his way." He made a mocking grin. "More likely, he'll ambush you on your way into Montfort or when you come back."

Shadoe's mouth tightened. "Everything is such a mess. Everything. I should have told Tom and Jesse the truth about Anne the day I buried her."

"Is that what you meant by this being all your fault?"

"Yes," Shadoe said with a slight nod. "It was wrong to live a lie. Can't you see that if Tom and Jesse had known that Joseph was to blame, then none of this would be happening?"

Lewis put down his fork. "You're thinking of Jesse hangin'."

"Goddammit, yes! It's my fault that boy was strung up and you know it as well as I do!"

"You're a fool to waste any thinkin' over it, Shadoe. You didn't steal those cows and horses, kill all those people. Pepper and his boys did, and, yes, just maybe Tom Woodward's behind the whole mess. And that's a big maybe." Lewis pointed a finger at him. "But just because Tom blamed you for Anne's death, for everything else, don't give him the right to destroy all these other lives—if he's the one. He should have drawn you out, faced you on a street, and called it to your face like a man."

Shadoe ran his fingertips over his brow, the bridge of his nose. "I'm going to end this mess once and for all," he muttered into his hands. "I'm going into town and tell Jesse the truth while he still breathes, and then I'm going to find Tom."

"Alone?"

Shadoe looked at Lewis through the web of taut fingers.

The answer came out slow. "A . . . lone."

When Lilly opened her eyes, she knew immediately that she had slept the whole day away. A murky gloom filled the air, and the frail light that somehow stretched through the window glass thinned quickly in her drowsy gaze.

She moved anxiously to look out the window. The sun was setting, a singular, caldron scar over the western edge of the tree-lined horizon.

She cursed herself for wasting time, for sleeping when she should have been with Shadoe, but she was still so tired, emotionally drained. Even now, after a day's rest, fatigue pounded like a fist over her head.

She quickly found her bag, slipped into a plain white blouse and dark blue skirt. On her feet, she wore her riding boots. Practical clothes for a woman who had planned to keep up with a fast-moving man.

And Shadoe was a fast-moving man. She doubted if he was there now. Why else would he have let her sleep all day? He had gone into town, or worse, he had gone gunning for Pepper Maddox.

Downstairs, she found Lewis sitting in the parlor, alone.

The moment he saw her, he pulled his pocket-watch from its fob and opened it. A soft melody played. "Eight o'clock," he told her with a plain expression.

She stepped into the room, slipped into a chair across from him, staring pointedly at his clear, green eyes. For as long as she had known Shadoe, she had known this man, too. Distant, a man of few words with all women, Lewis often appeared cold and unconcerned, but Lilly knew that he was very sensitive to Shadoe's needs.

"I shouldn't have rested so long," she began, her voice almost a whisper in the quiet house. "I slept too hard."

"A person who sleeps like that needs it, Miss McFall."

"I suppose so, but to miss the day?" Her lips were dry from the heat, and Lilly ran her tongue over them. "Where is everyone?"

Staring very casually at her, Lewis pushed his watch back into his trouser pocket. "I reckon the boy is sleepin' by now. He rode his new pony all afternoon, not to mention the two baths before and after." Lewis leaned back against the sofa. "The kid was exhausted when Lo Ching carried him upstairs."

"Lo Ching?" asked Lilly.

"Still with the boy."

She hesitated before asking the next question. Something about the way Lewis looked gave her warning. But she had to know, even if the news was that Shadoe had formed a posse and gone looking for the rest of the rustlers. "And where is Shadoe? I know that he's not here at the Double S."

Lewis dropped his gaze, and Lilly flinched. So many things could go wrong, she said to herself. So many things. She looked harshly at the foreman, the moment taking on a sense of apprehensiveness. Something had gone wrong.

"Where is he, Lewis? I have a right to know."

There was another stiff moment, then, "He went into town to see Jesse."

Lilly sighed with relief, and a smile broke across her face. "Is that all?" She almost giggled. "For heaven's sake, Lewis! The way you were looking, I thought he had gone gunning for Pepper Maddox," she exclaimed, her voice bursting with satisfaction. "Jesse! He went to tell Jesse the truth. Thank God!"

A strange look closed over Lewis's gaze, and Lilly caught sight of it. Something faultless yet brooding in his face.

Her smile faded, and she suddenly felt very foolish, though she wasn't sure why. "Shadoe did go to tell Jesse the truth about Joey, didn't he?"

Lewis nodded, but his peculiar expression held. "That he did, Miss McFall."

"And?" A pain surrounded her heart as she waited for Lewis to answer.

There was a weighty moment of silence.

"And . . . Tom," Lewis finally said. "He was seeing Tom, too."

"What?" Lilly slumped, weakened by his words.

"He took Dragon and went to Montfort to talk to Jesse, and then he said he was going to find Tom. Said he had some explaining to do. He was going to tell . . . tell everyone about it all. What happened in the past. He especially wanted to see Tom."

The last word slapped at her like an angry hand, and she swayed in the chair, suddenly dizzy and cold. Lewis jumped to his feet, moving to her side.

"How long? How long? How long?" Lilly kept murmuring over and over.

"He's been gone since right after noon."

"Oh God, no!" Lilly looked at Lewis. The news sent a white flash of pain through her head. A posse, yes. Pepper Maddox, yes, but Tom Woodward! And alone!

Lewis nodded, confirming her fears.

"But why did he go alone?"

"His decision," came the quick, earnest reply, but Lilly could see that Lewis was uneasy with his answer, troubled with Shadoe's determination to handle the affair by himself. He retreated from her, standing stiff, trying to look unmoved by her fear.

She shook her head at him. The gesture was accusing, unforgiving, violent. "We have to go after him—now. He's in danger. Tom's insane! He threatened Shadoe!"

Lewis took a breath. "Shadoe knows these things, Miss McFall," he reassured her. "He knows the boy's gone bad. Known for a long time."

She rose from the chair, reached out and grabbed Lewis's hands. Her body went rigid. "You don't understand, Lewis. In some crazy way Tom planned all this for revenge. His feelings for me, possessing Joey, buying the Double S, they were all to hurt Shadoe, to destroy him."

"I don't understand what you mean, Miss Lilly. Tom planned? How?"

"In his head. Twisted thoughts. Everything he has done in life for the last five years has been motivated by an obsessive need to revenge his sister's death. If Tom thinks for an instant that his plans have all failed, he'll stop at nothing to kill

Shadoe. He can't accept the truth. The lies are too prized, too fixed!" Her voice choked. "Nothing, Lewis . . . even if it means his own life. Tom will die putting a bullet in Shadoe."

"I promised him that I wouldn't leave you or the boy."

She broke away from him, angered. "Then I'll go after him myself!"

Lewis cursed lowly as Lilly repeated her threat.

"I mean it. I'm going after him. He shouldn't have gone into town alone!"

"Damn. Damn. Damn." The words rolled from Lewis's lips in a breath of submission. "All right, Miss McFall. One hour. We'll give Shadoe one more hour. In the meantime, we'll saddle some horses, and I'll bring one of the men into the house to watch Lo Ching and the boy." His lips thinned as he asked her, "Can you wait that long?"

Lilly pulled a halfhearted face, then nodded. "One hour."

Chapter 32

The sky was cloudless, a wide, black stretch spread thick with stars. Hot and sweaty, Shadoe stopped his horse in the middle of the road and pulled off his hat.

"Something's wrong," he told his dog. "What do you think, Dragon?"

He slipped the thong from his righthand gun, then mopping the hatband, he stared pointedly around him, looking for anything that was out of the ordinary.

He had that feeling, nothing substantial, just a cracked-up premonition that turned to mush in the pit of his stomach. The muscles in his body cranked up with a thought. *Someone is watching me.*

His gaze widened. He saw. Trepidation eddied. All too late. The shot that rang wildly singed him like fire, and Shadoe groaned as he fell from the saddle, crashing against the hardpan. Sweat rolled into his eyes, and a thin layer of dust, powdered by his fall, suddenly filled his nostrils. For a moment, he lay in the road, dazed by the bullet that had creased his arm, but when another shot rang out, splattering the dry dirt beside him, Shadoe drew his gun and fired.

Gunfire crackled again and again until the chambers were empty, and Shadoe knew that he was in trouble. He had no cover, but his adversary did. A snarl of low boulders just to the left of the road hid the assailant.

He hastily unfastened his gunbelt, popped several bullets out, then pushed them into his six-shooter. Crawling up on his knees, Shadoe took two dead shots at the boulders, then turned his lethal aim on his frightened horse. One shot and the animal fell to the ground. Shadoe grabbed his gunbelt and scrambled to his feet.

It was fair play now. The shots singed. The chambers turned red-hot.

Huddled behind his dead horse, Shadoe screamed curses as he loaded and reloaded, fired and fired. He was bleeding, and the bullets were running out.

It had to be Pepper, he told himself as he pushed the last two shells into the chamber. He fell on his belly, stretched against the sharp smell of his horse, lying in his own spent shells. He could hear Dragon barking, running back and forth in the darkness.

Damn the darkness! He couldn't see the enemy.

A salvo of shots fired, and Shadoe narrowed his gaze, groping for sight of an arm, a hand, anything. This was his last chance.

His mouth went dry, and he tried to swallow.

The dust and sweat made his skin itch. If only he could reach his Winchester. But he couldn't. It was buried under a ton of horseflesh.

Shadoe stared fixedly down the barrel of his gun, and the moment widened into minutes as he waited for something, anything. Then suddenly the black figure came at Shadoe in a charge of buzzing gunfire. Shadoe fired once, missed, then pulled the trigger a second time. The bullet exited the smoking gun, and the man fell, but before Shadoe could move, the assailant leaped straight to his feet and pulled a knife.

"Sonuvabitch!"

Shadoe reached for his knife, found the sleeve empty, glanced instinctively at the hardpan where he had fallen. A tiny flash of metal caught his eye. He cursed.

Before he had turned back, the man was on him. He was hit quickly across a rib, stabbed, and Shadoe felt the blood oozing, his blood, wet and sticky against his skin. He was hit again, this time across the upper sleeve of his shirt. Shadoe struggled, rolling, taking the man and the knife with him.

The two men twisted, rolled, and strained against each other. Dust filled the air, and running around them, Dragon yelped, barked, bared his teeth as he jumped skittishly at the two struggling forms.

Still fighting, Shadoe suddenly felt a dull ache growing in his chest, and as he grappled in the dirt, a strange and steadfast inertness swallowed all his efforts. His muscles wadded with fatigue. His limbs became woodlike. And the man seemed bigger, stronger, the world darker.

Inside he laughed, amused at the irony. All his

life, he had lived on the edge, wore a gun. He'd killed, and now, he could feel that he was near death.

He felt a slapping blow across his jaw, another, and then the world grew ink-black, his battle meaningless and distant as the mountains. He could vaguely hear Dragon snarling, faintly smell the dog's strong breath, hot and stinking against his own skin.

Then Shadoe was dreaming. It was early spring again, cool and light in his eyes, and he was years younger, riding high in the Land of Legends with his Lilly. There was no pain, no fear, no lies. Time was endless. . . .

The sound of a wounded animal, screaming and screaming, filled the night air, and the eerie screeches routed a flow of cold shivers directly up Lilly's spine. Her back tingled, her neck tensed.

"What was that?" she called, pulling her horse to a halt, listening. Lewis and one of his men drew up beside her.

The piercing howl came once more, and then silence, nothing but silence spinning in the blackness.

Lilly's breath clogged in her throat. "Wolf?" She flicked her eyes at Lewis.

"No . . . just a dog."

"Dog?"

They passed a look, and then Lewis raised his Winchester and fired a shot in the air. Spurring his horse in the flanks, he cried, "Dragon!"

With her hands over her face, Lilly cried. "Oh, please . . . please . . . don't leave me, don't leave me."

Shadoe opened his eyes, everything a blur, confusing, a rush of sound, surprise, Lilly gasping, screaming something, all shrill and vague. Still dreaming, perhaps.

He struggled to focus. His gaze jerked side to side. And finally, after a moment, Shadoe realized where he was. He was lying in his bed. Really awake. Somehow back, somehow safe at the Double S, somehow alive. And Lilly was staring at him, her gray eyes rounded. A stream of lighted tears poured over her pink cheeks. She looked frightened, and he hated it. Shadoe groaned, attempted to move, failed.

The morning sunlight spilled in, bright and hot against his skin. He felt scorched, thirsty. He couldn't swallow, but in his desperation, he whispered, "Tired . . . so tired . . . Lilly . . . love . . ."

Then he closed his eyes again. The red turned black against his lids, and he slipped once more into unconsciousness.

Dreams. . . .

Anne, sweet and beautiful. Anne sitting on her bed, singing a lullaby, waiting for him, smiling when she catches sight of his movements.

"You back already?" Voice honeyed, eager, filling his ears, ringing, saying his name in a low, cool tone, fine as desert sand on a winter's night. It doesn't stop, a thousand powdery grains pouring into his head. You back already? You back already? You back already?

It doesn't stop.

His name.

He reaches out, breathes in her vibrations, sees the color of her eyes, so blue and light, cornflowers in a late-spring garden, like her kisses, greeting him with tenderness. Those eyes, so full of tenderness, so full of life, then dull, suddenly right in front of him, blank, the cornflowers, the kisses, the smile, Anne— all gone.

Screams and hands on the pink and green of her dress, fingers running through her dark hair.

Her name.

It does not stop. It never stops, ringing, everywhere, out of the walls, out of the floor, out of lungs and hearts, out of mouths.

He looks up. He sees Joseph McFall standing at the top of the stairs.

Fast. Fast. Fast.

Everyone thinks and runs . . . keeps running.

Shadoe runs. . . .

"Nooooooooooooo—" Shadoe woke to the sound of his own cries. He bolted upright in the bed, shaking, sweating in the twisted linen. The moon poured its milky light over his knotted features, and instinctively, he turned to stare out the window at it, his eyes glazed, fixed on the silvery ball in the sky.

"Not again . . ."

A full moon, the only light in the room, but enough for Lilly to see him. She moved quickly from her chair, reaching for him as she sat on the bed. "Shadoe," she called in a whisper, taking him in her arms like a mother would clasp her child, comforting him with a gentle rocking motion, comforting herself. "Shadoe, I'm here. Don't worry, everything is going to be fine," she said, but her words gushed with doubts, uncertainties.

For the last two weeks, while recovering from his wounds, Shadoe had been plagued with persistent nightmares. Night after night, he had woke up screaming. And each night, Lilly observed that though Shadoe's physical wounds were healing, emotionally, he was very troubled.

He appeared listless, distant, uneasy, split to pieces in a way that she had never witnessed in a man. And Lilly sensed that she was losing him to something, something she couldn't see or feel, something she couldn't fight.

"Damn, I was dreaming . . . again," he moaned as she curled up against him. "The same damn dream."

For the moment, he clutched at her, his arms circling her, holding on like a struggling vine. His cheek rested on her hair. "I can't stop it. I can't stop it," Shadoe said, pressing his fingers into folds of her muslin gown, kneading the skin of her back. "I don't want to sleep anymore."

"Tell me the dream," Lilly said over his shoulder, her voice trembling. She wanted to know his pain, wanted to rid him of the torment. "Tell me what makes you so sad that you aren't able to sleep a whole night through."

"I can't. Not now. I hate the thought of it."

She pushed away from him, just enough to let him see her face. Her eyes flicked over his drawn features. There was a strange curl to his mouth, a hard, relentless grimace that frightened Lilly. If only he would make love to her, exorcise the demons with need and lust.

"Then kiss me, Shadoe."

His breath quickened at the request, and for a moment, he said nothing, did nothing, just stared into her eyes, fixed and pointed, as though to look away meant ceasing to exist, dying, literally dying.

The moment was incredible for Lilly. This was a

man on the edge of something . . . something dark
and dangerous and forbidden, and she was holding him, breaking the fall by the sheer force of
her gaze. Love had never meant so much. Loving
Shadoe. . . .

She wound her arms around his neck. A soft,
almost eerie feeling inundated her body. It was like
nothing she had felt before with him. A strangeness. A tenderness. Some achy need. And like a
gossamer web, it fell completely over Lilly. She
gasped. Her skin tingled at its touch. She was cold
and hot at the same time. Her heart began racing.

"I love you," she quickly whispered. "I have loved
you all my life. As a child loves a father. As a sister
loves a brother. As a woman loves a man. I love you
completely."

Shadoe's arms circled her waist, his fingers pressing into the gathers of her muslin gown. "Oh, Lilly,"
he muttered over and over, and then he pulled her
against him.

Her head fell back. He kissed her neck.

"Shadoe . . ."

"Lilly . . ."

Some more low-said words, vague and meaningless. Then they were falling, falling, back on
the bed, against the sheets, tumbling and reaching. Shadoe was clearly anxious now, wanting,
moaning, kissing her everywhere, on her neck,
her cheeks, her eyes, her lips, then her breasts,
kissing and licking the nipples right through the
fabric of her nightgown.

The moonlight came and went in her eyes.

Lilly felt Shadoe's needy hands, felt the buttons
slipping from the holes on her gown, and then she

felt him crawling all over her. Inch after inch she was covered with his flesh.

He smelled different, not the usual virile scent of leather and spice, but something all his, something sweet, and she took a deep breath, held it in her lungs until Shadoe's kiss took it from her.

After that, they were one. She raised her legs, crossing them behind his back.

They were falling again. Lilly somewhere she'd never been. Shadoe on top of her. So slow, so easy, that with every drag of his body, Lilly thought she would climax. But she didn't.

The moment of fulfillment carried on and on with a life of its own, and all Lilly could do was look at Shadoe, admire him, devour him as his body moved back and forth in hers.

She ran her hands over and over the outside of his slow-moving hips. So strong. How she loved the feel of his hard thighs beneath her fingers. "Oh, Shadoe, I'm half out of my head."

He smiled, a lazy grin, and Lilly shivered at the sight of it.

"Do you love me more than anything?" she asked him.

"Yes . . . yes."

"Say it . . ."

"I love you . . ."

"More than anything?"

His movements quickened. "I love you more than anything. Mercy, yes, I love you . . ." He closed his eyes, his breath growing ragged as his hips pressed thick and unyielding against hers.

Hasty movements. Hasty words.

"Open your eyes, Shadoe."

"I can't."

"Say my name."

"I can't."

"Move."

"I'm moving."

"Oh, Shadoe."

She was pulling his hair now, the long, unruly strands tangling between her urgent fingers. She was pulling him down against her, his exquisite weight crushing her body, pounding, and then she was moaning and pleading, closing her eyes, clinging to him like she was part of his body. And she was.

Shadoe pushed on a few moments, then collapsed against her. It was over, but the moment still reeled with beating hearts and violent breathing, with trickles of sweat and exhausted limbs.

"I can't breathe . . ."

With her soft complaint, Lilly heard Shadoe sigh, and then he was moving again, off her, rolling over, lying on his back. He reached up and brushed the hair back from his face in a sweep of fingers. His eyes were still closed.

Lilly thought he looked weary. She reached out, and with one finger, lightly rolled some of his hair around it.

Shadoe turned and looked at her.

Blue and full of love—that was all she could see in his eyes. He said her name. She smiled. So did he.

But it didn't last long. Before she could tell him that she loved him again, he was frowning, looking away from her.

"What's wrong?" she asked him.

"Everything," he told her. "Everything is wrong."

Chapter 33

"Everything? I don't understand? Look at what we just shared. How can everything be wrong?"

Shadoe was silent. Instead, he quickly sat up on the edge of the bed, reaching for some clothes on a nearby chair.

Somehow, Lilly wasn't surprised at his actions. She knew that he was on the edge of breaking, that will power alone was making his mind work.

She had hoped to save him with her love. But as he had told her once, love wasn't always everything.

Lilly rose from the bed and found her muslin gown. After she had slipped it over her head, she asked him bluntly, "Are we still talking about the dreams?"

"I can't sleep . . . I can't think," he moaned. "I think I might be going crazy. I feel as though I'm going crazy."

Lilly sat down on the bed next to him. Reaching

up, she stroked his face lightly with her fingers. A fresh scrub of beard ran rough against her skin. She liked the feel of it, coarse and uneven, damp with sweat and salt. "You can tell me anything. I love you."

He stared into her eyes, his gaze suddenly blank. Even his frown had crumbled, but his arm snaked around her waist. He was tense. "I'm not sure I should tell you . . . not anymore. I don't know. I don't know what to do!"

"Were you dreaming about the ambush? Are you reliving it over and over? The pain? The fear?"

"No."

She hesitated. "Is it Dragon?" The dog was dead and buried, brutally butchered by the assailant for some reason. Shadoe had buried it the first day that he was able to stand. Dragon lay in the little cemetery with his father and several of the old Spanish ranch hands.

Shadoe's arms dropped away from her, and he leaned back slightly. "No, not the dog."

"Not Dragon?" Lilly gently cupped his face in her hands. "Then what, love? Tell me. You can't go on like this." She gazed at him longingly. His eyes were so blue and clear, so filled with pain that it hurt her just to look at them, and terror washed over her.

"I don't want to talk about it," Shadoe commented in an apathetic tone. He shoved at her hands, and Lilly flinched as he moved slightly on the bed, as if to escape her. "Leave me alone, Lilly. For God's sake, just leave it alone for a while."

"No. Talk to me," she pleaded.

He said nothing, just looked away from her, staring out the window again.

Not tonight, she told herself while looking at him. She drew a long-suffering sigh. *I can't stand any more of this indifference. You aren't going to pull away from me . . . not tonight.*

Lilly moved over on the bed, putting a respectable distance between them.

"I can't go on like this, Shadoe," she suddenly told him, her voice rising to a higher pitch. "Since the attack, you don't look at me. You don't really want to touch me. Oh, I know that we made love . . . That isn't what I'm talking about. I'm talking about you not really being here with me. It's true. You act as though you don't want to care, that it hurts too much even to be in the same room with me. You're almost indifferent."

He swung his gaze to her, and Lilly could see that he was stunned by her approach. "What do you mean by that? I care about you. I touch you. I look at you. I can't keep from looking at you!"

"Lies. Just lies. Just like all your other damn lies."

Shadoe's eyes turned black and violent, and Lilly saw a muscle twitch in his jaw. Dead silence followed her accusations.

She almost smiled at him. At last! Some emotion. He was going to face her. Angry, yes! But he was going to talk to her!

Shadoe leaned over, staring pointedly at her, his wrathlike features set in stiff lines. "I'm looking at you now," he told her, but his tone gave her warning. It was chilly, frosted with an edge of caution, layered with resentment.

"Looking through me, maybe," she dared.

"What in damnation are you talking about?" Shadoe grabbed her shoulders, shook her a little.

"See me. I'm looking at you." He clutched her tighter. "Feel me. I'm touching you."

Lilly laughed at him. "Not really. Tell me the dream, Shadoe. Tell me all your secrets." She heard herself breathe, felt the pounding of her heart. "Come back to me. Be with me like you were all those years ago. I need you!"

Though he still touched her, his grasp relaxed, and Lilly saw the pain in Shadoe's face again. The anger she had so desperately wanted to see vanished.

Defeat rose and rose and rose, and Lilly trembled at the sound of his voice whispering, "No . . . no . . . no . . . I can't. I can't ever be what you want me to be. I need to go away . . . run . . . keep on running."

The words came at her like knives. Lilly looked at Shadoe, truly surprised. This was the man who had been her symbol of strength, her hero, but now he had the look of a beaten man, and the sight of it disgusted her. All her life, she had been fighting for him, for the memories, waiting, yearning for Shadoe to take her in his arms, to love her in spite of everyone and everything.

But now? At that very moment, she despised him, hated him for daring to hurt her again.

"You bastard!" she shouted. "You don't even care enough about me to share the pain, the loss. You like the secrets. They make you feel powerful. That's why you kept them all these years. They gave you strength and purpose, held your body up like chalk bones do!"

Shadoe grimaced, slammed his fist on the wall behind the bed. "You couldn't take the truth," he swore at her in a biting tone. "It'll stick in your gullet, strangle you."

"Try me."

He turned from her, his head falling back, and a long anguished breath rolled from his throat. He looked up at the dark sky, the silvered moonlight falling through the glass of the window, falling across his face, showing the pain and hurt.

"You want the truth. Well, here it is. Your wonderful brother, dear Joseph, killed Anne," Shadoe uttered. "I brought him . . . brought him up the back stairs at the Woodward house, left Anne in the room with him . . . even after—"

"What are you talking about?" Lilly interrupted.

The ugly words settled in her mind like a mirage in the hot desert sun, drifting, blurred, not real. "What's this about Joseph being at the Woodward house? He wasn't there."

Shadoe avoided her questions as though he didn't hear her voice. His gaze remained fixed on the sky. "They argued," he said in a monotonical voice. "Anne screaming and crying. I remember her, looking at me with those blue eyes, begging me to take him away, and all I did was stand there and let him abuse her, tell her things he didn't really mean. It made me feel good because she was choosing me over him. Oh God! The dream. That goddamn dream. It's been haunting me for years. Joseph at the top of the stairs."

Her stomach in knots, her legs shaking badly, Lilly struggled to drag herself across the bed to the other end. She felt sick to her stomach. This was not what she had expected. Talk about Anne, yes. But Joseph killing Anne? Not her brother, her strong and dashing brother, the same man who had cried and cried over Anne's death, swore he'd never love another.

Lilly shook her head. "It's not the truth! It's not," she suddenly blurted, looking at Shadoe with both anger and disbelief. "How dare you say such a thing when he is not here to defend himself! Kill Anne? It was an accident."

Shadoe turned and stared at her, a wide, vacant look in his eyes, a cold look that ran through Lilly like a blade of steel.

"Accident? Did anyone believe that when they talked about me? Oh, no, I was responsible. A murderer in the eyes of some." He laughed at her. "Oh, it's the truth, Lilly. Accept it, just like you accepted Joseph being both Anne's lover and Joey's father!"

"That was different," Lilly returned.

"Oh, different?" Shadoe laughed again, a harsh sound that made Lilly tremble. "I see. You could accept Joseph being Anne's lover because it meant that I never really betrayed you, didn't it? It was easily done, a blessing in disguise. Your pride could admit it."

Her mouth rounded a protest, but Shadoe held out his hand to stop her. "Well, it's all the damn truth. Joseph cursed Anne for marrying me—even when he didn't have enough guts to marry her himself. He ran after her when she went running down the hallway. He did, Lilly." Shadoe's voice rose to a scream. "She was so upset. He wanted her to leave me and go to England, be his mistress or something. She was so scared . . . so angry, and she fell . . ." Shadoe moaned. "Joseph watched her fall . . . Oh God! The sonuvabitch watched her fall. I saw him, standing there. She tripped. There was a hand, her hand, and it was reaching out. I heard her cry, and he just stood there—frozen—and let her go. And I was too far away." Shadoe rolled his head and moaned again. "Good Lord . . . I brought him to her. And that bastard let her die!"

"You're lying to me. It's not true. Joseph would have never done a thing like that! He would never have let anyone die intentionally. He was not a killer."

Shadoe ignored her. "And I went into town, Lilly, I told Jesse the truth. I told him everything, whispered it in his ear as he lay in the bed, bruised, beaten, hanging on to life with a thread." Shadoe clenched his hands into fists. "And the boy cried. All he could do was cry. I don't even know if he believed me."

"No," Lilly whimpered. "I don't believe you. I won't believe you. My brother may not be the kindest person in the world, but Joseph would never have hurt Anne, never hurt anyone like that."

"He was a killer. He murdered Sam Miller!"

At the sound of the words, Lilly slapped Shadoe's face, the impact stinging her own flesh.

Shadoe stiffened, and for a moment, his features were unreadable. No hate. No anger. Nothing. Lilly stared, thought she was going to faint. Her heart was beating so wildly that she couldn't breathe, felt dizzy.

"You finally got that slap," he retorted with a slight grin. "Does it feel as good to you as it does to me?"

Her throat thickened. "I didn't mean it."

"Oh, I think you did, Princess," Shadoe growled. "I think you liked it. You felt that I deserved it, and I did."

He looked at her for a long moment. Something

strange and hard flickered in his eyes, then burned
away, and Lilly felt her heart roll over at the sight
of it. He was pulling away from her again, leaving
her as surely as he had left her five years ago, and
part of her wanted him to go away.

"If it's true, why didn't you tell me, tell everyone
from the beginning?"

"I had my reasons. Good as they were, they just
aren't anymore. When I saw Jesse hanging from
the barn, I knew that I was wrong in keeping the
secrets, for taking the blame for something that I
didn't do. It wasn't me who shot Sam in the head.
It wasn't me who hurt Anne, and now . . . now Tom
has to be told, and unfortunately that may mean
killing him, or being killed. I mean to tell your
father, too." He paused, drew a heavy breath. Lilly
started to cry as she looked at him. "Your father
has to know what Joseph did. He has to realize
that his son never cared for anyone but himself.
If he understands this, then maybe he will really
believe that Joey is his own blood."

"You can't tell Papa! I won't let you," she suddenly cried through gritted teeth. "Papa's already
hurt enough!"

"Don't try to stop me. The rot is going to pour
one way or another. I'm tired of carrying Joseph's
spoils."

"But it's pointless! Pointless!"

"Damn you, Lilly. I knew you couldn't take
the truth!" Shadoe jumped up from the bed and
stomped across the room. "I want you to go
home."

"What?"

"You heard me. I want you to go back to Weatherly in the morning. You don't belong here with

me. I told you once that love was not enough. Now I can see that's true. It won't matter how much we love, how much we try, every time we look at one another, we'll see Joseph and Anne, the whole damn mess! I knew that I shouldn't have come back here!"

"No, Shadoe."

"Yes. We'll always end up fighting over the past, stuck in the same place with one another. I hate it! I tell you I hate it all!"

Lilly shook all over, angry, full of fear. "You don't mean that," she said with a whimper.

"I do, Lilly. I really mean it. There's too much trouble living here with you. I plan and plan. I even started building us a house at the Oasis, but every time we go there now, we'll see Jesse Woodward hanging from the rafters of the barn. It's too late for us. It was too late years ago." He paused, a frown smothering his darkened features, and his eyes flashed on her face.

"And there's the rustling," Shadoe added. "Pepper Maddox. Tom. You aren't safe at the Double S. No one is safe here anymore. I'm going to send the boy to San Francisco like I planned in the first place. If I live through this damn mess, I'm going to join him there."

"Leave me . . . leave me. How could you now? I was willing to give up everything for you."

"Not everything. I want to tell you something, Lilly, and I want it said plainly, the words branded in your mind so you won't ever forget them." He took a step toward her. "If Joseph ever comes back here, I'll kill him." A weighty pause passed. "Could you give up your brother's life for me?"

She couldn't talk. Lilly could barely breathe,

stunned in the steady stream of thought. How could he ask her such a thing? It was cruel and wicked. Kill Joseph?

"You must be mad! My lover murdering my brother? How could I live with that? How could my father live with that? It would kill him . . . kill Papa. You can't mean it?"

Shadoe made a little scornful sound. "Just what I thought. No matter what Joseph did, you could forgive him. A high-and-mighty McFall."

He turned and made his way to the door, opening it. He didn't look back, just stopped in the doorway as he spoke. "For what it's worth, I thought in the beginning that I was doing the right thing."

The tears fell in thick currents. Lilly blinked through them, watching his darkened shape. It shifted in the blur of her vision, in the welter of her confusion and heartache. She closed her eyes against it, closed her eyes and screamed, a fist in her mouth.

A long time passed. A very long time. When she opened her eyes, the shape and blur of a man was gone.

Later, Lilly sat alone in the dark and did some thinking.

Tears fell and fell. From somewhere came the sound of a clock ticking, and her mind clicked with its rhythm. Even though Shadoe's words had hit her hard, she knew they were true. Everything finally made sense, everything except . . . the senseless death of Sam Miller.

She couldn't understand how Sam Miller played a part in the mystery. Though Sam's death had been the one tiny clue that had begun her search for the truth, the incidents surrounding the event still eluded her, and Shadoe hadn't really told her enough to clear up the mystery.

Joseph had killed a man, and Shadoe had taken the blame. But what were the reasons behind such a senseless deed and such a cruel fate?

Lilly shuddered. Whatever the reasons were, they had to be horrible, for Shadoe had sworn to kill Joseph because of them.

Chapter 34

"Dammit, tell me the truth, Lo Ching!" Luke hollered feverishly.

Lilly took the last step off the stairs, and standing in the small foyer, peered into the other room, surprised at the sight of Luke Miller and Jackson Williams huddled in the parlor with Lo Ching. She scowled, inhaled the air which was already hot and heavy, even in the early-morning light.

"Dammit, Lo Ching," Luke continued, "I ain't asking you to betray anybody. I just need to talk to Shadoe."

Her eyes scanned the room, looking instinctively for the youngster, but not seeing Joey, she relaxed and gazed back at Luke.

Luke's face was puckered into a frown, and the impetuous horse breeder shifted on his feet, heels tapping on the floor nervously, as if he couldn't wait to get an answer. He had much the same look as he had had the night at the Oasis, but it lacked the violence and desperation.

"Where did he and Lewis go?" Luke questioned, still unaware that Lilly was listening.

"Where did who go?" Lilly asked abruptly, making her presence known. Entering the room, she looked at Lo Ching. She could see that he was distressed.

Luke and Jackson turned, both men casting Lilly a shocked and blunt stare. It was apparent to Lilly that they had not expected her to be at the Double S, not to mention her eavesdropping on their conversation.

"Miss Lilly?"

"Miss McFall?"

She smiled slowly, uneasily, and her voice was small and quiet as she said, "Hello, Luke. Deputy Williams." Lilly clasped her hands and looked at them with a little shrug. "What brings you out to the Double S this morning?"

They didn't answer, obviously speechless at her coming from the upstairs at seven o'clock in the morning. A sudden thought occurred to her, and her smile faded. "Is Jesse Woodward all right?"

Luke stuffed his hands in the pockets of his trousers. For a moment, he said nothing, but then a very warm grin opened over his darkly handsome features. And Lilly took note of the contrast. This was the man she knew, the guileless romantic of the Weatherly barbecue, the horseman who liked to play croquet with the ladies.

"He's better, Miss Lilly. Doc Brown says he may walk down that aisle with Molly Andrews after all," Luke told her in a gentle voice. "In fact, Jack and I were here to see how Shadoe was doing."

"Is that right?" Lilly laughed a bit, at herself, at them, at the irony of the situation. "As you can see, he's not here . . . more than fit enough to ride again. He's gone."

"Did he tell you where he might be going?" Luke prodded.

"No."

She eyed Lo Ching, saw the resistance in his Oriental eyes. He didn't want to tell Shadoe's business, but after the incident on the road, Lilly was reluctant to hide any of Shadoe's plans. He had barely survived being killed. Next time he might not be so fortunate.

"Did Mister Sinclair tell you where he was going, Lo Ching?" Lilly knew he wouldn't lie to her.

He hesitated, then answered in an obedient tone, "Yes, Miss Lilly. Mister Shadoe did."

"Then tell the gentlemen, Lo Ching. This isn't the time to be hiding anything."

The Chinaman made a nervous gesture with his hands, then nodded lightly at the two men. "He and Mister Lewis . . . they gone look for the man called Maddox and for Tom Woodward."

Luke sighed. "Well, he won't find Tom Woodward, that's for sure," he said coldly. He looked at Lilly, a strange expression in his big, dark eyes. "Tom's in Montfort with Jesse. Came riding in yesterday with a new man. Gonna move Jesse out to the ranch this morning. Left town at the same time that Jack and I did."

"But I thought—"

Luke cut her off with a wave of his hand. "You thought Tom was involved with Pepper and the others?" Luke shook his head. "Has an ironclad alibi for the rustling. He said Pepper had been rustling without his knowledge."

Lilly was dismayed. "And the sheriff believed him?"

"Yes, and so did your father," Luke replied, his tone carrying a trace of malice. "Mister McFall vouched for Tom *personally*. Said that Tom deserved a chance to defend himself, to prove that he had nothing to do with the trouble."

Lilly's mouth drooped in disbelief.

"I know what you're thinking, Miss Lilly, but Tom could be telling the truth," Luke said. "It's possible that Pepper and the boys were using Tom as a front. They're a sly bunch."

"But—"

Jackson interrupted, "It's true, Miss McFall." The deputy shifted his hat in his hands, and Lilly saw that he was restless and uneasy.

"Tom claimed that he'd been suspicious of Pepper and the others and that Jesse, too, was distrustful of Pepper and the Whittens. That's why the kid followed them from town."

"Is that what Jesse said?" Lilly asked, still feeling that it was all just too incredible.

"No. He didn't say that exactly. Still can't talk good enough to tell us what happened."

Lilly made a wry face as Jackson continued, "Anyways, it all has some sort of reason to it. If Tom had been in on the mess with Martin Whitten and Dice Jennings, why would those two beat Jesse like they did? It would have been just plain stupid for 'em to kill the ringleader's brother. Only sense I can make outta it is that Pepper must be the real culprit."

Lilly drew a shuddering breath. "If that's true, then I'm really relieved," she said, not quite convinced, but at the same time, wanting desperately to believe it.

It was one thing to deal with the fact that Tom hated Shadoe, that he wanted to kill him because of her and Anne, but to think that Tom Woodward had been the cause of all the rustling and murder in Harney County was quite another matter.

It was the first good news that she had heard in a long time. The only good news and for the moment, her mind, bone-weary and unhappy, accepted it. She had other worries.

Lilly turned to stare at Lo Ching. "Would you fix some coffee for the men? Some tea for me? It's going to be a long morning, I think."

The Chinaman nodded eagerly. "Want Lo Ching to make some breakfast, Miss Lilly?"

"No . . . not hungry, but thank you. Just tea and coffee, please."

Lo Ching made a clipped bow, then turned to go to the kitchen. When he was gone, Lilly glanced at Luke with a cautious eye, remembering why he was there in the first place. He wanted to see Shadoe.

"Was there any particular reason why you wanted to see Shadoe?"

Luke's expression suddenly turned empty, and he looked quickly at Jackson, as if he needed support.

"Well?" Lilly asked.

"We were just goin' to talk to him about the night of the attack," the deputy answered. "But I reckon we can talk to him about it another day."

"What about the attack?"

A silent moment followed her question.

"We picked up a trail while riding out yesterday," Jackson commented slowly. "Heading south toward number four. Blood, lots of blood, and then we found a small camp, some bandages. Pepper was hit."

"No!" Lilly snapped. "He couldn't have been. Shadoe was adamant about that. He didn't shoot Pepper. He was certain that he missed him . . . every shot." She shook her head and paced across the room, pivoting to stare at Jackson. "Shadoe knows that kind of thing. He told me that he missed Pepper. It must be someone else's trail."

"Rightly so, Miss McFall, but the blood's there, lots of it. Something happened to the man on that trail, which I might add is straight south of where Shadoe was ambushed."

Luke suddenly pounded a fist into the palm of his left hand. "Damn! Miss Lilly's right, Jack!" A wide smile came quickly to his lips.

Lilly looked at him, almost frightened by the sudden gesture. "What are you thinking, Luke?"

Jackson's features knotted in confusion. "How is she right?"

"Shadoe did miss his shot," Luke told them. "Don't you see? It's the right trail. It's even the same man. Pepper Maddox. But he ain't bleeding from no gunshot. The dog bit him!"

Lilly's eyes widened. In anger, she raised her hands to her head, dug them into her hair as she thought about Shadoe lying on the road, struggling for his life, stabbed, maybe dying. And Dragon. The good old dog had attacked the ambusher.

Her hands fell, fists covering her mouth in an act of sorrow, in an attempt to keep back the curses that were forming in her throat.

Poor Dragon, she cried to herself. She walked across the room, collapsing in a chair, thinking

of Shadoe and how much pain it had cost him to
bury that dog.

She glanced at Luke. "You're right, Luke. That's
it. That's why Pepper killed Dragon because the dog
was biting him. Dragon was protecting Shadoe."

"That dog was always a smart one," Jackson
commented.

Luke flicked Jackson a look, agreeing. "Dragon
could kill a man if he tried. He took a chewin' out
of Sam once when he and Shadoe got into a playful scuffle over a game of cards. I thought Dragon
was gonna chew Sam up for good . . ."

Lilly's eyes narrowed at the sound of Sam's name,
and she sank back in the chair, resting her head on
the back. The muscles at her nape tensed, tight as
strings on a fiddle. It took a conscious effort for
her to relax, but even after a moment passed, she
felt lightheaded. The heat, the excitement, and Sam
Miller's name echoed in her ears.

She reached up and ran her fingertips over her
brow, remembering with clarity and horror the
words that Shadoe had said the previous night.

Damn Shadoe. Damn the truth. Yes, she had
wanted the lies to come out before anyone else
was hurt. She wanted to resolve the past so that
the future could be bright and free. But her father?
Knowing about Joseph would destroy her father.

How could he do it? How could Shadoe love her
father, and at the same time, tell him that Joseph
had killed Sam Miller, and then had been responsible for the circumstances that had led to Anne's
tragedy? How could Joseph had done those things?
How? How? How?

She shook with the questions, and closing her
eyes, the faces of the dead came at her. Their

names pounded through her brain, and the present slipped away. Even Luke and Jackson's voices, as they talked on and on about Dragon and Sam, grew distant, drifted away in a blur of reflection.

Lilly was at the Weatherly barbecue, sipping lemonade, flirting and smiling at Luke, wanting to know what kept him from courting her, what kept him from talking about Sam's death. And then she was sitting in the buggy with him the morning of the church social, and Luke was hesitantly answering some of her carefully planned questions, finally admitting that Joseph was with Sam at the time of his death.

And the reflection ended there, cold, blunt reality. Everything was perfectly clear for the first time. Sam's death was becoming crystal clear in her mind. As disturbing as it was, it all suddenly made sense to Lilly. If Joseph had really murdered Sam, then that would explain all of it—Luke's never riding down to stay for too long at Weatherly, never courting her, never wanting to talk about Sam's death.

Lilly opened her eyes, blinked and stared pointedly at Luke. Everyone had always wondered how Luke had held the ranch together after Sam's death, where he had gotten the money to keep the fine breed of horses. Lilly winced, recalling Shadoe's insinuating comments about Luke's riding into town with her, evading her questions, making himself look good. He had even said that Luke could be bad, meaning that Luke had done something deceitful, too.

She sighed and breathed, the air rushing to her head. There could only be one answer—money. Luke had obviously taken money from Joseph as some sort of compensation for Sam's death.

The thought of it was horrible, but not because of Luke's action. He had been a heartbroken kid, suddenly with no family, on the verge losing everything.

But Joseph? Damn Joseph! Her brother had bought Luke's silence with McFall money.

Lilly's face knotted as she rose from the chair. "I was wondering if we could have a moment alone?" she abruptly asked Luke. Her voice was strained, and Luke faltered in the middle of a sentence, staring at her. Lilly gave him a firm gaze. "There's something that I want to ask you."

Luke stopped talking. He looked a little embarrassed, but mostly confused, and Lilly didn't offer him any explanation; instead she moved near him, looping her arm with his.

"Let's go for a walk," she told him.

They left Jackson, who watched curiously through the parlor window.

Chapter 35

They were walking very slowly, without direction. A faltering breeze, dry and hot, rolled over the land, sucking the water out of everything. Lilly shielded her eyes and looked momentarily up at the blue sky. She wished for a hat, any hat, even Shadoe's black plainsman would have done nicely. The sun beat hard on her face, and she had a headache.

"Too hot to breathe," Luke commented, and Lilly raised her eyes to his worn face. Even as he spoke, he was staring down at his boots, looking worried and anxious.

She sucked in a needed breath, felt the sweltering, dusty air hit the back of her throat. She swallowed and said with clear deliberation, "I need you to be honest with me. I'm in trouble. Serious trouble and Shadoe's in trouble, too."

Luke stopped, pulled his arm from hers. She watched him fumble with his trouser pockets, a nervous gesture of his. He didn't look at her. But she could see that he was clearly frowning. "What do you want to know?" he asked in a low, dull voice.

"For starters, I want to know why you were so determined about hanging Jesse? That's not like you, so you must have had a reason."

Luke grunted, finally looked her in the face. "I'm sorry about that, Miss Lilly." His gaze was thoughtful. "As I said before, I hated for you to see that, to see me that way."

"I understand—at least I think I do."

"I went a little crazy, that's all." He pointed to his head. "This temper of mine is bad at times, gets away from me. I was so sure that Jesse was involved, just like I was willing to believe that Tom was guilty, too."

"You still do."

The words were blunt and unexpected, and Luke's eyes suddenly widened in admiration. He looked pleased, though he didn't smile at her.

"It's hard for me to swallow that rubbish about Pepper rustling everyone's cows and horses without Tom knowing. Hogwash. I just said it for Jackson's sake. Have my own thoughts on the matter."

"You don't like Tom, do you?"

"No."

"You think he's guilty?"

"He's in on the rustling. I know it."

Her brows lifted. "What do you mean?"

"I was thinking about Tully's death and what he said before he died . . . the Land of Legends."

"Shadoe's lost canyon," Lilly murmured.

"You know it?"

"Yes. But I didn't want to say anything about it earlier. It was a secret, a place where Shadoe went to be alone. It was land his father gave him as a present. A land with treasure hidden in it or something. The Spanish called it the Land of Legends because it seemed that no one knew how to find it. Shadoe told my father and me about it one day many years ago. He promised to take us there to look for the Spanish gold."

"A lost canyon?" Luke was thinking. "Do you know where it is?"

"No, that's why I didn't say anything. I didn't know where it was. I don't think anyone does except maybe my father, and I'm not even sure of that."

"Then it all makes sense. I knew there was something odd about Tully crawling up in the rocks and hiding himself. It's clear that he was on the wrong side. So why did Pepper leave him alive, and why did he talk? That ain't Tully's way. Pepper's either."

"I don't follow," Lilly said.

Luke grimaced. "Cause something had gone wrong. Pepper'd take the stock straight down to Nevada . . . Winnamucca . . . somewhere, sell them cheap and head off north across the border with the money." Luke paused with a sigh. "But no one's reported any selling and buying of cows and horses, at least not by anyone who fit Pepper's description. In fact, no one has seen Pepper since the night of the lynching. And I bet no one sees him again. Probably dead somewhere. And those cows and horses are hidden in that canyon. It's Tom, I tell you. Tully knew that he was dangerous, and he was trying to warn us. Tom is crazy in some ways. He reminds me of my brother. Got an edge to him. It can kill a man, that edge."

"Did your brother have a temper like you?"

Luke raised his eyebrows. "My brother?" His face held a startled expression. "What does my brother's temper have to do with Tom?"

"Nothing," she told him bluntly. "But Sam's temper has a lot to do with my brother, doesn't it?"

Luke turned red, and the sight of it did nothing to ease Lilly's anxieties.

"Doesn't it, Luke? Doesn't Sam's temper have everything to do with Joseph? Tell me!"

He stepped back and shook his head, his black eyes never leaving her face. For a moment, he appeared lost, almost frightened, and Lilly thought he might leave without saying another word.

"It's not something you want to hear, Miss Lilly," he announced, frowning.

"I've already heard some of it. I just want you to confirm it, give me the details," she replied quickly.

"Oh, Miss Lilly. I was thinking that you didn't have to ever know. Who told?"

Her heart pounded in her chest rapidly. And as hot as it was, Lilly shivered. She was cold, cold with anxiety. Oh, she had thought herself prepared, but who could ever be ready and willing to hear that their brother was a murderer?

"Shadoe told me."

"Damn," Luke cursed. "And he made me promise."

"Joseph murdered Sam," she muttered.

Luke stared away from her, and Lilly turned away from him, too, her body and mind exploding with betrayal, with shame and misery. "But why? And why all the lies? Why would my brother kill Sam? It just seems so senseless."

"Simple," Luke said. He moved toward her, taking her arm in his. He squeezed her hand, forced her to meet his gaze, and said softly, "Anne Woodward was carrying a baby, Joseph's baby. When the news came about England, well, Miss Anne couldn't tell Joseph the truth. She knew he wasn't going to take her and she wasn't up to being a grand lady. That's how it all started."

"Anne didn't tell Joseph about the child?"

"No. Not at first. She told Sam. You know how Sam was back then. Miss Anne was the belle of Harney County. Every man was crazy about her in their own way, even Shadoe was. Why, we all loved her. She was so pretty and so sweet, and, well, a thing like that." Luke paused, moved a step back. "Well, being pregnant and not married could ruin a woman. Ruin her whole life. Can't you see what it meant for Miss Anne? For those who cared about her?"

"So Sam was going to rescue her, and have the belle of the ball."

"Yep." Luke smiled a little. "And he would've, too. Only Joseph heard a tale from Tom that Anne had left the house, angry, crying, and was riding up to our place."

"Did Tom know the truth?"

"No," Luke said. He dropped her arm and moved another step back. "Maybe Tom sensed it, cause he worried Joseph enough to come looking for Anne. Shadoe came with him. When Joseph found out that Anne was pregnant, and that she had not told him, well, he went crazy. He was fuming. I don't know what made him madder, Miss Lilly, Anne Woodward's being pregnant or Sam's planning to marry her. They got into an argument. You know Sam's temper. He let Joseph have it, every word an attack, and Sam was killed."

"Oh, God, I was such a fool!" Lilly began. "All this time, I thought I was so cunning, setting you up at the barbecue, later at the church picnic. I was so sure that Shadoe had accidentally killed Sam in some freakish moment." Lilly made a mocking laugh, and Luke stared at her, obviously anxious over her laughter.

"Silly fool. That's what I am. Just a silly young girl who didn't realize that by poking into the past, I was going to destroy my future. And I did, you know. I destroyed it."

"Don't, Miss Lilly."

She started to cry. "You see, Luke. I loved Shadoe so much. I just wanted him back."

"Miss Lilly—"

She cut him off, "How could you even stand to look at me, Luke? Joseph murdered your brother and then he gave you money to keep quiet. Oh, yes, I figured that little bit out all by myself. He gave you money to keep quiet, to buy off his guilt. How did you stomach it all these years?"

"I wanted to tell everyone, but Shadoe came to me, told me that it would hurt Miss Anne if the truth got out about Joseph not wanting her and such, and Joseph had convinced him that your father would never let him go to England with Sam's death hanging over him. We wanted Joseph to go away, so we kept our mouths shut. And then when Miss Anne died . . . Well, you know the rest of that sad history . . ." Luke's voice broke.

Lilly stiffened, and her gray eyes turned dark with anger. She cursed, her face stormy. "But Shadoe wants to tell my father now!"

"What?" Luke appeared bewildered.

"That's right. He wants my father to know that Joseph was responsible for Anne's death. But it was an accident. And it's pointless."

Luke shook his head, turned angry. "No. He's as responsible for Miss Anne's death as he is Sam's. No, Joseph was mad as hell when Shadoe married Miss Anne. I don't know why. You think he would have been relieved, Shadoe's making the ultimate sacrifice for everyone, but Joseph was always like that, Miss Lilly, a shallow, uncaring person. He didn't want Miss Anne for a wife, but he couldn't stand the thought of another man taking her, of raising the child he'd thought to abandon. Especially Shadoe. So when she and Shadoe came back from Winnamucca with the baby in the spring, Joseph went to her, persuaded Shadoe to take him up the back stairs at the Woodwards, and he argued with her. He wanted her to leave Shadoe and go to England with him. No talk of marriage. Why, she was already married, Joseph told her. She could just come and be his kept woman or something just as seedy." Luke spat, then pointed a finger at her. "Afterwards, he left without a word. Can you believe it . . . so cold?"

"No, no . . . no . . ."

"True. Every word of it."

"It's like he was a stranger."

"Joseph was. His whole life with you and his father was a lie. But we all knew it, those who ran with him. Two-sided, Joseph was. Only we couldn't tell you and Mister McFall. We respected you too much. And Shadoe loved you too much."

"I didn't know Joseph at all," Lilly said.

"No and neither did your father. Maybe your father should know the truth. Maybe Shadoe's right in telling him."

She stared hard at him. "But, Luke, it would kill my father to know the truth, to understand that Shadoe means to kill Joseph if he ever comes back to Oregon."

Luke's expression suddenly turned hard, and he took several steps away from her, looking nervously from Lilly to the house.

The sight of him pacing, looking almost frenzied, made Lilly's pulses quicken. She knew that look, caged anger. She had seen it on Shadoe's face the night before.

"Shadoe wouldn't kill Joseph," Luke told her in a grunt. "But I would."

Lilly was horrified. She blinked in the glare of sunlight. "You couldn't!"

Luke gave her an admonishing stare. "He deserves it, Miss Lilly. He shot Sam in the back of the head without a warning. That's the truth of it. Over nothing but the fact that Sam was in love with Anne Woodward, wanted to marry her." Luke shook his head, dismayed. "Don't you see the heartlessness of it? There was poor Miss Anne and the only way she thought to get out of her mess was to marry Sam, and Joseph took that away from her. How could she face her family and friends? Have a bastard child? It was a mean thing for Joseph to do. And Shadoe tried to fix it."

"Fix it . . ."

"Fix it for everybody."

"But to kill Joseph? Kill my brother if he comes back? I don't know—"

"You won't have to worry about that," Luke interrupted. "Joseph won't ever come back here. I already know that."

Lilly flushed at the contempt in his voice. "How do you know?"

"He told me so when he left. Shadoe made him leave to protect him and everyone from the truth. Shadoe told him to go and never look back, and I told him never to come back." Luke paused, drew a long breath. "But I intend to go there—to England—and settle with him. It's why I work so hard. I want to give him back his damn money."

"But, Luke, he's the Earl of Montfort. English nobility. You wouldn't have a chance in England."

"I can stand on my own."

"But my father?"

"Your father won't live forever," Luke said in a kinder voice. "He's an old man, had a hard life. I can wait. I've been waiting."

"But Shadoe will tell my father everything. I know he will."

"You can't stop Shadoe. The man took the blame that rightly belonged to Joseph. He's lived with it all these years. You can't ask him to keep the lie any longer."

Lilly stared at Luke. "But that's just what I intend to do. If it's the last thing I do, I'm going to keep my father from ever knowing the truth."

"You'll lose Shadoe, Miss Lilly. You'll lose him if you don't let him rid himself of the lies."

Lilly turned away and stared straight into the sun. The light burned her eyes. "I don't care anymore."

* * *

Lilly was sipping tea when she glanced out the window and saw the man riding up the road toward the house.

A strange man, thick and burly in stature. He had red hair, and Lilly wondered if he was one of the new hands who had been brought in since the rustling began. Immediately, her gaze shifted to Luke and Jackson, both busily saddling their horses, talking, unaware. They seemed relaxed.

She drank some more tea, turned, and looked at the boy who was sitting beside her. For the first time, she could see Joseph in his features. Not the coloring, that was Anne's completely, but around the eyes, the brows. Even around the mouth. She wondered why she had never seen them before, the lines and expressions that were clearly her brother's.

Joey stared up at her, and his pretty lips rounded into a sweet smile.

"Want some lunch?" she asked him.

He shook his head, but Lilly didn't see it. Hearing the sounds of hoofbeats, she turned, half expecting to see Luke and Jackson riding off with the stranger. Instead, she saw another strange rider, and then another, and then Luke and Jackson scrambling for the barn door.

"What in the world?"

The shots rang out quickly, so loud, pinging, shattering the glass of the parlor window.

Lilly screamed, jumped up from her chair. "Rustlers!" she shouted, and then, "Lo Ching!"

She grabbed Joey, hastily making her way for the kitchen. There was a cellar off the kitchen, a cellar with food and guns. A good place to hide.

The shots rang again. She jerked, and the youngster shrieked with panic. Lilly ran and rounding the corner of the room, she banged straight into the path of another unexpected visitor.

Joey hollered, and then he smiled, a big, bright grin as he looked up at the man. He held out his arms in a pleading gesture, and the man eagerly took him, giving the child a warm and loving embrace.

For a moment, Lilly just stared, confused. Then finally the word escaped from her throat in a questioning tone. Her throat was dry, and she had to swallow before she said it. "Tom?"

There was whiskey on his breath. His eyes twinkled with a hint of mischief, surprise. "Hello, Lilly," he said, sneering. "I never imagined that you would be here of all places. How fortunate for the both of us."

Chapter 36

Shadoe saw the smoke, even though he couldn't see the fire. And he knew. Oh God, what he knew.

He pulled his mouth into a thin hard line and stared across the river in the direction of the house that his father had built. It was a hollow gaze, fixed and unmistakably blind.

Silvery smoke billowed over the tops of the leafy trees that grew along the banks of the Blitzen River, its stink sharp and biting. Shadoe felt its heat and wretchedness. It filled his eyes, his nose, his mouth. It gnawed at him, balled in the middle of his gut like a tight, angry fist. He wanted to scream. But there were no words to utter. He wanted to move, but, somehow, he couldn't find the energy to do it. And he was afraid, more frightened than he had ever been in his life.

"He's burned it," Lewis was saying, his voice low and harsh against the slow drifting smoke. "That damn Pepper Maddox has burned the Double *S*."

Shadoe shook his head violently, and stared at his friend.

After a while, he found his voice and said, "Not Pepper. Tom."

James McFall gaped. For over two hours he had been watching through a blur of occasional tears, but he still couldn't believe. He didn't want to. The sight of the Double S headquarters burned to the ground seemed inconceivable to him. Simon Sinclair had built the place in a lifetime of both hard work and great joy.

At that very moment, James felt as though it was his own lifetime disappearing in a fine drizzle of cinders and smoke.

"This is madness," he said as quietly as possible, and Luke nodded in agreement as the two men stood together, staring rigidly at the blackened and splintered remains of the house and barn.

Around them buzzed several men and women. It seemed that everyone in Harney County had arrived at the ranch, eager to assist when the tragic news spread hurriedly throughout the area.

James, Hadley, and several others from Weatherly had been the first to reach the Double S, then came the entire Daniels family from the north, followed by Doctor Brown and several others. Even Sheriff Smith had arrived with a group of newly sworn deputies.

In his arms, James carried the young boy—Joey. The youngster had tired of the spectacle, and his head was resting against the older man's shoulder. Faint tears lay on Joey's hot and flushed cheeks. James knew that the boy wanted to sleep, but he also knew that the youngster was too frightened to close his eyes, and the old man patted the boy on the back, trying to reassure him that everything was going to be all right.

He is still Shadoe's son, thought James, *not Joseph's. Never Joseph's, not his own blood . . . All these years . . . No. Not his own blood.*

Then he thought of Lilly. James grimaced and stared at Luke. The plucky horse breeder had done everything to protect his daughter. But eventually, outnumbered and overwhelmed, he had failed.

Luke was clutching at his injured arm. The wound had been carelessly dressed with a wide strip of his checkered shirt. "Damn, the bastard really tried to kill me," Luke commented as he examined the binding. Blood dripped from his elbow onto the dirt.

"You need a doctor."

Luke scowled at James. "Lo Ching needs him a great deal more than I do. And so does Jackson."

"Then let Widow Daniels take a look at you. You'll bleed to death if you don't let someone attend to that . . . Clean the bullet out. Stitch you up."

"I'm not doing anything until I see Shadoe riding up." Luke gazed toward the direction of the river, his eyes full of pain and a sense of impatience. He had been hit twice, once across the ribs, a shallow flesh wound, once in the arm. The latter was dead through. "I want to tell him what happened myself. It can't come from anyone . . . from anyone else. Oh God, Lilly, what am I going to say?"

"You won't be able to tell him a bloody thing if you faint." James flicked his eyes toward the trickling blood, and his voice rose a pitch. "If you lose any more blood, you're sure to weaken, become unconscious."

"I'll take my chances, Mister McFall. No matter what, I'm going to be standing here to tell Shadoe about Miss Lilly. I owe him that much."

"You don't owe him a damn thing. It wasn't your fault that she was taken hostage. If anyone's, it's Shadoe's. He's the one who persuaded her to leave Weatherly in the first place."

Luke pursed his lips and pulled the binding tighter around his arm. His next words were bold. "You don't sound too worried. In fact, from the moment you arrived, you haven't asked two questions about your daughter."

It was true, and James couldn't explain it except that he hadn't really believed Luke's story about Tom's carrying Lilly off as some sort of sacrificial victim. It was too ridiculous a notion. Tom might use Lilly as a hostage, but he would never hurt her. Besides, if he believed it, he would panic, and getting hysterical didn't seem the appropriate form of action to take at the moment.

No, Luke was wrong. Everyone was wrong. Tom couldn't hurt Lilly. He loved her.

James was about to rebut Luke's opinion when he caught sight of the riders galloping in from the west. They appeared quickly from the thick grove of trees that extended for almost a mile to the edge of the river.

"There he is," came the hoarse comment, and Luke glanced with a lame smile.

"Hello, Shadoe," Luke called as several riders swung off their dusty mounts in front of him.

Without saying a word, Shadoe dropped his bridle strap, and hastily walked toward the remains of the house, his boots sending up spurts of dust. The sight of the smoldering ruins made his muscles knot. There wasn't a spot on his body that wasn't cracked with pain and raging hate.

He turned with a jerk, and stared pointedly at both James and Luke. He saw the boy. Relieved, he relaxed a bit, but only momentarily. He was thinking about Lilly, wondering. Had she left the Double *S* as he told her to? Was she at Weatherly, safe and far from this misery?

No . . . no . . . no . . . You know where she is, you fool!

"Where are the others?" he asked in a hurried breath.

Luke answered just as quick. "Lo Ching and Jackson are over there with the doctor. They're hurt pretty bad but they're going to be okay. Two others were hit. Another two dead. One . . . your man. The other was riding for Tom."

Luke was white to the lips as he spoke, and Shadoe hastily glanced at his arm, then noted the washed-out expression on the younger man's face.

"You seem to be hurt pretty bad yourself."

"I reckon. But I wanted to be standing when we talked."

James grimaced. His eyes shifted from man to man. "Would you two stop acting as though I'm not here? I do have a part in this as much as anyone else."

"Not with me, you don't," Shadoe told him. "I ain't got a damn thing to say to you." He grabbed Joey from James's arms.

The child clutched at him tightly, and Shadoe knew that Joey was confused and scared. But there was no time to see him happy, not now. Seconds were becoming minutes. Precious time was wasting away.

He hugged the youngster, whispered in his ear, and the boy lifted his head and smiled at his father. "Really, Papa?"

Shadoe even smiled. "Yes. But I want you to go with Lewis for a while. Okay?"

He didn't wait for an answer. Looking at Lewis, Shadoe told him in a rapid voice, "Take Joey into town, get him a room at the hotel . . . some supper . . . anything he wants to eat."

"You want me to stay in town?" Lewis asked, taking the child from Shadoe's arms.

Shadoe nodded. He pointed to some of his men. "You two ride with Lewis and stay in Montfort. Make sure there's no trouble." He paused with a sigh. "The rest of you come with me."

Luke frowned. "You going after Tom now?"

"Yessir, I am."

"He's got Lilly," Luke finally stammered in an exhausted breath. "He took her."

Shadoe stopped and stared at him. "Yes, I know. I knew that the minute I saw the smoke and realized that it was Tom instead of Pepper. He came to burn me out."

"And Miss Lilly?"

"He would have taken Lilly from anywhere, here, at Weatherly, in town. He would have gone for her. This whole mess is about revenge, and hurting Lilly would be the sweetest revenge of all."

James turned in cold fury to Shadoe. "That's not true!"

"You're a fool," Shadoe blurted before turning to walk through the crowd of men.

Both James and Luke followed on Shadoe's heels.

"I know Woodward. He would never harm Lilly!" James hollered at Shadoe, his voice breathless, his expression bewildered. "Tom just used her to get away."

Shadoe almost stopped, ready to slap some sense into the old man, but he didn't. Instead, he laughed as he walked quickly across the yard, his gaze searching for the two bodies Luke had mentioned earlier. He had a hunch. He wanted to see the dead man, the one who rode for Tom.

He found them near the smoking remnants of the barn. Two of his men were loading the bodies in the back of a buckboard. Sheriff Smith was carefully watching.

"You know them?" Shadoe asked the sheriff.

"Just the one who worked for you." When the second body was loaded, the sheriff flipped back the blanket and stared at the corpse. "This one, I don't know. But I heard he was in town a few weeks back."

Luke leaned over the side of the wagon, and James peered over his shoulder.

Shadoe's eyes fastened on the body, a steely glint in his stare. "I know him. Saw him in the saloon the night they brought Tully Brigman in dead. The man was playing poker with Maddox." He stepped back. "Damn," he muttered. "Where in the hell is Maddox?"

Luke squatted against the wagon. "I got a good idea," he grunted. His face knotted as he jerked, convulsed in a forward motion as he lost the fight with his stomach. Luke vomited on the ground.

"Get the doc!" the sheriff yelled, and one of the Double S ranch hands headed across the clearing to another buckboard.

Shadoe pulled Luke to his feet. "You all right?"

"Better . . . really . . . Get me some water."

Shadoe motioned and the other man left.

"You think you know where Maddox is?" Shadoe asked in an urgent tone. As much as he was worried about Luke and Lo Ching, he was even more anxious about Lilly. Wherever Maddox was, Tom was likely to be.

Luke gave him a thoughtful gaze. "It's a good guess."

James moved forward. "Luke, what do you mean?"

"When Tully was brought in . . . Remember the day of the church picnic?" Both Shadoe and James nodded at the same time. "Well, I was there. He kept mumbling something . . ."

"I heard about that," James said. "Wasn't it in Spanish?

Luke made a slight nod, drew a needed breath. "Anyways, I went looking for Miss Lilly. Tom had bid on her basket, and I found them in the grove of trees."

Shadoe's mind flooded with the thought.

Luke made a crippled grin. "Tom wasn't too eager to hear about Tully, and he was damn sure mad when he heard that Tully was speaking Spanish."

"What did Tully say?" Shadoe asked.

"I don't remember the Spanish, but Lilly translated it for me . . . something about the land of legends. Today she was telling me about it. This lost canyon of yours. I think they're holed up there."

Agitation, fear, memories and terror, slipped dreamily into his mind, and Shadoe let out a long, anguished sigh. For a heady moment, it was all he could do to keep his sanity, to keep his feet firmly on the ground. A moment later, he wanted to rip James's throat open with his bare hands. The old man had told! The fool!

He stared combatively at James, his eyes gleaming with rage as he felt the others' attention. "Old man, don't you see what's going on here?"

Silence, just silence, and then, "You told?" Shadoe whispered with a rare look of hurt and disbelief.

James's face was pinched white. "I never . . . never thought—"

"What the hell did you think? That canyon belongs to me. It's the only thing my father ever gave me—a hidden valley founded by those first *vaqueros*. I told you in trust. It is a sacred place to the Paiute, a place where you give thanks and do penance for your sins. Don't you see the irony in it? Penance for your sins . . ."

"He's going to kill her," James suddenly gasped, his voice choked and dry.

"You're damn right he is. Been planning it all along. And I was a fool . . . You were a fool. When I rode back into town, Tom knew that Lilly would never marry him and even if she didn't marry me, he realized soon enough that she'd marry Luke instead. No Woodward empire. No dynasty. It wasn't me he really wanted to kill. Not really. He's cracked. It was Lilly from the beginning. If he couldn't have her, no one would." Shadoe let out a curse and stomped his heel in the dirt. He stared at James who was visibly shaking. "Don't you see? Tom's crazy. So eaten up with want and need. He loves her. In his own way he loves her, and he's saving her from the likes of me."

Shadoe knotted one hand into an accusing fist. "And you told him about the canyon, a place where he could hide his cattle, a place where he could take Lilly and no one would ever find her. My secret place. Doesn't it stink of irony? Tom sees some sort of justice in it. The perfect form of revenge for everyone."

"Shut up! Shut up!" James screamed.

Shadoe closed his eyes against the harsh noise. A slice of pain shot through his head as he thought about the lost ravine deep in the Steens Mountains. One way in, and one way out. There was not a better place for bandits to hole up. He rubbed his throbbing forehead, then gave the older man a sidelong glance.

James was screaming for Hadley, his horse, some shells, a rifle, and his men. The old man looked almost crazy.

"No, just you and me," Shadoe suddenly announced.

Sheriff Smith, James, and Luke stared, their expressions wide, rigid, confused.

"Just McFall and me," Shadoe repeated. "Two men might get into that canyon, but a whole posse would be ambushed in the passage that leads in. Tom would know. He'd kill her before we had a chance to attack." Shadoe looked at the sheriff. "I have a plan that just might work."

Chapter 37

Cold and huddled next to the boulder, Lilly looked at Tom. He was licking his lips with a fumbling tongue, relishing the taste of whiskey on his mouth. She thought it disgusting, not just the way he looked, but the way he drank with ease as though he didn't have a care in the world.

For the last half-hour, he had been nursing a bottle of whiskey, and Lilly was surprised that he would drink at so dangerous a time. But then, maybe it gave him courage.

He rubbed his beard, a slow, thoughtful gesture that made Lilly nervous. Tom stared complacently at the bottle. "You're a fool for wastin' time thinkin' about someone comin' to save you."

At his words, Lilly was sick with shock. "Save me?" she questioned in a slow, almost broken voice. It was the first time that he had said anything to threaten her.

Tom smiled at her. "Yep. Save you. That's what

373

I said." His dark eyes were glazed, and even though it was almost dusk, she could see the madness in them. He was mad, and he was talking of someone saving her.

The weight of things suddenly thickened in her head. *I cain't let my love for you git in the way of it,* she heard Tom saying, and the words immediately took on a new and horrible meaning. He was going to kill her, had wanted to kill her for a long time.

She scowled, shook all over as she stared at him, still not quite able to grasp the fact that he was insane, that somehow everyone had miscalculated his rage.

Tears fell across her cheeks, and for a long moment she just sat and cried.

"Where are we?" she finally asked. An overwhelming sense of powerlessness filled her. She was desperate to know where she sat as though it would give her some sense of direction, a feeling of control.

"Tierra de leyendas," Tom said.

Lilly's mouth rounded as she labored for a breath. "The Land of Legends?"

"Don't you know where it is, Lilly?" There was a smirk on his face, and she nodded.

Oh God, this was Shadoe's place and she was going to die in it!

He laughed at her, and Lilly flinched. His voice seemed like flames, hot and painful against her face. She closed her eyes, struggling to think, her mind wandering over her years as a very young girl.

The Land of Legends? Fragments of a dream remembered: lava rocks and stunted sage, and clumps of orange and yellow flowers. It was springtime. There was fine bunch grass on the Catlow Valley and the Steens Mountains were alight in the distance, still covered in winter snow.

And Shadoe. Eyes so blue. Long brown hair. Strong hands. Always Shadoe. Her knight in shining armor, her prince of the cowboys, riding across the eeriness of the isolated flatlands, coming home to her . . . the promises. . . .

Lilly opened her eyes. A rush of new tears sprang from the corners of them, gray pools of knowledge. She whimpered, heard the whispers of a frothy breeze in her ears. For a moment, she even thought she heard the faint scrape of boot heel on the stones above. Shadoe was still in her head. He would always be in her head. He would be her last thought.

"This is Shadoe's land. His hidden valley," she told Tom with a sense of pride and peace.

Tom let out a loud, open-mouthed roar of laughter. He popped the cork back in the bottle, and rose to his feet. "Ain't that funny, Lilly?"

She was silent, still musing with recollections.

"Well, just think of it. I been hidin' the cattle and horses for months in this damn place. No one knows about it but Shadoe and your father. No one. One way in, one way out. I ain't got a man who can even find his way in here except Pepper." Tom pointed. "And he lies right about over there."

The gesture caught her attention. "You killed him?"

Tom gave a light shrug. "Well, he wanted to take the stock and clear out. Head north across the border to Canada. Leave everything. Forget everything. I couldn't have that. I had other plans."

Her voice cranked up a notch. "What plans?"

"My father's dreams. The land, the dynasty. Owning the valley. Controlling the water rights of the Blitzen and Donner Rivers. Those plans."

His words were sure and quick, and Lilly shivered. Her father's words. Those had been her father's very words, too. The land. The dynasty. She closed her eyes against the thought, wanting to scream. Men and their pride. Men and their dreams. Men and their madness. And this was surely madness! Tom would never have any of it.

"You're the fool," she told him as she opened her eyes. She reached up and wiped away the last of her tears. She wouldn't cry anymore, not for Tom, not for herself. She gave him a defiant stare. "You'll never have any of it."

With a painful look on his face, he rubbed his arm. He didn't seem to hear her. He looked lost as though he had drifted away into a world of his own. "There's only one key to this valley and that's you and now I have you all to myself. And if I cain't keep you, then nobody ain't."

His words were crazy, meaningless in purpose, and Lilly felt a nightmarish fright eddy over her, a heavy and malignant feeling of doom like dirt in the face, dirt in a grave—being buried alive.

Madness. She was looking at madness, and then Tom reached up and pulled a deep blue bandanna from his neck.

Tom smiled at her surprise. "You recognize it?"

She nodded, speechless. It was the blue bandanna that her brother had given Shadoe. Lilly's eyes widened as she stared at it, and she thought of how Shadoe had carried it all those years with him, wore it around his neck, even though Joseph had been so cruel and shallow. Why?

But then she quickly remembered her memories and fears. Then she had a sudden realization. *Oh, Shadoe, I understand everything. I know everything, and I am going to die without telling you. . . .*

It was true. She knew the story. She had unraveled the mystery, and now she understood his motivations. Shadoe had been the bastard son, and that was why he couldn't bear to think of Anne's child being a bastard. Shadoe had loved her father. Shadoe had wanted his own father's approval, and that was why he had really married Anne, out of love, obligation, and honor. He had given up everything for everyone else—especially her.

Oh, Shadoe, I will never tell you I love you again. I will never tell you that I'm sorry. . . .

And Lilly was. Shadoe had loved her, loved the proud daughter of an aristocratic man, but never felt quite worthy.

Oh, Shadoe, my love, everything you did was for me . . . for me and for my father. For the McFalls. . . .

The blue bandanna. Shadoe wore it not for love of Joseph, but out of love for her. That thought shocked Lilly into the full meaning of the situation, and she stared at Tom, her gaze fixed on his movements, watching intently as he rolled up his shirt sleeve, exposing several hurtful wounds.

"Dog bites!" Lilly's hands flew to her mouth.

"You didn't think I would give someone else the pleasure of killing him, did you?" Tom mocked.

"You bastard!"

From somewhere above, Shadoe came, slithering down a rope, then jumping, falling on the hardpan between Tom and Lilly.

It didn't take Lilly more than a heartbeat to realize what had happened, but Tom stood immovable, apparently confused by the attack.

Shadoe thrust up from the ground, standing steady, his eyes level with Tom's. "You killed my dog!" Shadoe screamed at him. Vengeance and rage filled his voice, and Shadoe quickly drew a knife from its sleeve, pointing the keen-edged blade at Tom's belly. "I ought to gut you here like an animal and leave you for the buzzards to pick."

"No!" came a clotted voice. "Save him for the sheriff." Hanging over the tip of the ledge above was James McFall. He held the rope in his hand.

"Papa!" Lilly cried, and in that moment of surprise, Tom pulled a gun.

Tom's shot missed Shadoe, hit the side of the rock, and ricocheted against the canyon walls. Shadoe dropped in a crouch at the sound of it.

There were screams and curses. Lilly's. Shadoe's. James's.

The old man slumped over, falling, falling, crashing down upon them. Tom's eyes flicked at the crumpled body of James McFall, and seizing the unguarded moment, Shadoe rose, half erect, propelling himself in a direct pitch at Tom's gun hand.

But Tom was ready. He met Shadoe's movement, slamming him in the jaw with the gun. Stunned, Shadoe fell flat on the ground.

Lilly screamed as Shadoe sprawled on his hands and knees. Tom gave him three quick, hard kicks, rolling Shadoe over on his back. Before Shadoe could move, the younger man took the butt of his gun and hit Shadoe across the crown. Shadoe moaned, and his eyes rolled in his head.

"No!" Lilly jumped at Tom, her arms wrapping

around his shoulders, her fingers clawing at his face.

He slapped at her, in every direction, annoyed, like she was a buzzing fly, but Lilly clung to him in her desperation. She reached, hooked a nail in his left eye, and jerked, felt a moment of exhilaration when a wetness poured over her fingertips. Blood.

"You bitch!" Tom cried at her. "I'll kill ya!"

He reached a hand around to her, pulling angrily at her dress until Lilly came plunging forward into his fierce grasp. Crazed, Tom threw her to the ground and jumped on top of her.

Lilly felt the breath rush out of her lungs. There was a strange pause as he stared at her, and then an even stranger smile. Lilly tried to move, to catch a glimpse of her father, but Tom reached down and grabbed her cheeks between his taut fingers.

"I ought to give you a good poke before you die," he threatened. "Would you like that, Lilly?"

She spat defiantly at him. Tom laughed. But the sound was soon drowned by another noise. Somehow, Shadoe was on Tom, pulling him from Lilly. She took a deep, shuddering breath and watched the blur of faces and hands entangled in front of her. A wave of nausea rolled through her body, and she struggled to her feet.

She had never thought to see Shadoe Sinclair so brutal and savage. She had never thought to see Tom Woodward die—and to be relieved for it.

But the sharp blade of cold steel left no doubt to the deed, no remorse, and no appeal.

Lilly watched and screamed, a silent voice that shook her very soul.

Tom fell against the earth, his throat sliced and bloodied—dead.

The moonlight waned, and the silence was worse than any sound. Lilly held her father's head in her lap, watching without tears as he struggled with his life. Somehow, she had no answer, no comfort, no voice at all for his pain and suffering, for her own.

But there was death in her heart, and it swallowed up all her previous feelings. She couldn't think of Shadoe, only of the father she loved. James held her hand tightly, took a long trembling breath. He still hadn't become conscious since his fall. Blood oozed from the bullet wound to his chest and he appeared older, fragile, childlike.

"I shouldn't have brought him," Shadoe said in an accusing tone.

He stooped, touching Lilly on the shoulder with his fingertips. It was a gentle gesture, meant to be kind and comforting, but she stiffened, openly jerked at the feel of his hand on her. She was angry, in shock.

"Then why did you?" she asked coldly as she glanced up at him.

Shadoe withdrew his hand, stared blankly at her face. "He wanted to come. I needed a man for the rope. It was the only way in. That simple."

Her father wheezed, and Lilly started.

"He was old and foolish." Lilly looked at Shadoe, a bewildered, disapproving expression in her eyes. She saw him flinch at the sight of it. Her white lips parted, and she felt so much pain. "You just wanted to see him suffer, to tell him about Joseph and Anne. You wanted him to know the truth so that Joseph would be offensive in his eyes."

Shadoe crouched down beside her, placed his handkerchief over the wound and pressed. "Maybe."

"I hate you for this."

"I know."

"I hate all of you," Lilly swore between gritted teeth. "Men and their pride. Their dreams of land and dominion."

"I have no such dreams," Shadoe muttered.

She opened her mouth to rebuke his claim, but the sound of her father's softened voice cut her to the bone. Lilly turned and stared at him.

His eyes were open, their gaze liquid and fixed, wide, gray eyes boring into her with a last strain of indomitability. Lilly's heart fluttered, and she whispered urgently, "Papa, it's Lilly. I'm going to take you home. We're both going home . . . to Weatherly."

He smiled, faintly, but it was there all the same, and Lilly squeezed his hand, consoled that her father had understood her.

"Lilly . . ."

She bent lower. "Yes, Papa?"

"I am sorry, child."

She shook her head at him. "No regrets. None. No apologies. Not now. I love you, Papa."

She felt his grasp tighten. "Where's Shadoe?" he asked.

"I'm here."

Shadoe leaned closer to where James could see his face.

"I'm dying . . ."

James's words shocked Lilly, and she was thoughtless for a minute, unable to respond in any manner, but Shadoe appeared saddened, even terrified at the sound of James's statement.

"You can't die, old man," he admonished in earnest. "I still have things to say to you. We aren't through with each other."

Lilly looked at Shadoe, a rush of blood coming to her face. She was hot all over, fired with imagination and distrust. His blue eyes met hers, and in that moment, she knew exactly what he was thinking. She could see it—the years he had spent away from his own father, the pain he had felt when he buried the elder Sinclair. All the unfinished words and gestures.

Regret and conscience. Those had been Shadoe's very words.

Oh, God, you can't tell him now. I won't let you. I swore that I wouldn't let you, and no matter what you did and why, I won't let you take this man's love of his son away.

"Don't," she said to him, the yearning of pity in her voice and eyes. "Don't . . ."

"Joseph?" James asked Shadoe. The older man reached out with his hand. "Joseph loved Anne, loved you?"

"Yes," Shadoe quickly replied.

"The boy? He's yours?"

"Yes. He's my son."

"Then . . . why . . . all the lies? Why?"

Shadoe's features turned stony and explicitly intense. Lilly held her breath for his answer. Would he still tell the truth? Would he send her father to his grave in bitterness?

Lilly waited in suspense, and the seconds passed in terror and slowness.

Shadoe sighed. All expression drained from his

face. "Because I wanted to be your son. Because I loved you. That's why I told the lies. I would have done anything for you—"

She sighed heavily. It was the truth, but Lilly knew that her father didn't understand. She heard Shadoe's voice break, heard tears. Not her own, though they streamed silently over her flushed cheeks. They were Shadoe's tears. In all her life, she had never expected to see him cry.

"I love you . . . Shadoe," James was saying weakly, and Lilly heard herself gasp at the unexpected words.

Shadoe bent over, clutched his knotted hands angrily to his face, and moaned. "Forgive me . . . forgive me," he whispered again and again.

"I for . . . give . . ." came the resolving lament, and then James McFall closed his eyes.

"He's gone," Shadoe said.

"No!"

Shadoe reached out for her, but she jerked away. "He's dead, Lilly."

"Noooooooooooo!"

The lost canyon thundered with echoes, the lonely and grief-filled shrieks of one man and one woman.

Chapter 38

It was morning when Lilly saw Weatherly again, and it wasn't a welcome sight.

Numbed, overcome with grief, physically exhausted from all that she had experienced, Lilly couldn't think, couldn't even feel; she just went through the motions of existing.

For her, life had suddenly became a blur of disassociation. It was as if someone else was living her life, and she was tucked away somewhere inside her own mind, warm and safe for the moment, watching the living move by her at a guarded distance.

When she entered the house, Martha walked her up the stairs to her room, a gradual climb of one step after the other. Between them, there were no words, no tears, just silence, thick and somehow strangely cold.

Shivering, Lilly immediately collapsed across the bed and into a deep sleep.

No dreams this time. No nightmares, nothing but peace.

And for days, she slept.

Then one morning, four days later, she donned her best black silk, and in the early-afternoon sun, she buried James McFall in the family vault next to his wife.

It was the first time that she had seen Shadoe since the incident in the canyon, and Lilly found that she had trouble looking at him.

Not hate, or regret, not even simple anger, but fearfulness kept her from embracing him, from telling him that she was grateful that he had spared her father the truth about Joseph, that she loved him. But she was afraid, and a horrible fear it was.

When Shadoe reached to touch her hand as they strolled back to the house from the little cemetery, Lilly slapped it away, and later when he doggedly pursued her into the house, she fled up the stairs, fighting back the tears in her eyes.

She couldn't face Shadoe now. It would mean facing too much pain. Everything had changed, and it seemed that nothing would melt the chill in her heart.

Shadoe didn't follow Lilly up the stairs. Instead, he rode to the Oasis, climbed up on the roof of his newly constructed house, and began banging the nails, one hard drive after the other.

The minutes flew by in the pounding, and slowly it dawned on Shadoe that he had splintered the pine plank. The one-by-six collapsed under the last nail, shattered into several pieces. He uttered a low curse, then turned and stared into the distance toward Weatherly . . . and Lilly.

Sun and sky spread for miles.

He dropped the hammer, crouched in a low stoop, letting his mind run free with the thought of her in his arms again. Then he screamed, a silent cry.

It's over. It's done, and she's dying. Oh, Lilly, what is it gonna take to bring you back to the living, bring you back to me again?

Silence, and then Shadoe heard, "You, you damn silly fool!" It was Lilly's voice calling out to him.

Shadoe moved as agile as a cat, his hands on the ladder, then a quick leap to the ground.

She lay on the bed, dressed in black, her head propped on several feather-filled pillows.

When Shadoe came pounding on her bedroom door like a madman, she didn't even move, just stared at it, her body stiff, her mind soundless to the noise and demands.

The door slammed open, then slammed shut again, and Shadoe stood in her room.

Lilly immediately looked away, avoided his searching eyes, those bright blue eyes that preyed upon her with every stare.

"Where's Aunt Martha?" she asked, her voice deliberately chilly, nonchalant.

But Shadoe didn't answer.

More silence, cold and thick. Lilly shivered.

"You look good in black, Princess," Shadoe said as he moved across the room. "Black as the ace of spades, that dress of yours." He stopped by the bed, and stroked the silky skirt. "Soft, too."

"Go away . . . please."

"A trifle upset, are you?"

Lilly turned, struggled to hold back the rage and passion that she was feeling. If the dam broke, she would surely drown.

"Y . . . e . . . s."

Shadoe smiled at her. "Now that's a worthless gesture." He waved a hand, a mockery-filled motion. "This sight reminds me of one of those poor-pitiful-me scenarios. That's what it looks like to me. You're feeling sorry for yourself."

She gritted her teeth, clutched at the handkerchief in her hand. "You're being cruel, Shadoe. I don't need this . . . not now. Can't you see that I'm not in the mood for conversation?" She scowled, feigned an earnest look at the door. "Where's Aunt Martha?"

"Out. Gone. Poof! She's disappeared. I think the ole castle is empty, except for you and me, darlin'."

Lilly jerked up from the pillows. Her hands flapped to her breasts. "Where would she go?" Her voice changed midstream, from a note of panic to one of pity. "Aunt Martha knows that I might need her."

Shadoe sat on the edge of the bed. "You need me. That's all you need, Princess. Just like I need you."

She shook her head in a violent gesture. "You bastard! I buried my father today! Don't you understand what is going on? I feel as though I'm dead, too." She paused, literally sucked in a choked breath. Tears welled in the corners of her eyes. "The dead don't feel, and they certainly don't love. You bury them. And if they somehow still breathe, you dig them up and watch them walk around . . . wounded, haunted, ghosts. Well, I'm one of the walking wounded." She took his hand, touched it to her cheek. "I breathe surely but I'll never love again. I can't."

Shadoe raised his hand, pushing the stray curls from her eyes, and Lilly trembled at his touch, felt the familiar fire that he ignited in her. It ran like lightning from the top of her skull down to her toes. But it was a slow burn afterwards.

"Lies. All lies. As good as the ones I've lived with these past five years," Shadoe said. His hands played with her hair while his gaze roamed over her face, watching her, and Lilly couldn't look away. His eyes seemed filled with questions.

"You don't understand," she managed in protest.

"Yes, I do." Shadoe nodded as he snaked his hand around the back of her head. With fingers tangled in her hair, he drew her close to him.

Lilly's nose pressed against his face. The smell of him engulfed her, and, unaware, she brushed the tip of her nose back and forth against his warm skin.

"You're afraid, that's all. Afraid to care. Even afraid that you'll never feel again," Shadoe continued. His voice turned hoarse. "You think . . . No, that's not the right word . . . You fear that life and love won't be the same. I thought that years ago when Anne died. I was wrong."

Shadoe turned desperate. "Princess, I need you. I'm going crazy thinking that you are pulling away from me. Don't leave me. Love me. Be with me. I can't make it without you. I hurt so bad, too—"

"Oh, Shadoe," Lilly whispered urgently.

His lips reached for hers, his teeth gently nibbling at her lips, softly coaxing her into a kiss.

Life, fear, and love were in his kiss. And like a raging river, it washed over Lilly. Wet and warm, his tongue between her teeth, he claimed her mouth, at first tenderly, then recklessly.

She was surely drowning.

Instinctively, Lilly hooked her arms over his shoulders as if the gesture could hold her high above the tide of emotions, but they both fell and fell and fell, inundated with touch and taste and smell.

Shadoe was making love to her, and one minute Lilly's eyes filled with tears, the next minute, laughter.

Moments later, her head hanging off the edge of the bed, Lilly felt the rush, felt Shadoe, his skin, his heat, his muscles constricting, his seed, liquid and flowing, and full of life. She heard his voice, and it called her beautiful and love and wife.

Then Lilly heard her own cries. From the past, the present, came the screams of a thousand memories that shouted, *The wounds will heal. Be happy. Look not to the past, but toward tomorrow. . . .*

Epilogue

The valley settled into peace and quiet in the fall. Most of the missing stock were recovered, including Lilly's young feisty mare. In late November, some of the remaining rustlers were finally jailed. Those who escaped fled over the northern borders, nameless and without money. The trouble was over.

By December, snow blew across Harney County, Oregon. But even in the bitter cold, Shadoe finished his house at the Oasis, and on a windy Christmas morning, he and Lilly, along with Joey and Lo Ching, moved in as a family, one name, one love, one dream.

Others, too, went on with their lives. Dan Hadley quietly married Widow Daniels and moved up near Malheur Lake. Lewis Smith took over as foreman of Weatherly, and Jackson Williams became Montfort's new sheriff when Sheriff Smith sudden-ly retired after breaking both his legs in the raging and final struggle with the rustlers in the Steens. The fearless young lawman quickly rescued Naomi from the life of the saloon by marrying her, an act that shocked the whole town, and overshadowed one very important deed. On the day that the saloon girl became Jackson's wife, Luke Miller left town, beginning his long journey to England.

Luke's departure did not go unnoticed by Jesse Woodward. As the snow fluttered in his face, he watched the train leave and wondered how Lilly Sinclair would take the news. The hate and revenge had been a long time coming for everyone, including Luke, and now, the forgiveness would take time, too.

But Jesse had forgiven. Seeing death so close had taught him that hate and revenge were not so honeyed to the taste. To let bygones be bygones was far more sweet. Shadoe had saved his life, told him the truth about Anne and Joseph McFall. It was enough.

Oh, yes, there were flowers on all the graves back in the summer, and there were grief and tears for everyone, but the snow had fallen, white and clean, and it was Christmas. Jesse and Molly were even riding out to the Oasis for merrymaking with Shadoe, Lilly, and several other guests.

"Jesse Woodward, you come back here right this minute!"

"I ain't wearing it, Molly," the young man called over his shoulder. "I done told you once was enough when we got hitched. I ain't wearing another silly ole hat." He reached for his brown plainsman from the hook by the front door and plastered it on his neatly combed hair.

"But it's Christmas!"

Jesse turned in the front foyer, almost laughing when he saw Molly standing right behind him, a smile in her determined eyes, the hat in her hands.

"Oh, Molly, you gonna ruin my Christmas for sure, making me wear that darn thing."

"Please, Jesse," she pleaded. "Paw paid three dollars and sixty cents for this fine derby." She ran her hand over it almost in adoration. "The finest wool felt. You'll look just like a perfect gentleman with your brown suit and starched shirt."

Jesse grimaced as he took his hat from his head and hung it back on the hook. "All right, but I promise you this is the last time that you are gonna git me dressed up like I'm ready for the undertaker."

Molly looked pleased as he took the derby from her hand and gently pressed it on the crown of his head. "I feel like a fool!"

Molly giggled. "But so handsome a fool." She reached out, grabbed one of his hands, and pressed it to her swollen belly. "Feel that?"

A smile leaped to his face. "Sure do. That girl is a real kicker. Got some spirit!"

Molly slapped playfully at his hand. "You mean *boy*, Jesse. This baby's gonna be a boy baby."

"No, it's a little girl . . . Dark hair and big blue eyes . . . Anne . . . our little Annie. I done dreamed about her."

"But all men want a boy baby."

"Not me." Jesse pulled Molly into his arms and whispered over her shoulder, "She's coming into the world just in time to live and to be married to Sinclair's young Joey."

Molly pushed away, her face full of surprise as she stared at him. "I never thought to hear those words from you. A Woodward married to a Sinclair?"

Jesse looked down at her with a faint ironical smile. A moment passed, and they just looked at one another, silent, then Jesse pulled her tightly to him again.

His eyes closed as he thought, *A Woodward married to a McFall. Kissing cousins. Anne's tragedy will find new meaning, for her child and my child will one day inherit the whole valley.*

Jesse sighed. The name of the future was Sinclair, but the blood would be Woodward and McFall. Even if Tom had known the truth, he would have never accepted it just like old James McFall. Some people could never let go of their cherished illusions.

But Jesse had, and the truth gave him a man's peace and hope, a man's pride and dream.

One day, in the new century, there would be a dynasty in Harney County. Promises at last fulfilled.

LOVE SPELL

THE MAGIC OF ROMANCE
PAST, PRESENT, AND FUTURE....

Dorchester Publishing Co., Inc., the leader in romantic fiction, is pleased to unveil its newest line—Love Spell. Every month, beginning in August 1993, Love Spell will publish one book in each of four categories:

1) *Timeswept Romance*—Modern-day heroines travel to the past to find the men who fulfill their hearts' desires.

2) *Futuristic Romance*—Love on distant worlds where passion is the lifeblood of every man and woman.

3) *Historical Romance*—Full of desire, adventure and intrigue, these stories will thrill readers everywhere.

4) *Contemporary Romance*—With novels by Lori Copeland, Heather Graham, and Jayne Ann Krentz, Love Spell's line of contemporary romance is first-rate.

Exploding with soaring passion and fiery sensuality, Love Spell romances are destined to take you to dazzling new heights of ecstasy.

COMING IN SEPTEMBER 1993
HISTORICAL ROMANCE
TEMPTATION
Jane Harrison

He broke her heart once before, but Shadoe Sinclair is a temptation that Lilly McFall cannot deny. And when he saunters back into the frontier town he left years earlier, Lilly will do whatever it takes to make the handsome rogue her own.

_0-505-51906-2 $4.99 US/$5.99 CAN

CONTEMPORARY ROMANCE
WHIRLWIND COURTSHIP
Jayne Ann Krentz writing as Jayne Taylor
Bestselling Author of *Family Man*

When Phoebe Hampton arrives by accident on Harlan Garand's doorstep, he's convinced she's another marriage-minded female sent by his matchmaking aunt. But a sudden snowstorm traps them together for a few days and shows Harlan there's a lot more to Phoebe than meets the eye.

_0-505-51907-0 $3.99 US/$4.99 CAN

COMING IN OCTOBER 1993
HISTORICAL ROMANCE
DANGEROUS DESIRES
Louise Clark

Miserable and homesick, Stephanie de la Riviere will sell her family jewels or pose as a highwayman—whatever it takes to see her beloved father again. And her harebrained schemes might succeed if not for her watchful custodian—the only man who can match her fiery spirit with his own burning desire.

__0-505-51910-0 $4.99 US/$5.99 CAN

CONTEMPORARY ROMANCE
ONLY THE BEST
Lori Copeland
Author of More Than 6 Million Books in Print!

Stranded in a tiny Wyoming town after her car fails, Rana Alcott doesn't think her life can get much worse. And though she'd rather die than accept help from arrogant Gunner Montay, she soon realizes she is fighting a losing battle against temptation.

__0-505-51911-9 $3.99 US/$4.99 CAN

LEISURE BOOKS
ATTN: Order Department
276 5th Avenue, New York, NY 10001

Please add $1.50 for shipping and handling for the first book and $.35 for each book thereafter. PA., N.Y.S. and N.Y.C. residents, please add appropriate sales tax. No cash, stamps, or C.O.D.s All orders shipped within 6 weeks via postal service book rate. Canadian orders require $2.00 extra postage and must be paid in U.S. dollars through a U.S. banking facility.

Name _____

Address _____

City _____ State _____ Zip _____

I have enclosed $_____ in payment for the checked book(s). Payment <u>must</u> accompany all orders.☐ Please send a free catalog.